PRAISE FOR COLLEEN HOOVER

"What a glorious and touching read, a forever keeper. The kind of book that gets handed down."

—*USA Today* on *It Ends with Us*

"*Confess*, by Colleen Hoover, is a beautiful and devastating story that will make you feel so much."

—*Guardian*

"*It Ends with Us* tackles [a] difficult subject . . . with romantic tenderness and emotional heft. The relationships are portrayed with compassion and honesty, and the author's note at the end that explains Hoover's personal connection to the subject matter is a must-read. Packed with riveting drama and painful truths, this book powerfully illustrates the devastation of abuse—and the strength of the survivors."

—*Kirkus*, starred review

"Hoover joins the ranks of such luminaries as Jennifer Weiner and Jojo Moyes, with a dash of Gillian Flynn. Sure to please a plethora of readers."

—*Library Journal*, starred review, for *November 9*

"Hoover builds a terrific new-adult world here with two people growing in their careers and discovering mature love."

—*Booklist*, starred review, for *Ugly Love*

"Betrayals, secrets, and shifting family loyalties keep the pages turning in this excellent contemporary from Hoover . . . This is Hoover at her very best."

—*Publishers Weekly*, starred review, for *Regretting You*

REMINDERS OF HIM

OTHER TITLES BY COLLEEN HOOVER

Layla
Heart Bones
Regretting You
Verity
All Your Perfects
Without Merit
Too Late
It Ends with Us
November 9
Confess
Ugly Love
Hopeless
Losing Hope
Finding Cinderella: A Novella

Maybe Someday Series

Maybe Someday
Maybe Not: A Novella
Maybe Now

Slammed Series

Slammed
Point of Retreat
This Girl

REMINDERS OF HIM

A NOVEL

COLLEEN HOOVER

This is a work of fiction. Names, characters, organizations, places, events, and incidents are either products of the author's imagination or are used fictitiously.

Published by Montlake, Seattle

www.apub.com

ISBN-13: 9781542025607
ISBN-10: 1542025605

Cover design by Caroline Teagle Johnson

Printed in the United States of America

This book is for Tasara.

CHAPTER ONE

KENNA

There's a small wooden cross staked into the ground on the side of the road with the date of his death written on it.

Scotty would hate it. I bet his mother put it there.

"Can you pull over?"

The driver slows down and brings the cab to a stop. I get out and walk back to where the cross is. I shake it side to side until the dirt loosens around it, and then I pull it out of the ground.

Did he die in this very spot? Or did he die in the road?

I didn't pay attention to the details during the pretrial. When I heard he had crawled several yards away from the car, I started humming so I wouldn't hear anything else the prosecutor said. Then, to avoid having to sit through details if the case went to trial, I pleaded guilty.

Because technically, I was.

I may not have killed him with my actions, but I definitely killed him with my inaction.

I thought you were dead, Scotty. But dead people can't crawl.

I walk back to the cab with the cross in hand. I set it on the back seat next to me and wait for the driver to pull back onto the road, but he doesn't. I glance at him in the rearview mirror, and he's staring at me with a raised brow.

"Stealing roadside memorials has to be some kind of bad karma. You sure you want to take that?"

I look away from him and lie. "Yes. I'm the one who put it there." I can still feel him staring at me as he pulls back onto the road.

My new apartment is only two miles from here, but it's in the opposite direction from where I used to live. I don't have a car, so I decided to find a place closer to downtown this time so I can walk to work. If I can even find a job. It'll be difficult with my history and lack of experience. And, according to the cabdriver, the bad karma I'm probably carrying around right now.

Stealing Scotty's memorial might be bad karma, but one could argue that leaving a memorial up for a guy who verbally expressed his hatred for roadside memorials could be bad karma as well. That's why I had the driver take the detour down this back road. I knew Grace probably left something at the location of the wreck, and I felt I owed it to Scotty to remove it.

"Cash or card?" the driver asks.

I look at the meter and pull cash and a tip out of my purse and hand it to him after he parks. Then I grab my suitcase and the wooden cross I just stole and make my way out of the cab and up to the building.

My new apartment isn't part of a huge complex. It's just a single-standing unit flanked by an abandoned car lot on one side and a convenience store on the other. Plywood covers a downstairs window. Beer cans in various stages of decay litter the property. I kick one aside so that it doesn't get stuck in the wheels of my suitcase.

The place looks even worse than it did online, but I expected as much. The landlord didn't even ask for my name when I called to see if they had any vacancies. She said, "We always have vacancies. Bring cash; I'm in apartment one." Then she hung up.

I knock on apartment one. There's a cat in the window staring at me. It's so motionless I start to wonder if it's a statue, but then it blinks and slinks away.

The door opens, and an older, tiny woman stares up at me with a disgruntled look about her. She has curlers in her hair and lipstick smeared to her nose. "I don't need anything you're selling."

I stare at the lipstick, noting how it's bleeding into the wrinkles hugging her mouth. "I called last week about an apartment. You said you'd have one available."

Recognition flashes on the woman's prune-like face. She makes a *hmph* sound while looking me up and down. "Didn't expect you to look like this."

I don't know what to make of her comment. I look down at my jeans and T-shirt while she walks away from the door for a few seconds. She comes back with a zipper pouch. "Five fifty a month. First and last month's rent is due today."

I count out the money and hand it to her. "There's no lease?"

She laughs, stuffing the cash into her pouch. "You're in apartment six." She points a finger up. "That's right above me, so keep it down, I go to bed early."

"What utilities are included?"

"Water and trash, but you cover electric. It's on now—you have three days to get it switched into your name. Deposit is two fifty to the light company."

Fuck. Three days to come up with $250? I'm starting to question my decision to come back so soon, but when I was released from transitional housing, I had two choices: spend all my money trying to survive in that town, or drive the three hundred miles and spend all my money in this one.

I'd rather be in the town that holds all the people once connected to Scotty.

The woman takes a step back into her apartment. "Welcome to Paradise Apartments. I'll bring you a kitten once you get settled."

I immediately put my hand on her door to prevent her from closing it. "Wait. What? A kitten?"

"Yeah, a *kitten*. Like a cat, but smaller."

I step away from her door like it'll somehow protect me from what she just said. "No, thank you. I don't want a kitten."

"I have too many."

"I don't want a kitten," I repeat.

"Who wouldn't want a kitten?"

"Me."

She huffs, like my response is completely unreasonable. "I'll make you a deal," she says. "I'll leave the electric on for two weeks if you take a kitten." *What in the hell kind of place is this?* "Fine," she says, responding to my silence as if it's a negotiation tactic. "The *month*. I'll leave the electric on for the whole month if you just take one kitten." She walks into her apartment but leaves the door open.

I don't want a kitten at all, ever, but not having to spend $250 on an electricity deposit this month would be worth several kittens.

She reappears with a small black-and-orange kitten. She places it in my hands. "There ya go. My name is Ruth if you need anything, but try not to need anything." She goes to close her door again.

"Wait. Can you tell me where I can find a pay phone?"

She chuckles. "Yeah, back in 2005." She closes her door completely.

The kitten meows, but it's not a sweet meow. It sounds more like a cry for help. "You and me both," I mutter.

I make my way toward the stairs with my suitcase and my . . . kitten. Maybe I should have held out a few more months before coming back here. I worked to save up just over $2,000, but most of that was spent on moving here. I should have saved up more. What if I don't find a job right away? And now I'm tasked with the responsibility of keeping a kitten alive.

My life just became ten times more difficult than it was yesterday.

I make it up to the apartment with the kitten clinging to my shirt. I insert the key in the lock and have to use both hands to pull on the door and get the key to turn. When I push open the door to my new apartment, I hold my breath, afraid of what it's going to smell like.

I flip on the light switch and look around, releasing my breath slowly. There's not much of a smell. That's both good and bad.

There's a couch in the living room, but that's literally all there is. A small living room, an even smaller kitchen, no dining room. No bedroom. It's an efficiency apartment with a closet and a bathroom so small the toilet touches the tub.

The place is a dump. A five-hundred-square-foot absolute shithole, but it's a step up for me. I've gone from sharing a one-hundred-square-foot cell with a roommate, to living in transitional housing with six roommates, to a five-hundred-square-foot apartment I can call my own.

I'm twenty-six years old, and this is the first time I've ever officially lived somewhere alone. It's both terrifying and liberating.

I don't know if I can afford this place after the month is up, but I'm going to try. Even if that means applying to every business I walk past.

Having my own apartment can only serve to help as I plead my case to the Landrys. It'll show I'm independent now. Even if that independence will be a struggle.

The kitten wants down, so I put her on the floor in the living room. She walks around, crying out for whoever she left downstairs. I feel a pang in my chest as I watch her searching corners for a way out. A way back home. A way back to her mother and siblings.

She looks like a bumblebee, or something out of Halloween, with her black and orange splotches.

"What are we going to name you?"

I know she'll more than likely be nameless for a few days while I think about it. I take the responsibility of naming things very seriously. The last time I was responsible for naming someone, I took it more seriously than I've ever taken anything. That could have been because the whole time I sat in my cell during my pregnancy, all there was to do was think about baby names.

I chose the name Diem because I knew as soon as I was released, I was going to make my way back here and do everything in my power to find her.

Here I am.

Carpe Diem.

CHAPTER TWO

Ledger

I'm pulling my truck into the alley behind the bar when I notice the nail polish still on the fingernails of my right hand. *Shit.* I forgot I played dress-up with a four-year-old last night.

At least the purple matches my work shirt.

Roman is tossing bags of trash into the dumpster when I exit the truck. He sees the gift sack in my hand and knows it's for him, so he reaches for it. "Let me guess. Coffee mug?" He peeks inside.

It's a coffee mug. It always is.

He doesn't say thank you. He never does.

We don't acknowledge the sobriety these mugs symbolize, but I buy him one every Friday. This is the ninety-sixth mug I've bought him.

I should probably stop because his apartment is full of coffee mugs, but I'm too far in to give up now. He's almost at one hundred weeks sober, and I've been holding on to that one-hundredth-milestone mug for a while now. It's a Denver Broncos mug. His least favorite team.

Roman gestures toward the back door of the bar. "There's a couple inside harassing other customers. You might want to keep an eye on them."

That's odd. We don't normally have to deal with unruly people this early in the evening. It isn't even six o'clock yet. "Where are they sitting?"

"Next to the jukebox." His eyes fall to my hand. "Nice nails, man."

"Right?" I hold up my hand and wiggle my fingers. "She did pretty good for a four-year-old."

I open the back door of the bar and am met with the grating sound of my favorite song being slaughtered by Ugly Kid Joe through the loudspeakers.

Surely not.

I walk through the kitchen and into the bar and immediately spot them. They're hunched over the jukebox. I quietly make my way over to them and see she's punching in the same four numbers again and again. I look over their shoulders at the screen while they giggle like mischievous children. "Cat's in the Cradle" is set to play thirty-six times in a row.

I clear my throat. "You think this is funny? Forcing me to listen to the same song for the next six hours?"

My father spins around when he hears my voice. "Ledger!" He pulls me in for a hug. He smells like beer and motor oil. And limes, maybe? *Are they drunk?*

My mother backs away from the jukebox. "We were trying to fix it. We didn't do this."

"Sure, you didn't." I pull her in for a hug.

They never announce when they're going to show up. They just appear and stay a day or two or three and then head out in their RV again.

Their showing up drunk is new, though. I glance over my shoulder, and Roman is behind the bar now. I point to my parents. "Did you do this to them, or did they show up this way?"

Roman shrugs. "A little of both."

"It's our anniversary," my mother says. "We're celebrating."

"I hope you guys didn't drive here."

"We didn't," my father says. "Our car is with the RV in the shop getting routine maintenance, so we took a Lyft." He pats my cheek.

"Wanted to see you, but we've been here two hours waiting for you to show up, and now we're leaving because we're hungry."

"This is why you should warn me before you drop into town. I have a life."

"Did you remember our anniversary?" my father asks.

"Slipped my mind. Sorry."

"Told you," he says to my mother. "Pay up, Robin."

My mother reaches into her pocket and hands him a ten-dollar bill.

They bet on almost everything. My love life. Which holidays I'll remember. Every football game I've ever played. But I'm almost positive they've just been passing the same ten-dollar bill back and forth for several years.

My father holds up his empty glass and shakes it. "Get us a refill, bartender."

I take his glass. "How about an ice water?" I leave them at the jukebox and make my way behind the bar.

I'm pouring two glasses of water when a girl walks into the bar looking somewhat lost. She glances around the room like she's never been here before, and then when she notices an empty corner at the opposite end of the bar, she makes a beeline for it.

I stare at her the entire time she's walking through the bar. I stare at her so hard I accidentally overfill the glasses and water goes everywhere. I grab a towel and wipe up my mess. When I look at my mother, she's looking at the girl. Then at me. Then at the girl.

Shit. The last thing I need is for her to try to set me up with a customer. She tries to play matchmaker plenty when she's sober, so I can't imagine how bad the tendency might be after a few drinks. I need to get them out of here.

I take the waters to them and then hand my mother my credit card. "You guys should go down to Jake's Steakhouse and have dinner on me. Walk there so you can sober up on the way."

"You are so nice." She clutches at her chest dramatically and looks at my father. "Benji, we did so well with him. Let's go celebrate our parenting with his credit card."

"We did do well with him," my father says in agreement. "We should have more kids."

"Menopause, honey. Remember when I hated you for an entire year?" My mother grabs her purse, and they take the glasses of water with them as they go.

"We should get rib eye since he's paying," my father mutters as they walk away.

I release a sigh of relief and then make my way back to the bar. The girl is tucked quietly into the corner, writing in a notebook. Roman isn't behind the bar right now, so I'm assuming no one has taken her order yet.

I gladly volunteer as tribute.

"What can I get you?" I ask her.

"Water and a Diet Coke, please." She doesn't look up at me, so I back away to fulfill her order. She's still writing in her notebook when I return with her drinks. I try to get a glimpse of what she's writing, but she closes her notebook and lifts her eyes. "Thank . . ." She pauses in the middle of what I think is her attempt at saying *thank you*. She mutters the word *you* and sticks the straw in her mouth.

She seems flustered.

I want to ask her questions, like what her name is and where she's from, but I've learned over the years of owning this place that asking questions of lonely people in a bar can quickly turn into conversations I have to maul my way out of.

But most of the people who come in here don't capture my attention like she has. I gesture toward her two drinks and say, "Are you waiting for someone else?"

She pulls both drinks closer. "Nope. Just thirsty." She breaks eye contact with me and leans back in her chair, pulling her notebook with her and giving it all her attention.

I can take a hint. I walk to the other end of the bar to give her privacy.

Roman returns from the kitchen and nudges his head in her direction. "Who's she?"

"I don't know, but she isn't wearing a wedding ring, so she's not your type."

"Very funny."

CHAPTER THREE

KENNA

Dear Scotty,

They turned the old bookstore into a bar. Can you believe that shit?

I wonder what they did with the sofa we used to sit on every Sunday.

I swear, it's like this whole town is one huge Monopoly board, and after you died, someone came along and picked up the board and scrambled all the pieces around.

Nothing is the same. Everything seems unfamiliar. I've been walking around downtown taking it all in for the last couple of hours. I was on my way to the grocery store when I got sidetracked by the bench we used to eat ice cream on. I sat down and people watched for a while.

Everyone seems so carefree in this town. The people here just wander around like their worlds are right-side-up—like they aren't about to fall off the pavement and land in the sky. They just move from one moment to the next, not even aware of the mothers walking around without their daughters.

I probably shouldn't be in a bar, especially my first night back. Not that I have an issue with alcohol. That one horrible night was an exception. But the last thing I need your parents to find out is that I stopped by a bar before I stopped by their house.

But I thought this place was still the bookstore, and bookstores usually have coffee. I was so disappointed when I walked inside because it's been a long day of traveling here on a bus and then the cab. I was hoping for more caffeine than a diet soda can provide.

Maybe the bar has coffee. I haven't asked yet.

I probably shouldn't tell you this, and I promise it'll make sense before I finish this letter, but I kissed a prison guard once.

We got caught and he got transferred to a different unit and I felt guilty that our kiss got him in trouble. But he talked to me like I was a person and not a number, and even though I wasn't attracted to him, I knew he was attracted to me, so when he leaned in to kiss me, I kissed him back. It was my way of saying thank you, and I think he knew that, and he was okay with it. It had been two years since I had been touched by you, so when he pressed me against the wall and gripped my waist, I thought I'd feel more.

I was sad that I didn't.

I'm telling you this because he tasted like coffee, but a better kind of coffee than the prison coffee they served to the prisoners. He tasted like expensive eight-dollar coffee from Starbucks, with caramel and whipped cream and a cherry. It's why I kept kissing him. Not because I enjoyed the kiss, or him, or his hand on my waist, but because I missed expensive flavored coffee.

And you. I miss expensive coffee and you.

Love,

Kenna

"You want a refill?" the bartender asks. He has tattoos that slide all the way into his shirtsleeves. His shirt is deep purple, a color you don't see in prison very often.

I never thought about that until I was there, but prison is really drab and colorless, and after a while, you start to forget what the trees look like in the fall.

"Do you have coffee?" I ask.

"Sure. Cream and sugar?"

"Do you have caramel? And whipped cream?"

He tosses a rag onto his shoulder. "You bet. Soy, skim, almond, or whole milk?"

"Whole."

The bartender laughs. "I was kidding. This is a bar; I have a four-hour-old pot of coffee and your choice of cream or sugar or both or none."

The color of his shirt and the way it complements his skin tone are no longer impressive. *Asshole.* "Just give me whatever," I mutter.

The bartender backs away to retrieve my basic prison coffee. I watch as he lifts the pot out of the holder and brings it close to his nose to sniff it. He makes a face, then dumps it out in the sink. He flicks the water on while refilling a guy's beer while starting a new pot of coffee while closing out someone else's tab while smiling just enough but not too much.

I've never seen someone move so fluidly, like he has seven arms and three brains and they're all going at once. It's mesmerizing watching someone who's good at what they do.

I don't know what I'm good at. I don't know that there is anything in this world I could make look effortless.

There are things I *want* to be good at. I want to be a good mother. To my future kids, but mostly to the daughter I already brought into this world. I want to have a yard that I can plant stuff in. Stuff that will flourish and not die. I want to learn how to talk to people without wishing I could retract every word I said. I want to be good at feeling things when a guy touches my waist. I want to be good at life. I want to make it look effortless, but up until this point, I've made every aspect of life appear entirely too difficult to navigate.

The bartender glides back to me when the coffee is ready. As he's filling the mug, I look at him and actually absorb what I'm seeing this time. He's good looking in a way that a girl who is trying to get custody of her daughter should want to stay away from. He's got eyes that have seen a thing or two, and hands that have probably hit a man or two.

His hair is fluid like his movements. Long, dark strands that hang in his eyes and move in whatever direction he moves. He doesn't touch his hair; he hasn't since I've been sitting here. He just lets it get in his way, but then he'll flick his head every now and then, the slightest little movement, and his hair goes where he needs it to. It's thick hair, agreeable hair, want-my-hands-in-his-hair hair.

My mug is full of coffee now, but he lifts a finger and says, "One sec." He swivels and opens a minifridge and then pulls out whole milk. He pours some into the mug. He puts the milk back, opens another fridge—*surprise*, whipped cream. He reaches behind him, and when his hand reappears, he's holding a single cherry that he places carefully on top of my drink. He slides it closer to me and spreads out his arms like he just created magic.

"No caramel," he says. "Best I could do for not-a-coffee-shop."

He probably thinks he just made a bougie drink for a spoiled girl who's used to having eight-dollar coffee every day. He has no idea how long it's been since I've had a decent cup of coffee. Even in the months I spent in transitional housing, they served prison coffee to the prison girls with prison pasts.

I could cry.

I *do* cry.

As soon as he gives his attention to someone at the other end of the bar, I take a drink of my coffee and close my eyes and cry because life can be so fucking cruel and hard, and I've wanted to quit living it so many times, but then moments like these remind me that happiness isn't some permanent thing we're all trying to achieve in life, it's merely a thing that shows up every now and then, sometimes in tiny doses that are just substantial enough to keep us going.

CHAPTER FOUR

LEDGER

I know what to do when a child cries, but I don't know what to do when a grown woman cries. I stay as far away from her as I can while she drinks her coffee.

I haven't learned much about her since she walked in here an hour ago, but one thing I know for certain is she didn't come here to meet anyone. She came here for solitude. Three people have tried to approach her in the last hour, and she held up a hand and shot them down without making eye contact with any of them.

She drank her coffee in silence. It's barely seven in the evening, so she might just be working her way up to the hard stuff. I kind of hope not. I'm intrigued by the idea that she came to a bar to order things we rarely serve while turning down men she never even made eye contact with.

Roman and I are the only ones working until Mary Anne and Razi get here. The place is getting busier, so I can't give her the attention I want to give her, which is *all* my attention. I make it a point to spread myself out just enough so that it doesn't seem like I'm in her space too much.

As soon as she finishes the coffee, I want to ask her what she's having next, but instead I make her sit with her empty mug for a good ten minutes. I might make it fifteen before I work my way back to her.

In the meantime, I just steal glances at her. Her face is a work of art. I wish there was a picture of it hanging on a wall in a museum somewhere so I could stand in front of it and stare at it for as long as I wanted. Instead, I'm just getting in peeks here and there, admiring how all the same pieces of a face that make up all the other faces in the world just seem to coordinate better on her.

People rarely come to a bar at the start of a weekend evening in such a raw state, but she isn't dressed up. She's wearing a faded Mountain Dew T-shirt and jeans, but the green in the shirt matches the green in her eyes with such perfection it's as if she put all her effort into finding the perfect color of T-shirt, when I'm pretty sure she gave that shirt no thought at all. Her hair is russet. All one sturdy color. All one length, right below her chin. She slides her hands through it every now and then, and every time she does, it looks like she's about to fold in on herself. It makes me want to walk around the bar and lift her up and give her a hug.

What's her story?

I don't want to know.

I don't need to know.

I don't date girls I meet in this bar. Twice I've broken that rule, and twice it's bitten me in the ass.

Besides, there's something terrifying about this one. I can't quite put my finger on it, but when I talk to her, I feel like my voice is trapped in my chest. And not in a way that I'm left breathless by her, but in a more substantial way, as though my brain is warning me not to interact with her.

Red flag! Danger! Abort!

But why?

We make eye contact when I reach for her mug. She hasn't looked at anyone else tonight. Only me. I should feel flattered, but I feel scared.

I played professional football and own a bar, yet I'm scared of a little eye contact with a pretty girl. That should be my Tinder bio. *Played for the Broncos. Owns a bar. Scared of eye contact.*

"What next?" I ask her.

"Wine. White."

It's a hard balance owning a bar and being sober. I want everyone else to be sober, but I also need customers. I pour her the glass of wine and set it in front of her.

I remain near her, pretending to use a rag to dry glasses that have been dry since yesterday. I notice the slow roll of her throat as she stares down at the glass of wine, almost as if she's unsure. That split second of hesitation, or maybe it's regret, is enough to make me think she might struggle with alcohol. I can always tell when people are tossing away their sobriety by how they look at their glass.

Drinking is only stressful to alcoholics.

She doesn't drink the wine, though. She quietly sips on the soda until it's empty. I reach for the empty glass at the same time she does.

When our fingers touch, I feel something else trapped in my chest other than my voice. Maybe it's a few extra heartbeats. Maybe it's an erupting volcano.

Her fingers recoil from mine and she puts her hands in her lap. I pull the empty glass of soda away from her, as well as the full glass of wine, and she doesn't even look up to ask me why. She sighs, like maybe she's relieved I took the wine away. Why did she even order it?

I refill her soda, and when she isn't looking, I pour the wine in the sink and wash the glass.

She sips from the soda for a while, but the eye contact stops. Maybe I upset her.

Roman notices me staring at her. He leans an elbow onto the counter and says, "Divorce or death?"

Roman always likes to guess the reasons people come in alone and seem out of place. The girl doesn't seem like she's here because of a divorce. Women usually celebrate those by coming to bars with groups of friends, wearing sashes that say *Ex-Wife*.

This girl does seem sad, but not sad in a way that would indicate she's grieving.

"I'm gonna say divorce," Roman says.

I don't respond to him. I don't feel right guessing her tragedy, because I'm hoping it isn't divorce or death or even a bad day. I want good things for her because it seems like she hasn't had a good thing in a long, long time.

I stop staring at her while I tend to other customers. I do it to give her privacy, but she uses it as an opportunity to leave cash on the bar and sneak out.

I stare for several seconds at her empty barstool and the ten-dollar tip she left. She's gone and I don't know her name and I don't know her story and I don't know that I'll ever see her again, so here I am, rushing around the bar, through the bar, toward the front door she just slipped out of.

The sky is on fire when I walk outside. I shield my eyes, forgetting how assaulting the light always is when I step out of the bar before dark.

She turns around right when I spot her. She's about ten feet from me. She doesn't have to shield her eyes because the sun is behind her, outlining her head like it's topped with a halo.

"I left money on the bar," she says.

"I know."

We stare at each other for a quiet moment. I don't know what to say. I just stand here like a fool.

"What, then?"

"Nothing," I say. But I immediately wish I would have said, *"Everything."*

She stares at me, and I never do this, I *shouldn't* do this, but I know if I let her walk away, I won't be able to stop thinking about the sad girl who left me a ten-dollar tip when I get the feeling she can't afford to leave me a tip at all.

"You should come back tonight at eleven." I don't give her a chance to tell me no or explain why she can't. I go back inside the bar, hoping my request makes her curious enough to show back up tonight.

CHAPTER FIVE

KENNA

I'm sitting on an inflatable mattress with my unnamed kitten, contemplating all the reasons I shouldn't go back to that bar.

I didn't come back to this town to meet guys. Even guys as good looking as that bartender. I'm here for my daughter and that's it.

Tomorrow is important. Tomorrow I need to feel Herculean, but the bartender unintentionally made me feel weak by pulling away my glass of wine. I don't know what he saw on my face that made him want to take the wine away from me. I wasn't going to drink it. I only ordered it so I could feel a sense of control in *not* drinking it. I wanted to look at it and smell it and then walk away from it feeling stronger than when I sat down.

Now I just feel unsettled because he saw how I was looking at the wine earlier, and the way he pulled it away makes me think he assumes I have an active issue with alcohol.

I don't. I haven't had alcohol in years because one night of alcohol mixed with a tragedy ruined the last five years of my life, and the last five years of my life have led me back to this town, and this town makes me nervous, and the only thing that calms my nerves is doing things that make me feel like I'm still in control of my life and my decisions.

That's why I wanted to turn down the wine, dammit.

Now I'm not going to sleep well tonight. I have no reason to feel accomplished because he made me feel the complete opposite. If I want to sleep well tonight, I'm going to need to turn down something else I want.

Or some*one.*

I haven't wanted anyone in a long, long time. Not since I first met Scotty. But the bartender was kind of hot, and he had a great smile, and he makes great coffee, and he already invited me to come back, so it'll be simple to show up and turn him down.

Then I'll sleep well and be prepared to wake up and face the most important day of my life.

I wish I could take my new kitten with me. I feel like I need a sidekick, but she's asleep on the new pillow I bought at the store earlier.

I didn't buy much. The inflatable mattress, a couple of pillows and sheets, some crackers and cheese, and some cat food and litter. I decided I'm only going to live two days at a time in this town. Until I know what tomorrow will bring, there's no sense in my wasting any of the money I've been working six months to save up. I'm already running low, which is why I choose not to call a cab.

I leave the apartment to walk back to the bar, but I don't carry my purse or my notebook with me this time. I just need my driver's license and my apartment key. It's about a mile-and-a-half walk from my apartment to the bar, but it's nice out and the road is well lit.

I'm a little concerned that someone might recognize me at the bar, or even on my walk there, but I look completely different than I did five years ago. I used to care more about self-maintenance, but five years in prison has made me less concerned about hair dye and extensions and false lashes and artificial nails.

I didn't live in this town long enough to make many friends outside of Scotty, so I doubt many people even know who I am. I'm sure plenty of them know *of* me, but it's hard to be recognized when you aren't even missed.

Patrick and Grace might recognize me if they saw me, but I only met them once before going to prison.

Prison. I'll never get used to saying that word. It's such a hard word to say out loud. When you lay the letters out on paper individually, they don't seem that harsh. But when you say the word out loud, "*Prison,*" it's just so damn severe.

When I think about where I've been for the last five years, I like to refer to it in my head as *the facility*. Or I'll think of my time there as *When I was away*, and leave it at that. To say *"When I was in prison"* is not something I'll ever get used to.

I'll have to say it this week when I look for a job. They'll ask, "Have you ever been convicted of a crime?" I'll have to say, "Yes, I spent five years in prison for involuntary manslaughter."

And they'll either hire me or they won't. They probably won't.

There's a double standard for women, even behind bars. When women say they've been to prison, people think *trash, whore, addict, thief.* But when men say they've been to prison, people add badges of honor to the negative thoughts, like trash, *but badass*, addict, *but tough*, thief, *but impressive.*

There's still a stigma with the men, but the women never get out with stigmas *and* badges of honor.

According to the clock on the courthouse, I make it back downtown at eleven thirty. Hopefully he's still here even though I'm half an hour late.

I didn't pay attention to the name of the bar earlier, probably because it was daylight out and I was shocked it was no longer a bookstore, but there's a small neon sign above the door that reads **WARD'S**.

I hesitate before going back inside. My return presence is more or less sending this guy a message. A message I'm not sure I want him to receive. But the alternative is my going back to that apartment and being alone with my thoughts.

I've spent enough time alone with my thoughts over the past five years. I'm craving people and noise and all the things I haven't had, and my apartment reminds me a little of prison. There's a lot of loneliness and silence there.

I open the door of the bar. It's louder and smokier and somehow darker than it was earlier. There are no empty seats, so I weave through people, find the restroom, wait in the hall, wait outside, weave some more. Finally, a booth opens up. I cross the room and sit in it alone.

I watch the bartender flow behind the bar. I like how unbothered he seems. Two guys get into an argument, but he doesn't care—he just points to the door and they leave. He does that a lot. Points at things, and people just do the things he points out for them to do.

He points at two customers while making eye contact with the other bartender. That bartender walks up to them and closes out their tabs.

He points to an empty shelf, and one of the waitresses nods, and then a few minutes later she has the shelf restocked.

He points at the floor, and the other bartender disappears through the double doors and reappears with a mop to clean up a spill.

He points to a hook on the wall, and another waitress, a pregnant one, mouths, "*Thank you*," and she hangs up her apron and goes home.

He points, and people do, and then it's last call, and then it's time to close. People trickle out. No one trickles in.

He hasn't looked at me. Not even once.

I second-guess being here. He seems busy, and maybe I read him wrong earlier. I just assumed when he told me to come back that he said it for a reason, but maybe he tells all his customers that.

I stand up, thinking maybe I need to trickle out, too, but when he sees me stand, he points. He makes a simple motion with his finger, indicating for me to sit back down, so I do.

I'm relieved to know my intuition was right, but the emptier the bar gets, the more nervous I grow. He assumes I'm a grown-ass woman, but I barely feel like an adult. I'm a twenty-six-year-old teenager, inexperienced, starting from scratch.

I'm not sure I'm here for the right reasons. I thought I could just walk in, flirt with him, and then walk away, but he's more tempting than any bougie coffee. I came here to turn him down, but I had no idea that he would be pointing all night, or that he would point at me. *I had no idea pointing was sexy.*

I wonder if I would have found it sexy five years ago, or if I'm pathetically easy to please now.

By midnight, we're the only two people left. The other employees have gone, the door is now locked, and he's carrying a case of empty glasses to the back.

I pull my leg up and wrap my arms around it. I'm nervous. I didn't come back to this town to meet a guy. I'm in this town with a much bigger purpose. One he looks like he could derail with the point of a finger.

I'm only human, though. Humans need companions, and even though I didn't return to this town to meet people, this guy is hard to ignore.

He walks through the double doors with a different shirt on. He's no longer wearing the purple collared shirt with the rolled-up sleeves that all the other employees were wearing. He put on a white T-shirt. So simple, but so complicated.

He smiles when he reaches me, and I feel that smile slip over me with the warmth of a weighted blanket. "You came back."

I try to act unaffected. "You asked me to."

"You want something to drink?"

"I'm okay."

He touches his hair now, pushing it back, staring down at me. There's a war in his eyes, and I am by no means Switzerland, but he comes to me anyway. Sits next to me. *Right* next to me. My heart beats faster, even faster than when Scotty came to my register for a fourth time all those years ago.

"What's your name?" he asks.

I don't want him to know my name. He looks like he could be the age Scotty would be now if Scotty were alive, which means he might recognize my name, or me, or remember what happened. I don't want anyone to know me, or remember, or warn the Landrys that I'm in town.

It isn't a small town, but it isn't huge either. My presence won't go unnoticed for long. I just need it to go unnoticed for long *enough*, so I lie, sort of, and give him my middle name. "Nicole."

I don't ask him what his name is because I don't care. I'll never use it. I'll never come back here after tonight.

I pull at a strand of my hair, nervous at being so close to someone after so long. I feel like I've forgotten what to do, so I just blurt out what I came here to say. "I wasn't going to drink it."

He tilts his head, confused by my confession, so I clarify.

"The wine. Sometimes I . . ." I shake my head. "It's dumb, but I do this thing where I order alcohol specifically to walk away from it. I don't have a drinking problem. It's more like an issue with control, I think. Makes me feel less weak."

His eyes scan my face with the slightest hint of a smile. "I respect that," he says. "I rarely drink for similar reasons. I'm around drunk people every night, and the more I'm around them, the less I want to be among them."

"A bartender who doesn't drink? That's rare. Right? I'd think bartenders would have one of the highest rates of alcoholism. Easy access."

"That's actually the construction industry. Which probably isn't good for my odds. I've been building a house for several years now."

"You're really setting yourself up for failure."

He smiles. "Looks that way." He relaxes into the booth a little more. "What do you do, Nicole?"

This is the moment I should walk away. Before I say too much, before he asks more questions. But I like his voice and his presence, and I feel like staying here would be distracting, and I really need a distraction right now.

I just don't want to talk. Talking will only get me in trouble in this town.

"Do you really want to know what I do for a living?" I'm sure he'd rather have his hand up my shirt than hear whatever it is a girl would say in this moment. And since I don't want to admit that I do nothing for a living because I've been locked up for five years, I slide onto his lap.

It surprises him, almost as if he really did expect us to sit here and chat for the next hour.

His expression changes from mild shock to acceptance. His hands fall to my hips, and he grips them. I shiver from the contact.

He adjusts me so that I'm sitting a little farther up, and I can feel him through his jeans, and I'm suddenly not as confident that I can walk away as I was five seconds ago. I thought I could kiss him and then tell him good night and saunter home with pride. I just wanted to feel a little bit powerful before tomorrow, but now he's dragging his fingers across the skin on my waist, and it's making me weaker and weaker, and so fucking *thoughtless*. Not thoughtless as in uncaring, but thoughtless as in empty inside my head, and feeling everything in my chest, like a ball of fire is building inside of me.

His right hand slides up my back, and I gasp because I feel his touch surge through me like a current. This guy is touching my face now, running his fingers down my cheekbone, and then his fingertips across my lips. He's staring at me like he's trying to figure out where he knows me from.

Maybe that's just my paranoia at work.

"Who are you?" he whispers.

I already told him, but I repeat my middle name anyway. "Nicole."

He smiles but then loses the smile and says, "I know your name. But where'd you come from? Why have we never met before tonight?"

I don't want his questions. I have no honest answers. I move a little closer to his mouth. "Who are *you*?"

"Ledger," he says, right before he rips open my past, pulls out what's left of my heart, drops it on the floor, and then kisses me.

⸻

People say you fall in love, but *fall* is such a sad word when you think about it. Falls are never good. You fall on the ground, you fall behind, you fall to your death.

Whoever was the first person to say they fell in love must have already fallen out of it. Otherwise, they'd have called it something much better.

Scotty told me he loved me halfway into our relationship. It was the night I was supposed to meet his best friend for the first time. I had already met his parents, and he was excited for that, but not nearly as excited as he was to introduce me to the guy he considered a brother.

That meeting never happened. I can't remember why; it's been a long time. But his friend had to cancel, and Scotty was sad, so I baked him cookies and we smoked a joint and then I gave him head. Best girlfriend ever.

Until I killed him.

But this was three months before he would die, and on that particular night, even though he was sad, he was very much alive. He had a beating heart and a rapid pulse and a heaving chest and tears in his eyes when he said, *"I fucking love you, Kenna. I love you more than I've ever loved anyone. I miss you all the time, even when we're together."*

That stuck with me. *"I miss you all the time, even when we're together."*

And I thought that was the *only* thing that stuck with me that night, but I was wrong. Something else stuck with me. A name. *Ledger.*

The best friend who never showed. The best friend I never got to meet.

The best friend who just put his tongue in my mouth and his hand up my shirt and his name in my chest.

CHAPTER SIX

Ledger

I don't understand attraction.

What is it that draws people to each other? How can dozens of women walk through the doors to this bar every week and I don't feel the urge to give any of them a second glance? But then this girl waltzes in, and I can't take my fucking eyes off her.

Now I can't take my mouth off her.

I don't know why I'm breaking my self-imposed rule: "no pursuing customers." But there's something about her that indicates I'll only have one chance. I get the feeling she's either passing through town or doesn't plan on coming back in here. Tonight seems like an exception to whatever her normal routine may be, and I feel like skipping an opportunity to be with her will be that one regret in life I'll still think back on when I'm an old man.

She seems like a quiet person, but not the shy kind of quiet. She's quiet in a fierce way—a storm that sneaks up on you, and you don't know it's there until you feel the thunder rattle your bones.

She's quiet, but she's said just enough to make me want the rest of her words. She tastes like apples, even though she had coffee earlier, and apples are my favorite fruit. They're probably my favorite food *period*, now.

We kiss for several seconds, and even though she made the first move, she still seemed surprised when I pulled her to my mouth.

Maybe she expected me to wait a little longer before tasting her, or maybe she wasn't expecting it to feel like this—*I hope it feels like this for her*—but whatever caused that tiny gasp right before my mouth met hers, it wasn't because she didn't want the kiss.

She pulls away, briefly indecisive, but then she seems to make up her mind because she leans in and kisses me again with even more conviction.

That conviction disappears, though. Too fast. She pulls away for a second time, and this time her eyes are full of regret. She shakes her head quickly and places her palms on my chest. I cover her hands with mine right when she says, "I'm sorry."

She slides off me, the inside of her thigh rubbing across my zipper, making me even harder, as she scoots out of the booth. I reach for her hand, but her fingers trickle out of mine as she backs away from the table. "I shouldn't have come back."

She turns away from me and heads toward the door.

I deflate.

I didn't commit her face to memory, and I don't like the thought of her leaving without me, being able to remember the exact shape of the mouth that was just on mine.

I push out of the booth and follow her.

She can't get the door open. She jiggles the handle and tries to push it like she can't get away from me fast enough. I want to beg her to stay, but I also want to help her get away from me, so I pull down on the top lock while reaching in front of her with my foot to push up on the floor lock. The door opens and she spills outside.

She inhales a big gulp of air and then spins and faces me. I scan her mouth, wishing I had a photographic memory.

Her eyes are no longer the same color as her shirt. They're a lighter green now because she's tearing up. Once again I find myself not knowing what to do. I've never seen a girl so all over the place in such a short amount of time, and none of it feels forced or dramatic. With every move she makes and every feeling she has, it's as if she wants to reel them back in and tuck them away.

She seems embarrassed.

She's gasping for breath, trying to wipe away the few tears that are beginning to form, and since I have no idea what the fuck to say, I just hug her.

What else can I do?

I pull her to me, and for a second, she stiffens, but that's almost immediately followed up by a sigh as she relaxes.

We're the only people around. It's after midnight, everyone is home sleeping, watching a movie, making love. But I'm here on Main Street, hugging a really sad girl, wondering why she's sad, wishing I didn't think she was so beautiful.

Her face is pressed against my chest, and her arms are tight around my waist. Her forehead comes right up to my mouth, but she's tucked under my chin.

I rub her arms.

My truck is right around the corner. I always park in the alley, but she seems upset and I don't want to encourage her to follow me to an alley when she's crying. I lean against an awning post and pull her with me.

Two minutes pass, maybe three. She doesn't let go. She molds against me, soaking up the comfort my arms and chest and hands are giving her. I'm rubbing her back, up and down, my voice still trapped in my throat.

Something is wrong with her, something I'm not sure I even want to know at this point, but it's something I can't just leave her on the sidewalk and drive away from.

I don't think she's crying anymore when she says, "I need to go home."

"I'll give you a ride."

She shakes her head and pulls away from me. I keep my hands on her arms, and I notice when she folds her arms over her chest that she touches my right hand with two of her fingers. It's just a quick swipe, but it's deliberate, like she wants to get one last tiny feel of me before she leaves.

"I don't live far. I'll walk."

She's crazy if she thinks she's walking home. "It's too late to be walking by yourself." I point toward the alley. "My truck is ten feet away." For obvious reasons, that gesture makes her hesitate, but then she accepts the hand I'm reaching out to her, and she follows me around the corner.

When my truck comes into view, she stops walking. I turn around, and she's staring at my truck with concern in her eyes.

"I can call you an Uber if you'd prefer that. But I swear, I'm just offering you a ride home. No expectations."

She looks down at her feet, but continues walking toward my truck. I open my passenger door for her, and when she climbs inside, she doesn't face forward. She's still facing me, and her legs are preventing me from closing the door. She's looking at me like she's torn. Her eyebrows are drawn apart. I'm not sure I've ever seen anyone look so effortlessly sad.

"Are you okay?"

She leans her head against the seat and stares at me. "I will be," she says quietly. "Tomorrow is a big day for me. I'm just nervous."

"What's tomorrow?" I ask her.

"A big day for me."

She obviously doesn't plan on elaborating, so I nod, respecting her privacy.

Her focus moves to my arm. She touches the hem of my sleeve, so I put my hand on her knee because I want it somewhere on her, and her knee seems like the safest place until she lets me know where else she might want my hand.

I don't know what her intentions are. Most people show up to bars and make their intentions clear. You can tell who comes in for a hookup and who comes in to get shit faced.

I can't tell with this girl. It seems like she accidentally opened the door and ended up in my bar and has no idea what she wants from tonight.

Maybe she just wants to skip tonight and get straight to whatever big thing she's got going on tomorrow.

I'm waiting for a signal from her on what she wants me to do next, because I thought I was taking her home, but she hasn't faced forward. It's like she wants me to kiss her again. But I don't want to make her cry again. *But I want to kiss her again.*

I touch her face, and she leans into my hand. I'm still not positive she's comfortable, so I hesitate until she scoots closer to me. I position myself between her legs, and then she tightens her thighs around my hips.

I can take a hint.

I swipe my tongue across her lips, and she pulls me in until her sweet breath is in my mouth. She tastes like apples still, but her mouth is saltier and her tongue is more decisive. She leans into my kiss, and I lean into the truck, into her, and she slowly falls back across the seat, pulling me with her. I hover over her, standing between her legs, pressing myself against her.

The way she sucks in small gasps of air while I kiss her is driving me insane.

She guides my hand up her shirt and I grab her breast and she wraps her legs around me and then my jeans are against hers and we're rocking back and forth like we're in fucking high school and this is our only place to go.

I want to pull her back into the bar and tear off her clothes, but this is enough. More than this would be way too much. For her. Or maybe too much for me. I don't know, I just know her mouth and this truck are enough.

After a minute of making out in the dark, I pull away from her mouth just enough to see that her eyes are closed and her lips are parted. I keep my steady rhythm against her, and she lifts her hips, and I swear the friction between our clothes is enough to start an actual fire. It's so hot between her thighs, and I don't think I can finish like this. I'm not sure she can either. We're just going to drive ourselves crazy if we don't find a way to get even closer, or stop altogether.

I would invite her to my house, but my parents are in town, and I'm not bringing anyone near those two.

"Nicole," I whisper. I feel uncomfortable even suggesting this, but I can't keep making out with her in an alley like she isn't worth a bed. "We could go back inside."

She shakes her head and says, "No. I like your truck," right before pulling my mouth back to hers.

If she likes my truck, I *love* my truck. My truck is my second-favorite thing in the world right now.

Her mouth is my first.

She moves my hand to the button on her jeans, so I oblige and unbutton them while my tongue is dragging across hers. I slip my hand into the front of her jeans until my fingers slide over her panties. She moans, and it's so loud against the silent soundtrack of this sleepy town.

I move her panties aside with my fingers, and I'm met with smooth skin and heat and a whimper. When I inhale, I can hear the shakiness of my own breaths.

I bury my mouth against her neck just as headlights turn onto the street next to us.

"Shit." My truck is parked in the alley, but we aren't hidden from the view of the street. We suddenly find ourselves scrambling as we're snapped back to reality. I pull my hand out of her jeans, and she buttons them. I help her up, and then she faces forward while straightening out her hair.

I close her door and walk around the truck as the car approaches and comes to a slow roll, then a stop, right in front of the alley. I glance up at the car and see Grady in his cruiser. He's rolling down the window, so I walk away from my truck and up to his car.

"Busy night?" he asks as he leans toward the passenger seat so that he can see me from the driver's side of the car.

I look behind me at Nicole in the truck and then back at him. "Yep. Just closed. You on until morning?"

He turns down his radio. "Whitney took a new shift at the hospital, so I'm back on nights for now. I like it. It's quiet."

I tap his hood and then take a step back. "Good to hear. I gotta go. See you tomorrow on the field?"

Grady can tell something is up. I'm usually not this quick to brush him off. He leans forward, looking around me, attempting to see whoever is in my truck. I lean to the right and block his view. "Have a good night, Grady." I point down the road, letting him know he's welcome to continue his patrol.

He grins. "Yep. You too."

I'm not trying to hide her. I just know his wife is a gossip, and I don't really want to be the talk of the T-ball field tomorrow.

I climb into my truck, and she's got her feet up on the dash. She's looking out her window, avoiding eye contact with me. I don't want her to feel awkward. That's the last thing I want. I reach over and tuck a strand of hair behind her ear. "You okay?"

She nods, but the nod is stiff, and so is she, and so is her smile. "I live next to Cefco."

That gas station is almost two miles away. She told me earlier she lived close by, but two miles at midnight isn't close. "Cefco off Bellview?"

She shrugs. "I think so. I can't remember all the street names. I just moved here today."

That explains why she isn't familiar to me. I want to say something like, *"Where'd you come from? What brings you to town?"* But I say nothing, because she seems to want me to say nothing.

Two miles only takes two minutes when there's no traffic, and two minutes isn't all that long, but it sure does feel like an eternity when you're spending it in a truck with a girl you almost fucked. And it wouldn't have been a good fuck. It most certainly would have been a quick, sloppy, selfish, couldn't-have-been-good-for-her fuck.

I want to apologize, but I'm not sure what I'd be apologizing for, and I don't want her to think I regret it. The only thing I regret is that I'm taking her home and not to my house.

"I live there," she says, pointing at Paradise Apartments.

I don't come to this part of town very often. It's in the opposite direction of my house, so I rarely drive down this road. I honestly thought they condemned this place.

I pull into the parking lot, and I intend to kill the engine and open her door for her, but she's already out of the truck before I even get it turned off.

"Thanks for the ride," she says. "And . . . for the coffee." She closes the door and spins around like that's how we're supposed to part.

I open my door. "Hey. Wait."

She pauses but waits to turn around until I've reached her. She's hugging herself, chewing on her lip, scratching nervously at her arm. She looks up at me. "You don't have to say anything."

"What do you mean?"

"I mean . . . I know what that was." She waves a hand at my truck. "You don't have to ask for my number, I don't even have one."

How does she know what that was? *I* don't know what that was. My mind is still trying to process it. Maybe I should ask her. *"What was that? What does it mean? Can it happen again?"*

I'm in uncharted territory. I've had one-night stands before, but things were discussed and agreed to prior to the sex. And it's always happened in a bed, or something close to it.

But with her, the make-out just happened, and then it was interrupted, and it was in an alley of all places. I feel like an asshole.

I have no idea what to say. I don't know where to put my hands because I feel like I should be hugging her goodbye, but it seems like she doesn't want me near her now. I slip my hands into the pockets of my jeans. "I want to see you again." It's not a lie.

Her eyes flicker from mine to her apartment building. "I'm not . . ." She sighs, and then she just says, "No, thank you."

She says it so politely, I can't even be upset.

I stand in front of her apartment building and watch her walk away until she goes up the stairs and into an apartment and I can't see her anymore. And even then, I stay in the same spot because I think I'm shocked or, at the least, jarred.

I don't know her at all, but I find her more intriguing than anyone else I've met in a long time. I want to ask her more questions. She never even answered the one question I asked about her life. Who the hell is she?

Why do I feel the need to find out more about her?

CHAPTER SEVEN

KENNA

Dear Scotty,

When they say it's a small world, they aren't kidding. Tiny. Miniscule. Overcrowded.

I'm only telling you this because I know you can't actually read these letters, but I saw Ledger's truck tonight and I thought I was going to cry.

Actually, I was already crying because he said his name and I realized who he was and I was kissing him and I felt so guilty, so I embarrassingly ran outside and almost had a panic attack.

But yeah. That damn truck. I can't believe he still has it. I still remember the night you pulled up in it to take me on our first date. I laughed because it was such a bright orange that I couldn't understand what kind of person would willingly choose that color.

Over three hundred letters I've written to you and I only realized tonight while skimming the letters that not one of them details the first moment we met. I wrote about our actual first date, but never mentioned the first time we laid eyes on each other.

I was working as a cashier at Dollar Days. It was the first job I applied for when I moved away from Denver. I knew no one, but I didn't mind it. I was in a new state and a new town and no one held any preconceived notions of me. No one knew my mother.

When you came through my line, I didn't notice you right away. I rarely looked at the customers, especially if they were guys my age. Guys my age had only disappointed me up to that point. I thought maybe I was supposed to be attracted to older men, or maybe even women, because no guy I had ever met who was my age made me feel good about myself. Between the catcalls and the sexual expectations, I had lost complete faith in the male population of my generation.

We were a small store, and everything in the store was just a dollar, so people usually came through with carts full of stuff. You came through my line with one dinner plate. I wondered what kind of person only bought one dinner plate. Surely most people expect to have friends occasionally, or at least the hope for friends. But buying one plate felt like you expected to always eat alone.

I rang up the plate and wrapped it before placing it in a sack and handing it to you.

It wasn't until the second time you came through my line a few minutes later that I finally looked at your face. You were buying a second dinner plate. It made me feel better for you. I rang up the second plate, you handed me your dollar and some change, I handed you the sack, and that's when you smiled.

You had me in that moment, although you probably didn't realize it. Your smile was like warmth sliding over me. It was dangerous and it was comfortable, and I didn't know what to do about those warring feelings, so I looked away from you.

Two minutes later, you were standing in line again with a third plate.

I rang you up. You paid. I wrapped your plate and handed you your sack, but this time I spoke. "Come back soon," I said.

You grinned and said, "If you insist."

You circled the register and went back to the aisle that contained the plates. I didn't have any other customers, so I watched the aisle until you reappeared with a fourth plate and brought it to the register.

I rang up the plate and said, "You know, you can buy more than one thing at a time."

"I know," you said. "But I only need one plate."

"Then why is this the fourth one you've bought?"

"Because I'm trying to work up the nerve to ask you out."

I had hoped that was why. I handed you your sack, wanting your fingers to touch mine. They did. It felt exactly as I imagined, like our hands were magnetic. It took a lot of effort just to pull my hand back.

I tried to act nonchalant about your flirtation, because that's just what I'd always done with men, so I said, "It's against store policy for employees to date customers."

There wasn't any firmness or truth to my voice at all, but I think you liked the game we were playing, so you said, "Okay. Give me a minute to rectify that." You walked to the only other cashier in the store. You were only a few feet away, so I heard you say, "I need to return these plates, please."

The other cashier had been on the phone with a customer during your four trips to the register, so I'm not sure she knew you were being facetious. She glanced at me from her register and made a face. I shrugged like I didn't know what was up with the guy who had four different receipts for four plates, and then I turned away from her to wait on another customer.

You came through my line a few minutes later and slapped a return receipt on the counter. "I'm no longer a customer. What now?"

I picked up the receipt, pretending to read it carefully. I handed it back to you and said, "I get off work at seven."

You folded the receipt and didn't look at me when you said, "See you in three hours."

I should have told you six, because I ended up getting off work early. I spent the extra hour in the store next door buying a new outfit. You still hadn't shown up at twenty minutes past seven, so I had given up and was walking to my car when you sped into the parking lot and pulled up next to me. You rolled down your window and said, "Sorry I'm late."

I was perpetually late, so I was in no place to judge you on your tardiness, but I sure did judge you based on your truck. I thought maybe you were insane or overconfident. It was an older Ford F-250. Big double cab, the ugliest color of orange I'd ever seen. "I like your truck." I wasn't sure if I was telling the truth or if I was lying. It was such an ugly truck it made me hate it. But because it was so ugly, it made me love that you were picking me up in it.

"It's not mine. It's my best friend's truck. My car is in the shop."

I was relieved it wasn't yours, but also a little disappointed because I found the color so amusing. You motioned for me to get in the truck. You looked proud and smelled like a candy cane.

"Is that why you're late? Your car broke down?"

You shook your head and said, "No. I had to break up with my girlfriend."

My head swung in your direction. "You have a girlfriend?"

"Not anymore." You shot me a coy look.

"But you had one when you asked me out earlier?"

"Yes, but by the time I purchased my third dinner plate, I knew I was going to break up with her. It was overdue," you said. "We've both been wanting out of it for a while. We were just too comfortable to call it off." You flipped on your blinker and pulled into a gas station and up to a gas pump. "My mother will be sad. My mother really likes her."

"Mothers don't usually like me," I admitted. Or maybe it was more of a warning.

You smiled. "I can see that. Mothers prefer to imagine their sons with wholesome-looking girls. You're too sexy to make a mother feel comfortable."

I wasn't one to get offended by a guy calling me sexy. I worked hard that day to look sexy. I spent a lot of money on the bra and low-cut shirt I had purchased thirty minutes earlier with the goal of making my breasts look store bought.

I appreciated the compliment, even if you were being a little tacky.

As you got out to fill your friend's truck up with gas, I thought about the wholesome-looking girl whose heart you just broke simply because I agreed to go on a date with you, and I felt a bit like a snake in that moment.

But even though I felt like a snake, I didn't plan on slithering away. I liked your energy so much, I planned to coil myself around you and never let go.

When Ledger said his name against my lips earlier tonight, I almost said, "Scotty's Ledger?" But the question would have been pointless, because I knew in that instant that he was your Ledger. How many Ledgers can there be? I've never met one before.

I was overwhelmed with questions, but Ledger kissed me and it ripped me in half, because I wanted to kiss him back, but even more than that I wanted to ask him questions about you. I wanted to say, "What was Scotty like as a child? What did you love about him? Did he ever talk about me? Do you still talk to his parents? Have you met my daughter? Can you help me put all the pieces of my broken life back together?"

But I couldn't speak because your best friend had his searing hot tongue in my mouth and it felt like he was branding me with the word CHEATER.

I don't know why it felt like I was cheating on you. You've been dead five years, and I kissed the prison guard, so it's not like you were even my last kiss. But my kiss with the prison guard didn't make me feel like I was cheating on you. That could be because the prison guard wasn't your best friend.

Or maybe I felt like a cheater because I actually felt Ledger's kiss. It trickled all over me the way your kisses used to do, but then there was that added element of feeling like a cheater, or a liar, or trash, because Ledger didn't know me at all. To Ledger, he was being kissed by the transient girl he couldn't stop staring at all night.

To me, I was being kissed by the hot bartender whose best friend died because of me.

Everything exploded. I felt like I was shattering. I was allowing Ledger to touch me, knowing full well he'd probably rather stab me if he knew who I was. Pulling away from his kiss felt a little like trying to put out a forest fire with a nuclear bomb.

I wanted to apologize, I wanted to escape.

I felt like collapsing, thinking about how Ledger probably knew you better than I did. I hated that the one guy I ran into in this town is the one guy I should be avoiding.

Ledger didn't turn away when I cried, though. He did what you would have done. He put his arms around me and let me be however I needed to be, and it felt nice because I hadn't been held like that since you.

I closed my eyes and pretended your best friend was my ally. That he was on my side. I pretended he was holding me despite what I'd done to you, and he wanted to help me heal.

I also let it happen because if Ledger is back in this town, and he's still driving the truck I met you in all those years ago, then that means he's a fan of routine.

And there's a huge possibility that our daughter is part of Ledger's routine.

Is it possible I'm only one person away from Diem?

If you could see the pages I'm writing this letter on, you'd see the tearstains. Crying seems to be the only thing left in life that I'm good at. Crying and making bad decisions.

And, of course, I'm good at writing you bad poetry. I'll leave you with one I wrote on the bus ride back to this town.

I have a daughter I have never held.

She has a scent I have never smelled.

She has a name I have never yelled.

She has a mother who has already failed.

Love,

Kenna

CHAPTER EIGHT

LEDGER

I didn't park in the garage when I got home last night. Diem likes to wake up and look out her window in the mornings to make sure I'm home, and when I leave my truck in the garage, Grace says it makes Diem sad.

I've lived across the street from them since Diem was eight months old, but if I don't count the years I moved out of this house and lived in Denver, I've technically been in this house my entire life.

My parents haven't lived here in several years, even though they're both passed out in the guest room right now.

They bought the RV when my father retired, and they travel the country now. I bought the house from them when I moved back, and they loaded up and left. I figured it would last a year at the most, but it's been over four years now, and they aren't showing any signs of slowing down.

I just wish they'd warn me before they show up. Maybe I should download a GPS app to their phones so I'll have some kind of warning in the future. Not that I don't like their visits. It would just be nice to be able to prepare for them.

This is why I'm building a privacy gate at my new house.

Eventually.

It's slow going because Roman and I are doing a lot of the work ourselves. Every Sunday from sunup until sundown, I drive up to Cheshire Ridge with Roman and we work on it. I contract out for the more difficult stuff, but we've completed a good chunk of the build ourselves. After two years of Sundays, the house is finally starting to come together. I'm maybe six months from moving in.

"Where are you going?"

I spin around when I reach the garage door. My father is standing outside the guest bedroom. He's in his underwear.

"Diem has T-ball. You guys want to come?"

"Nope. Too hungover for kids today, and we really need to get back on the road."

"You're already leaving?"

"We'll be back in a few weeks." My father gives me a hug. "Your mother is still asleep, but I'll tell her you said bye."

"Maybe give me a heads-up before the next visit and I'll take off work."

My father shakes his head. "Nah, we like seeing the surprise on your face when we show up unannounced." He heads into the bathroom and closes the door.

I walk through the garage and toward Patrick and Grace's house across the street.

I'm hoping Diem isn't in a talkative mood because my concentration is going to be shit today. All I can think about is the girl from last night and how much I want to see her again. I wonder if it would be weird if I left a note on her door?

I knock on Patrick and Grace's front door and then walk in. We're all back and forth at each other's houses so much, at one point we got tired of saying, *"It's open."* It's always open.

Grace is in the kitchen with Diem. Diem is sitting in the center of the table with her legs crossed and a bowl of eggs on her lap. She never sits in chairs. She's always on top of things, like the back of the couch, the kitchen bar, the kitchen table. She's a climber.

"You're still in your pajamas, D." I take the bowl of eggs from her and point down the hallway. "Get dressed, we gotta go." She runs to her room to put on her T-ball uniform.

"I thought the game was at ten," Grace says. "I would have had her ready."

"It is, but I've got Gatorade duty, so I have to run by the store, and then I have to swing by and pick up Roman." I lean against the counter and grab a tangerine. I peel it open while Grace starts the dishwasher.

She blows a piece of hair out of her face. "She wants a swing set," she says. "One of those ridiculously big ones like the one you used to have in your backyard. Her friend Nyla from school got one, and you know we can't say no. It'll be her fifth birthday."

"I still have it."

"You do? Where?"

"It's in the shed in pieces, but I can help Patrick put it back together. Shouldn't be too hard."

"You think it's still in good shape?"

"Was when I took it apart." I fail to tell her Scotty is the reason I took it apart. I got angry every time I looked at it after he died.

I put another piece of tangerine in my mouth and reroute my thoughts. "I can't believe she'll be five."

Grace sighs. "I know. Unreal. Un*fair*."

Patrick pops into the kitchen and tousles my hair like I'm not almost thirty and three inches taller than him. "Hey, kid." He reaches around me and grabs one of the tangerines. "Did Grace tell you we can't make the game today?"

"I haven't yet," Grace says. She rolls her eyes, her annoyed gaze landing on me. "My sister is in the hospital. Elective surgery, she's fine, but we have to drive to her house and feed her cats."

"What's she getting done this time?"

Grace waves a hand at her face. "Something with her eyes. Who knows? She's five years older than me, but looks ten years younger."

Patrick covers Grace's mouth. "Stop. You're perfect." Grace laughs and shoves his hand away.

I've never seen them fight. Not even when Scotty was a kid. My parents bicker a lot, and it's mostly in fun, but I've never even seen Grace and Patrick bicker in the twenty years I've known them.

I want that. Someday. I don't have time for it yet, though. I work too much and feel like I'm slowly running myself into the ground. I need to make a change if I ever want to keep a girl long enough to have what Patrick and Grace have.

"Ledger!" Diem yells from her bedroom. "Help me!" I walk down the hallway to go see what she needs. She's on her knees in her closet, digging around. "I can't find my other boot—I need my boot."

She's holding one red cowboy boot and rummaging around for the other. "Why do you need boots? You need your cleats."

"I don't want to wear my cleats today. I want to wear my boots."

Her cleats are next to her bed, so I grab them. "You can't wear boots to play baseball. Here, hop on the bed so I can help you put on your cleats."

She stands up and flings the second red boot onto her bed. "Found it!" She giggles and climbs onto her bed and starts putting on her boots.

"Diem. It's baseball. People don't wear boots to play baseball."

"I am, I'm wearing boots today."

"No, you can't—" I shut up. I don't have time to argue with her, and I know once she gets to the field and sees all the other kids with their cleats, she'll let me take off her boots. I help her put on the boots and take the cleats with us when I carry her out of the room.

Grace meets us at the door and hands Diem a juice pouch. "Have fun today." She kisses Diem on the cheek, and then Grace's eyes go to Diem's boots.

"Don't ask," I say as I open their front door.

"Bye, Nana!" Diem says.

Patrick is in the kitchen, and when Diem fails to tell him goodbye, he stomps dramatically toward us. "What about NoNo?"

Patrick wanted to go by *Papa* when Diem started talking, but for whatever reason, she called Grace *Nana* and Patrick *NoNo*, and it was so funny Grace and I enforced it enough that it finally stuck.

"Bye, NoNo," Diem says, giggling.

"We may not get back before you," Grace says. "You mind keeping her if we aren't?"

I don't know why Grace always asks me. I've never said no. I'll never *say* no. "Take your time. I'll take her somewhere for lunch." I put Diem down when we get outside.

"McDonald's!" she says.

"I don't want McDonald's," I say as we cross the street toward my truck.

"McDonald's drive-through!"

I open the back door to my truck and help her into her booster seat. "How about Mexican food?"

"Nope. McDonald's."

"Chinese? We haven't had Chinese food in a long time."

"McDonald's."

"I'll tell you what. If you wear your cleats when we get to the game, we can eat McDonald's." I get her seat belt buckled.

She shakes her head. "No, I want to wear my boots. I don't want lunch anyway—I'm full."

"You'll be hungry by lunchtime."

"I won't, I ate a dragon. I'm gonna be full forever."

Sometimes I worry about how many stories she tells, but she's so convincing I'm more impressed than concerned. I don't know at what age a child should know the difference between a lie and using their imagination, but I'll leave that up to Grace and Patrick. I don't want to stifle my favorite part of her.

I pull onto the street. "You ate a dragon? A *whole* dragon?"

"Yeah, but he was a baby dragon, that's how he fit in my stomach."

"Where'd you find a baby dragon?"

"Walmart."

"They sell baby dragons at Walmart?"

She proceeds to tell me all about how baby dragons are sold at Walmart, but you have to have a special coupon, and only kids can eat them. By the time I make it to Roman's, she's explaining how they're cooked.

"With salt and shampoo," she says.

"You aren't supposed to eat shampoo."

"You don't *eat* it—you use it to cook the dragon."

"Oh. Silly me."

Roman gets in the truck, and he looks about as excited as someone going to a funeral. He hates T-ball days. He's never been a kid person. The only reason he helps me coach is that none of the other parents would do it. And since he works for me, I added it to his schedule.

He's the only person I know who gets paid to coach T-ball, but he doesn't seem to feel guilty about it.

"Hi, Roman," Diem says from the back seat in a singsong voice.

"I've only had one cup of coffee; don't talk to me." Roman is twenty-seven, but he and Diem have met somewhere in the middle with their love-hate relationship, because they both act twelve.

Diem starts tapping the back of his headrest. "Wake up, wake up, wake up."

Roman rolls his head until he's looking at me. "All this shit you do to help little kids in your spare time isn't going to gain you any points in an afterlife because religion is a social construct created by societies who wanted to regulate their people, which makes heaven a concept. We could be sleeping right now."

"Wow. I'd hate to see you *before* coffee." I back out of his driveway. "If heaven is conceptual, what is hell?"

"The T-ball field."

CHAPTER NINE

KENNA

I've been to six different places trying to find a job, and it isn't even ten in the morning yet. They've all gone the same. They give me an application. Ask me about my experience. I have to tell them I have none. I have to tell them why.

Then they apologize, but not before looking me up and down. I know what they're thinking. It's the same thing my landlord, Ruth, said when she saw me for the first time. *"Didn't expect you to look like this."*

People think women who go to prison have a certain look. That we're a certain way. But we're mothers, wives, daughters, *humans*.

And all we want is to just catch one fucking break.

Just one.

The seventh place I try is a grocery store. It's a little farther from my apartment than I'd like, almost two and a half miles, but I've exhausted everything else between this store and my apartment.

I'm sweating when I enter the store, so I freshen up in the bathroom. I'm washing my hands in the sink when a short woman with silky black hair enters the bathroom. She doesn't go into a stall. She just leans against the wall and closes her eyes. She has a name badge on: **AMY**.

When she opens her eyes, she notices I'm staring at her shoes. She's wearing a pair of moccasins with white and red beads in the shape of a circle on top of them.

"You like?" she asks, lifting her foot and tilting it from one side to the other.

"Yeah. They're beautiful."

"My grandmother makes them. We're supposed to wear sneakers here, but the general manager has never said anything about my shoes. I think he's scared of me."

I look down at my muddy sneakers. I recoil at the sight of them. I didn't realize I was walking around with such dirty shoes.

I can't apply for a job like this. I take one of them off and start washing it in the sink.

"I'm hiding," the woman says. "I don't normally hang out in bathrooms, but there's an old lady in the store who always complains about everything, and I'm honestly just not in the mood for her bullshit today. I have a two-year-old and she didn't sleep all night and I really wanted to call in sick today, but I'm the shift manager, and shift managers don't call in sick. We show up."

"And hide in bathrooms."

She grins. "Exactly."

I switch shoes and start washing the other one. I have a lump in my throat when I say, "Are you guys hiring? I'm looking for a job."

"Yeah, but it's probably not anything you're interested in."

She must not see the desperation on my face. "What are you hiring for?"

"Grocery bagger. It's not full time, but we usually leave those spots open for teenagers with special needs."

"Oh. Well, I don't want to take a job away from anyone."

"No, it's not that," she says. "We just don't have many applicants because of the low hours, but we really are in need of part-time help. It's about twenty hours a week."

That won't even pay rent, but if I worked hard enough, I could possibly work my way into a different position. "I can do it until someone with special needs applies. I could really use the money."

Amy looks me up and down. "Why are you so desperate? The pay is shit."

I put my shoe back on. "I, um . . ." I tie my shoe, stalling the inevitable admission. "I just got out of prison." I say it fast and confidently, like it doesn't bother me as much as it does. "But I'm not . . . I can do this. I won't let you down and I won't be any trouble."

Amy laughs. It's a loud laugh, but when I don't laugh with her, she folds her arms over her chest and tilts her head. "Oh, shit. You're serious?"

I nod. "Yeah. But if it's against policy, I totally get it. It's not a big deal."

She waves a flippant hand. "Eh, we don't really have a policy. We aren't a chain—we can hire whoever we want. To be honest, I'm obsessed with *Orange Is the New Black*, so if you'll promise to let me know which parts of the show are bullshit, I'll give you an application."

I could cry. Instead, I fake a smile. "I've heard so many jokes about that show. I guess I need to watch it."

Amy rolls her head. "Yes. Yes, yes. Best show, best cast; come with me."

I follow her to the customer service desk at the front of the store. She digs around in a drawer and finds an application, then hands it to me along with a pen. "If you fill it out while you're here, I can get you in for Monday orientation."

I take the application from her, and I want to thank her, I want to hug her, I want to tell her she's changing my life. But I just smile and quietly take my application to a bench by the front door.

I fill out my full name but put quotation marks around my middle name, so they'll know to call me Nicole. I can't be wearing a name tag that says **Kenna** in this town. Someone will recognize it. Then they'll gossip.

I get halfway through the first page when I'm interrupted.

"Hey."

My fingers clench the pen tightly when I hear his voice. I slowly lift my head, and Ledger is standing in front of me with a grocery cart full of about a dozen packs of Gatorade.

I flip the application over, hoping he didn't already see my name across the top of it. I swallow and attempt to appear to be in a more stable mood than all the moods he witnessed from me yesterday.

I gesture toward the Gatorade. "Special at the bar tonight?"

A subtle relief seems to wash over him, like he was expecting me to tell him to fuck off. He taps one of the packs of Gatorade. "T-ball coach."

I look away from him, because for some reason that answer makes me uneasy. He doesn't look like a T-ball coach. Those lucky mothers.

Oh, no. He's a T-ball coach. Does he have a kid? A kid and a wife?

Did I almost sleep with a married T-ball coach?

I tap the pen on the back of the clipboard. "Are you, um . . . you aren't married, are you?"

His grin tells me no. He doesn't even need to say it, but he shakes his head and says, "Single," then motions toward the clipboard on my lap. "You applying for a job?"

"Yep." I glance toward the customer service desk, and Amy is eyeing me. I need this job so bad, but I'm afraid this might make it look like I'm going to be distracted by sexy bartenders while I'm on the clock. I look away from her, wondering if Ledger's standing here talking to me is hurting my chances. I flip the clipboard back over, but tilt it so that he isn't able to see my name. I start writing in my address, hoping he walks away.

He doesn't. He pushes his cart to the side so a guy can get around him, and then he leans his right shoulder against the wall and says, "I was hoping I'd run into you again."

I'm not going to do this right now.

I'm not going to lead him on when he has no idea who I am.

I'm also not going to risk this job by fraternizing with customers.

"Can you go?" I whisper it, but loud enough for him to hear it.

He makes a face. "Did I do something wrong?"

"No, I just really need to finish this."

His jaw tightens, and he pushes off the wall. "It's just that you act like you're mad, and I feel kind of bad about last night . . ."

"I'm fine." I look back at the customer service desk, and Amy is still staring. I face Ledger and plead with him. "I *really* need this job. And right now, my potential new boss keeps looking over here, and no offense, but you're covered in tattoos and look like trouble, and I need her to think I'm not going to give her any issues at all. I don't care what happened last night. It was mutual. It was fine."

He nods slowly and then grips the handle of his shopping cart. "It was *fine*," he repeats, seemingly offended.

For a moment, I feel bad, but I'm not going to lie to him. He put his hand down my jeans, and if we hadn't been interrupted, we probably would have ended up fucking. *In his truck.* How spectacular could it have been?

But he's right—it was more than *fine*. I can't even look at him without staring at his mouth. He's a good kisser, and it's toying with my head right now because I have so many more important things going on in my life than his mouth.

He stands silent for a couple of seconds and then reaches into a sack in his cart. He pulls out a brown bottle. "I bought caramel. In case you come back." He tosses the bottle into the cart. "Anyway. Good luck." He looks uneasy when he turns and walks out the door.

I try to continue filling out the form, but I'm shaking now. I feel like I've got a bomb strapped to me and it ticks down in his presence, getting closer and closer to exploding my secrets all over him.

I finish filling out the application, but my handwriting is sloppy because of my trembling hands. When I return to customer service and hand it to Amy, she says, "He your boyfriend?"

I play dumb. "Who?"

"Ledger Ward."

Ward? The bar is called Ward's. He owns the bar?

I shake my head, answering Amy's question. "No, I hardly know him."

"Shame. He's a hot commodity around here since he and Leah broke up."

She says that like I'm supposed to know who Leah is. I guess in a town this size, most people know most people. I glance back at the door Ledger disappeared through. "I'm not in the market for a hot commodity. Just a lukewarm job."

Amy laughs and then browses my application for a moment. "Did you grow up here?"

"No, I'm from Denver. I came here for college." That's a lie—I never went to college—but it's a college town, and my intentions were to eventually go. That just never happened.

"Oh, yeah? What's your degree in?"

"Didn't finish. That's why I'm back," I lie. "Registering for next semester."

"This job is perfect for that; we can work around your classes. Be here Monday at eight for orientation. Do you have a driver's license?"

I nod. "Yeah, I'll bring it." I leave out the fact that I just got my driver's license last month, after months of working to get it reinstated. "Thank you." I try to say that with as little eagerness in my voice as possible, but so far things are working out. I have an apartment and now a job.

Now I just need to find my daughter.

I turn to walk away, but Amy says, "Wait. Do you want to know how much you're making?"

"Oh. Yeah, of course."

"Minimum wage. Ridiculous, I know. I don't own this place, or I'd raise it." She leans forward and lowers her voice. "You know, you can probably get a job at the Lowe's warehouse. They pay twice that starting out."

"I tried online last week. They won't hire me with my record."

"Oh. Bummer. Well. See you Monday, then."

Before I go, I tap my fist on the counter and ask a question I probably shouldn't ask. "One more thing. You know the guy I was talking to? Ledger?"

She raises an amused brow. "What about him?"

"Does he have kids?"

"Just a niece or something. She comes in here with him sometimes. Cute girl, but I'm pretty sure he's single and childless."

A niece?

Or could it be his deceased best friend's daughter?

Does he shop here with my daughter?

I somehow force a smile through the onslaught of emotions suddenly spiraling through me. I thank her again, but then I leave in a hurry, hoping by some miracle Ledger's truck is still outside and that my daughter is in the truck with him.

I look around the parking lot, but he's already gone. My stomach sinks, but I can still feel the adrenaline disguised as hope running through my body. Because now I know he coaches T-ball, and Diem more than likely plays on his team, because why else would he coach if he doesn't have children of his own?

I debate going straight to the T-ball field, but I need to do this right. I want to speak with Patrick and Grace first.

CHAPTER TEN

LEDGER

I'm in the dugout pulling the equipment out of the bag when Grady slips his fingers through the chain-link fence, gripping it. "So? Who was she?"

I pretend not to know what he's talking about. "Who was who?"

"The girl you had in your truck last night."

Grady's eyes are bloodshot. It looks like the night shift change is taking a toll on him. "A customer. I was just giving her a ride home."

Grady's wife, Whitney, is standing next to him now. At least the rest of the mom brigade isn't with her, because I can tell immediately by the way she's looking at me that everyone on the T-ball field is already talking. I can only be confronted by one couple at a time. "Grady said you had a girl in your truck last night."

I shoot Grady a look, and he holds his hands up helplessly, like his wife yanked the information out of him.

"It was no one," I repeat. "Just giving a customer a ride home." I wonder how many times I'm going to have to repeat this today.

"Who was she?" Whitney asks.

"No one you know."

"We know everyone around here," Grady says.

"She's not from here," I say. I might be lying; I might be telling the truth. I wouldn't know since I know very little about her. Other than what she tastes like.

"Destin has been working on his swing," Grady says, changing the subject to his son. "Wait'll you see what he can do."

Grady wants to be the envy of all the other fathers. I don't get it. T-ball is supposed to be fun, but people like him put so much competitiveness into it and ruin the sport.

Two weeks ago, Grady almost got into a fight with the umpire. He probably would have hit him if Roman hadn't pushed him off the field.

Not sure getting that heated over a T-ball game is a good look for anyone. But he takes his son's sports very seriously.

Me . . . not so much. Sometimes I wonder if it's because Diem isn't my daughter. If she were, would I get angry over a sport that doesn't even keep score? I don't know that I could love a biological child more than I love Diem, so I doubt I'd be any different when it comes to their sports. Some of the parents assume that since I played professional football I'd be more competitive. I've dealt with competitive coaches my whole life, though. I agreed to coach this team specifically to prevent some competitive asshole from coming in and setting a bad example for Diem.

The kids are supposed to be warming up, but Diem is standing behind home plate shoving T-balls into the pockets of her baseball pants. She's got two in each pocket, and now she's trying to shove a third in. Her pants are starting to sag from the weight.

I walk over to her and kneel. "D, you can't take all the T-balls."

"They're dragon eggs," she says. "I'm going to plant them in my yard and grow baby dragons."

I toss the balls one at a time to Roman. "That's not how dragons grow. The momma dragon has to sit on the eggs. You don't bury them in the yard."

Diem bends forward to pick up a pebble, and I notice she has two balls stuffed down the back of her shirt. I untuck her shirt, and the balls fall to her feet. I kick them to Roman.

"Did *I* grow in an egg?" she asks.

"No, D. You're a human. Humans don't grow in eggs—we grow in . . ." I stop talking because I was about to say, "*We grow in our mother's bellies,*" but I'm always careful to avoid any talk of mothers or fathers around Diem. I don't want her to start asking me questions I can't answer.

"What do we grow in?" she asks. "Trees?"

Shit.

I put my hand on Diem's shoulder and completely ignore her question because I have no idea what Grace or Patrick has told her about how babies are made. This isn't my wheelhouse. I wasn't prepared for this conversation.

I yell for all the kids to go to the dugout, and luckily Diem is distracted by one of her friends and walks away from me.

I blow out a breath, relieved the conversation ended where it did.

I dropped Roman off at the bar to spare him a trip to McDonald's.

And yes, we're at McDonald's even though Diem didn't wear her cleats at all during the game, because she gets her way with me more often than she doesn't.

Choose your battles, they say. But what happens when you never choose *any*?

"I don't want to play T-ball anymore," Diem says out of the blue. She's dipping her french fry into honey when she makes that decision. The honey dribbles down her hand.

I try to get her to eat her fries with ketchup because it's a lot easier to clean, but she wouldn't be Diem if she didn't do everything the hardest way possible.

"You don't like T-ball anymore?"

She shakes her head and licks her wrist.

"That's fine. But we only have a few more games, and you made a commitment."

"What's a commitment?"

"It's when you agree to do something. You agreed to be a part of the team. If you quit in the middle of the season, your friends will be sad. You think you can make it through the rest of the season?"

"If we can have McDonald's after all the games."

I narrow my eyes in her direction. "Why do I feel like I'm getting swindled?"

"What does *swindled* mean?" she asks.

"It means you're trying to trick me into getting you McDonald's."

Diem grins and eats her last fry. I put all our trash on the tray. I grab her hand to lead her out of the store and remember the honey. Her hands are as sticky as a flytrap. I keep wet wipes in my truck for this very reason.

A couple of minutes later, she's buckled up in her booster seat and I'm scrubbing her hands and arms with the wet wipe when she says, "When is my mom getting a bigger car?"

"She drives a minivan. How big of a car does she need?"

"Not Nana," Diem says. "My mom. Skylar said my mom never comes to my T-ball games, and I told her she will when she gets a bigger car."

I stop wiping her hands. She never brings up her mother. This is twice in one day we've brushed the conversation.

I guess she's getting to that age, but I have no idea what Grace or Patrick has told her about Kenna, and I have absolutely no idea why she's asking about her mother's car.

"Who told you your mom needed a bigger car?"

"Nana. She said my mom's car isn't big enough and that's why I live with her and NoNo."

That's confusing. I shake my head and throw the wipes in a sack. "I don't know. Ask your nana." I close her door and text Grace as I'm circling around to the driver's side of my truck.

Why does Diem think her mother isn't in her life because she needs a bigger car?

We're a few miles away from McDonald's when Grace calls. I make sure not to answer it on speaker. "Hey. Diem and I are on our way back." It's my way of letting Grace know I can't say much on my end.

Grace sucks in a breath like she's getting ready for a long explanation to my text. "Okay, so last week, Diem asked me why she doesn't live with her mother. I didn't know what to say, so I told her she lives with me because her mother's car isn't big enough to fit all of us. It was the first lie I could come up with. I panicked, Ledger."

"I'd say so."

"We plan on telling her, but how do you tell a child her mother went to prison? She doesn't even know what prison is."

"I'm not judging," I say. "I just want to make sure we're on the same page. We should probably come up with a more accurate version of the truth, though."

"I know. She's just so young."

"She's starting to get curious."

"I know. Just . . . if she asks again, tell her I'll explain it to her."

"I did. Prepare for questions."

"Great," she says with a sigh. "How did the game go?"

"Good. She wore the red boots. *And* got McDonald's."

Grace laughs. "You're a sucker."

"Yeah. Tell me something new. See you soon." I end the call and glance into the back seat. Diem's face is full of concentration.

"What are you thinking, D?"

"I want to be in a movie," Diem says.

"Oh yeah? You want to be an actress?"

"No, I want to be in a movie."

"I know. That's called being an actress."

"Then, yeah, that's what I want to be. An actress. I want to be in cartoons."

I don't tell her cartoons are just voices and drawings. "I think you'd be a great cartoon actress."

"I will be. I'm gonna be a horse or a dragon or a mermaid."

"Or a unicorn," I suggest.

She grins and looks out her window.

I love her imagination, but she definitely didn't get it from Scotty. His mind was more concrete than a sidewalk.

CHAPTER ELEVEN

KENNA

I've never seen a picture of Diem. I don't know if she looks like me or Scotty. Are her eyes blue or brown? Is her smile honest like her father's? Does she laugh like me?

Is she happy?

That's my only hope for her. I want her to be happy.

I have complete faith in Grace and Patrick. I know they loved Scotty, and it's obvious they love Diem. They loved her before she was even born.

They started fighting for custody the day they were told I was pregnant. The baby didn't even have fully developed lungs, but they were already fighting for its first breath.

I lost the custody battle before Diem was even born. There aren't many rights a mother has when she's sentenced to several years in prison.

The judge said, because of the nature of our situation and the duress I'd caused to Scotty's family, he could not, in good conscience, honor my request for visitation rights. Nor would he force Scotty's parents to maintain the relationship between my daughter and me while I was in prison.

I was told I could petition the court for rights upon my release, but since my rights were terminated, there's probably very little I can do.

Between Diem's birth and my release almost five years later, there has been little anyone could, or would, do for me.

All I have is this intangible hope I try to cling to with childlike hands.

I was praying Scotty's parents just needed time. I assumed, ignorantly, that they would eventually see a need for me to be in Diem's life.

There wasn't much I could do from my isolated position in the world, but now that I'm out, I've thought long and hard about how I should go about this. I have no idea what to expect. I don't even know what kind of people they are. I only met them once when Scotty and I were dating, and that didn't go over very well. I've tried to find them online, but their profiles are extremely private. There wasn't a single picture of Diem online that I could locate. I even looked up all of Scotty's friends whose names I could remember, but I couldn't remember very many, and all *their* profiles were private.

I knew very little about Scotty's life before he met me, and I wasn't with him long enough to truly get to know his friends or his family. Six months out of the twenty-two years he lived.

Why is everyone from his life so locked down? Is it because of me? Are they afraid of this very thing happening? Me showing up? Me hoping to be a part of my daughter's life?

I know they hate me, and they have every right to hate me, but part of me has been living with them for the past four years in Diem. My hope is that they've found a sliver of forgiveness for me through my daughter.

Time heals all wounds, right?

Except I didn't leave them with a simple wound. I left them with a casualty. One so heartbreaking there's a possibility it will never be forgiven. It's hard not to cling to hope, though, when all I've been able to do or look forward to is this moment.

It's either going to complete me or destroy me. There is no in-between.

Four more minutes before I find out.

I'm more nervous in this moment than I was in the courtroom five years ago. I grip the rubber starfish tightly in my hand. It's the only toy they had for sale at the gas station next door to my apartment. I could have had the cabdriver take me to Target or Walmart, but they're both in the opposite direction of where I'm hoping Diem still lives, and I can't afford that much cab fare.

After I got hired at the grocery store today, I walked home and took a nap. I didn't want to show up while Diem wasn't at Grace and Patrick's, and if Amy is right and Ledger doesn't have kids, it's a reasonable assumption that the little girl he coaches in T-ball is my daughter. And judging by the amount of Gatorade he bought, he was preparing for a long day with a lot of teams, which, using deductive reasoning, would mean it would be hours before Diem was back home.

I waited as long as I could. I know the bar opens at five, which means Ledger will likely be taking Diem home before then, and I really don't want Ledger to be there when I arrive, so I timed my cab ride to get me there at five fifteen.

I didn't want to arrive later than that because I don't want to show up when they're having dinner, or after she's gone to bed. I want to do everything right. I don't want to do anything that will make Patrick or Grace feel more threatened by my presence than they probably already will be.

I don't want them to ask me to leave before I can even plead my case.

In a perfect world, they'll open their front door for me and allow me to reunite with the daughter I've never held.

In a perfect world . . . their son would still be alive.

I wonder what I'll see in their eyes when they find me at their front door. Will it be shock? Hatred?

How much does Grace despise me?

I try to put myself in Grace's shoes sometimes.

I try to imagine the hatred she holds for me—what it must feel like from her perspective. Sometimes I lie in bed and close my eyes and try to justify all the reasons this woman is keeping me from knowing my daughter so that I don't hate her back.

I think, *Kenna—imagine you're Grace.*

Imagine you have a son.

A beautiful young man that you love more than life, more than any afterlife. And he's handsome, and he's accomplished. But most importantly, he's kind. Everyone tells you this. Other parents wish their children could be more like your son. You smile because you're proud of him.

You're so proud of him, even when he brings home his new girlfriend, the one you heard moaning too loud in the middle of the night. The girlfriend you saw looking around the room while everyone else was praying over dinner. The girlfriend you caught smoking at eleven at night on your back patio, but you didn't say anything; you just hoped your perfect son would outgrow her soon.

Imagine you get a phone call from your son's roommate, asking if you know where he is. He was supposed to show up for work early that day, but for whatever reason he didn't show.

Imagine your worry, because your son shows. He always shows.

Imagine he doesn't answer his cell phone when you call to see why he didn't show.

Imagine you start to panic as the hours stretch on. Normally, you can feel him, but you can't feel him today; you feel full of fear and empty of pride.

Imagine you start to make phone calls. You call his college, you call his employer, you'd even call the girlfriend you don't much care for, if only you knew her number.

Imagine you hear a car door slam, and you breathe a sigh of relief, only to fall to the floor when you see the police at your door.

Imagine hearing things like "I'm sorry," and "accident," and "car wreck," and "didn't make it."

Imagine yourself not dying in that moment.

Imagine being forced to go on, to live through that awful night, to wake up the next day, to be asked to identify his body.

His lifeless body.

A body you created, breathed life into, grew inside of you, taught to walk and talk and run and be kind to others.

Imagine touching his cold, cold face, your tears falling onto the plastic bag he's tucked into, your scream stuck in your throat, silent like the screams you've had in nightmares.

And yet you still live. Somehow.

Somehow you go on without the life you made. You grieve. You're too weak to even plan his funeral. You keep wondering why your perfect son, your kind son, would be so reckless.

You are so devastated, but your heart keeps beating, over and over, reminding you of all the heartbeats your son will never feel.

Imagine it gets even worse.

Imagine that.

Imagine when you think you're at rock bottom, you're introduced to a whole new cliff you get to fall off when you're told your son wasn't even driving the car that was going way too fast on the gravel.

Imagine being told the wreck was her fault. The girl who smoked the cigarette and didn't close her eyes during dinner prayer and moaned too loud in your quiet house.

Imagine being told she was careless and so unkind with the life you grew.

Imagine being told she left him there. "Fled," they said.

Imagine being told they found her the next day, in her bed, hungover, covered in mud and gravel and your kind son's blood.

Imagine being told your perfect son had a perfect pulse and might have lived a perfect life if only he could have had that wreck with a perfect girl.

Imagine finding out it didn't have to be this way.

He wasn't even dead. Six hours they estimated he had lived. Several feet he had crawled, searching for you. Needing your help. Bleeding. Dying.

For hours.

Imagine finding out that the girl who moaned too loud and smoked the cigarette on your patio at eleven o'clock at night could have saved him.

One phone call she didn't make.

Three numbers she never dialed.

Five years she served for his life, like you didn't raise him for eighteen, watch him flourish on his own for four, and maybe could have gotten fifty more years with him had she not cut them short.

Imagine having to go on after that.

Now imagine that girl . . . the one you hoped your son would grow out of . . . imagine after all the pain she's caused you, she decides to show back up in your life.

Imagine she has the nerve to knock on your door.

Imagine she smiles in your face.

Asks about her daughter.

Expects to be a part of the tiny little beautiful life your son miraculously left behind.

Just imagine it. Imagine having to look into the eyes of the girl who left your son to crawl several feet during his death while she took a nap in her bed.

Imagine what you would say to her after all this time.

Imagine all the ways you could hurt her back.

It's easy to see why Grace hates me.

The closer I get to their house, the more I'm starting to hate me too.

I'm not even sure why I'm here without being more prepared. This isn't going to be easy, and even though I've been preparing myself for this moment every day for five years, I've never actually rehearsed it.

The cabdriver turns the car onto Scotty's old street. I feel like I'm sinking into the back seat with a heaviness unlike anything I've ever experienced before.

When I see their house, my fear becomes audible. I make a noise in the back of my throat that surprises me, but it's taking all the effort inside me to keep my tears at bay.

Diem could be inside that house right now.

I'm about to cross a yard that Diem has played in.

I'm about to knock on a door that Diem has opened.

"Twelve dollars even," the driver says.

I fish fifteen dollars out of my pocket and tell him to keep the change. I feel like I float out of the car. It's such a weird feeling; I glance into the back seat to make sure I'm not still sitting there.

I contemplate asking the driver to wait, but that would be prematurely admitting defeat. I'll figure out how to get home later. Right now, I cling to the impossible dream that it'll be hours before I'm asked to leave.

The driver pulls away as soon as I close the door, and I'm left standing on the opposite side of the street from their house. The sun is still hanging bright in the western sky.

I wish I'd have waited until dark. I feel like an open target. Vulnerable to whatever is about to come at me.

I want to hide.

I need more time.

I haven't even practiced what I'm going to say yet. I've thought about it constantly, but I've never practiced out loud.

My breaths become harder and harder to control. I put my hands on the back of my head and breathe in and out, in and out.

Their living room curtains aren't open, so I don't feel like my presence is known yet. I sit down on the curb and take a moment to gather myself before walking over there. I feel like my thoughts are scattered at my feet and I need to pick them up one at a time and place them in order.

1. Apologize.
2. Express my gratitude.
3. Beg for their mercy.

I should have dressed better. I'm in jeans and the same Mountain Dew T-shirt I had on yesterday. It was the cleanest outfit I had, but now that I'm looking down at myself, I want to cry. I don't want to meet my daughter for the first time while wearing a Mountain Dew T-shirt. How are Patrick and Grace expected to take me seriously when I'm not even dressed seriously?

I shouldn't have rushed over here. I should have given this more thought. I'm starting to panic.

I wish I had a friend.

"Nicole?"

I turn toward the sound of his voice. I crane my neck until my eyes meet Ledger's. Under normal circumstances, seeing him here would shock me, but I'm already at max capacity for things to feel, so my thought process is more along the lines of an apathetic *"Great. Of course."*

There's a sharp intensity in the way he's looking at me that sends a chill up my arms. "What are you doing here?" he asks.

Fuck. Fuck. Fuck. "Nothing." Fuck. My eyes flicker across the street. Then I look behind Ledger, at what I'm assuming is his house. I remember Scotty saying Ledger grew up across the street from him. *What are the odds that he would still live here?*

I have no idea what to do. I stand up. My feet feel like weights. I look at Ledger, but he's no longer looking at me. He's looking across the street at Scotty's old house.

He runs a hand across his jaw, and there's a fresh disturbing look on his face. He says, "Why were you staring at that house?" He's looking at the ground, then across the street, then toward the sun, but then his eyes land on me after I've failed to answer his question, and he's a completely different person than the man I saw at the grocery store today.

He's no longer the fluid guy who moves around the bar like he's on Rollerblades.

"Your name isn't Nicole." He says it like it's a depressing realization.

I wince.

He's put it all together.

Now he looks like he wants to rip it all apart.

He points at his house. "Go." The word is sharp and demanding. I take a step into the street, away from him. I feel myself begin to tremble, just as he steps into the street and closes the gap between us. His eyes are on the house across the street again as he reaches his arm around me, pressing a firm hand into my lower back. He begins pushing me along with him as he points toward the house opposite where my daughter lives. "Get inside before they see you."

I expected he'd eventually put the pieces together. I just wish he would have made the connection last night. Not right now, when I'm only fifteen feet away from her.

I look at his house, then look at Patrick and Grace's house. I have no method of escaping him. The last thing I want to do right now is cause a scene. My goal was to arrive peacefully and make this go as smoothly as possible. Ledger seems to want the opposite.

"Please leave me alone," I say through clenched teeth. "This is none of your business."

"The *fuck* it isn't," he hisses.

"Ledger, *please*." My voice shakes from both fear and tears. I'm scared of him, scared of this moment, scared of the idea that this is going to be so much more difficult than I feared. Why else would he be pushing me away from their property?

I look back at Patrick and Grace's house, but my feet keep moving toward Ledger's house. I would put up a fight, but at this point, I'm no longer sure I'm ready to face the Landrys. I thought I was ready when I got into the cab earlier, but now that I'm here and Ledger is mad, I'm absolutely *not* ready to face them. It's obvious from the last few minutes that my arrival might have been somewhat anticipated and is not at all welcomed.

They were likely notified when I was released into transitional housing. They had to be expecting this to happen eventually.

My feet are no longer weights. I feel like I'm floating again, high in the air like a balloon, and I'm following Ledger as if he's pulling me along by a string.

I feel embarrassed to be here. Embarrassed enough to follow behind Ledger like I have no voice or thoughts of my own. I certainly don't have any confidence in this second. And my shirt is too stupid for a moment of this magnitude. *I'm* stupid for thinking this was the way to go about it.

Ledger closes his door once we're inside his living room. He looks disgusted. I don't know if it's at the sight of me, or if he's thinking about last night. He's pacing the living room, one palm pressed against his forehead.

"Is that why you showed up at my bar? You were trying to trick me into leading you to her?"

"No." My voice is pathetic.

He slides his hands down his face in frustration. He pauses and then just mutters, "God dammit."

He is so mad at me. *Why do I always make the worst decisions?*

"You've been in town for one day." He swipes keys off a table. "You really thought this was a good idea? Showing up this soon?"

This soon? *She's four years old.*

I clench an arm over my churning stomach. I don't know what to do. What do I do? What *can* I do? There has to be something. Some kind of compromise. They can't just collectively decide what's best for Diem without consulting me.

Can they?

They can.

I'm the unreasonable one in this scenario. I've just been too scared to admit it. I want to ask him if there's anything I can do to get them to hear me out, but the way he's glaring at me makes me feel completely in the wrong. I begin to wonder if I'm even in a position to ask questions.

His focus falls to the rubber starfish in my hand. He walks over to me and holds out his hand. I place the starfish in his palm. I don't know why I hand it over. Maybe if he sees I showed up with a toy, he'll know I'm here with good intentions.

"Really? A *teething* ring?" He tosses it on his couch like it's the stupidest thing he's ever seen. "She's *four*." He walks toward his kitchen. "I'm taking you home. Wait until I pull my truck into the garage. I don't want them to see you."

I no longer feel like I'm floating. I feel heavy and frozen, like my feet are trapped in the concrete slab of his house.

I glance out the living room window toward Patrick and Grace's house.

I'm so close. All that separates us is a street. An empty street with no traffic.

It's clear to me what's going to happen next. Patrick and Grace want nothing to do with me, to the point Ledger knew to intercept my arrival. This means there won't be any negotiating. The forgiveness I was hoping had found its way to them never made it here.

They still hate me.

Apparently, so does everyone else in their lives.

The only way I'm going to be able to see my daughter is if, by some miracle, I can take it through the court system, and that's going to take money I don't yet have and years I can't bear the thought of passing by. I've already missed so much.

If I want to see Diem at all, ever, this is my only chance. If I want the opportunity to beg Scotty's parents for forgiveness, it's now or never.

Now or never.

Ledger probably won't notice I'm not following him to his garage for another ten seconds, at least. I might make it before he catches up to me.

I slip outside and run as fast as I can across the street.

I'm in their yard.

My feet are sprinting across grass Diem has played on.

I'm beating on their front door.

I'm ringing their doorbell.

I'm trying to look through the window to get a glimpse of her.

"Please," I whisper, knocking harder. My whisper turns into panic as I hear Ledger approaching me from behind. "I'm sorry!" I yell, beating on the door. My voice is a fearful plea now. "I'm sorry, I'm sorry, please let me see her!"

I'm being pulled, and then carried, back to the house across the street. Even through my struggle to get out of his arms, I'm staring at that front door as it gets smaller and smaller, hoping for even a half-second glimpse of my little girl.

I don't see any movement at all in their house before I'm no longer outside. I'm back inside Ledger's house, being dropped onto his couch.

He's holding his phone, pacing his living room as he dials a phone number. It's only three digits. *He's calling the police.*

I panic. "No." *Plead.* "No, no, no." I lunge across his living room in an attempt to grab at his phone, but he just puts a hand on my shoulder and steers me back to the couch.

I sit down and bury my elbows into my knees, bringing my fingers to a shaky point against my mouth. "Please don't call the police. *Please.*" I sit still, wanting to appear unthreatening, hoping he just looks me in the eye long enough to feel my pain.

His eyes meet mine just as tears begin to fall down my cheeks. He pauses before completing the call. He stares me down . . . studying me. Searching my face for a promise.

"I won't come back." If he calls the police, this will not look good for me. I can't have anything added to my record, even though I've broken no laws that I know of. But just being here unwanted is enough of a mark against me.

He takes a step closer. "You *cannot* come back here. Swear to me we'll never see you again, or I'll call the police right now."

I can't. I can't promise him that. What else is there in my life other than my daughter? She's all I have. She's why I'm still alive.

This can't be happening.

"*Please,*" I cry, not knowing what I'm even begging for. I just want someone to listen to me. To hear me out. *To understand how much I'm suffering.* I want him to be the man I met in the bar last night. I want him to pull me to his chest, to make me feel like I have an ally. I want him to tell me it's going to be okay, even though I know with everything in me that it will never, ever be okay.

The next several minutes are a defeated blur. I'm a mess of emotions.

I get into Ledger's truck, and he drives me away from the neighborhood my daughter has been raised in her whole life. I'm finally in the same town as her after all these years, but I've never felt farther away from her than I do in this moment.

I press my forehead to the passenger window and I close my eyes, wishing I could start over from the beginning.

The *very* beginning.

Or at least fast-forward to the end.

CHAPTER TWELVE

LEDGER

It's typical for people to be praised in death. Heralded to the point of heroism sometimes. But nothing anyone said about Scotty was embellished for the sake of remembering him fondly. He was everything everyone said about him. Nice, funny, athletic, honest, charismatic, a good son. A great friend.

Not a day goes by that I don't wish I could have traded places with him, in life and in death. I'd give up the life I've been living in an instant if it meant he could have just one day with Diem.

I don't know that I'd be this angry—this protective over Diem—if Kenna had just simply caused the accident. But she did so much more than that. She was driving when she shouldn't have been, she was speeding, she was drinking, she flipped the car.

And then she left. She left Scotty there to die, and she walked home and crawled into bed because she thought she could get away with it. He's dead because she was scared she'd get in trouble.

And now she wants forgiveness?

I can't think about the details of Scotty's death right now. Not with her sitting next to me in this truck, because I'd rather be dead than allow her the satisfaction of knowing Diem. If it means driving us both off a bridge, I might just be vengeful enough to do that right now.

The fact that she thought it would be okay to show up is baffling to me. I'm pissed she's here, but I think my anger is amplified by the knowledge that she knew who I was last night. When we kissed, when I held her.

I shouldn't have ignored my gut. There was something off about her. She doesn't look like the Kenna I saw in the articles five years ago. Scotty's Kenna had long blonde hair. But I never really looked at her face back then. I never met her in person, but I feel like even just seeing a mug shot of the girl who killed my best friend should have stuck in my head more.

I feel stupid. I'm angry, I'm hurt, I feel taken advantage of. Even today in the store, she knew who I was, yet gave me no hint as to who *she* was.

I crack my window to get some fresh air, hoping it'll calm me down. My knuckles are white as I grip the steering wheel.

She's staring out the window, unresponsive. She may be crying. I don't know.

I don't fucking care.

I don't.

She isn't the girl I met last night. That girl doesn't exist. She was pretending with me, and I fell right into her trap.

Patrick expressed concern several months ago when we found out she was released. He thought this might happen—that she might show up wanting to meet Diem. I even put in a Ring camera on my house that points at their front yard. It's how I knew someone was sitting on the curb.

I told Patrick he was silly to worry. *"She wouldn't show up. Not after what she did."*

I grip the steering wheel even tighter. Kenna might have brought Diem into the world, but that's where her claim to Diem ends.

When her apartments come into view, I pull the truck into a spot and put it in park. I don't kill the engine, but Kenna doesn't make a move to exit my truck. I figured she'd jump out before I even came to a complete stop like she did last night, but it looks like there's something she wants to say. Or maybe she just dreads going into that apartment as much as she probably dreads staying in this truck.

She's staring at her hands folded together in her lap. She brings her hand to the seat belt and releases it, but when she's free from it, she remains in the same position.

Diem looks like her. I always assumed she did since I didn't see much of Scotty in Diem's features, but until tonight I had no idea just how much she resembles her mother. They have the same reddish shade of brown hair, straight and flat, not a wave or a curl in sight. She has Kenna's eyes.

Maybe that's why I saw red flags last night. My subconscious recognized her before I could.

When Kenna's eyes slide over to mine, I feel a tug of disappointment inside of me. Diem looks *so much* like her when she's sad. It's like I'm looking into the future at who Diem is going to someday be.

I don't like that the one person I dislike the most in this world reminds me of the person I love the most.

Kenna wipes her eyes, but I don't lean over and open the glove box to retrieve a napkin. She can use the Mountain Dew shirt she's been wearing for two days.

"I didn't know you before I showed up at your bar last night," she says with a trembling voice. "I swear." Her head falls back against the headrest, and she stares straight ahead. Her chest rises with a deep inhale. She exhales at the exact moment my finger meets the unlock button. My cue for her to exit.

"I don't care about last night. I care about Diem. That's it."

I watch a tear as it skates down her jaw. I hate that I know what those tears taste like. I hate that part of me wants to reach over and wipe it away.

I wonder if she cried as she was walking away from Scotty that night?

She moves with a graceful sadness, leaning forward, pressing her face into her hands. Her movement fills my truck with the scent of her shampoo. It smells like fruit. *Apples.* I rest my elbow on my doorframe and lean away from her, covering my mouth and my nose with my hand. I look out my window, not wanting to know anything else about her. I don't want to know what she smells like, what she sounds like, what her tears look like, what her pain makes me feel like.

"They don't want you in her life, Kenna."

A cry mixes with a gasp that sounds like it's filled with years of heartache when she says, "She's my *daughter*." Her voice decides to reconnect with her spirit in this moment. It's no longer a wisp of air escaping her mouth. It's full of panic and desperation.

I grip my steering wheel, tapping it with my thumb while I think of how to say what I need for her to understand.

"Diem is *their* daughter. Your rights were terminated. Get out of my truck, and then do us all a favor and go back to Denver."

I don't know if the sob that escapes her is even real. She wipes her cheeks and then opens the door and steps out of my truck. She faces me before closing the door, and she looks so much like Diem; even her eyes have grown a shade lighter like Diem's do when she cries.

I feel that look deep within me, but I know it's only because of how closely she resembles Diem. *I'm hurting for Diem. Not for this woman.*

Kenna looks torn between walking away, responding to me, or screaming. She hugs herself and looks at me with two huge, devastated eyes. She tilts her face up toward the sky for a second, inhaling a shaky breath. "*Fuck* you, Ledger." The sting of agony in her voice makes me flinch internally, but I remain as stoic as possible on the outside.

Her words weren't even a yell. They were just a quiet and piercing statement.

She slams my truck door, and then slaps my window with both of her palms. "Fuck you!"

I don't wait for her to say it a third time. I throw the truck in reverse and pull back onto the street. My stomach is in a knot that feels tethered to her fist. The farther I get from her, the more I feel it unravel.

I don't know what I expected. I've had this vision of her in my head all these years. A girl with no remorse for what she's done. A mother with no attachment to the child she brought into the world.

Five years of preconceived yet solid notions aren't easy to let go of. Kenna has been one way and one way only in my mind. Unremorseful. Uninvolved. Uncaring. Unworthy.

I can't reconcile the emotional turmoil she seems to suffer from not being part of Diem's life with the lack of regard she held for Scotty's life.

I drive away while thinking of a million things I should have said. A million questions I still don't have answers to.

"Why didn't you call for help?"

"Why did you leave him there?"

"Why do you think you deserve to cause another upheaval in the lives you've already destroyed?"

"Why do I still want to hug you?"

CHAPTER THIRTEEN

KENNA

I feel like I'm living my worst-case scenario. Not only did I not get to meet my daughter today, but the only person who might have been able to lead me to her is now enemy number one.

I hate him. I hate that I let him touch me last night. I hate that in the brief time I spent with him yesterday, I gave him all the ammunition to label me a liar, a whore, an alcoholic. As if *murderer* wasn't enough.

He's going to go straight to Grace and Patrick and reinforce their hatred for me. He's going to help them build an even sturdier, taller, thicker wall between me and my daughter.

I have no one on my side. Not a single person.

"Hi."

I pause halfway up the stairwell. There's a teenage girl sitting at the top of the stairs. She has Down syndrome, and she's smiling at me adorably, like this isn't the worst day of my life. She's wearing the same type of work shirt that Amy had on at the grocery store. She must work there. Amy said they give grocery bagger positions to people with special needs.

I wipe tears from my cheeks and mutter, "Hi," and then sidestep around her. I would normally make more of an effort to be neighborly, especially if I'm going to be working with this girl, but I have more tears in my throat than words.

I open my apartment door, and once I'm inside, I slam it shut and fall facedown onto my half-deflated mattress.

I can't even say I'm back to square one. I feel like I'm at square *negative* one now.

My door swings open, and I immediately sit up. The girl from the stairs walks into my apartment uninvited. "Why are you crying?" She closes the door behind her and leans against it, scanning my apartment with curious eyes. "Why don't you have any stuff?"

Even though she just barged in without permission, I'm too sad to be upset about it. She doesn't have boundaries. Good to know.

"I just moved in," I say, explaining my lack of stuff.

The girl walks to my refrigerator and opens it. She sees the half-eaten package of Lunchables I left this morning, and she grabs it. "Can I have this?"

At least she waits for permission before she eats it. "Sure."

She takes a bite out of a cracker, but then her eyes get wide and she tosses the Lunchables on the counter. "Oh, you have a kitten!" She walks over to the kitten and picks her up. "My mom won't let me have a kitten—did you get it from Ruth?"

Any other time, I'd welcome her. Really. But I just don't have the strength to be friendly during one of the worst moments of my life. I need to have a decent breakdown, and I can't do that with her here. "Can you please go?" I say it as nicely as possible, but asking someone to leave you alone can never not sting.

"One time when I was like five, I'm seventeen now, but when I was five, I had a kitten, but it got worms and died."

"I'm sorry." *She still hasn't closed the refrigerator.*

"What's her name?"

"I haven't named her yet." *Did she not hear me ask her to leave?*

"Why are you so poor?"

"What makes you think I'm poor?"

"You don't have any food or a bed or stuff."

"I've been in prison." Maybe that'll scare her off.

"My dad is in prison. Do you know him?"

"No."

"But I haven't even told you his name."

"I was in an all-female prison."

"Able Darby. That's his name, do you know him?"

"No."

"Why are you crying?"

I get off the mattress and walk to the refrigerator and shut it.

"Did someone hurt you? Why are you crying?"

I can't believe I'm going to answer her. I feel like this makes me even more pathetic, to just vent to a random teenager who walked into my apartment without my permission. But it seems like it would feel good to say it out loud. "I have a daughter, and no one will let me see her."

"Did she get kidnapped?"

I want to say yes, because sometimes it feels that way. "No. My daughter lived with people while I was in prison, but now that I'm out, they don't want me to see her."

"But you want to?"

"Yes."

She kisses the kitten on top of its head. "Maybe you should be glad. I don't really like little kids. My brother puts peanut butter in my shoes sometimes. What's your name?"

"Kenna."

"I'm Lady Diana."

"Is that really your name?"

"No, it's Lucy, but I like Lady Diana better."

"Do you work at the grocery store?" I ask her, pointing at her shirt.

She nods.

"I start work there on Monday."

"I've worked there for almost two years. I'm saving to buy a computer, but I haven't saved anything yet. I'm gonna go eat dinner now." She hands me the kitten and starts walking toward my door. "I have some sparklers. When it gets dark later, do you want to light them with me?"

I lean against my counter and sigh. I don't want to say no, but I also have a feeling my breakdown is going to last at least until morning. "Maybe another time."

Lady Diana leaves my apartment. I lock the door this time, and then I immediately grab my notebook and write a letter to Scotty because it's the only thing that can prevent me from crumbling.

> Dear Scotty,
>
> I wish I could tell you what our daughter looks like, but I still have no idea.
>
> Maybe it's my fault for not being honest with Ledger about who I was last night. He seemed to take that as some type of betrayal when he realized who I was today. I didn't even get to see your parents because he was so angry I was there.
>
> I just wanted to see our daughter, Scotty. I just wanted to look at her. I'm not here to take her from them, but I don't think Ledger or your parents have any idea what it's like to carry a human inside of you for months, only to have that tiny little human ripped away from you before you even get to meet them.
>
> Did you know that when an incarcerated woman gives birth, if they're almost finished with their sentence, they sometimes get to keep their babies with them? This mostly happens in jails, where the sentences are shorter. It sometimes happens in prisons, but it's rare.

In my case, I was just beginning my sentence when I gave birth to Diem, which made it to where she wasn't allowed to stay with me in the prison. She was a preemie, and as soon as she was born, they noticed her breathing wasn't where they wanted it to be, so they immediately whisked her away and transferred her to the NICU. They gave me an aspirin, some oversized pads, and eventually took me back to the facility with empty arms and an empty womb.

Depending on the circumstances, some mothers are allowed to pump, and their breastmilk is stored and delivered to their baby. I wasn't one of the lucky ones. I wasn't allowed to pump, and I wasn't allowed anything that would help my milk dry up.

Five days after Diem was born, I was in the prison library, crying in a corner because my milk had come in, my clothes were soaking wet, and I was still emotionally devastated and physically spent.

That's when I met Ivy.

She had been there for a while, knew all the guards well, all the rules, how far she could bend them and who would let her. She saw me crying while holding a book about postpartum depression. Then she saw my soaking wet shirt, so she took me to a bathroom and helped me clean up. She meticulously folded up paper towels into squares and handed them to me one by one while I layered them inside my bra.

"Boy or girl?" she asked.

"Girl."

"What'd you name her?"

"Diem."

"That's a good name. A strong name. She healthy?"

"She was a preemie, so they took her as soon as she was born. But a nurse said she was doing well."

Ivy winced when I said that. "They gonna let you see her?"

"No. I don't think so."

Ivy shook her head, and I didn't know it then, but Ivy had a way of communicating entire conversations through all the different ways she shook her head. I'd slowly learn them over the years, but that day, I didn't know the way she shook her head translated to, "Those bastards."

She helped me dry my shirt, and when we got back to the library, she sat me back down and said, "Here's what you're gonna do. You're gonna read every book in this library. Pretty soon you'll start to live in the lavish worlds inside these books, rather than the bleak world inside this prison."

I was never a big reader. I didn't like her plan. I nodded, but she could tell I wasn't listening to her.

She pulled a book off the shelf and handed it to me. "They took your baby from you. You won't ever get over that. So, you decide right now, right here. Are you gonna live in your sadness or are you gonna die in it?"

That question punched me in my stomach—the stomach that no longer contained my daughter. Ivy wasn't giving me a pep-talk. In a lot of ways, it was the opposite. She wasn't saying I would move past what I was feeling, or that things would get easier. She was telling me this was it—the misery I felt was my new normal. I could either learn to live with it or I could let it consume me.

I swallowed and said, "I'm gonna live in it."

Ivy smiled and squeezed my arm. "There you go, Momma."

Ivy didn't know it, but she saved me that day with her brutal honesty. She was right. My normal would never be the same. It hadn't been the same since I lost you, and losing our daughter to your parents just pushed me even further from center.

The way I felt when they took her from me back then is the exact same defeated misery I feel right now.

Ledger has no idea how much his actions tonight have broken the last few pieces of me.

Ivy has no idea how much her words from almost five years ago are still somehow saving me.

Maybe that's what I'll name the kitten. Ivy.

Love,

Kenna

CHAPTER FOURTEEN

Ledger

I've received three calls from Patrick on my drive back to the house, but I haven't answered any of them because I'm too angry at Kenna to have a conversation about her over the phone. I was hoping the Landrys didn't hear her beating on their door, but it's obvious they did.

Patrick is waiting in my yard when I pull back into my driveway. He's talking before I even get out of the truck.

"What does she want?" he asks. "Grace is a mess. Do you think she's going to try to fight the termination? The lawyer said it would be impossible." He's still spitting questions at me as he follows me into the kitchen.

I toss my keys on the table. "I don't know, Patrick."

"Should we get a restraining order?"

"I don't think you have grounds to do that. She hasn't threatened anyone."

He paces the kitchen, and I watch as he seems to grow smaller and smaller. I pour him a glass of water and hand it to him. He downs the whole thing and then takes a seat on one of the barstools. He drops his head into his hands. "The last thing Diem needs is for that woman to be in and out of her life. After what she did to Scotty . . . we can't . . ."

"She won't show up here again," I say. "She's too afraid of having the cops called on her."

My comment only heightens his worry. "Why? Is she trying to keep her record clean in case she *can* take us to court?"

"She lives in a shithole. I doubt she has money to hire an attorney."

He stands up. "She's *living* here?"

I nod. "Paradise Apartments. I don't know how long she plans to stay."

"Shit," he mutters. "This is going to destroy Grace. I don't know what to do."

I don't have any advice for him. As involved as I am in her life, I'm not Diem's father. I haven't been the one raising her since she was born. This isn't my fight, even though I've somehow immersed myself in the middle of it.

I may not have legal say, but I have opinions. Strong ones. As much as the entire situation doesn't have one single positive outcome for all parties involved, the simple truth is that being a part of Diem's life is a privilege, and Kenna lost that privilege the night she decided her freedom was worth more than Scotty's life.

Grace isn't strong enough to face Kenna. Patrick may not be strong enough, either, but Patrick has always made sure to at least pretend to be as strong as Grace needs him to be.

He'd never act this distraught in front of Grace. He saves this side of himself for the moments Scotty's death gets to be too much. The moments he needs to escape and cry alone in my backyard.

Sometimes I can see them both start to unravel. It always happens in February, the month of Scotty's birthday. But then Diem's birthday comes around in May, and it breathes new life back into them.

That's what Kenna needs to understand. Grace and Patrick are only alive because of Diem. She's the thread that keeps them from unraveling.

There's no room for Kenna in this picture. Some things can be forgiven, but sometimes an action is so painful the memory of it can still crush a person ten years down the road. Patrick and Grace get by because Diem and I help them forget about what happened to Scotty long enough for them to get through each day. But if Kenna is around, his death will slap them in the face over and over and over again.

Patrick's eyes are closed, and his hands are in a point against his chin. It looks like he's saying a silent prayer.

I lean forward over the bar and try to keep my voice reassuring. "Diem is safe for now. Kenna is too scared to have the cops called on her and too broke to start a custody battle. You've got the advantage. I'm sure after tonight she'll cut her losses and head back to Denver."

Patrick stares at the floor for about ten seconds. I can see the weight of everything he's been through settled squarely on his shoulders.

"I hope so," he says. He heads for the front door, and once he's gone, I close my eyes and exhale.

Every reassuring thing I just said to him was a lie. Based on what I know of Kenna now—however little knowledge that may be—I get the feeling this is far from over.

"You seem distracted," Roman says. He takes a glass from me and starts pouring a beer a customer has had to order from me three times already. "Maybe you should take a break. You're slowing us down."

"I'm fine."

Roman knows I'm not fine. Every time I look at him, he's watching me. Trying to figure out what's going on with me.

I try to work for another hour, but it's Saturday night and it's loud, and even though we have a third bartender on Saturday nights, Roman is right, I'm slowing us down and making it worse, so I eventually go take the damn break.

I sit on the steps in the alley, and I look up at the sky and wonder what the hell Scotty would do right now. He was always so levelheaded. I don't think he got that from his parents, though. Maybe he did, I don't know. Maybe it's harder for them to think with a level head when they have such broken hearts.

The door opens behind me. I look over my shoulder, and Roman is slipping outside. He sits next to me. He doesn't say anything. That's his way of opening the floor for me to speak.

"Kenna is back."

"Diem's mother?"

I nod.

"Shit."

I rub my eyes with my fingers, relieving some of the pressure from the headache that's been building all day. "I almost had sex with her last night. In my truck, after the bar closed."

He has no immediate reaction to that. I glance over at him, and he's just staring blankly at me. Then he brings a hand to his face and rubs it over his mouth.

"You *what*?" Roman stands up and walks out into the alley. He's staring at his feet, processing what I've just said. He looks as shocked as I felt when I put two and two together outside my house. "I thought you hated Diem's mother."

"I didn't know she was Diem's mother last night."

"How could you not know? She was your best friend's girlfriend, right?"

"I never met her. I saw a picture of her once. And maybe her mug shot, I think. But she had long blonde hair back then—looked completely different."

"Wow," Roman says. "Did she know who *you* were?"

I still don't know the answer to that, so I just shrug. She didn't seem surprised to see me outside my house earlier. She just seemed upset.

"She showed up and tried to meet Diem today. And now . . ." I shake my head. "I fucked up, Roman. Patrick and Grace don't need this."

"Does she have any rights as a parent?"

"Her rights were terminated because of the length of her prison sentence. We've just been hoping she wouldn't show up and want to be a part of her life. I mean, they feared it. We all did. I guess we just assumed we'd have some kind of warning."

Roman clears his throat. "I mean, to be fair, the woman gave birth to Diem. I think that was your warning." Roman likes to play devil's advocate in everything he does. It doesn't surprise me he's doing it now. "What's the plan? Are they going to let Diem meet her mother now that they know she wants to be involved?"

"It would be too hard on Patrick and Grace if Kenna were in their lives."

Roman makes a face. "How's Kenna going to take that?"

"I don't really care how Kenna feels. No grandparent should be forced to have to set up visitation with their son's murderer."

Roman raises a brow. "*Murderer.* That's a bit dramatic. Her actions led to Scotty's death, sure. But the girl isn't some cold-blooded murderer." He kicks a pebble across the pavement. "I always thought they were a little too harsh on her."

Roman didn't know me back when Scotty died. He only knows the story. But if he had been around five years ago to see how it affected everyone, and he still somehow managed to say what he just said, I'd have punched him for it.

But he's just being Roman. Devil's advocate. Uninformed.

"What happened when she showed up? What'd they say to her?"

"She didn't make it that far. I intercepted her in the street and dropped her off at her apartment. Then I told her to go back to Denver."

Roman shoves his hands in his pockets. I watch his face, looking for the judgment. "How long ago was this?" he asks.

"It's been a few hours."

"You aren't worried about her?"

"Who? Diem?"

He shakes his head with a small laugh, like I'm not following. "I'm talking about Kenna. Does she have family here? Friends? Or did you drop her off alone after telling her to fuck off?"

I stand up and brush the back of my jeans. I know what he's getting at, but it's not my problem. *At least that's what I keep telling myself.*

"Maybe you should go check on her," he suggests.

"I'm not going to *check* on her."

Roman looks disappointed. "You're better than this."

I can feel my pulse hammering in my throat. I don't know if I'm more pissed at him or at Kenna right now.

Roman takes a step closer. "She's responsible for the *accidental* death of someone she was in love with. As if that wasn't hard enough, she went to prison for it and was forced to give up her own child. She finally shows back up hoping to meet her, and you do God knows what with her in your truck, and then you prevent her from meeting her daughter, and *then* you tell her to fuck off. No wonder you've been slamming shit around all night." He walks back up the steps, but before he goes inside, he turns to me and says, "You're the reason I'm not dead in a ditch somewhere, Ledger. You gave me a chance when everyone else gave up on me. You have no idea how much I look up to you for that. But it's really hard to look up to you right now. You're acting like an asshole." Roman walks back inside the bar.

I stare at the door after it closes, and then I hit it. "Fuck!"

I start pacing in the alley. The more I pace, the guiltier I feel.

I've been unequivocally on Patrick and Grace's side since the day I found out what happened to Scotty, but the more seconds that pass between Roman's words and my next decision, the more uneasy I feel about it all.

There are two possibilities running through my head right now. The first is that Kenna is exactly who I've always believed her to be, and she showed up here selfishly, only thinking of herself and not at all thinking of what her presence would do to Patrick and Grace, or even Diem.

The second possibility is that Kenna is a devastated, grieving mother who simply aches for a child she desperately wants to do right by. And if that's the case, I don't know that I'm okay with how I left things tonight.

What if Roman is right? What if I ripped away every ounce of hope she had left? If so, where does that leave her? Alone in an apartment with no future to look forward to?

Should I be worried?

Should I check on her?

I pace the alley behind the bar for several more minutes, until I finally ask myself the question that keeps circling back around. *What would Scotty do?*

Scotty always saw the best in people, even in those who I failed to find good in at all. If he were here, I can only imagine how he would be rationalizing all of this.

"You were too harsh, Ledger. Everyone deserves the benefit of the doubt, Ledger. You won't be able to live with yourself if she takes her own life, Ledger."

"Fuck," I mutter. "Fuck, fuck, *fuck*."

I don't know Kenna's personality at all. The reaction she had earlier could just be dramatics for all I know. But she could also be in a really dark place, and I can't sleep with that on my conscience.

I feel unsettled and frustrated as I get in my truck and head back to her place.

Maybe I should feel a sense of relief that I now think Roman was wrong, but I just feel pissed.

Kenna isn't holed up inside her apartment. She's outside, looking like she doesn't have a care in this world. She's playing with fucking *fireworks*. Sparklers. Her and some girl, twirling around in the grass like she's a kid and not a grown-ass adult who, just hours earlier, acted like her world was coming to an end.

She didn't see me pull up because her back was to the parking lot, and she hasn't noticed I've been sitting here for several minutes.

She lights another sparkler for the girl, who then proceeds to make a mad dash with her sparkler and leave trails of light with her as she disappears around the corner.

Once Kenna is alone, she presses her palms to her eyes and tilts her face up to the sky. She stands like that for a few seconds. Then she wipes her eyes with her T-shirt.

The girl reappears and Kenna smiles, then the girl disappears, and Kenna lets her face fall back into a frown.

She's just turning it on and off and on and off, and I don't like that I like that she's pretending not to be sad every time that girl comes running back to her. Maybe Roman *was* right.

The girl returns once more and hands her another sparkler. As she's lighting it, Kenna looks up and spots my truck. Her whole body seems to shrivel, but she forces a smile toward the girl and makes a motion for the girl to run around the building. As soon as the girl is gone again, Kenna begins to head in my direction.

It's obvious I've been sitting here watching her. I don't even try to hide that. I unlock my door right before she reaches my truck and climbs inside.

She slams the door. "Are you here with good news?"

I shift in my seat. "No."

She opens the door and starts to get out.

"Wait, Kenna."

She pauses, and then closes the door and remains in my truck. It's so quiet. She smells like gunpowder and matches, and there's a strange current inside this truck that's so palpable I expect the whole damn truck to explode. But it doesn't. Nothing happens. No one speaks.

I finally clear my throat. "Are you gonna be okay?" My concern is buried beneath a stone-cold exterior, so I know my question seems forced, as if I don't care what the response might be.

Kenna tries to get out of the truck again, but I grab her wrist. Her eyes meet mine.

"Are you gonna be *okay*?" I repeat.

She stares hard at me with her swollen, red eyes. "Are you . . ." She shakes her head, seemingly confused. "Are you here because you're afraid I might *kill* myself?"

I don't like how she seems to want to laugh at my concern. "Am I worried you aren't in a good headspace?" I ask, reframing her question. "Yeah. I am. I wanted to make sure you were okay."

Her head tilts slightly to the right as she turns her whole body so that she's facing me in her seat. Her shoulder-length strands of straight hair lean with her. "That's not it," she says. "You're worried if I end my life, you'll be left feeling guilty that you've been so unbearably cruel to me. *That's* why you came back. You don't care if I *actually* kill myself—you just don't want to be the impetus for my decision." She shakes her head with a shallow laugh. "You did it. You checked on me. Your conscience is clear now, goodbye."

Kenna goes to open her door, and the girl she was lighting sparklers for suddenly appears at her passenger window. Her nose is pressed against the glass.

"Roll down this window," Kenna says to me.

I turn my key so that I can roll down her window. The girl leans in, smiling at us. "Are you Kenna's dad?"

Her question is so out of left field, I can't help but laugh. Kenna laughs too.

Diem has Scotty's laugh and smile. Kenna's laugh is her own. One I haven't heard before this second. One I want to hear again.

"He's definitely not my dad," Kenna says. She cuts her eyes to mine. "He's the guy I told you about earlier. The one keeping me from my little girl." Kenna opens her door and hops out.

She slams my truck door, and then the teenage girl leans in the passenger window and says, "Jerk."

Kenna grabs the girl's hand and pulls her away from the truck. "Come on, Lady Diana. He's not on our side." Kenna walks away with the girl and she doesn't look back, no matter how much I want her to and *don't* want her to, and *fuck, my brain is a pretzel.*

I'm not sure I could be on her side even if I wanted to be. This whole situation contains so many nooks and crannies and corners I get the feeling *choosing sides* is going to be the downfall of all of us.

CHAPTER FIFTEEN

KENNA

Here's the thing.

It shouldn't matter if a mother isn't perfect. It shouldn't matter if she's made one big, horrible mistake in the past, or a lot of little ones. If she wants to see her child, she should be allowed to see her, even if it's just once.

I know from experience that if you're going to grow up with an imperfect mother, it's better to grow up knowing your imperfect mother is fighting for you than to grow up knowing she doesn't give a shit about you.

There were two years of my life—not consecutive—that were spent in foster care. My mother wasn't an addict or an alcoholic. She just wasn't a very good mother.

Her neglect was validated when I was seven and she left me alone for a week when some guy she met at the dealership where she worked offered to fly her to Hawaii.

A neighbor noticed I was home alone, and even though my mother told me to lie if anyone asked, I was too scared to lie when the social worker showed up at our door.

I was placed into a foster family for nine months while my mother worked to get her rights back. There were a lot of kids and a lot of rules and it felt more like a strict summer camp, so when my mother finally regained custody of me, I was relieved.

The second time I was placed in foster care, I was ten. I was the only foster child, placed with a woman in her sixties named Mona, and I stayed with her for almost a year.

Mona wasn't anything spectacular, but the simple fact that she watched movies with me every now and then, cooked dinner every night, and did laundry was more than my own mother ever did. Mona was average. She was quiet, she wasn't very funny, she wasn't even all that fun, but she was *present*. She made me feel taken care of.

I realized during the year that I was with Mona that I didn't need my mother to be spectacular, or even great. I just wanted my mother to be adequate enough to not have the state intervene in her parenting. That isn't too much for a child to ask of the parent who gave them life. *"Just be adequate. Keep me alive. Don't leave me alone."*

When my mother regained custody of me for the second time and I had to leave Mona, it was different than the first time I was returned to her. I wasn't excited to see her. I had turned eleven while living with Mona, and I came home with all the appropriate emotions an eleven-year-old would develop with a mother like mine.

I knew that I was going back to an environment where I would have to fend for myself, and I wasn't happy. I was being returned to a mother who wasn't even adequate.

Our relationship never got back on track after that. My mother and I couldn't have a conversation without it turning into a fight. After a few years of this, when I was around fourteen, she eventually stopped trying to parent me, and instead it felt like I had become her enemy.

But I was self-sufficient by then and didn't need my mother coming in twice a week and pretending she had any say over me when she knew nothing about my life, or who I was as a person. We lived together until I graduated high school, but we were not friends and there was no relationship between us whatsoever. When she spoke to me, her words were insults. Because of that, I eventually just stopped speaking to her. I preferred the neglect over the verbal abuse.

By the time I met Scotty, it had been two years since I'd heard her voice.

I thought I'd never speak to her again, not because we had some huge falling-out, but because our relationship was a burden and I think we both felt like we'd been set free when that relationship broke down.

I didn't realize how desperate I would one day become, though.

We had gone almost three years without speaking when I reached out to her from prison. I was desperate. I was seven months pregnant, Grace and Patrick had already filed for custody, and because of the length of my sentence, I found out they were also petitioning for termination of my parental rights.

I understood why they were doing it. The baby would need somewhere to go, and I preferred the Landrys over anyone else I knew, especially my mother. But to find out they wanted to terminate my rights permanently was terrifying. That meant I wouldn't see my daughter at all. I wouldn't have say over her, even after my release. But because I had such a long sentence, and there was no one else I could grant custody of my daughter to, I had to reach out to the only family member who could possibly help me.

I thought maybe, if my mother fought for visitation rights as a grandparent, I could at least be left with some control over what happened to my daughter in the future. And maybe if my mother had visitation rights with my daughter, she could bring my baby to the prison after she was born so I would at least be able to know her.

When my mother walked into the visitation room that day, she had a smug smile on her face. It wasn't a smile that said, "I've missed you, Kenna." It was a smile that said, *"This doesn't surprise me."*

She looked pretty, though. She was wearing a dress, and her hair had gotten so long since I'd last seen her. It was odd seeing her for the first time as her equal, rather than as a teenager.

We didn't hug. There was still so much tension and animosity between us we didn't know how to interact.

She sat down and motioned toward my stomach. "This your first?"

I nodded. She didn't seem excited to be a grandmother.

"I googled you," she said.

That was her way of saying *I read what you did.* I dug my thumbnail into my palm to stop myself from saying something I'd regret. But every word I wanted to say was a word I'd regret, so we sat there in silence for the longest time while I tried to figure out where to start.

She tapped her fingers on the table, growing impatient with my silence. "So? Why am I here, Kenna?" She pointed at my stomach. "You need me to raise your child?"

I shook my head. I didn't want her to raise my child. I wanted the parents who raised a man like Scotty to raise my child, but I also wanted to *see* my child, so as much as I wanted to get up and walk away from her in that moment, I didn't.

"No. The paternal grandparents are getting custody of her. But . . ." My mouth was dry. I could feel my lips sticking together when I said, "I was hoping you'd petition for visitation rights as the grandmother."

My mother tilted her head. "Why?"

The baby moved at that moment, almost as if she was begging me not to ask this woman to have anything to do with her. I felt guilty, but I was out of options. I swallowed and put my hands on my stomach. "They want to terminate my rights. If they do that, I'll never get to see her. But if you have rights as a grandmother, you could bring her here to see me every now and then." I sounded like the six-year-old version of myself. Scared of her, but still in need of her.

"It's a five-hour drive," my mother said.

I didn't know where she was going with that comment.

"I have a life, Kenna. I don't have time to take your baby on five-hour road trips to see her mother in prison every week."

"I . . . it wouldn't have to be weekly. Just whenever you can."

My mother shifted in her seat. She looked angry with me, or annoyed. I knew she'd be bothered by the drive, but I thought once she saw me, she'd at least think the drive was worth it. I was at least hoping she'd show up wanting to redeem herself. I thought maybe, after finding out she was going to be a grandmother, she'd feel like she got a do-over, and she'd actually *try* this time.

"I haven't received one phone call from you in three years, Kenna. Now you're asking for favors?"

I didn't get a single phone call from her, either, but I didn't bring that up. I knew it would only make her angry. Instead, I said, "*Please.* They're going to take my baby."

There was nothing in my mother's eyes. No sympathy. No empathy. I realized in that moment that she was glad she'd gotten rid of me and had no intention of being a grandmother. I'd expected it. I was just hoping she'd grown a conscience in the years since I'd last seen her.

"Now you'll know how I felt every time the state took you from *me*. I went through so much to get you back both times, and you never appreciated it. You never even said thank you."

She really wanted a *thank-you*? She wanted me to thank her for being so shitty at being a parent that the state took me from her *twice*?

I stood up and left the room in that moment. She was saying something to me as I left, but I couldn't hear her because I was so angry at myself for being desperate enough to call her. She hadn't changed. She was the same self-centered, narcissistic woman I had grown up with.

I was on my own. Completely.

Even the baby still growing in my stomach didn't belong to me.

CHAPTER SIXTEEN

Ledger

Patrick and I started building the swing set in my backyard today. Diem's birthday isn't for a few more weeks, but we figured if we could get it put together before her party, she and her friends would have something to play on.

The plan sounded feasible, but neither of us knew building a swing set would be a lot like building an entire damn house. There are pieces everywhere, and without instructions, it's caused Patrick to mutter *fuck* at least three times. He rarely ever uses that word.

We've avoided talk of Kenna up to this point. He hasn't brought it up, so I haven't brought it up, but I know it's all he and Grace have been thinking about since she showed up on our street yesterday.

But I can tell the silence on that subject is about to end, because he stops working and says, "Welp."

That's always the word Patrick uses before he's about to start a conversation he doesn't want to have, or if he's about to say something he knows he shouldn't say. I picked up on it when I was just a teenager. He'd walk into Scotty's room to tell me it was time for me to go home, but he'd never actually say what he intended to say. He'd just talk around it. He'd tap the door and say, *"Welp. Guess you two have school tomorrow."*

Patrick sits in one of my patio chairs and rests his tools on the table. "It's been quiet today," he says.

I've learned to decipher the things he doesn't say. I know he's referring to the fact that Kenna hasn't shown back up.

"How's Grace?"

"On edge," he says. "We spoke to our lawyer last night. He assured us there's nothing she can legally do at this point. But I think Grace is more concerned she'll do something stupid, like swipe Diem from the T-ball field when none of us are looking."

"Kenna wouldn't do that."

Patrick laughs half-heartedly. "None of us know her, Ledger. We don't know what she's capable of."

I know her better than he thinks I do, but I'll never admit that. But Patrick may also be right. I know what it's like to kiss her, but I have no idea who she is as a human.

She seems to have good intentions, but I'm sure Scotty thought the same thing about her before she walked away from him when he needed her the most.

I'm getting loyalty whiplash. One minute I feel horrible for Patrick and Grace. The next, I feel horrible for Kenna. There has to be a way everyone can compromise without Diem being the one to suffer.

I take a drink of water to pad the silence, and then I clear my throat. "Are you at all curious about what she wants? What if she's not trying to take Diem? What if she just wants to meet her?"

"Not my concern," Patrick says abruptly.

"What is?"

"Our suffering is my concern. There's no way Kenna Rowan can fit into our lives, or Diem's life, without it affecting our sanity." He's focusing on the ground now, as if he's working all this out in his head as it's coming out of his mouth. "It's not that we think she'd be a bad mother. I certainly don't think she'd be *good.* But what would this do to Grace if she were to have to share that little girl with that woman? If she had to look her in the eye every week? Or worse . . . what if Kenna somehow made a judge feel sorry for her and her rights were reinstated? Where would that leave Grace and me? We already lost Scotty. We can't lose Scotty's daughter too. It's not worth the risk."

I get what Patrick is saying. Completely. But I also know that after getting to know Kenna just over the last couple of days, the hatred I had for her is starting to turn into something else. Maybe that hatred is turning into empathy. I feel like that could possibly happen to Patrick and Grace if they gave her a chance.

Before I can even think of something to say, Patrick reads the expression on my face. "She killed our son, Ledger. Don't make us feel guilty for not being able to forgive that."

I wince at Patrick's response. I've somehow hit a nerve with my silence, but I'm not here to make him feel guilty for the decisions they've made. "I would never do that."

"I want her out of our lives and out of this town," Patrick says. "We won't feel safe until both of those things happen."

Patrick's whole mood has changed. I feel guilty for even suggesting they entertain Kenna's reasoning. She got herself here, and instead of expecting everyone in Scotty's life to conform to her situation, the easier and less damaging thing would be for her to accept the consequences of her actions and respect the decision Scotty's parents have made.

I wonder what Scotty would have wanted if he could have seen this outcome. We all know the wreck, while preventable, was also an accident. But was he mad at her for leaving him? Did he die hating her?

Or would he be ashamed of his parents—*and me*—for keeping Kenna from Diem?

I'll never have that answer, and neither will anyone else. It's why I always find something else to focus on when I start wondering if we're all going against what Scotty would have wanted.

I lean back in the patio chair and stare at the jungle gym that will hopefully start to take shape soon. As I stare at it, I think of Scotty. This is exactly why I tore it down.

"Scotty and I smoked our first cigarette in that jungle gym," I say to Patrick. "We were thirteen."

Patrick laughs and leans back in his chair. He seems relieved that I've changed the subject. "Where did you two get cigarettes at thirteen?"

"My dad's truck."

Patrick shakes his head.

"We drank our first beer there. We got high for the first time there. And if I remember correctly, Scotty had his first kiss there."

"Who was she?" Patrick asks.

"Dana Freeman. She lived down the street. She was my first kiss too. That was the only fight me and Scotty ever got into."

"Who kissed her first?"

"I did. Scotty swooped in like a fucking eagle and took her from me. Pissed me off, but not because I liked her. I just didn't like that she chose him over me. We didn't speak for like eight whole hours."

"Well, it's only fair. He was so much better looking than you."

I laugh.

Patrick sighs, and now we're both thinking about Scotty and it's bringing the energy down. I hate how often this happens. I wonder if it'll ever start to happen less.

"Do you think Scotty wished I was different?" Patrick asks.

"What do you mean? You were a great dad."

"I've worked in an office crunching sales figures my whole life. Sometimes I wondered if he ever wished I was something better, like a firefighter. Or an athlete. I wasn't the type of dad he could brag about."

I feel bad that Patrick thinks Scotty would have wanted him to be any different than he was. I think back to the many conversations Scotty and I had about our future, and one of those conversations sticks out to me.

"Scotty never wanted to move away," I say. "He wanted to meet a girl and have kids and take them to the movies every weekend and to Disney World every summer. I remember thinking he was crazy when he said that, because my dreams were way bigger. I told him I wanted to play football and travel the world and own businesses and have a steady cash flow. I wasn't about the simple life like he was," I say to Patrick. "I remember, after I told him how important I wanted to be, he said, 'I don't want to be important. I don't want the pressure. I want to slide under the radar like my dad, because when he comes home at night, he's in a good mood.'"

Patrick is quiet for a while, but then he says, "You're full of shit. He never said that."

"I swear," I say with a laugh. "He said things like that all the time. He loved you just the way you were."

Patrick leans forward and stares at the ground, clasping his hands together. "Thank you for that. Even if it isn't true."

"It's true," I say, reassuring him. But Patrick still seems sad. I try to think of one of the lighter stories about Scotty. "One time, we were sitting inside the jungle gym, and out of nowhere, this pigeon landed in the yard. It was only three or four feet away from us. Scotty looked at it and said, 'Is that a fucking *pigeon*?' And I don't know why, maybe because we were both high, but we laughed so hard at that. We laughed until we cried. And for years, up until he died, every time we'd see something that didn't make sense, Scotty would say, 'Is that a fucking *pigeon*?'"

Patrick laughs. "*That's* why he always said that?"

I nod.

Patrick starts laughing even harder. He laughs until he cries.

And then he just cries.

When the memories start to hit Patrick like this, I always walk away and leave him alone. He's not the type who wants comfort when he's sad. He just wants solitude.

I go inside and close the door, wondering if it'll ever get better for him and Grace. It's only been five years, but will he still need to cry alone in ten years? Twenty?

I want so badly for them to heal, but the loss of a child is a wound that never heals. It makes me wonder if Kenna cries like Patrick and Grace do.

Did she feel that kind of loss when they took Diem from her?

Because if she did, I can't imagine Grace and Patrick would willingly allow her to continue to feel it, since they know what it feels like firsthand.

CHAPTER SEVENTEEN

KENNA

Dear Scotty,

I started my new job today. I'm here now, actually. I'm at orientation and it's really boring. I'm two hours into videos about how to properly bag groceries, stack eggs, keep meats separated, and I'm trying to keep my eyes open, but I haven't been sleeping well.

Luckily, I figured out that the orientation videos still play if I minimize the video tab. I'm writing you this letter using Microsoft Word.

I used the printer here to print off all the old letters I typed into Google Docs when I was in prison. I shoved them into my bag and put them in my employee locker to hide them because I doubt I'm supposed to be printing things.

Almost everything I remember about you is documented. Every important conversation we had. Every impactful moment that happened after you died.

I spent five years typing letters to you, trying to recall all the memories I had with you in case Diem wants to know about you someday. I know your parents have more to share with her about you than I do, but I still feel like the part of you I knew is worth sharing.

When I was walking around downtown the other day, I noticed the antique store was no longer there. It's a hardware store now.

It made me think of the first time we went there and you bought me all those tiny little rubber hands. We were a few days from our six-month anniversary, but we were celebrating it early because I had to work the weekend shift and wouldn't get off work in time for us to go out.

We'd both said I love you by that point. We were past our first kiss, our first time to make love, our first fight.

We had just eaten at a new sushi restaurant downtown and were browsing antique stores, mostly window-shopping because it was still light out. We were holding hands, and every now and then you would stop and kiss me. We were in that sickening stage of relationships—the stage I'd never reached with anyone before you. We were happy, in love, full of hormones, full of hope.

It was bliss. A bliss we thought would last forever.

You pulled me into the antique store at one point during our walk and said, "Pick something out. I'll buy it for you."

"I don't need anything."

"This isn't about you. It's about me, and I want to buy you something."

I knew you didn't have a lot of money. You were about to graduate college and you planned to start graduate school full-time. I was still working at Dollar

Days making minimum wage, so I walked toward the jewelry display, hoping I could find something cheap. Maybe a bracelet, or a pair of earrings.

But it was a ring that caught my eye. It was dainty and gold and looked like it belonged on the finger of someone straight out of the 1800s. There was a pink stone in the center of it. You noticed the moment I spotted it because I sucked in a breath.

"You like that one?" you asked.

It was in a case with all the other rings, so you asked the guy behind the counter if we could see it. The man took it out and handed it to you. You slipped it on the ring finger of my right hand and it fit perfectly. "It's so pretty," I said. It was honestly the prettiest ring I'd ever seen.

"How much is it?" you asked the guy.

"Four grand. I could probably knock a couple hundred off. It's been in the case for a few months."

Your eyes bulged at that price. "Four grand?" you asked in disbelief. "Is it a fucking pigeon?"

I sputtered laughter because I had no idea why you always said that phrase, but it was at least the third time I'd heard you say it. I also laughed because the ring was four thousand freaking dollars. I'm not sure I'd ever had anything on my body worth four thousand dollars.

You grabbed my hand and said, "Hurry. Take it off before you break it." You gave it back to the man. There was a display of tiny rubber hands next to the register. They were little gag gifts that slipped onto the tips of fingers so you'd have fifty fingers instead of ten. You grabbed one and said, "How much are these?"

The man said, "Two bucks."

You bought me ten of them. One for each finger. It was the stupidest gift anyone had ever given me, but by far my favorite.

When we stepped out of the store, we were both laughing. "Four thousand dollars," you muttered, shaking your head. "Does that ring come with a car? Do all rings cost that much? Do I need to start saving for our engagement now?" You were slipping the rubber hands on the tips of my fingers as you ranted about the price of jewelry.

But your rant made me smile, because it's the first time you ever mentioned the word engagement. I think you noticed what you said because you got quiet after that.

When all the rubber hands were on my fingers, I touched both of your cheeks. It looked so ridiculous. You were smiling when you wrapped your hands around my wrists and kissed my palm.

Then you kissed the palms of all ten of my rubber hands.

"I have so many fingers now," I said. "How will you afford to buy rings for all fifty of my fingers?"

You laughed and pulled me against you. "I'll figure out a way. I'll rob a bank. Or I'll rob my best friend. He'll be rich soon, that lucky bastard."

You were referring to Ledger, although I'm not sure I knew that at the time, because I didn't know Ledger. He had just signed a contract with the Broncos. I knew very little about sports, though, and nothing about your friends.

We were consumed by each other so much we hardly made time for anyone else. You were in class most days and I worked most days, so the little time we were able to spend together, we spent together alone.

I figured that would eventually change. We were just at points in our lives where we were each other's priority, and neither of us saw that as a bad thing because it felt so good.

You pointed at something in the window of the store across the street and then you grabbed one of the tiny plastic hands and you held it as we headed in that direction.

I had this fantasy that you would someday propose to me and then we'd get married and have babies and raise them together in this town because you loved it here, and I would have loved anywhere you wanted to be. But you died, and we didn't get to live out our dream.

And now we never will, because life is a cruel, cruel thing, the way it picks and chooses who to bully. We're given these shitty circumstances and told by society that we, too, can live the American dream. But what they don't tell us is that dreams almost never come true.

It's why they call it the American dream rather than the American reality.

Our reality is that you're dead, I'm in orientation for a shitty job making minimum wage, and our daughter is being raised by people who aren't us.

Reality is depressing as fuck.

So is this job.

I should probably get back to it.

Love,

Kenna

Amy put me on the floor after I finished the three hours of orientation videos. I was nervous at first because I was expecting to shadow someone my first day, but Amy said, "Make sure the heavy stuff goes on the bottom, treat the bread and eggs like infants, and you'll be fine."

She was right. I've been bagging groceries and carrying them out for customers for two hours now, and so far, it's just your average low-paying job.

No one warned me there could be job hazards on the first day, though.

That job hazard is named Ledger, and even though I haven't laid eyes on him, I just spotted his ugly orange truck in the parking lot.

My pulse speeds up because I don't want him to make a scene. I haven't seen him since he showed up at my apartment Saturday night to check on me.

I think I handled myself pretty well. He seemed remorseful for treating me the way he did, but I kept my cool and acted unfazed, even though his showing back up definitely fazed me.

It gave me a little bit of hope. If he feels bad enough for how he treated me, maybe there's a chance he could eventually grow empathetic toward my situation.

I'm sure it's a small chance, but it's still a chance.

Maybe I *shouldn't* avoid him. Being in his presence might make him realize I'm not the monster he thinks I am.

I walk back inside the store and return the grocery cart to the rack. Amy is behind the customer service counter.

"Can I take a bathroom break?"

"You don't have to ask permission to pee," she says. "Remember how we met? I fake pee every hour when I'm here. It's the only way I stay sane."

I really like her.

I don't have to use the restroom. I just want to walk around and see if I can spot Ledger. Part of me hopes he's here with Diem, but I know he isn't. He saw me applying for a job here, which means he'll likely never bring Diem inside this store ever again.

I eventually find him in the cereal aisle. I was planning to just spy on him so I can keep tabs on him while he shops, but he's at the same end of the aisle I appear at, and he spots me as soon as I see him. We're just four feet apart from one another. He's holding a box of Fruity Pebbles.

I wonder if those are for Diem.

"You got the job." Ledger says this without any hint as to whether he even cares that I got the job, or if he's bothered by it. I'm sure if he's that bothered by it, he would have shopped somewhere else today. It's not like he didn't know I was trying to get a job here.

He's going to have to find a new store if it bothers him because I'm not going anywhere. I can't. No one else will hire me.

I look up from the box of cereal in his hands and immediately wish I hadn't. He looks different today. Maybe it's the fluorescent lighting or the fact that when I'm in his presence, I'm attempting not to look at him too closely. But here in the cereal aisle, the lights seem to illuminate him.

I hate that he looks better under fluorescent lighting. How is that even possible? His eyes are friendlier, his mouth is even more inviting, and I don't like that I'm thinking good things about the man who physically pulled me away from the house my daughter was in.

I leave the cereal aisle with a new lump in my throat.

I changed my mind; I don't want to be nice to him. He's already spent five years judging me. I'm not going to change his view of me in the aisle of a grocery store, and I get too flustered in his presence to give him any semblance of a good impression.

I try to time things so that I'm not available when he checks out, but as karma would have it, the other grocery baggers on duty are all busy. I get called to his lane to bag his groceries, which means I'll have to walk them out to his truck and converse with him and be nice.

I don't make eye contact with him, but I can feel him watching me as I separate his food into sacks.

There's something intimate about knowing what everyone in this town is buying for their kitchens. I feel like I can almost define a person based on their groceries. Single women buy a lot of healthy food. Single men buy a lot of steak and frozen dinners. Large families buy a lot of bulk meat and produce.

Ledger gets frozen dinners, steak, Worcestershire sauce, Pringles, animal crackers, Fruity Pebbles, milk, chocolate milk, and a lot more Gatorade. Based on his selections, I conclude he's a single guy who spends a lot of time with my daughter.

The last items the cashier rings up are three cans of SpaghettiOs. I'm jealous he knows what my daughter likes, and that jealousy shows in the way I toss the cans into the sack and then into the cart with a thud.

The cashier side-eyes me as Ledger pays for the groceries. Once he gets his receipt, he folds it up and puts it in his billfold while walking to the cart. "I can get it."

"I have to do it," I say flatly. "Store policy."

He nods and then leads the way to his truck.

I don't like that I still find him attractive. I try to look everywhere but at him as we make our way across the parking lot.

When I was in his bar the other night, before I knew he was the owner, I couldn't help but notice how diverse the employees were. That made me appreciate whoever the owner was. The other two bartenders, Razi and Roman, are both Black. One of the waitresses is Hispanic.

I like that he's a figure in my daughter's life. I want her to be raised by good people, and even though I barely know Ledger, so far he seems like a decent human.

When we reach his truck, Ledger takes the Gatorades and puts them in the back while I unload the rest of his groceries into the back seat opposite the side where Diem's booster seat is. There's a pink-and-white scrunchie on the floorboard. When I'm finished loading his sacks, I stare at the scrunchie for a few seconds and then reach for it.

There's a strand of brown hair wrapped around it. I pull at the hair until it comes loose from the scrunchie. The strand is about seven inches long and is the exact same color as mine.

She has my hair.

I feel Ledger approach me from behind, but I don't care. I want to climb into this back seat and stay here with her booster seat and her hair scrunchie and see if I can find any other remnants of her that'll give me hints as to what she looks like and what kind of life she lives.

I turn around, still staring at the scrunchie. "Does she look like me?" I glance up at him, and his eyebrows are drawn apart as he looks at me. His left arm is resting on the top of his truck, and I feel caged between him, the door, and the grocery cart.

"Yeah. She does."

He doesn't say *how* she looks like me. Is it her eyes? Her mouth? Her hair? All of her? I want to ask him if we have similar personalities, but he doesn't know me at all.

"How long have you known her?"

He folds his arms over his chest and looks down at his feet like he doesn't feel comfortable answering these questions. "Since they brought her home."

The jealousy that rolls through me is almost audible. I suck in a trembling breath and push back my tears with another question. "What's she like?"

That question makes him sigh heavily. *"Kenna."* All he says is my name, but it's enough to know he's done answering my questions. He looks away from me and scans the parking lot. "Do you walk to work?"

Convenient change of subject. "Yes."

He's looking at the sky now. "It's supposed to storm this afternoon."

"Lovely."

"You could Uber." His eyes come back to mine. "Did they have Uber before you . . ." His voice trails off.

"Went to prison?" I finish with a roll of my eyes. "Yes. Uber existed. But I don't have a phone, so I don't have the app."

"You don't have a phone?"

"I had one but I dropped it last month, and I can't get a new one until I get a paycheck."

Someone uses a key fob to unlock the car a space over from us. I glance around and see Lady Diana walking toward the car with an older couple and a cart full of groceries. We aren't in their way, but I use it as an excuse to close his door.

Lady Diana sees Ledger as she's opening the trunk. She grabs the first sack and mutters, "Jerk."

It makes me smile. I glance at Ledger, and I think he might even be smiling. I don't like that he doesn't seem like an asshole. It would be a lot easier to hate him if he were an asshole.

"I'm keeping the scrunchie," I say as I turn the cart around.

I want to tell him that if he's still going to insist on shopping here, he should bring my daughter next time. But when I'm in his presence, I can't decide if I should be polite because he's the only thing linking me to my daughter, or if I should be mean because he's one of the things keeping me *from* my daughter.

Saying nothing when I want to say everything is probably my best bet for now. I glance back at him before I head into the store, and he's still leaning against his truck, watching me.

I go inside and return the cart to the rack and then pull my hair up with Diem's scrunchie and wear it for the rest of my shift.

CHAPTER EIGHTEEN

Ledger

There are a dozen chocolate cupcakes staring at me when I walk inside the bar.

"Dammit, Roman."

Every week he goes to the bakery down the street and buys cupcakes. He only buys them so he'll have an excuse to see the woman who owns the bakery, but he doesn't even eat them. Which means that leaves me with the task of eating them. I usually take the ones that survive the night to Diem.

I grab one of the cupcakes just as Roman walks through the double doors from the back of the bar. "Why don't you just ask her out? I've put on ten pounds since you first saw her."

"Her husband might not like that," Roman says.

Oh, yeah. She's married. "Good point."

"I've never even spoken to her, you know. I just keep buying cupcakes from her because I think she's hot, and apparently I like to torture myself."

"You definitely enjoy self-torture. You still work here for some reason."

"Exactly," Roman says flatly. He leans against the counter. "So? What's the update on Kenna?"

I look over his shoulder. "Anyone else here yet?" I don't want to talk about Kenna around anyone. The last thing I need is for it to get back to the Landrys that I've interacted with her outside of the one time they know of.

"No. Mary Anne comes on at seven and Razi is off tonight."

I take a bite of the cupcake and talk with a mouthful. "She works at the grocery store on Cantrell. She has no car. No phone. I'm starting to think she doesn't even have family. She walks to work. These cupcakes are fucking delicious."

"You should see the woman who bakes them," Roman says. "Have Diem's grandparents decided what to do?"

I put the other half of the cupcake back in the box and wipe my mouth with a napkin. "I tried talking to Patrick about it yesterday, but he doesn't even want the topic up for discussion. He just wants her out of town and out of their lives."

"What about you?"

"I want what's best for Diem," I say immediately. I've *always* wanted what's best for Diem. I just don't know if what I used to think was best for her is still what's best for her.

Roman doesn't say anything. He's staring at the cupcakes. Then he says, "Fuck it," and he grabs one.

"You think she cooks as good as she bakes?"

"Hopefully one day I find out. Almost one out of every two couples divorce," he says, his voice hopeful.

"I bet Whitney could find you a nice single girl to date."

"Fuck you," he mutters. "I'd rather wait until Cupcake Girl's marriage falls apart."

"Does Cupcake Girl have a name?"

"Everyone has a name."

It's the slowest night we've had in a long time, probably because it's Monday and it's raining. I don't usually notice every time the door to the bar opens, but since there are only three customers right now, all eyes go to her when she slips inside and out of the rain.

Roman notices her too. We're both staring in her direction when he says, "I have a feeling your life is about to get incredibly complicated, Ledger."

Kenna walks toward me, her clothes soaking wet. She takes the same seat she sat in the first time she was here. She pulls Diem's scrunchie out of her hair and then leans over the bar and grabs a handful of napkins. "Well. You were right about the rain," she says, drying her face and her arms. "I need a ride home."

I'm confused, because the last time she got out of my truck, she was so angry with me I was positive she'd never be inside of it again. "From me?"

She shrugs. "You. An Uber. A cab. I don't care. But first I want a coffee. I hear you guys carry caramel now."

She's in a feisty mood. I hand her a clean rag and start making her a coffee while she dries off. I look at the time, and it's been at least ten hours since I was in the store. "Did you just now get off work?"

"Yeah, someone called in, so I worked a double."

The grocery store closes at nine, and it likely takes her an hour to walk home. "You probably shouldn't be walking home this late."

"Then buy me a car," she retorts.

I glance over at her, and she raises an eyebrow like that was a dare. I top her coffee with a cherry and slide it over to her.

"How long have you owned this bar?" she asks.

"A few years."

"Didn't you used to play some kind of professional sport?"

Her question makes me laugh. Maybe because my short two-year stint as an NFL player is usually the only thing people around here want to talk about with me, but Kenna makes it seem like a passing thought. "Yeah. Football for the Broncos."

"Were you any good?"

I shrug. "I mean, I made it to the NFL, so I didn't suck. But I wasn't good enough to get my contract renewed."

"Scotty was proud of you," she says. She looks down at her drink and cups her hands around it.

She was pretty closed off the first night she came in, but her personality is starting to slip here and there. She eats her cherry and then takes a sip of the coffee.

I want to tell her she can go upstairs to the apartment Roman stays in so she can dry her clothes, but it feels wrong being nice to her. It's been a constant battle in my head for the last couple of days, wondering how I can be attracted to someone I've hated for so long.

Maybe it's because the attraction happened last Friday, before I knew who she was.

Or maybe it's because I'm starting to question my reasons for having hated her for so long.

"You don't have friends in this town who can give you a ride home from work? Family?"

She sets down her coffee. "I know two people in this town. One of them is my daughter, but she's only four and can't drive yet. The other one is you."

I don't like that her sarcasm somehow makes her more attractive. I need to stop interacting with her. I don't need her to be here in this bar. Someone might see me talking to her, and word could get back to Grace and Patrick. "I'll give you a ride home when you finish your coffee."

I walk to the other end of the bar just to get away from her.

Kenna and I head outside to my truck about half an hour later. The bar closes in an hour, but Roman said he'd take care of it. I just need to get Kenna out of the bar, and out of my presence so no one can tie us together.

It's still raining, so I grab an umbrella and I hold it over her. Not that it'll make a huge difference. She's still soaking wet from her walk here.

I open the passenger door for her, and she climbs inside the truck. It's awkward when we make eye contact, because there's no way we aren't both thinking about the last time we were together on this side of the truck.

I shut her door and try not to think about that night, or what I thought of her, or how she tasted.

Her feet are against the dash when I settle into the driver's seat. She's fidgeting with Diem's hair scrunchie as I pull onto the street.

I can't stop thinking about what she said—about Diem being the only person in this town she knows besides me. If that's true, Diem isn't even really someone she knows. She just knows Diem is here and that she exists, but the only person she really knows in this town is me.

I don't like that.

People need people.

Where is her family? Where is her mother? Why has none of her family tried to reach out and get to know Diem? I've always wondered why no one, not even another grandparent or aunt or uncle, has tried contacting Grace or Patrick about meeting Diem.

And if she doesn't have a cell phone, who does she talk to?

"Do you regret kissing me?" she asks.

My focus swings from the road and over to her as soon as she asks that. She's staring at me expectantly, so I look at the road again, gripping my steering wheel.

I nod, because I do regret it. Maybe not for the reasons she thinks I regret it, but I regret it all the same.

It's quiet all the way to her apartment after that. I put my truck in park and glance over at her. She's looking down at the scrunchie in her hand. She slides it onto her wrist, and without even making eye contact with me, she mutters, "Thanks for the ride." She opens her door and is out of my truck before I find my voice to tell her good night.

CHAPTER NINETEEN

KENNA

I think about kidnapping Diem sometimes. I'm not sure why I don't follow through with it. It's not like there's a worse life for me than the one I'm currently living. At least when I was in prison, I had a reason I was unable to see my daughter.

But right now, the only reason is the people raising her. And it hurts to hate the people raising her. I don't want to hate them. When I was in prison, it was harder to blame them, because I was so grateful she had people who were taking care of her.

But from right here in this lonely apartment, it's hard not to think of how great it would be to take Diem and go on the run. Even if it was just for a few days before I got caught. I could give her everything while I had her. Ice cream, presents, maybe a trip to Disney World. We'd have a lavish weeklong celebration before I turned myself in, and she'd remember it forever.

She'd remember *me*.

And then, by the time I got out of prison for kidnapping her, she'd be an adult. And she'd probably forgive me, because who wouldn't appreciate a mother who would risk going back to prison just to experience one good week with their daughter?

The only thing preventing me from taking her is the possibility that Patrick and Grace might change their minds someday. What if they have a change of heart and I get to meet Diem without having to break the law to do it?

And there's also the fact that she doesn't know me at all. She doesn't even love me. I'd be ripping her from the only parents she knows, and while that might sound appealing to me, it would more than likely be horrifying for Diem.

I don't want to make selfish decisions. I want to be a good example for Diem, because someday she'll find out who I am and that I wanted to be in her life. It might be thirteen years from now before she's able to decide for herself whether or not she wants anything to do with me, and for that reason alone, I'm going to live the next thirteen years in a way that will hopefully make her proud.

I snuggle up to Ivy and try to fall asleep, but I can't. There are so many thoughts swimming around in my head, and none of my thoughts ever settle. I've had insomnia since the night Scotty died.

I spend my nights awake, thinking about Diem and Scotty.

And now, thoughts of Ledger are added to the mix.

Part of me is still so mad at him for intercepting me at their house this past weekend. But part of me feels a sense of hope when I'm around him. He doesn't seem to hate me. Yes, he regrets kissing me, but I don't care about that. I don't even know why I asked him that question. I just wonder if he regrets it because he was Scotty's best friend, or because of what I did to Scotty. Probably both.

I want Ledger to see the side of me that Scotty saw so that I might have someone on my side.

It's really fucking lonely when the only friends you have are a teenager and a kitten.

I should have made more of an effort with Scotty's mom when he was alive. I wonder if that would have made a difference.

The night I met Scotty's parents was probably the strangest night of my life.

I'd seen families like theirs on television, but never in person before. I honestly didn't know they existed. Parents who got along and seemed to like each other.

They met us in the driveway. It had been three weeks since Scotty had been home, and they looked like they hadn't seen him in years. They hugged him. Not like a hello hug, but an *I missed you* hug. A *you're the best son in the world* hug.

They hugged me, too, but it was a different hug. Quick, *hello, nice to meet you* hug.

When we went inside the house, Grace said she needed to finish up dinner, and I know I should have told her I'd help, but I didn't know my way around a kitchen, and I was afraid she'd smell the inexperience on me. So instead, I stuck to Scotty's side like glue. I was nervous and I felt out of place, and he was the closest to a home that I could get.

They even prayed. Scotty said the prayer. It was so earth shattering for me to be sitting at a dinner table, listening to a guy thank God for his meal and his family and me. It was too surreal to keep my eyes closed. I wanted to take it all in, to see what other people looked like as they prayed. I wanted to stare at this family because it was hard to wrap my head around the idea that if I married Scotty, this would be mine. I would have these parents, and this meal would be something I helped cook, and I'd learn how to thank God for my food and for Scotty. I wanted it. I craved it.

Normalcy.

Something I was wholly unfamiliar with.

I saw Grace peek up right at the end of the prayer, and she caught me looking around. I immediately closed my eyes, but at that point Scotty said, "Amen," and everyone picked up their forks, and Grace already had an opinion of me, and I was too scared and too young to know how to change it.

It seemed hard for them to look at me during dinner. I shouldn't have worn the shirt I had on. It was low cut. Scotty's favorite. I spent the whole meal hunched over my plate, embarrassed about myself and all the things I wasn't.

After dinner, Scotty and I sat out on his back porch. His parents went to bed, and as soon as their bedroom light turned off, I breathed a sigh of relief. I felt like I was being graded.

"Hold this," Scotty said, handing me his cigarette. "I have to pee." He smoked occasionally. I didn't mind it, but I didn't smoke. It was dark out, and he walked around to the side of the house. I was standing on his back porch leaning against the railing when his mother appeared at the back door.

I straightened up and tried to hide the cigarette behind my back, but she'd already seen it. She walked away and then returned with a red Solo cup a moment later.

"Use this for your ashes," she said, handing it to me out the back door. "We don't have an ashtray. None of us smoke."

I was mortified, but all I could say was "Thank you," and then I took the cup from her. She closed the back door just as Scotty came back for his cigarette.

"Your mother hates me," I said, handing him the cigarette and the cup.

"No, she doesn't." He kissed me on the forehead. "The two of you will be best friends someday." He took a final drag of his cigarette, and then I followed him back inside the house.

He carried me up the stairs on his back, but when I saw all the pictures of him that lined the stairwell, I made him stop at each one so I could look at them. They were so happy. The way his mother looked at him in the photos is the same way she looked at him as an adult.

"What kid is that cute?" I asked him. "They should have had three more of you."

"They tried," he said. "Apparently I was a miracle baby. Otherwise, they probably would have had seven or eight."

That made me sad for Grace.

We got to his room, and Scotty dropped me onto his bed. He said, "You never talk about your family."

"I don't have one."

"What about your parents?"

"My father is . . . somewhere. He got tired of paying child support, so he bolted. My mother and I don't get along. I haven't spoken to her in a couple of years."

"Why?"

"We just aren't compatible."

"What do you mean?" Scotty sprawled out next to me on the bed. He seemed genuinely curious about my life, and I wanted to tell him the truth, but I also didn't want to scare him away. He grew up in such a normal household; I wasn't sure how he would feel knowing I didn't.

"I was alone a lot," I said. "She always made sure I had food, but she neglected me to the point I was put in foster care twice. Both times they sent me back to live with her, though. It's like she was shitty, but not shitty *enough*. I think after growing up and seeing other families, I started to realize she wasn't a good mother. Or even a good person. It became really hard to coexist. It was like she felt I was her competition and not on her team. It was exhausting. After I moved out, we stayed in touch for a while, but then she just stopped calling. And I stopped calling her. We haven't spoken in two years." I looked at Scotty, and he had the saddest look on his face. He didn't say anything. He just brushed my hair back and stayed quiet. "What was it like having a *good* family?" I asked him.

"I'm not sure I knew how good it was until just now," he replied.

"Yes, you did. You love your parents. And this house. I can tell."

He smiled gently. "I don't know if I can explain it. But being here . . . it's like I can be my truest, most authentic self. I can cry. I can be in a bad mood, or sad, or happy. Any of those moods are accepted here. I don't feel that anywhere else."

The way he described it made me sad I never had it. "I don't know what that's like," I said.

Scotty bent down and kissed my hand. "I'll give it to you," he said. "We'll get a house together someday. And I'll let you pick everything out. You can paint it however you want. You can lock the door and only let the people in that you want in there. It'll be the most comfortable place you've ever lived."

I smiled. "That sounds like heaven."

He kissed me then. Made love to me. And as quiet as I tried to be, the house was even quieter.

The next morning when we were leaving, Scotty's mother couldn't look me in the eye. Her embarrassment seeped into me, and I knew for certain in that moment she didn't like me.

As we were pulling out of his driveway, I pressed my forehead against the passenger window of Scotty's car. "That was mortifying. I think your mother heard us last night. Did you see how tense she was?"

"It's jarring for her," Scotty said. "She's my mother. She can't imagine me screwing *any* girl; it has nothing to do with you in particular."

I fell back against the seat and sighed. "I liked your dad."

Scotty laughed. "You'll love my mother too. Next time we visit them, I'll make sure and fuck you *before* we get here so she can pretend I don't do things like that."

"And maybe stop smoking."

Scotty grabbed my hand. "I can do that. Next time, she'll love you so much, she'll be pushing for a wedding and grandbabies."

"Yeah," I said wistfully. "Maybe." But I doubted it.

Girls like me just didn't seem to fit in with *any* family.

CHAPTER TWENTY

Ledger

It's been three days since she was in the bar, and three days since I was last in the grocery store. I told myself I wasn't going to come back here. I decided I'd just start shopping at Walmart again, but after having dinner with Diem last night, I spent the entire night thinking about Kenna.

I've noticed since she's been back in town that the more time I spend with Diem, the more curious I am about Kenna.

I compare Diem's mannerisms to hers now that I have something to compare them to. Even Diem's personality seems to make more sense now. Scotty was straightforward. Concrete. He wasn't very imaginative, but I saw that as a good quality. He wanted to know how things worked, and he wanted to know why. He didn't waste time on anything that wasn't science based.

Diem is the opposite of that, and I've never wondered if she got that from her mother until now. Is Kenna concrete like Scotty was, or does she like to use her imagination? Is she artistic? Does she have dreams outside of being reunited with her daughter?

More importantly, *is she good?*

Scotty was good. I always assumed Kenna wasn't because of that one night. That one cause and effect. That one terrible choice she made.

But what if we were just looking for someone to blame because we were all hurting so much?

It never once occurred to me that Kenna might have been hurting as much as we were.

I have so many questions for her. Questions I shouldn't want answers to, but I need to know more about that night and more about her intentions. I have a feeling she isn't going to leave town without a fight, and as much as Patrick and Grace want to brush this under the rug, it's not something that's going to go away.

Maybe that's why I'm here, sitting in my truck, watching her load groceries into cars. I'm not sure if she's noticed I've been lurking in the parking lot for half an hour. She probably has. My truck doesn't necessarily blend in with its surroundings.

There's a knock on my window that makes me jump. My eyes meet Grace's. She's holding Diem on her hip, so I open my door.

"What are you doing here?"

Grace shoots me a confused look. I'm sure she was expecting my response to be more on the excited side than concerned. "We're getting groceries. We saw your truck."

"I want to go with you," Diem says. She reaches for me, and I slide out of the truck as I take her from Grace's arms. I immediately scan the parking lot to make sure Kenna isn't outside.

"You need to leave," I say to Grace. She parked in the row in front of me, so I walk toward her car.

"What's wrong?" Grace asks.

I face her and make sure to choose my words carefully. "She works here."

There's confusion in Grace's face before the realization hits. As soon as she grasps who I'm referring to, the color begins to drain from her cheeks. "What?"

"She's on shift right now. You need to get Diem out of here."

"But I want to go with *you*," Diem says.

"I'll come pick you up later," I say, gripping the door handle. Grace's car is locked. I wait for her to unlock it, but she's frozen in place like she's in a trance. "Grace!"

She quickly refocuses and then starts digging in her purse for her keys.

That's when I see Kenna.

That's when Kenna sees me.

"Hurry," I say, my voice low.

Grace's hands are shaking as she starts clicking her key fob.

Kenna has stopped walking. She's just standing in the middle of the parking lot, staring at us. When she realizes what she's seeing—that her daughter is just yards from her—she abandons her customer's grocery cart and starts heading in our direction.

Grace gets the doors unlocked, so I swing the back door open and put Diem in her booster seat. I don't know why I feel like I'm racing against time. It's not like Kenna could take her with both of us right here. I just don't want Grace to have to face her. Not in front of Diem.

This also isn't the time or the place for Kenna to meet her daughter for the first time. It would be too chaotic. It would scare Diem.

"Wait!" I hear Kenna yell.

Diem isn't even buckled in all the way when I say, "Go," and shut her door.

Grace puts the car in reverse and pulls out of the parking spot as soon as Kenna reaches us. Kenna passes me and rushes after the car, and as much as I want to grab her and pull her back, I keep my hands off her because I still feel remorse for pulling her away from their front door.

Kenna gets close enough to their car to tap the back of it and plead, "Wait! Grace, wait! Please!"

Grace doesn't wait. She drives away, and it's painful to watch Kenna debate on running after the car. When she finally realizes she isn't going to stop them, she turns around and looks at me. Tears are streaming down her cheeks.

She covers her mouth with her hands and starts to sob.

It's conflicting, being thankful she didn't make it to us in time, but also heartbroken for her that she didn't make it to us in time. I want Kenna to meet her daughter, but I don't want Diem to meet her mother, even though they're one and the same.

I feel like Kenna's monster and Diem's protector.

Kenna looks like she's about to collapse from agony. She's in no shape to finish her shift. I point to my truck. "I'll give you a ride home. What's your boss's name? I'll let her know you aren't feeling well."

She wipes her eyes with her hands and says, "Amy," as she walks defeatedly toward my truck.

I think I know the Amy she's referring to. I've seen her in the store before.

The cart Kenna abandoned is still in the same spot. The elderly woman Kenna was walking groceries out for is just standing by her car, staring at Kenna as she climbs into my truck. She's probably wondering what in the hell all the commotion was.

I run to the cart and push it over to the woman. "Sorry about that."

The woman nods and unlocks her trunk. "I hope she's okay."

"She is." I load the groceries into her car and then return the cart to the store. I make my way to the customer service desk and find Amy behind the counter.

I try to smile at her, but there's too much shifting around inside of me to even fake a smile at this point. "Kenna isn't feeling well," I lie. "I'm giving her a ride home. I just wanted to let you know."

"Oh, no. Is she okay?"

"She will be. Do you know if she has anything I need to grab for her? Like a purse?"

Amy nods. "Yeah, she uses locker twelve in the break room." She points to a door behind the customer service desk.

I round the desk and walk through the door to the break room. The girl from Kenna's apartment complex is sitting at the table. She looks up at me, and I swear she scowls. "What are you doing in our break room, jerk?"

I don't try to defend myself. She has her mind made up about me, and at this point, I agree with her. I open locker twelve and go to grab Kenna's purse. It's more like a tote bag, and the top is wide open, so I see a thick stack of pages shoved inside.

It looks like a manuscript.

I tell myself not to look, but my eyes unwittingly land on the first line on the front page.

Dear Scotty

I want to read more, but I close the bag and respect her privacy. I go to leave the break room and say to the girl, "Kenna is sick. I'm taking her home, but do you think you can check on her this evening?"

The girl's eyes are focused hard on me. She finally nods. "Okay, jerk."

I want to laugh, but there are too many things suppressing that laugh right now.

When I get back to Amy, she says, "Let her know I clocked her out, and to call me if she needs anything."

She has no phone, but I nod. "I will. Thank you, Amy."

When I reach the truck, Kenna is curled up in the passenger seat, facing more toward the window. She flinches when I open the door. I set the tote bag between us, and she pulls it to her side. She's still crying, but she doesn't say anything to me, so I don't say anything to her. I wouldn't even know what to say. I'm sorry? Are you okay? I'm an asshole?

I pull out of the parking lot and don't even make it half a mile down the road when Kenna mutters something that sounds like "Pull over."

I look at her, but she's looking out the window. When I don't put on my blinker, she repeats herself. "Pull over." Her voice is demanding now.

"You'll be home in two minutes."

She kicks my dash. "Pull over!"

I don't say anything else. I do what she says. I flip on my blinker and pull over to the shoulder.

She grabs her tote bag, gets out of the truck, and then slams the door. She starts walking in the direction of her apartment. When she gets several feet in front of my truck, I put it in drive and move along the shoulder, rolling down my window.

"Kenna. Get back in the truck."

She keeps walking. "You told her to leave! You saw me coming and you told her to leave! Why do you keep *doing* this to me?" I continue driving at the pace she's walking until she finally turns and faces me through the window. *"Why?"* she demands.

I press on the brakes until we're even. My hands are starting to shake. Maybe it's the adrenaline, maybe it's the guilt.

Maybe it's the anger.

I put my truck in park because she looks like she's ready to tackle this. "Do you really think you can confront Grace in the parking lot of a *grocery* store?"

"Well, I tried to do it at their house, but we both know how that turned out."

I shake my head. The location isn't what I'm referring to.

I don't *know* what I'm referring to. I work to gather my thoughts. I'm confused because I think she might be right. She tried to approach them peacefully the first time, and I stopped her then too.

"They aren't strong enough for whatever it is you're here for, even if you aren't here to take her from them. They aren't even strong enough to share her with you. They've given Diem a good life, Kenna. She's happy and she's safe. Is that not enough?"

Kenna looks like she's holding her breath, but her chest is heaving. She stares at me for a moment and then walks toward the back of the truck so that I can't see her face. She stands still for a while, but then she walks into the grass on the side of the road and just sits down. She pulls up her knees and hugs them as she stares out over an empty field.

I don't know what she's doing, or if she needs time to think. I give her a few minutes alone, but she doesn't move or stand up, so I finally get out of the truck.

When I reach her, I don't say anything. I quietly sit down next to her.

The traffic and the world continue to move behind us, but in front of us is a big open field, so we both stare straight ahead and not at each other.

She eventually looks down and pulls a small yellow flower out of the grass. She rolls it in her fingers, and I find myself watching her now. She inhales a slow breath, but doesn't look at me when she releases it and starts to speak.

"Other mothers told me what it would be like," she says. "They told me they'd take me to the hospital to give birth, and that I'd get two days with her. Two whole days, just me and her." A tear falls down her cheek. "I can't tell you how much I looked forward to those two days. It was the only thing I had to look forward to. But she was born early . . . I don't know if you know that, but she was a preemie. Six weeks. Her lungs were . . ." Kenna blows out a breath. "Right after she was delivered, they had to transfer her to the NICU at another hospital. I spent my two days alone in a recovery room with an armed guard keeping watch over me. And when my two days were up, they sent me back to the prison. I never got to hold her. I never even got to look into the eyes of the human Scotty and I made."

"Kenna . . ."

"Don't. Whatever you're about to say, don't. Trust me, I'd be lying if I said I didn't come here with the ridiculous hope that I would be welcomed into her life and even given some kind of role. But I also know she's where she belongs, so I would have been grateful for anything. I would have been so grateful to finally get to *look* at her, even if that's all I was ever allowed to do. Whether you or Scotty's parents think I deserve that or not."

I close my eyes because her voice is painful enough. Looking at her and seeing the agony on her face when she talks makes it so much worse.

"I am so grateful to them," she says. "You have no idea. The whole time I was pregnant, I never had to worry about what kind of people would raise her. They were the same two people who raised Scotty, and he was perfect." She's quiet for a couple of seconds, so I open my eyes. She's staring right at me when she shakes her head and says, "I'm not a bad person, Ledger." Her voice is full of so much regret. "I'm not here because I think I deserve her. I just wanted to *see* her. That's all. That's *it*." She uses her shirt to dry her eyes, and then she says, "Sometimes I wonder what Scotty would think if he could see us. It makes me hope that an afterlife doesn't exist, because if it does, Scotty is probably the only sad person in heaven."

Those words hit me in the gut, because I'm terrified she might be right. It's been my biggest fear since she showed back up and I started viewing her as the woman Scotty was in love with rather than the woman who left him to die.

I stand up and leave Kenna alone in the grass. I walk to my truck and open my console. I get my phone and take it back to where Kenna is sitting.

I sit down next to her again and open my photo app and then open the folder where I keep all the videos I've taken of Diem. I pull up the most recent one I took of her at dinner last night, and I hit play and hand the phone to Kenna.

I never could have imagined what it would be like for a mother to lay eyes on her child for the first time. The sight of Diem on the screen steals Kenna's breath. She slaps a hand over her mouth and begins to cry. She cries so hard, she has to set the phone on her legs so she can use her shirt to clear her eyes of tears.

Kenna becomes a different person right in front of my eyes. It's as if I'm witnessing her become a mother. It might be the most beautiful thing I've ever seen.

I feel like an absolute fucking monster for not helping her experience this moment sooner.

I'm sorry, Scotty.

She watched four videos while sitting in the grass on the side of the road. She cried the whole time, but she also smiled a lot. And she laughed every time Diem would speak.

I let her hold my phone and continue to watch more of them as I drove her home.

I walked her upstairs to her apartment because I would have felt too bad taking my phone away from her, so she's been watching videos for almost an entire hour. Her emotions are all over the place. She's laughing, she's crying, she's happy, she's sad.

I have no idea how I'll get my phone back. I don't know that I want to.

I've been in her apartment for so long Kenna's kitten is now asleep in my lap. I'm on one end of the couch and Kenna is on the other, and I'm just watching her watch the videos of Diem, full of pride like a father, because I know Diem is healthy and articulate and funny and happy, and it feels good to watch Kenna realize all these things about her daughter.

But, at the same time, I feel like I'm betraying two of the most important people in my life. If Patrick and Grace knew I was here right now, showing Kenna videos of the child they've raised, they'd likely never speak to me again. I wouldn't blame them.

There's just no way to navigate this situation in a way that I don't feel like I'm betraying *someone*. I'm betraying Kenna by keeping Diem from her. I'm betraying Patrick and Grace by giving Kenna a glimpse of Diem. I'm even betraying Scotty, although I don't quite know how yet. I'm still trying to figure out where those feelings of guilt are coming from.

"She's so happy," Kenna says.

I nod. "She is. She's very happy."

Kenna looks up at me, wiping her eyes with a crumpled-up napkin I handed her in the truck. "Does she ever ask about me?"

"Not specifically, but she is starting to wonder where she came from. Last weekend she asked if she grew in a tree or in an egg."

Kenna smiles.

"She's still young enough that she doesn't really understand family dynamics. She has me and Patrick and Grace, so right now, I don't know that she really feels like anyone is missing. I don't know if that's what you want to hear. It's just the truth."

Kenna shakes her head. "It's fine. It actually makes me feel good that she doesn't know I'm missing in her life yet." She watches another video and then reluctantly hands me the phone. She pushes off the couch to walk to her bathroom. "Please don't leave yet."

I nod, assuring her I'm not going anywhere. When she closes the bathroom door, I move Kenna's kitten and stand up. I need something to drink. The last couple of hours have somehow made me feel dehydrated even though Kenna is the one who has been crying.

I open Kenna's refrigerator, but it's empty. Completely empty. I open her freezer and it's empty too.

When she steps out of her bathroom, I'm looking through her empty cabinets. They're as barren as her apartment.

"I don't have anything yet. I'm sorry." She seems embarrassed when she says that. "It's just . . . it took everything I had to move here. I'll get paid soon, and I plan to move eventually, to somewhere better, and I'm getting a phone and—"

I lift a hand when I realize she thinks I'm judging her ability to provide for herself. Or maybe for Diem. "Kenna, it's fine. I admire the determination that got you here, but you need to eat." I slide my phone into my pocket and head toward the door. "Come on. I'll buy you dinner."

CHAPTER TWENTY-ONE

KENNA

Diem does look like me. We have the same hair, the same eyes. She even has the same slender fingers I have.

I was glad to see she got Scotty's laugh and smile. Watching the videos of her was like a refresher course in the history of Scotty. It's been so long, and I had no pictures of him in prison, so I was beginning to forget what he looked like. But I saw him in her, and I'm thankful for that.

I'm grateful to know that when Patrick and Grace look at Diem, they can still see some semblance of their own son. I always worried that if she looked too much like me, they might not see remnants of him.

I thought I'd feel different after finally seeing her. I was hoping there would be a sense of closure within me, but it's almost as if someone has stretched open the wound. I thought seeing her happy would make me happier, but in a way, it's made me even sadder, in a completely selfish way.

It's not that difficult to love a child you gave birth to, even if you've never laid eyes on them. But it's extremely difficult to finally see what they look like and sound like and *are* like, and then be expected to just walk away from that.

But that's exactly what they all expect me to do. It's what they *want* me to do.

The thought of it makes my stomach feel like it's full of tight, knotted ropes, and they're all about to snap.

Ledger was right, I needed food. But now that I'm sitting here with food, all I can do is think about the last couple of hours, and I don't know if I can eat. I'm nauseous, full of adrenaline, emotional, exhausted.

Ledger went through a drive-through and ordered us burgers. We're sitting in his truck in the parking lot of a park, eating our food.

I know why he didn't want to take me anywhere public. His being seen with me probably wouldn't go over well with Diem's grandparents. Not that I know a whole lot of people in this town, but I knew enough people back then that there's a chance I could be recognized.

If I haven't been already. I had a few coworkers back then, and even though I never met Ledger, I did meet a handful of Scotty's other friends. And since it's a small town, I could possibly be recognized by anyone who was nosy enough to pass around my mug shot.

People love a good rumor, and if there's anything I'm good at, it's being fodder for gossip.

I don't blame anyone but myself. Everything would be different if I wouldn't have panicked that night. But I did, and these are the consequences, and I've accepted that. I spent the first couple of years of my sentence replaying every decision I've ever made, wishing I could go back and get a second shot.

Ivy once said to me, *"Regret keeps you stuck on pause. So does prison. When you get out of here, make sure you hit play so you don't forget to move forward."*

I'm scared to move forward, though. What if the only way I can move forward is without Diem?

"Can I ask you a question?" Ledger says. I glance over at him, and he's already finished his food. I haven't even taken three bites of my burger.

Ledger is good looking, but not in the way Scotty was. Scotty was more the boy next door. Ledger isn't the boy next door. Ledger looks like the guy who might beat up the boy next door. He's rough around the edges, and the fact that he owns a bar doesn't soothe that image any.

He doesn't come off quite the way he looks when he opens his mouth, though, and that's the most important thing.

"What happens if they won't let you meet her?" he asks.

I'm definitely not hungry now. Just the thought of it is nauseating. I shrug. "I guess I'll move away. I don't want them to feel like I'm a threat." I force myself to eat a french fry, only because I don't know what else to say.

Ledger takes a sip of his tea. The truck is quiet. It feels like there might be an apology hanging in the air between us, but I'm not sure who it belongs to.

Ledger claims it when he shifts in his seat and says, "I feel like I owe you an apology for stopping you from—"

"It's okay," I say, cutting him off. "You were doing what you thought you needed to do to protect Diem. As mad as I am for my own sake . . . I'm happy Diem has people in her life who protect her that fiercely."

He's staring at me with his head slightly tilted. He processes my response, tucking it away somewhere without giving me any clue as to what he's thinking. He nudges his head toward my uneaten food. "You aren't hungry?"

"I think I'm too wound up to eat right now. I'll take it home." I put my burger back in the sack, along with the rest of my fries. I fold the sack up and set it on the seat between us. "Can I ask *you* a question?"

"Of course."

I lean my head against the seat and study his face. "Do you hate me?" I'm surprised when the question leaves my mouth, but I need to know where his head is at. Sometimes, like when we were at his house, it feels like he hates me as much as Scotty's parents do.

But then sometimes, like right now, he looks at me like he might empathize with my situation. I need to know who my enemies are, and I need to know if there's anyone on my team. If I only have enemies, what am I even still doing here?

Ledger leans into his driver's side door, resting his elbow on the windowsill. He stares straight ahead and rubs his jaw. "I formed an opinion of you in my head after Scotty's death. All these years, it's like you've been some random person online—someone I could make strong judgments about and place blame on without actually having to know. But now that we're face to face . . . I don't know that I want to say all the things to you I've always wanted to say."

"But you still feel them?"

He shakes his head. "I don't know, Kenna." He shifts in his seat so that his attention is more directed at me. "That first night you walked into my bar, I thought you were the most intriguing girl I'd ever met. But then when I saw you the next day in front of Patrick and Grace's house, I thought you were the most disgusting person I'd ever met."

His honesty fills my chest with embarrassment. "And tonight?" I ask quietly.

He looks me in the eye. "Tonight . . . I'm starting to wonder if you're the saddest girl I've ever met."

I smile what is probably the most painful-looking smile, simply because I don't want to cry. "All of the above."

His smile is almost as painful. "I was afraid of that." There's a question in his eyes. Lots of questions. So many questions, I have to look away from his face to avoid them.

Ledger gathers his trash and gets out of the truck and walks it over to a trash can. He lingers outside his truck for a moment. When he reappears at the driver's side door, he doesn't get in. He just grips the top of the truck and stares at me. "What happens if you have to move away? What are your plans? Your next step?"

“I don’t know,” I say with a sigh. “I haven’t thought that far ahead. I’ve been too afraid to let go of the hope that they’ll change their minds.” That’s starting to feel like the direction this is going, though. And Ledger of all people knows where their heads are at. “Do you think they’ll ever give me a chance?”

Ledger doesn’t answer. He doesn’t shake his head or nod. He just completely ignores the question and gets in his truck and backs out of the parking lot.

Leaving me without an answer is still an answer.

I think about this the entire way home. When *do* I cut my losses? When do I accept that maybe my life won’t intersect with Diem’s?

My throat is dry and my heart is empty when we pull back into the parking lot of my apartment unit. Ledger gets out of the truck and comes around to open my door. He just stands there, though. He looks like he wants to say something, the way he shuffles back and forth on his feet. He crosses his arms over his chest and looks down at the ground.

“It wasn’t a good look, you know. To his parents, to the judge, to everyone in that courtroom . . . you just seemed so . . .” He can’t finish his sentence.

“I seemed so *what*?”

His eyes connect with mine. “Unremorseful.”

That word knocks the breath out of me. *How could anyone think I was unremorseful?* I was absolutely devastated.

I feel like I’m about to start crying again, and I’ve cried enough today. I just need out of his truck. I grab my bag and my to-go food, and Ledger steps aside so that I can exit his truck. When my feet are on the ground, I start walking because I’m trying to catch my breath, and I can’t and don’t know how to respond to what he just said.

Is that why they refuse to let me see my daughter? They think I didn’t *care*?

I can hear his footsteps following me, but it forces me to walk even faster until I’m up the stairs and inside my apartment. I set my stuff down on the counter, and Ledger is standing in the doorway to my apartment.

I grip the edge of the counter next to the sink and process what he's just said. Then I face him with the distance of the room between us. "Scotty was the greatest thing that ever happened to me. I wasn't unremorseful. I was too devastated to speak. My lawyers, they told me I needed to write an allocution statement, but I hadn't been able to sleep in weeks. I couldn't get a single word out on paper. My brain, it was . . ." I press a hand to my chest. "I was *shattered*, Ledger. You have to believe that. Too shattered to even defend myself, or care what happened to my life. I wasn't unemotional, I was *broken*."

And it happens again. The tears. I'm so sick of the fucking tears. I turn away from him because I'm sure he's sick of them too.

I hear my door close. *Did he leave?* I spin around, but Ledger is standing inside my apartment. He's walking slowly toward me, and then he leans against the counter next to me. He folds his arms over his chest, crosses his legs at the ankles, and then just stares at the floor silently for a moment. I grab the napkin off the counter that I was using earlier.

Ledger eyes me. "Who would it benefit?" he asks.

I wait for more clarification, because I don't know what he's asking me.

"It wouldn't benefit Patrick or Grace having to share custody of Diem with you. It would bring a level of stress to their lives that I'm not sure they can emotionally handle. And Diem . . . would it benefit her? Because right now, she has no idea anyone is even missing from her life. She has two people she considers her parents already, and all of *their* family who love her. She also has me. And if you were allowed visitation, yes, it might mean something to her when she's older. But right now . . . and I'm not being hateful, Kenna . . . but you would change the peaceful existence they've worked so hard to build since Scotty died. The stress your presence would bring to Patrick and Grace would be felt by Diem, no matter how hard they tried to hide it from her. So . . . who would your presence in Diem's life benefit? Besides yourself?"

I can feel my chest tightening at his words. Not because I'm angry at him for saying them, but because I'm scared he's right.

What if she's better off without me in her life? What if my presence would just be an intrusion?

He knows Patrick and Grace better than anyone, and if he says my presence is going to change the good dynamic they've built, who am I to argue with that?

I already feared everything he just said, but it feels painful and embarrassing hearing the words actually come from him. He's right, though. My presence here is selfish. He knows it. *They* know it.

I'm not here to fill some void in my daughter's life. I'm here to fill a void in *mine.*

I blink back tears and blow out a calming breath. "I know I shouldn't have come back here. You're right. But I can't just up and leave. It took everything I had to get here, and now I'm stuck. I have nowhere to go and no money to get there because the grocery store is only part time."

The empathy has returned to his face, but he's quiet.

"If they don't want me here, I'll leave. It's just going to take time because I don't have the money, and every business in this town has turned me down because of my past."

Ledger pushes off the counter. He clasps his hands behind his head and paces a few steps. I don't want him to think I'm asking for money. That would be the most mortifying result of this conversation.

But if he offered me money, I'm not sure I'd turn it down. If they want me to leave badly enough to pay for my exit, I'll cut my fucking losses and go.

"I can give you eight hours on Friday and Saturday nights." He looks like he regrets the offer as soon as it leaves his mouth. "It's just kitchen work. Mostly dishes. But you have to stay in the back of the bar. No one can know you work there. If the Landrys find out I'm helping you . . ."

I realize he's offering me this opportunity to get me out of town quicker. He's not doing me a favor; he's doing Patrick and Grace a favor. I try not to think about the *whys*, though. "I won't tell anyone," I say quickly. "I swear."

The hesitant look on Ledger's face conveys his regret. It looks like he's about to say *never mind*, so I hurry up and spit out a *thank you* before he can backtrack. "I get off work at four o'clock Friday and Saturday. I can be there by four thirty."

He nods, and then says, "Come in through the back door. And if anyone asks, tell them your name is Nicole. That's what I'll tell the other employees."

"Okay."

He shakes his head like he's just made the biggest mistake of his life, and then he heads to the front door. He says, "Good night," but his voice is clipped when he says it. Then he closes the door behind him.

Ivy is rubbing against my ankles, so I bend down and pick her up. I bring her up to my chest and cuddle her.

Ledger might have just offered me a job to get me out of town, but I sit down on my couch with a smile, because I got to see my daughter's face today. No matter how depressing the rest of the day was, I finally got a piece of something I've been praying five years for.

I grab my notebook and write the most important letter I've ever written to Scotty.

> Dear Scotty,
> She looks like both of us, but she laughs like you.
> She's perfect in every way.
> I'm so sorry you never got to meet her.
> Love,
> Kenna

CHAPTER TWENTY-TWO

LEDGER

Kenna is supposed to show up any minute. Roman has been off since the night I hired her, so I haven't had a chance to warn him. But I've been debating on changing my mind about hiring her since the second I made *up* my mind.

Roman just arrived, and Kenna said she'd be here around four thirty, so now is probably a good time to bring it up to him so he's not blindsided.

I'm slicing up limes and oranges to make sure we have enough garnishes for the night. Roman hasn't even made it behind the bar yet when I say, "I fucked up." I meant to say, "*I hired Kenna*," but I feel like they both have the same meaning.

Roman eyes me suspiciously.

I can't have this conversation while I'm slicing fruit, so I put the knife down before I hack off a finger. "I hired Kenna. Part time, but no one can know who she is. Call her Nicole in front of the other employees." I pick up the knife again because I'd rather look at the limes than at the expression Roman is giving me right now.

"Um. Wow. *Why?*"

"It's a long story."

I hear his keys and his phone as he drops them on the bar and then scoots out a stool. "Good thing we both work until midnight. Start talking."

I walk to the edge of the bar and glance back into the kitchen to make sure we're still alone. No one else has arrived yet, so I give him a quick rundown of what happened in the grocery store parking lot, and how I showed her videos of Diem and then took her for burgers and somehow ended up feeling sorry for her and offered her a job to help her get out of town.

I get the whole story out, and the whole time, he's completely silent.

"I asked her to stay in the back, away from the customers," I say. "I can't risk Grace or Patrick finding out she works here. I'm not worried about them showing up; they never come here. But I'd still like her to stay in the back. She can do the dishes and help Aaron."

Roman laughs. "So, you essentially hired a barback who can back but not bar?"

"There's plenty to do back there to keep her busy."

I hear Roman swipe his phone and his keys off the bar. Right before he disappears through the double doors to the kitchen, he says, "I don't want to hear another word about the fucking cupcakes ever again."

He's gone before I can point out that his being obsessed with the married baker down the street is a little different than my giving Kenna a job to get her out of town faster.

The doors to the back swing open a couple of minutes later, and Roman says, "Your new hire just arrived."

When I make it to the kitchen, Kenna is standing by the alley door holding her tote, gripping her wrist with the opposite hand. She looks nervous, but different. She's got lip gloss on or something. I don't know, but her mouth is all I can seem to focus on, so I clear my throat and look away from her and casually say, "Hey."

"Hi," she says.

I point to a closet where the employees keep their stuff while on shift. "You can put your bag in there."

I grab her an apron and keep it as professional as I can. "I'll give you a quick tour." She follows me quietly as I show her around the kitchen. I explain the process of how to stack the dishes once she washes them. I give her a brief tour of our stock room. I show her where my office is. I take her out to the alley to show her which dumpster is ours.

We're making our way back to the alley door when Aaron walks up. He pauses when he sees me standing in the alley with Kenna.

"Aaron, this is Nicole. She'll be helping you out in the kitchen."

Aaron narrows his eyes, looking Kenna up and down. "Do I need help in the kitchen?" he asks, confused.

I look at Kenna. "We have a limited menu of food on the weekends, but Aaron takes care of all of it. Just be available if he needs the help."

Kenna nods and reaches out a hand to Aaron. "Nice to meet you," she says. Aaron returns the handshake, but he's still eyeing me suspiciously.

I look at her and point at the door, letting her know I want a minute with Aaron. Kenna nods and slips back inside. I give my focus to Aaron. "She'll only be here a few weeks at the most. She needed a favor."

Aaron holds up a hand. "Enough said, boss." He squeezes my shoulder as he passes me and heads inside.

I've shown Kenna everything I need to show her to keep her busy for one night. And she has Aaron now. He'll take care of her.

I don't want to walk through the back and have to look at her again, so I make my way through the front door. Razi and Roman are covering most of tonight because I have to leave. I didn't take into consideration when I hired Kenna and told her to show up tonight that I already had plans and wouldn't even be here for most of her shift.

"I'll be back around nine," I tell Roman. "I'm going to dinner with them after the recital."

Roman nods. "Mary Anne asks questions," he says. "She's been wanting us to hire her nephew as a barback. This isn't going to sit well with her."

"Just tell Mary Anne that Kenna is . . . *Nicole* is temporary. That's all she needs to know."

Roman shakes his head. "You didn't really think this one through, Ledger."

"I thought about it plenty."

"Maybe, but you thought about it with the wrong fucking head."

I ignore his observation and leave.

Diem decided she wanted to try a dance class a few months ago. Grace says it's because her best friend takes dance, and it's not because Diem actually *likes* dance.

After seeing her recital tonight, it's clear dancing isn't her passion. She was all over the place. I'm not even sure she's paid one second of attention in dance class, because while all the other kids were at least attempting the routine, Diem was running back and forth on the stage recreating moves from her favorite movie, *The Greatest Showman*.

The entire audience was laughing. Grace and Patrick were mortified but were trying not to laugh. At one point, Grace leaned over and whispered, "Make sure she never watches that movie again."

I was filming it, of course.

The whole time I was filming Diem, I had this underlying sense of anticipation at the thought of showing Kenna. But Diem's moments aren't mine to share. I need to remember that, no matter how good it felt on the side of the road to see Kenna finally get a glimpse of Diem a few days ago.

Patrick and Grace legally make all decisions for Diem, and rightfully so. If I found out someone close to me was sharing information about Diem after clearly knowing I asked them not to, I'd be more than livid. And I'd immediately cut that person out of my life.

I can't take that chance with Patrick and Grace. I'm already doing enough behind their backs by just giving Kenna this job.

"I don't think I want to take dance anymore," Diem says. She's still wearing her purple leotard, but there's queso dripping down the front of it now. I wipe it off her because she's on the same side of the booth as me.

"You can't quit dance yet," Grace says. "We've already paid for three more months."

Diem likes to try new things. I don't look at her willingness to quit all the things she tries as a negative personality trait. I think it's a strength that she wants to try every sport she can.

"I want to do that thing with the swords," Diem says, swinging her fork back and forth in the air.

"Fencing?" Patrick asks. "They don't have fencing lessons in this town."

"Ledger can teach me," Diem says.

"I don't have swords. And I don't have time. I already coach your T-ball team."

"T-ball is hell," Diem says.

I choke on my laugh.

"Don't say that," Grace whispers.

"That's what Roman said," Diem retorts. "I have to go to the bathroom."

The bathrooms are within view of our seats, so Diem slides under the table and scoots out of the booth. Grace keeps a close eye on her as she walks to the bathroom door. It's a single-stall bathroom that Diem can lock behind her, which is the only reason Grace isn't following her.

Grace usually accompanies Diem to the restroom, but Diem has been demanding her independence lately. She makes Grace wait outside the bathroom now, and when we come to this restaurant, we always ask to be seated near the bathroom hallway so Grace can allow Diem the space to do things on her own while still keeping a close eye on her.

When Patrick starts to speak, I can tell half of Grace's attention is still on the bathroom door. "We filed a restraining order against Diem's mother."

I hold back my reaction, but it's hard. I swallow those words with my bite of food and then take a sip of water. "Why?"

"We want to be prepared for whatever she decides to do," Patrick says.

"But what would she try to do?" I can tell by the way Grace cocks her head that maybe I shouldn't have said that. But would a judge even grant a restraining order simply because it's filed? I figure it would take more than Kenna's presence for a restraining order to be approved.

Grace says, "She chased us down in the grocery store parking lot. I don't feel safe, Ledger."

Oh. I forgot about that yet somehow still feel the need to defend her like it was my fault we were all in that predicament in the first place.

"We spoke to Grady," Patrick says. "He said he could have the judge expedite it, and she'll probably be served this week."

I have so much I want to say, but now isn't the time to say it. I have no idea when the *right* time to say it is. Or if I even need to say anything at all.

I take another drink and don't respond to their news. I just sit silent, trying not to give off traitor vibes. Because that's exactly what I am right now. There's no way around it.

"Let's change the subject," Grace says, watching Diem as she heads back to the table. "How's your mother, Ledger? I didn't even get to talk to her while she was in town."

"Good. They're heading to Yellowstone, so they'll probably drop into town on their way back through."

Diem is climbing onto Grace's lap when Grace says, "I'd love to see her. Let's plan dinner for when they're here."

"I'll let her know."

Grace hands Diem a french fry and says, "The date is coming up. How are you feeling?"

I blink twice. I know she's not referring to anything related to Scotty, but I have no idea what she's talking about.

"Leah?" Grace says. "The cancelled wedding?"

"Oh. That." I shrug. "I'm fine. She's fine. Things are better this way."

Grace frowns a little bit. She always liked Leah, but I don't think she knew the real Leah very well. Not that Leah is a bad person. I wouldn't have proposed to her if I thought she was.

She just wasn't good enough for Diem, and if Grace knew that, she'd thank me for calling off the engagement rather than continue to bring it up in hopes I change my mind.

"How's the house coming along?" Patrick asks.

"Fine. I think I'm just a few months out from having it move-in ready."

"When are you putting your current house up for sale?"

The thought of that makes me sink an inch deeper into my seat. Putting it up for sale will feel like selling off a piece of myself, for so many reasons. "I don't know yet."

"I don't want you to move," Diem says.

Those six words hit me right in the heart.

"But you'll get to go stay with him at his *new* house," Grace says, attempting to reassure her. "He won't be far."

"I like the house he has now," Diem says with a pout. "I can walk there all by myself."

Diem is staring at her hands. I want to reach over and pull her out of Grace's lap and hug her and tell her I'll never leave her, but it would be a lie.

I wish I would have waited just six months before deciding to build that house back when Diem was younger. Six months would have been plenty of time to know that the little girl Grace and Patrick were raising would infiltrate my life and my heart as if I made her myself.

"Diem will be fine," Grace reassures me. She must be deciphering the look on my face right now. "It's twenty minutes. Hardly anything will change."

I stare at Diem, and she looks up at me, and I swear I can see tears in her eyes. But she closes them and curls into Grace before I can be sure.

CHAPTER TWENTY-THREE

KENNA

I found out from the paperwork he left me to sign that Ledger is paying me way more than what the grocery store pays me.

Because of that, and because it's just in my nature, I've been busting my ass all night. I've been reorganizing everything. No one said I needed to, but I wash dishes faster than they come back to me, so between bouts of dirty dishes, I've been reorganizing the shelves, the stock room, all the dishes in the cabinets.

I've had five years of practice. I didn't tell Ledger about my kitchen experience, because it's always awkward to talk about, but I worked in the kitchen when I was away. A couple dozen bar patrons is a walk in the park compared to hundreds of women.

I wasn't sure how it would feel being stuck back here with Aaron at first because he looks intimidating, with stocky shoulders and dark, expressive eyebrows. But he's a teddy bear.

He said he's been working here since Ledger opened the doors several years ago.

Aaron is a married father of four and works two jobs. Maintenance at the high school during the week, and kitchen duty on Fridays and

Saturdays here. All his children are grown and out of the house now, but he says he keeps this job because he saves up his paychecks and he and his wife like to take an annual vacation to visit her family in Ecuador.

He likes to dance while he works, so he keeps the speakers turned up, and he yells when he talks. Which is entertaining, since he's usually talking about the other employees. He told me Mary Anne has been dating a guy for seven years and they're about to have a second child together, but she refuses to marry him because she hates his last name. He divulged that Roman is obsessed with a married woman who owns the bakery down the street, so he's constantly bringing cupcakes to work.

He's just about to tell me all about the other bartender, Razi, when someone walks through the kitchen doors and says, "Holy shit." I spin around and find the waitress, Mary Anne, looking around the kitchen. "You did all this?"

I nod.

"I didn't realize what a mess it was until now. Wow. Ledger will be impressed with his rash decision when he gets back."

I didn't even know he was gone. I can't see up front, and none of the bartenders have been back to the kitchen at all.

Mary Anne puts her hand on her stomach and walks to a refrigerator. She looks to be around five months along. She opens a Tupperware container and grabs a handful of grape tomatoes. She pops one in her mouth and says, "Tomatoes are all I crave. Marinara sauce. Pizza. Ketchup." She offers me one, but I shake my head. "Tomatoes give me heartburn, but I can't stop eating them."

"Is this your first?" I ask her.

"No, I have a two-year-old boy. This one's also a boy. You have any kids?"

I never know how to answer this question. It hasn't come up much since I was released from prison, but the few times it has, I usually say I do and then immediately change the subject. But I don't want anyone here to start asking questions, so I just shake my head and keep the focus on her. "What are you naming him?"

"Not sure yet." She eats another tomato and then puts the container back in the refrigerator. "What's your story?" she asks. "You new around here? You married? You seeing anyone? How old are you?"

I have different answers for every question coming at me, so I nod, then shake my head, and I end up looking like my head is wobbling like a bobblehead doll by the time she stops firing questions at me.

"I just moved to town. I'm twenty-six. Single."

She raises a brow. "Does Ledger know you're single?"

"I guess."

"Huh," she says. "Maybe that explains it."

"Explains what?"

Mary Anne and Aaron exchange a look. "Why Ledger hired you. We've been wondering."

"Why did he hire me?" I'd like to know what she thinks is the reason.

"I don't mean this to come off in a negative way," she says, "but we've had the same employees for over two years now. He's never mentioned needing more help, so *my* theory is that he hired you to make Leah jealous."

"Mary Anne." Aaron says her name like it's a warning.

She waves him off. "Ledger was supposed to get married this month. He acts like he's okay that the wedding was called off, but something has been bothering him lately. He's been acting weird. And then you apply for a job and he just hires you on the spot when we don't even need the help?" She shrugs. "Makes sense. You're gorgeous. He's heartbroken. I think he's filling a void."

It actually doesn't make sense at all, but I get the feeling Mary Anne is the curious type, and I don't want to say anything to make her even more curious about my presence here.

"Ignore her," Aaron says. "Mary Anne craves gossip as much as she craves tomatoes."

She laughs. "It's true. I like to talk shit. I don't mean anything by it; I'm just bored."

"Why was his wedding called off?" I ask her. Apparently, she's not the only curious one in this kitchen.

She shrugs. "I don't know. Leah, his ex, told people they weren't compatible. Ledger doesn't talk about it. He's a hard egg to crack."

Roman peeks through the double doors, and his presence steals her attention. "The frat boys need you, Mary Anne."

She rolls her eyes and says, "Ugh. I hate college kids. They're terrible tippers."

Aaron suggests I take a break about three hours into my shift, so I decide to spend it sitting on the steps in the alley. I wasn't sure if I'd get a break, or what my hours would even be tonight, so I grabbed some chips and a bottled water before I left the grocery store earlier.

It's quieter in the alley, but I can still hear the bass of the music. Mary Anne came back to chat again earlier and she saw I had pieces of paper towel stuck in my ears to drown out the music while I worked. I lied and told her I get migraines easily, but I really just hate most music.

Every song is a reminder of something bad in my life, so I'd rather hear no songs at all. She says she has a pair of headphones she can bring me tomorrow. So far, the music is the only part of this job I don't like. That was one good thing about prison—I rarely heard music.

Roman opens the back door and seems momentarily surprised to find me on the steps, but he walks over to the other side of the alley and flips a bucket upside down. He sits on it and stretches his leg out, putting pressure on his knee. "How's your first night?" he asks.

"Good." I've noticed Roman limps when he walks, and now he's stretching his leg like he's in pain. I don't know if it's a new injury, but I feel like if it is, he might need to take it easier than he has been tonight. He's a bartender; they never sit. "Did you hurt your leg?"

"It's an old injury. It flares up with the weather." He hikes up his pant leg and reveals a long scar on his knee.

"Ouch. How'd that happen?"

Roman leans back against the brick on the side of the building. "Pro football injury."

"You played pro football too?"

"I played for a different team than Ledger did. I'd rather die than play for the Broncos." He gestures toward his knee. "This happened about a year and a half in. Ended my football career."

"Wow. I'm so sorry."

"Hazard of the job."

"How'd you end up working here with Ledger?"

He eyes me carefully. "I could ask the same of you."

Fair enough. I don't know how much Roman knows about my story, but Ledger did mention he's the only one here who knows who I am. I'm sure that means he knows everything.

I don't want to talk about myself.

Luckily, I don't have to because the alley fills with light from Ledger's truck as he pulls into his usual parking spot. For whatever reason, Roman uses this moment to escape back inside and leave me out here alone.

I tense with Roman's disappearance and Ledger's return. I'm embarrassed I'm sitting outside on the steps. As soon as Ledger opens the door of his truck, I say, "I've been working. I swear. You just happened to pull up right when I took a break."

Ledger smiles as he gets out of the truck, like my explanation is unnecessary. I don't know why I have a physical reaction to that smile, but it sends a swirl through my stomach. His presence always creates this hum right under my skin, like I'm buzzing with nervous energy. Maybe it's because he's my only link to my daughter. Maybe it's because I think about what happened between us in this alley every time I close my eyes at night.

Maybe it's because he's my boss now, and I really don't want to lose this job, and here I am not doing anything, and I suddenly feel like a pathetic asshole.

I liked it much better when he wasn't here. I was more relaxed.

"How's it going tonight?" He leans against his truck like he's in no hurry to get inside.

"Good. Everyone's been nice."

He raises an eyebrow like he doesn't buy that. "Even Mary Anne?"

"Well. She's been nice to *me*. She kind of talked a little shit about you, though." I'm smiling so he knows I'm teasing. But she did imply he only hired me because he thinks I'm pretty and he's trying to make his ex jealous. "Who's Leah?"

Ledger's head falls back against his truck, and he groans. "Which one of them brought up Leah? Mary Anne?"

I nod. "She said you were supposed to get married this month."

Ledger looks uncomfortable, but I'm not going to be the one to cut this conversation short on account of his discomfort. If he doesn't want to talk about it, he doesn't have to. But I want to know, so I wait expectantly for him to muster up an answer.

"It was honestly so stupid when I look back on it," he says. "The whole breakup. We got in an argument about kids we don't even have yet."

"And that ended your engagement?"

He nods. "Yep."

"What was the argument?"

"She asked me if I was going to love my future kids more than I love Diem. And I said no, I would love them all the same."

"That made her angry?"

"It bothered her how much time I spent with Diem. She said when we started a family of our own one day, I'd have to spend less time focusing on Diem and more time on *our* family. It was like an epiphany. I realized she didn't see Diem fitting into a potential future family like I did. After that, I sort of just . . . checked out, I guess."

I don't know why I expected their breakup to be over something more serious. People don't usually break up over hypothetical situations, but it says a lot about Ledger that he was able to see his own happiness is tied to Diem's happiness, and he wouldn't settle for anyone who didn't respect that.

"Leah sounds like a terrible bitch." I'm half kidding when I say it, which is why Ledger laughs. But the more I think about it, the more irritated I get. "Seriously, though. Screw her for thinking Diem isn't worthy of the same love as kids who don't even *exist* yet."

"Exactly. Everyone thought I was crazy for breaking up with her, but to me it was a precursor to all the potential problems we'd be facing down the road." He smiles at me. "Look at you being an overprotective mother. I don't feel so crazy now."

As soon as he says that—acknowledges me as Diem's mother—my face falls. It was a simple sentence, but it meant everything to hear it come from him.

Even if it slipped out by accident.

Ledger straightens up and then locks his truck. "I better get inside; the parking lot looked packed."

He never said what he left to go do for several hours tonight, but I have a feeling he was doing something with Diem. But he could have also been on a date, which unnerves me almost as much.

I'm not allowed to be in my own daughter's life, but whoever Ledger decides to date gets to be in her life, and that automatically makes me jealous of whatever girl that ends up being.

At least it won't be Leah.

Screw her.

Roman brings a crate full of glasses to the back and sets them by the sink for me. "I'm heading out," he says. "Ledger said he'd give you a ride home if you don't mind waiting. He's got about half an hour of shit left to do."

"Thanks," I say to Roman. He takes off his apron and tosses it into a basket where all the other employee aprons have ended up for the night. "Who cleans those?" I don't know if that's supposed to be my job. I'm not even really sure what all my job entails. Ledger wasn't here to train me throughout the night, and everyone else kind of pointed out things here and there that I could do, so I've just been doing everything I can get my hands on.

"There's a washer and dryer upstairs," Roman says.

"There's another level to the bar?" I haven't seen any stairs.

He points at the door that leads out to the alley. "Access to the stairs is outside. Half of the space is storage, the other half is a studio apartment with a washer and dryer."

"Do I need to take them up and wash them?"

He shakes his head. "I usually do that in the mornings. I live there." He pulls his shirt off to toss it in the basket just as Ledger walks into the kitchen.

Roman is shirtless now, changing into his street clothes, and Ledger is staring straight at me. I know it looks like I was staring at Roman as he was changing, but we were having an active conversation. I wasn't staring at him because he was momentarily shirtless. Not that it matters, but it embarrasses me, so I turn around and focus on the remaining dishes.

Roman and Ledger have a conversation I can't hear, but I do hear it when Roman tells Ledger good night and leaves. Ledger disappears back into the front of the bar.

I'm alone, but I prefer it that way. Ledger makes me more nervous than comfortable.

I finish my work and wipe everything down for a final time. It's half past midnight, and I have no idea how much longer Ledger has until he's finished. I don't want to bother him, but I'm too tired to walk home, so I wait for the ride.

I grab my stuff and push myself onto the counter. I pull out my notebook and my pen. I don't know that I'll ever do anything with the letters I write to Scotty, but they're cathartic.

> Dear Scotty,
> Ledger is an asshole. We've clarified that. I mean, the guy turned a bookstore into a bar. What kind of monster would do that?
>
> But . . . I'm beginning to think he has a sweet side too. Maybe that's why you two were best friends.

"What are you writing?"

I slam my notebook shut at the sound of his voice. Ledger is removing his apron, eyeing me. I shove my notebook into my bag and mutter, "Nothing."

He tilts his head, and his eyes fill with curiosity. "Do you like to write?"

I nod.

"Would you say you're more artistic or more scientific?"

That's an odd question. I shrug. "I don't know. Artistic, I guess. Why?"

Ledger grabs a clean glass and walks over to the sink. He fills it with water and then takes a sip. "Diem has a wild imagination. I always wondered if she got that from you."

My heart fills with pride. I love when he reveals little tidbits about her. I also love knowing someone in her life appreciates her imagination.

I had a vivid imagination when I was younger, but my mother stifled it. It wasn't until Ivy encouraged me to open that part of myself back up that I actually felt like someone supported it.

Scotty would have, but I don't even think he knew I was artistic. He met me at a time when that part of me was still in a deep sleep.

It's awake now, though. Thanks to Ivy. I write all the time. I write poems, I write letters to Scotty, I write book ideas I don't know that I'll ever get around to fleshing out. Writing might actually be what saved me from myself.

"I mostly just write letters." I regret saying it as soon as I say it, but Ledger doesn't react to that confession.

"I know. Letters to Scotty." He sets his glass of water on the table beside him and then folds his arms over his chest.

"How do you know I write him letters?"

"I saw one," he says. "Don't worry, I didn't read it. I just saw one of the pages when I grabbed your bag out of your locker."

I wondered if he saw that stack of papers. I was worried he might have peeked, but if he says he didn't read them, for some reason I believe him.

"How many letters have you written him?"

"Over three hundred."

He shakes his head in disbelief, but then something makes him smile. "Scotty hated writing. He used to pay me to write his reports for him."

That makes me laugh, because I wrote a paper or two for him when we were together.

It's weird talking with someone who knew Scotty in a lot of the same ways I knew him. I've honestly never experienced this before. It feels good, thinking about him in a way that makes me laugh instead of cry.

I wish I knew more about Scotty outside of who he was with me.

"Diem might grow up to be a writer someday. She likes to make up words," Ledger says. "If she doesn't know what something is called, she just invents a word for it."

"Like what?"

"Solar lights," he says. "The kind that line sidewalks? We don't know why, but she calls them *patchels*."

That makes me smile, but it also makes me ache with jealousy. I want to know her like he does. "What else?" My voice is quieter because I'm trying to hide the fact that it's shaking.

"The other day she was riding her bike, and her feet kept slipping on the pedals. She said, 'My feet won't stop flibbering.' I asked her what *flibbering* meant, and she said it's when she wears flip-flops, and her feet slip out of them. And she thinks *soaking* means 'very.' She'll say, 'I'm soaking tired,' or, 'I'm soaking hungry.'"

It hurts too much to even laugh at that. I force a smile, but I think Ledger can sense that stories about a daughter I'm not allowed to know are ripping me in two. He stops smiling and then walks to the sink and washes the glass. "You ready?"

I nod and hop off the table.

On the drive home, he says, "What are you going to do with the letters?"

"Nothing," I say immediately. "I just like writing them."

"What are the letters about?"

"Everything. Sometimes nothing." I look out my window so he can't read the truth on my face. But something in me makes me want to be honest with him. I want Ledger to trust me. I have a lot to prove. "I'm thinking about compiling them and putting them into a book someday."

That gives him pause. "Will it have a happy ending?"

I'm still looking out the window when I say, "It'll be a book about my life, so I don't see how it could."

Ledger keeps his eyes on the road when he asks, "Do any of the letters talk about what happened the night Scotty died?"

I put space between his question and my answer. "Yes. One of them does."

"Can I read it?"

"No."

Ledger's eyes meet mine briefly. Then he looks in front of him and flips on his blinker to turn onto my street. He pulls into a parking spot and leaves his truck running. I don't know if I should get out immediately, or if there's anything left to be said between us. I put my hand on the door handle.

"Thank you for the job."

Ledger taps the steering wheel with his thumb and nods. "I'd say you earned it. The kitchen hasn't been that organized since I've owned the building, and you've only worked one shift."

His compliment feels good. I absorb it and then tell him good night.

As much as I want to look back at him when I get out of his truck, I keep my focus ahead of me. I listen for him to back out, but he doesn't, which makes me think he watches me as I walk all the way up to my apartment.

Once I'm inside, Ivy immediately runs up to me. I pick her up and leave the lights off as I walk to the window to peek out.

Ledger is just sitting in his truck, staring up at my apartment. I immediately press my back against the wall next to the window. Finally, I hear his engine rev up as he backs out of the parking spot.

"Ivy," I whisper, scratching her head. "What are we doing?"

CHAPTER TWENTY-FOUR

Ledger

"Ledger!"

I glance up from packing the equipment, and I immediately start packing faster. The mom brigade is walking toward me. When they come at me in group formation like this, it's never good. There are four of them, and they have matching chairs with each of their children's names on the backs of them. They're either going to tell me I'm not playing their kids enough, or they're about to try to set me up with one of their single friends.

I glance at the playground, and Diem is still out there playing chase with two of her friends. Grace is keeping an eye on her, so I get the last helmet in the bag, but it's too late to pretend I didn't notice they were trying to get my attention.

Whitney speaks first. "We heard Diem's mother showed back up."

I make brief eye contact with her, but try not to show any sort of surprise that they know Kenna is in town. None of them actually knew Kenna in the brief time she dated Scotty. None of these women even knew Scotty.

But they know Diem, and they know me, and they know the story. So, they think they're entitled to the truth. "Where'd you hear that?"

"Grace's coworker told my aunt," one of the mothers says.

"I can't believe she actually had the nerve to come back," Whitney says. "Grady said Grace and Patrick filed a restraining order."

"They did?" I play dumb, because it's better than letting them know how much I know. They'll just ask more questions.

"You didn't know?" Whitney asks.

"We talked about it. Wasn't sure if they went through with it."

"I don't blame them," she says. "What if she tries to take Diem?"

"She wouldn't do that," I say. I throw the bag in my truck and slam the tailgate shut.

"I wouldn't put it past her," Whitney says. "Addicts do crazy shit."

"She isn't an addict." I say it too adamantly. Too quickly. I can see suspicion in Whitney's eyes.

I wish Roman were at this game. He couldn't make it today, and he's usually my excuse to escape the mom brigade. Some of them are friends with Leah, so they don't flirt with me directly, out of respect for her. But Roman isn't off limits, so I usually leave him to the wolves when they show up.

"Tell Grady I said hello." I walk away from them and head toward Grace and Diem.

I don't know how to defend Kenna in these kinds of situations. I don't know that I *should*. But it feels wrong allowing everyone to continue to think the worst of her.

I didn't tell Kenna I was picking her up today, but I didn't know I was until I was on my way to the bar and realized it was almost time for her shift at the grocery store to end.

I pull into the parking lot, and it's not even two whole minutes before she walks outside. She doesn't notice my truck. She walks toward the road, so I drive across the parking lot to intercept her.

She sees my truck, and I swear she makes a face when I point to the passenger door. She mutters "Thanks" when she opens the door. And then, "You don't have to give me rides. I'm fine walking."

"I just left the ball field; it was on my way."

She sets her purse between us and then pulls on her seat belt. "Is she any good at T-ball?"

"Yeah. I don't think she likes the game as much as she likes hanging out with her friends, though. But if she stuck with it, I think she'd be pretty good."

"What else does she do besides T-ball?"

I can't blame Kenna for being curious. I've put myself in this position by already sharing too much with her, but now the moms have planted a seed in my head.

What if she's only asking so she can get a handle on Diem's schedule? The more she knows about Diem's activities, the easier it would be for her to show up and take her. I feel guilty even thinking that, but Diem is my number one priority in life, so I'd feel even shittier not feeling a little overprotective.

"I'm sorry," Kenna says. "I shouldn't ask you questions you don't feel comfortable answering. It's not my place."

She looks out her window as I pull onto the street. She does this thing where she flexes her fingers and then grips her thighs. Diem does the same thing with her fingers. It's incredible how two people who have never met can have so many of the same mannerisms.

It's too loud in the truck, and I feel like I need to warn her, so I roll up my window as I pick up speed. "They filed a restraining order against you."

I see her look at me out of the corner of my eye. "Are you serious?"

"Yes. I wanted to give you a heads-up before you get served papers."

"Why would they do that?"

"I think what happened at the grocery store scared Grace."

She shakes her head and looks back out her window. She doesn't say anything else until we pull up to the alley behind the bar.

I feel like I've set her up for failure tonight by putting her in a bad mood as soon as she got in my truck. I shouldn't have told her about the restraining order right before her shift, but I feel like she has the right to know. She honestly hasn't done anything to deserve being served a restraining order, but the simple fact that she exists in the same town as Diem is reason enough for the Landrys to file one on her.

"She takes dance," I say, answering her earlier question about Diem. I put my truck in park and pull up the video from her recital. "That's where I was last night. She had a recital." I hand Kenna the phone.

She watches the first several seconds with a straight face and then bursts into laughter.

I hate that I love watching Kenna's face when she watches videos of Diem. It does something to me. Makes me feel something I probably shouldn't be feeling. But I like the feeling, and it makes me wonder what it would be like getting to witness Kenna and Diem interact in real life.

Kenna watches the video three times with a huge smile on her face. "She's horrible!"

It makes me laugh. There's a joy to her voice that isn't usually there, and I wonder if that joy would always be present if Diem were a part of Kenna's life.

"Does she like dance?" Kenna asks.

I shake my head. "No. After the recital was over, she said she wanted to quit and do 'that thing with the swords.'"

"Fencing?"

"She wants to try everything. All the time. But she never sticks to anything because she gets bored with it and thinks the next thing will be more interesting."

"They say boredom is a sign of intelligence," Kenna says.

"She's very smart, so that would make sense."

Kenna smiles, but as she hands me back my phone, her smile falters. She opens the door and heads toward the back door, so I follow suit.

I open the back door for her, and we're greeted by Aaron. "Hey, boss," he says. "Hey, Nic."

Kenna walks over to him, and he lifts a hand. They high-five like they've known each other a lot longer than just one shift.

Roman walks into the back holding a tray of empty bottles. He nods at me. "How'd it go?"

"No one cried and no one vomited," I say. That's what we consider a successful day in T-ball.

Roman gets Kenna's attention. "She had gluten-free. I put three of them in the fridge for you."

"*Thank* you," Kenna says. It's the first hint of excitement I've ever seen come from her that had nothing to do with Diem. I have no idea what they're talking about. I was gone for a few hours last night, and it's like she developed personal relationships with everyone here.

And why is Roman buying her three of whatever it is they're talking about?

Why am I having a slight visceral reaction to the thought of Kenna and Roman becoming close? Would he hit on her? Would I even have a right to be jealous? When I got back to the bar last night, they were taking their break at the same time. Did Roman do that on purpose?

Right when I have that thought, Mary Anne shows up for her shift. She hands Kenna a pair of what look like noise-cancelling headphones. Kenna says, "You're a lifesaver."

"I knew I had an extra pair at home," Mary Anne says. She passes me and says, "Hey, boss," before heading to the front.

Kenna hangs the headphones around her neck and then ties her apron. The headphones aren't even attached to anything, and she doesn't have a phone. I'm confused about how she's going to listen to music with them.

"What are those for?" I ask her.

"To drown out the music."

"You don't want to hear music?"

She faces the sink, but not before I see her expression falter. "I hate music."

She hates *music*? Is that even a thing? "Why do you hate music?"

She looks at me over her shoulder. "Because it's sad." She covers her ears with the headphones and starts running water in the sink.

Music is the one thing that grounds me. I couldn't imagine not being able to connect with it, but Kenna is right. Most songs are about love or loss, two things that are probably incredibly difficult for her to absorb in any medium.

I leave her to her duties and head to the front to start on mine. We haven't opened just yet, so the bar is empty. Mary Anne is unlocking the front door, so I pause next to Roman. "Three what?"

He glances at me. "Huh?"

"You said you put three of something in the fridge for Kenna."

"*Nicole*," he corrects, looking across the room at Mary Anne. "And I was talking about cupcakes. Her landlord can't have gluten, and she's trying to stay on her good side."

"Why?"

"I don't know, something about her electric bill." Roman side-eyes me and then walks away.

I'm glad she's getting along with everyone, but there's also a small part of me that regrets leaving for most of my shift last night. I feel like they all got to know Kenna in a way I don't know Kenna. I don't know why that bothers me.

I go to the jukebox to start up a few songs before the crowd arrives, and I analyze each song I choose. It's a digital jukebox with access to thousands of songs, but I realize it would take me all night to find even a handful that wouldn't remind Kenna of Scotty or Diem in some way.

She's right. In the end, if there's nothing good going on in your life, almost every song becomes depressing, no matter what it's about.

I put it on shuffle to match my mood.

CHAPTER TWENTY-FIVE

Kenna

I got a paycheck. It was small, and the way the paydays worked out, it was only for a partial week, but it was enough to finally get a new phone.

I'm sitting on the picnic table outside my apartment browsing apps. I opened at the grocery store today, so I had several hours between that shift and my shift at the bar tonight, so I'm just passing time outside. I try to get as much vitamin D as I can, considering my outdoor time was scheduled and limited for five solid years. I should probably buy vitamin D supplements so my body can catch up.

A car pulls into a parking spot, and I look up in time to see Lady Diana waving wildly at me from the front seat. We work different shifts most days, which is unfortunate. It would be nice to be able to ask her mother for a ride to and from work, but my hours are longer than Lady Diana's. Ledger has given me rides a handful of times, but I haven't seen him at all since he dropped me off at my apartment after my second shift last Saturday night.

I've never met Lady Diana's mother. She looks to be a little older than me, maybe midthirties. She smiles and follows Lady Diana across the grass until they reach me. Lady Diana gestures toward the phone in my hand. "She got a phone—why can't I have a phone?"

Her mother sits next to me. "She's an adult," her mother says, glancing at me. "Hi. I'm Adeline."

I never know how to introduce myself. I'm Nicole at both of my jobs, but I introduced myself as Kenna to Lady Diana the first time, and also as Kenna to the landlord, Ruth. This is going to catch up to me eventually, so I somehow need to figure out a way to make the lie a truth.

"Kenna," I say. "But I go by Nicole." That feels okay. It's kind of a lie. Kind of the truth.

"I got a new boyfriend at work today," Lady Diana says to me. She's bouncing on her toes, full of energy. Her mother groans.

"Oh, yeah?"

Lady Diana nods. "His name is Gil, he works with us, he's the guy with the red hair, he asked me to be his girlfriend. He has Down syndrome like me and he likes video games and I think I'm gonna marry him."

"Slow down," her mother says. Lady Diana spoke in one solid run-on sentence, so I'm not sure if her mother is telling her to slow down when she speaks or slow down on the wedding plans.

"Is he nice?" I ask her.

"He has a PlayStation."

"But is he nice?"

"He has lots of Pokémon cards."

"Is he nice, though?" I repeat.

She shrugs. "I don't know. I'll have to ask him."

I smile. "Yes. Do that. You should only marry people who are nice to you."

Adeline looks at me. "Do you know this kid? *Gil?*" She says his name with contempt, and it makes me laugh.

I shake my head. "No, but I'll keep an eye out for him." I look at Lady Diana. "And I'll make sure he's nice."

Adeline looks relieved. "Thank you." She stands up. "Are you coming to the lunch on Sunday?"

"What lunch?"

"We're having a small lunch here for Mother's Day; I told Lady Diana to invite you."

I feel the sting in the mention of that holiday. I've tried not to think about it. It'll be the first time I've experienced it outside of prison and in the same town as Diem.

Lady Diana says, "Kenna's daughter was kidnapped, so I didn't invite her."

I immediately shake my head. "She wasn't kidnapped. I just . . . it's a long story. I don't have custody of her right now." I am mortified. Adeline can tell.

"Don't worry, the lunch is for everyone who lives here," Adeline says. "We mostly host it for Ruth since her kids live so far away."

I nod, because I feel like if I agree to come, she won't pressure me, and then maybe I won't have to explain why Lady Diana said my daughter was kidnapped. "What can I bring?"

"We've got it covered," she says. "It was good to meet you." She starts to walk away, but spins around. "Actually, do you know anyone with an extra table and a few chairs? I think we're gonna need more seating."

I want to say no, since I don't know anyone but Ledger. But I don't want her to think I'm as lonely as I am, so I just nod and say, "I can ask around."

Adeline tells me it was nice to finally meet me, and then she walks toward their apartment, but Lady Diana lingers behind. When her mother is gone, she reaches for my phone. "Can I play a game?"

I hand her the phone, and she sits in the grass next to the picnic table. I need to get ready for my shift at Ward's. "I'm gonna go change.

You can play with my phone until I get back down." Lady Diana nods but doesn't look at me.

I'd love to be able to save for a car so I no longer have to walk to work, but being forced to save up in order to just move away and make the Landrys more comfortable is really eating into my financial plans.

⸻

I get to the bar early, but the back door is unlocked.

I feel confident in what I need to do after having worked here last week. I put on my apron and start to get the sink water ready when Roman walks to the back.

"You're early," he says.

"Yeah. Wasn't sure how bad traffic would be."

Roman laughs. He knows I don't have a car.

"Who used to wash dishes before Ledger hired me?" I ask him.

"Everyone. We all pitched in when we had a spare second, or we'd wait until the end of the night and take turns staying late to clean." He grabs his apron. "I doubt we'll ever want to go back down an employee after this. It's nice actually getting to leave when the bar closes."

I wonder if Roman knows my position is only temporary. He probably does.

"It's gonna be busy tonight," he warns. "Last day of finals were today. I have a feeling we're gonna see a rush of college kids."

"Mary Anne will love that." I pour liquid soap into the bin. "Hey. Quick question." I face him. "There's a luncheon at my apartment on Sunday. They need an extra table. Do you guys happen to have one here?"

Roman nudges his head toward the ceiling. "Up in storage, I think." He looks at his phone screen. "We still have a while before we open. Let's go check."

I turn off the water and follow him out to the alley. He pulls a ring of keys from his pocket and flips through them. "Excuse the mess," he says, inserting a key into the door. "I usually keep it a little cleaner up here in case we have a runt, but it's been a while." He pulls the door open to reveal a well-lit stairwell.

"What's a runt?" I ask as I follow him up to the apartment. The stairwell curves after the last step, and the door opens up to a space about the size of the back kitchen of the bar. It's the same floor plan, but it's finished out to actually be a living space.

"Runts are what we call the leftover drunk people at the end of the night that no one claims. Sometimes we put them on the couch up here until they sober up and remember where they need to go." He flips on a light, and the couch is the first thing I see. It's old and worn, and I can tell it's comfortable just by looking at it. There's a stand with a flat-screen TV on it a few feet away from a king-size bed.

It's an efficiency apartment, complete with a kitchen and a small dining room with a window that overlooks the street in front of the bar. It's twice the size of mine and actually has a little charm.

"It's cute." I point to the counter in the kitchen when I see at least thirty coffee mugs lined up against the wall. "You addicted to coffee or just coffee mugs?"

"It's a long story." Roman flips through his keys again. "There's a storage area behind this door. Last time I looked, there was a table, but I can't make any promises." He gets the door unlocked, and when he pulls it open, there are two six-foot tables stacked vertically against the wall. I help him as he pulls one out. "You need both of them?"

"One will do." We lean the table against the couch, and then he closes and locks the door.

We both lift one end to carry it downstairs. "We can leave it at the bottom of the stairwell for now and then throw it in the back of Ledger's truck tonight," he says.

"Awesome. Thank you."

"What kind of luncheon is it?"

"Just a potluck." I don't want to admit it's for Mother's Day. It would seem like I'm celebrating the holiday, and I don't want to be judged.

Not that Roman seems like the judgmental type. He actually seems like a decent person, and he's handsome enough that I'd probably look at him differently if I didn't already know what it was like to kiss Ledger.

I can't look at another man's mouth without wishing I was looking at Ledger's. I hate that I still find him as attractive as I did the first night I walked into his bar. It would be so much easier to be attracted to someone else. *Anyone* else.

Roman props the table up at the bottom of the stairwell. "Do you need chairs?"

"Chairs. Shit. Yes." I didn't think about chairs. He heads back upstairs, and I follow him. "So, how do you and Ledger know each other?"

"He's the one who injured me playing football."

I pause at the top of the stairs. "He ended your football career, and now you're . . . *friends*?" I'm not sure I follow how that trajectory could have occurred.

Roman eyes me carefully as he unlocks the storage room door again. "You really don't know this story?"

I shake my head. "I've been sort of preoccupied for several years."

He laughs quietly. "Yeah. I guess so. I'll give you the condensed version." He opens the door and starts grabbing chairs. "I had to have knee surgery after the injury," Roman says. "I was in a lot of pain. Got addicted to pain pills and spent every penny I made in the NFL on my addiction." He sets two chairs outside the door and then grabs two more. "Let's just say I fucked up my life pretty good. Word got back to Ledger, and he tracked me down. I think he felt somewhat responsible, even though what he did to my knee was an accident. But he showed up when everyone else bowed out. He made sure I got the help I needed."

I don't know what to do with all the information he just handed me. "Oh. Wow."

Roman has all six chairs stacked against the wall before he closes the door. He grabs four and I grab two, and we head back down. "Ledger gave me a job and rented this apartment to me when I got out of rehab two years ago." We set the chairs against the wall before walking outside. "I honestly don't even remember how it started, but he'd give me a coffee mug on the weekly anniversary of my sobriety. He still gives me a mug every Friday, but now he just does it to be an asshole because he knows I'm running out of space."

That's honestly kind of adorable. "Hopefully you like coffee."

"I survive on coffee. You don't want to be around me if I haven't had it." Roman's eyes lock on something behind me. I turn around to find Ledger standing between his truck and the back door to the bar. He's staring at us.

Roman doesn't pause like I do. He keeps walking toward the back door to the bar. "Kenna is borrowing a table and some chairs for a thing she's having Sunday. We put them at the bottom of the stairwell. Grab them before you leave."

"*Nicole*," Ledger says, correcting Roman.

"Nicole. Whatever," Roman says. "Don't forget. Tables. Chairs. Ride home." He disappears into the bar.

Ledger looks at the ground for a moment before staring at me. "What kind of thing do you need a table for?"

I shove my hands in my back pockets. "It's just a lunch on Sunday. At my apartment." He continues to stare at me as if he wants more of an explanation.

"Sunday is Mother's Day."

I nod and start walking toward the door. "Yep. Might as well celebrate with the mothers at my apartment since I can't celebrate the day with my own daughter." My voice is clipped when I walk inside. Maybe a bit accusatory. The door falls shut behind me with a thud, and

I walk straight to the sink and turn on the water. I grab the headphones Mary Anne let me borrow last week, but this time I plug them into my phone now that I finally have one. I loaded up an audiobook to get me through the shift.

I can feel a slight breeze meet my neck when Ledger enters the building. I wait a few seconds and then look over my shoulder to see where he is and what he's doing.

He's walking toward the front, staring straight ahead the whole time. I can't tell what he's thinking when he wears that stoic expression. The thing about Ledger's expressions is I haven't really seen many of them since the first night he was working. He seemed loose and carefree that night behind the bar. But since the moment he found out who I was, he seems inflexible in my presence. Almost like he's doing everything he can to keep me from knowing his thoughts.

CHAPTER TWENTY-SIX

Ledger

The joints in my body feel locked in place as I attempt to execute the motions of the evening with a stiffness that should be the result of a hangover. But I'm not hungover. Just . . . irritated? Is that what this is?

I'm reacting like an asshole. I know it and Roman knows it, but my maturity can't seem to catch up and take over.

How long has Kenna been here? How long were they in Roman's apartment? Why did she seem short with me? Why the fuck do I care?

I don't know what to do with these feelings, so I wad them up and try to keep them stuffed in my throat, or my stomach, or wherever people tuck away this shit. I don't need to start this shift with an attitude. It's the end of finals week. Tonight is going to be insane enough as it is.

I turn on the jukebox and the first song that comes on is one left over from last night's queue. "If We Were Vampires," by Jason Isbell.

Great. An epic love song. Just what Kenna needs.

I walk to the back and notice she's got her headphones on. I grab all the fruit I normally slice at the beginning of my shift and take it to the front.

I'm slicing up a lime, possibly a little too angrily, when Roman says, "You good?"

"I'm fine." I try to say it like I would normally say it, but I don't know how I would normally say it because Roman never has to ask me if I'm good. I'm usually always good.

"Rough day?" he asks.

"Great day."

He sighs and reaches over, pulling the knife out of my hand. I press my palms into the counter and turn to look at him. He's leaning casually on his elbow, twirling the knife in a circle with his finger while he stares at me. "It was nothing," he says. "She borrowed a table and some chairs. We were upstairs for three minutes."

"I didn't say anything."

"You didn't have to." He releases an exasperated laugh. "Shit, man. I didn't peg you for the jealous type."

I reach for my knife and start slicing through the limes again. "It has nothing to do with jealousy."

"What is it, then?" he asks.

I'm about to answer him, probably with some bullshit lie, but the door swings open and four guys spill into the bar. Loud, ready to celebrate, possibly already drunk. I cut our conversation short and prepare for a shift I'm not at all in the mood for.

Eight long hours later, Roman and I are in the alley loading the table and chairs into the back of my truck. We've barely had time to think tonight, much less finish our conversation from earlier.

Not much is said between us. We're both tired, and I think Roman is treading carefully, but the more I think about him and Kenna being in his apartment together, the more it bothers me.

I could see Roman being attracted to her. And I don't know Kenna that well, but she'd probably be desperate enough to attach herself to anyone who could be an excuse for her to stay in this town.

I feel guilty even having that thought.

"We gonna talk about this?" Roman asks.

I slam my tailgate shut, and then I grip my truck with one hand and my jaw with the other. I choose my words cautiously as I begin to speak. "If you start something up with her, she'll find an excuse not to leave town. The whole point of her working here is so she can save up money and leave."

Roman rolls his head, like rolling his eyes wouldn't convey his irritation enough. "You think I'm trying to hook up with her? You think I would do that to you after everything you've done for me?"

"I'm not making her off limits because I'm jealous. I need her to leave town so Patrick and Grace's life can go back to normal."

Roman laughs. "You are so full of shit. You played in the NFL. You own a lucrative business. You're building a ridiculous fucking house. You aren't broke, Ledger. If you wanted her to leave town, you would have written her a check to get rid of her."

I'm tense as fuck, so I tilt my head to the side until my neck pops. "She wouldn't have taken a handout."

"Did you even try?"

I didn't have to. I know Kenna, and she wouldn't have taken a handout. "Just be careful with her, Roman. She'd do anything to be in Diem's life."

"Well, at least we agree on *that* part," he says, right before disappearing into the stairwell to his apartment.

Fuck him.

Fuck him because he's right.

As much as I can try to deny it, I'm not acting this way because I'm worried Kenna will stay in town longer. I'm upset because the thought of her leaving has me more on edge than the thought of her sticking around.

How did this happen? How did I go from absolutely loathing this woman to feeling something else entirely? Am I that pathetic a friend to Scotty? Am I that disloyal to Patrick and Grace?

I didn't hire Kenna because I want her to leave. I hired her because I like being in her presence. I hired her because I think about kissing her again every time my head meets the pillow at night. I hired her because I'm hoping Patrick and Grace have a change of heart, and I want to be around if that happens.

CHAPTER TWENTY-SEVEN

KENNA

My face is on fire when I back away from the door.

I heard every word Ledger said to Roman. I even heard some of the words he didn't say.

I walk to the storage room and grab my bag as soon as I hear him walking up the back steps. When he opens the door, I can't help but wonder what thoughts are going through his head when his eyes land on me.

Since the moment he offered me this job, I've been convinced it's because he hates me and wants me to leave town, but Roman is right. He could pay me off and send me on my way if that's really what he wanted.

Why *am* I still here?

And why is he warning Roman about me, like my intentions aren't good? I didn't ask for this job. He *offered* it to me. That he would think I'd use Roman to get to my daughter feels like a slap in the face, if that's even what he was insinuating. I'm not sure what he was insinuating, or if he was just being oddly territorial over me.

"You ready?" Ledger asks. He flips off the lights and holds open the back door for me. As I pass him, there's a different kind of tension between us. It isn't a tension necessarily related to Diem anymore. It's a tension that seems to exist simply because we're in each other's presence.

As we head to my apartment, I feel short of air. I want to roll down the window, but if I do, I'm worried he'll know it's because I can't seem to breathe properly in his presence.

I glance at him a couple of times, attempting to be discreet, but there's a new tightness to his jaw that isn't usually there. Is he thinking about everything Roman said to him? Is he upset because he agrees, or upset because Roman was completely off the mark?

"Did you get served with the restraining order this week?" he asks.

I clear my throat to make room for the tiny *no* I speak out loud. "I googled it on my phone and read that it can take about one to two weeks for a restraining order request to process."

I'm looking out my window when Ledger says, "You got a phone?"

"Yeah. A few days ago."

He grabs his own phone and hands it to me. "Put in your info."

I don't like how bossy that seems. I don't grab his phone. Instead, I look at it, and then at him. "What if I don't want you to have my number?"

He pegs me with his stare. "I'm your boss. I need a way to contact my employees."

I huff because I hate that he makes a valid point. I grab his phone and text myself so I'll have his number, too, but when I save my information, I list myself as Nicole rather than Kenna. I don't know who has access to his phone. Better safe than sorry.

I set his phone back in his phone holder as he pulls into my parking lot.

He swings open his door as soon as he kills his truck. He grabs the table, and I try to help him, but he says, "I've got it. Where do you want it?"

"Do you mind taking it upstairs?"

He heads that way, and I grab a couple of chairs. By the time I make it to my stairwell, he's already heading back down to grab the rest of the chairs. He steps to the side, pressing his back against the railing to make room for me, but when I pass him, I can smell him. He smells like limes and bad decisions.

The table is propped up next to my apartment door. I unlock my door and then set the chairs next to the wall. I look out the window, and Ledger is grabbing the rest of the chairs from his truck, so I glance around my apartment to see if anything needs rectifying before he comes back up. There's a bra on the couch, so I cover it up with a pillow.

Ivy is at my feet meowing, and I notice her food and water bowls are empty. I'm refilling them as Ledger taps on the door and then opens it. He brings the chairs and then the table inside.

"Anything else?" he asks.

I set Ivy's water bowl down in the bathroom, and she goes straight for it. I close the door and shut her in the bathroom so she doesn't try to escape through the open front door. "No. Thanks for the help." I walk to the door so I can lock it after Ledger leaves, but he just stands by it, gripping the door handle.

"What time do you get off work at the grocery store tomorrow?"

"Four."

"Our T-ball game should end around then. I can give you a ride, but I might be a little late."

"It's okay. I can walk. The weather is supposed to be nice."

He says, "Okay," but he lingers in the doorway for an uncomfortable beat.

Should I tell him I overheard him?

I probably should. If there's one thing spending five years without a life taught me, it's that I don't want to waste a single second of the life I have left being scared of confrontation. My cowardice is a big part of why my life has turned out the way it has.

"I wasn't trying to eavesdrop," I say, wrapping my arms around myself. "But I heard your conversation with Roman."

Ledger's eyes flick away from my face, like that makes him uncomfortable.

"Why did you tell him to be careful around me?"

Ledger presses his lips together in thought. His throat slowly rolls with his swallow, but he still doesn't say anything. He just looks torn as his face takes on what looks like a world of pain. He leans his head against the doorframe and looks down at his feet. "Was I wrong?" His question is barely above a whisper, but it feels like a scream echoing inside of me. "Would you not do anything for Diem?"

I blow out a frustrated breath. That feels like a trick question. Of course I'd do anything for her, but not at the expense of others. *I don't think.* "That's not a fair question."

He locks eyes with me again, and I can feel my pulse beginning to pound.

"Roman is my best friend," he says. "No offense, but I barely know you, Kenna."

He might not know me, but he feels like the *only* person *I* know.

"I still don't know if what happened between us the first night you showed up at my bar was authentic, or if it was all an act to get to Diem."

I rest my head against the wall and watch Ledger's expression. He's looking at me with patience, and not at all with judgment. It's like he truly does want to know if the kiss we shared was authentic. It's almost as if it *meant* something to him.

It was authentic, but it also wasn't.

"I didn't know who you were until you said your name," I admit. "I was literally sitting on your lap when I realized you knew Scotty. Seducing you wasn't part of some master plan."

He gives my answer time to sink in, and then he nods gently. "That's good to know."

"Is it?" I flatten my back against the wall. "Because it doesn't feel like it even matters. You still don't want me to meet my daughter. You're still hoping I leave town." *None of it matters.*

Ledger dips his head until our eyes meet again. He's looking at me pointedly when he says, "There is nothing in this world that would make me happier than you getting to meet Diem. If I knew how to change their minds, I would do it in a heartbeat, Kenna."

My breath shakes upon release. His confession is everything I needed to hear. I close my eyes because I don't want to cry and I don't want to watch him leave, but until this moment, I wasn't sure if he even wanted me in Diem's life.

I feel the heat of his arm next to my head, and I keep my eyes closed, but I'm sucking in small gasps of air. I can hear his breaths, and then I can feel them on my cheek, and then my neck, as if he's moving in on me.

I feel surrounded by him in this moment, and I'm scared if I open my eyes, I'll realize it's all in my head and that he actually walked out of my open apartment door. But then he exhales, and the warmth rolls down my neck and shoulder. I barely crack open my eyes to find him towering over me, his hands on either side of the wall beside my head.

He's just hovering, like he can't decide whether he should leave or reenact our kiss from the night we met. Or maybe he's just waiting on me to make some kind of move, or decision, or mistake.

I don't know what compels me to lift my hand and place it on his chest, but when I do, he sighs as if that's exactly what he wanted me to do. But I don't know if I'm touching his chest because I want to push him away, or because I want to pull him closer.

Either way, there's a warmth between us that builds with his sigh, and he rests his forehead lightly against mine.

There have been so many choices and consequences and feelings packed into the space we've kept between us since we met, but Ledger pushes through all of it and presses his lips to mine.

Heat pulses through me like a heartbeat, and I sigh into his mouth. His tongue skims my top lip, fogging my thoughts. He cradles my head and deepens our kiss, and it's intoxicating. His mouth is warmer than I remember it being the first time we kissed. His hands feel more gentle; his tongue feels less daring.

There's a carefulness in his kiss—one I'm too afraid to dissect because I already feel so much it's dizzying. The warmth of him envelops me, and just when I start to cling to him, he pulls away.

I suck in air while he studies my face. It's as if he's trying to get a read on my expression, scanning me for signs of regret or desire.

I'm sure he can see both. I want his kiss, but the thought of having to say goodbye to more than just the idea of Diem is enough to stop me from allowing this to happen. Because the closer I grow to Ledger, both emotionally and physically, the more I'd be putting his relationship with Diem at risk.

As much as his kiss makes me feel, it's nothing compared to the heartache that would follow if the Landrys found out he's seeing me behind their backs. I can't have that hanging over my head.

He starts to lean in again, making my entire body feel unstable, but I somehow find the strength to shake my head. "Please don't," I whisper. "It hurts enough already."

Ledger pauses right before his mouth connects with mine. He draws back and lifts his hand, gently gliding his fingertips over my jaw. "I know. I'm sorry."

We both fall quiet. Unmoving. I wish I was processing how to make this work between us, but I'm processing how to not let it hurt, because it *can't* work.

He eventually pushes off the wall, stepping away from me. "I feel so fucking . . ." He runs a hand through his hair as he searches for the right word. "Helpless. *Useless.*" He walks out the door after settling on both words. "I'm sorry," I hear him mutter as he walks away.

I close my door, lock it, and then release every breath I've held in tonight. My heart is pounding. The apartment seems really warm now.

I turn down the thermostat and let Ivy out of the bathroom. We curl up on the couch together, and I grab my notebook.

> Dear Scotty,
>
> Do I owe you an apology for what just happened?
>
> I'm not quite sure what just happened. Ledger and I definitely had a moment, but was it a good one? A bad one? It felt more sad than anything.
>
> What if it happens again? I'm not sure I'm going to be strong enough to ask him not to touch me in all the ways we'd probably be touching each other right now if I didn't blurt out the words "Please don't."
>
> But if we act on anything we're feeling, he's eventually going to have to choose. And he won't choose me. I wouldn't let him, and I'd think so much less of him if he didn't choose Diem.
>
> And what's to come of me when that happens? I'll not only lose my chance with Diem, but I'll lose Ledger too.
>
> I've already lost you for good. That's hard enough.
>
> How many losses can one person take before they just throw in the fucking towel, Scotty? Because it sure is starting to feel like I'm all out of wins, here.
>
> Love,
>
> Kenna

CHAPTER TWENTY-EIGHT

LEDGER

Diem's arms are tight around my neck as I give her a piggyback ride across the parking lot toward Grace's car. The T-ball game just ended, and Diem is making me carry her because she said her legs were *soaking sore*.

"I want to go to work with you," she says.

"You can't. Kids aren't allowed in bars."

"I go to your bar with you sometimes."

"Yeah, when we're closed," I clarify. "That doesn't count. We'll be open tonight, and it's busy and I won't be able to keep an eye on you." Not to mention, her mother who she doesn't even know exists will be there. "You can come work for me when you turn eighteen."

"That's a long, long, long time away; you'll be dead."

"Hey, now," Grace says defensively. "I'm a lot older than Ledger, and I don't plan on being dead when you're eighteen."

I get Diem secured into her car seat. "How old will I be when everybody dies?" she asks.

"Nobody knows when anyone will die," I tell her. "But if we all live until we're old, we'll all be old together."

"How old will I be when you're two hundred?"

"*Dead* old," I say.

Her eyes grow wide, and I immediately shake my head. "We'll *all* be dead. No one lives to be two hundred."

"My teacher is two hundred."

"Mrs. Bradshaw is younger than *me*," Grace pipes up from the front seat. "Stop telling lies."

Diem leans forward and whispers, "Mrs. Bradshaw really is two hundred."

"I believe you." I kiss her on top of the head. "Good job today. Love you."

"I love you, too; I want to go to work with . . ." I close Diem's door before she finishes her sentence. I don't normally rush them off this way, but as we were walking through the parking lot, I received a text from Kenna.

All it said was, Please come get me.

It's not quite four yet. She said she didn't need a ride when I asked her yesterday, so my concern was immediately heightened when I got the text.

I'm already to my truck when Grace and Diem drive away. Patrick couldn't make the game today because he's working on the jungle gym. I was planning on going home for a couple of hours to see the progress and help before I went to the bar, but now I'm on my way to the grocery store to check on Kenna.

I'll text Patrick when I get there to let him know I'm not stopping by. We're almost finished with the jungle gym. Diem's birthday is coming up, which means today was supposed to be the big day. Leah's and my wedding. We planned on going to Hawaii just a week after the wedding, and I remember being stressed that we wouldn't be back for Diem's birthday party.

That was another point of contention between Leah and me. She didn't like that Diem's fifth birthday was almost as big a deal to me as our honeymoon.

I'm sure Patrick and Grace would have been willing to move the birthday party, but Leah acted like Diem's fifth birthday was a major conflict with our honeymoon before she even inquired about them moving the party, and that ended up becoming one of the first of many red flags.

I gave Leah the trip to Hawaii after our breakup. I had already paid for it, but I'm not sure if she's still going. Hopefully she is, but it's been three months since we've even spoken. I feel like I have no clue what's going on in her life now. Not that I *want* to know. It's strange, being involved in every facet of another human being, and then suddenly not knowing anything.

It's also strange thinking you know someone but then later realizing maybe you didn't know them at all. I feel that with Leah, and I'm starting to feel that about Kenna, but in the opposite way. With Kenna, I feel like I judged her too poorly in the beginning. With Leah, I feel like I judged her too favorably.

I probably should have texted Kenna to let her know I was on my way, because I spot her walking alone on the side of the road about a quarter of a mile away from the store. Her head is down, and she's got both hands gripping the strap of her tote bag on her shoulder. I pull over on the opposite side of the road, but she doesn't even notice my truck, so I tap on the horn. It gets her attention. She looks both ways and then crosses the road and climbs into my truck.

A heavy sigh emanates from her when she closes her door. She smells like apples, just like she smelled last night in the doorway of her apartment.

I could fucking punch myself for last night.

She drops her bag between us and pulls an envelope out of it. She shoves it at me. "I got it. The restraining order. I was served as I was walking out of the store to put groceries into someone's car. It was mortifying, Ledger."

I read over the forms, and I'm confused about how a judge even granted it, but when I see Grady's name, it all makes sense. He probably vouched for Patrick and Grace and might have even embellished the truth a little bit. He's that type. I bet his wife is loving this. I'm surprised she didn't bring it up at the ball field today.

I fold it back up and stick it in her purse. "It doesn't mean anything," I say, attempting to comfort her with my lie.

"It means everything. It's a message. They want me to know they aren't changing their minds." She pulls on her seat belt. Her eyes and cheeks are red, but she isn't crying. It looks like she's probably cried it out already, and I got to her in the aftermath.

I pull back onto the road feeling heavy. What I said last night about feeling useless—it's the most accurate term for what I am right now. I can't help Kenna, other than how I'm already helping her.

Patrick and Grace aren't changing their minds, and any time I try to approach the subject with them, they're immediately defensive. It's difficult, because I agree with why they don't want Kenna around, but I also vehemently disagree.

They would cut me out of Diem's life before they would agree to add Kenna into it. That's what scares me the most. If I push the subject too much, or if they find out I'm even remotely on Kenna's side, I'm afraid they'll start viewing me as a threat, the same way they view Kenna.

The worst part is, I don't blame them for how they feel about Kenna. The impact of her choices has been detrimental to their lives. But the impact of *their* choices is becoming detrimental to *her* life.

Fuck. There's no good answer. I've somehow immersed myself in the depths of an impossible situation. One that doesn't leave a single solution that won't lead to at least one person suffering.

"Do you want to take the night off work?" I completely understand if she doesn't feel up to it, but she shakes her head.

"I need the hours. I'll be fine. It was just embarrassing, even though I knew it was coming."

"Yeah, but I figured Grady would have the decency to serve you at home. It's not like your home address isn't at the top of the order." I turn right at the next light to get to the bar, but something tells me Kenna might need an hour or so before she moves from one shift to the next. "You want a snow cone?"

I'm not sure if that's a stupid resolution to an issue this serious, but snow cones are always the answer for me and Diem.

Kenna nods, and I think I might even see a hint of a smile. "Yeah. A snow cone sounds perfect."

CHAPTER TWENTY-NINE

KENNA

I'm leaning my head against the passenger window of his truck, watching him stride up to the snow cone stand with his tattoos and his sex appeal to order two rainbow snow cones. Why does he have to do nice things that make him so attractive?

I came here once with Scotty, but Scotty didn't look out of place ordering snow cones. We sat at a picnic table that used to be to the left of the snow cone stand, but it's a parking lot now, and the picnic table is nowhere to be seen. All the seating areas have been replaced by plastic tables with pink umbrellas.

I only texted Ledger and asked for a ride because of Amy.

She found me in the bathroom about to have a panic attack and asked what was wrong. I couldn't bear to tell her someone had filed a restraining order against me. Instead, I just told her the truth. That I sometimes have panic attacks, but that it would pass, and I was sorry, and then I pathetically begged her not to fire me.

She looked so sad for me, but she also laughed. "Why would I fire you? You're the only worker I have who actually *wants* to work double shifts. So you had a panic attack, big deal." She talked me into finding a ride home because she didn't trust me to have to walk all that way. I didn't want to tell her Ledger is the only person I know in town, so I texted him, more to reassure her that I wouldn't be alone. It felt good to be worried about by someone.

There's a lot I know I need to be grateful for, and Amy is one of those things. It's just really hard to be grateful when there's only one thing I want in my life, and I feel like I'm just getting further and further from that.

Ledger returns to the truck with our snow cones. There are sprinkles on mine, and I know that's a small thing, but I make note of it. Maybe if I acknowledge all the good things, no matter how small, they'll add up to make the bad thing in my life less painful.

"Do you ever bring Diem here?" I ask him.

He uses his spoon to point down the street. "The dance studio is about a block that way," he says. "I drop her off and Grace picks her up. She's hard to say no to, so I'm a regular here." He sticks his spoon in his mouth and then opens his wallet and pulls out a business card. There are tiny little snow cones hole-punched around it. "Close to getting a free one," he says, tucking it back in his wallet.

It makes me laugh. "Impressive." I wish I would have gone up to order with him just so I could see him hand in his snow cone punch card.

"Banana and lemonade." He looks over at me after taking a bite. "That's her favorite combination."

I smile. "Is yellow her favorite color?"

He nods.

I stick my spoon into the yellow part of my snow cone and dig out a bite. These little tidbits he gives me are something else I'm appreciative of. They're tiny parts of the whole, and maybe if he gives me enough of them, it won't hurt as bad when I have to leave.

I try to think about something to talk about that isn't Diem. "What does the house you're building look like?"

Ledger picks up his phone and checks the time, and then puts his truck in reverse. "I'll take you to see it. Razi and Roman can cover us for a while."

I take another bite and don't say anything, but I don't think he realizes what his willingness to show me his new house means to me.

The Landrys might have filed a restraining order against me, but at least Ledger trusts me.

I have that to cling to, and I cling to it hard.

Once we're at least fifteen miles outside of town, we turn into an area with a big wooden entryway that says *Cheshire Ridge*, and then we begin to make our way up a winding road. The trees cover the road like they're hugging it. The sides of the road are dotted with mailboxes every quarter to half a mile.

None of the houses can be seen from the road. The mailboxes are the only clues that people even live out here, because the trees are so dense. It's peaceful and secluded. I can see why he chose this area.

We come to a piece of property that's so thick with trees you can't even see most of the driveway from the road. There's a stake in the ground where I assume the mailbox will eventually go. There are columns that look like they'll end up being a privacy gate someday.

"Do you have close neighbors out here?"

He shakes his head. "Not for a half mile, at least. The property is on a ten-acre tract."

We pull onto the property, and eventually, a house begins to take shape through the trees. It isn't what I expected. This house isn't your average large manor-style home with a peaked roof. It's spread out and flat and unique, built of some kind of material I don't recognize.

I didn't peg Ledger to want something so modern and unusual. I don't know why I pictured a log cabin or something more traditional.

Maybe because he mentioned he and Roman were building it, and I just expected it to be a little less . . . complicated.

We get out of the truck, and I try to imagine Diem out here, running around this yard, playing on the patio, roasting marshmallows in the firepit out on the back deck.

Ledger shows me around, but I can't grasp this type of lifestyle, not even for my daughter. The countertops in the outdoor kitchen that overlook the backyard are probably worth more than everything I've ever owned in my entire life added up.

There are three bedrooms, but the main bedroom is the highlight for me, with a ridiculous closet almost as big as the bedroom itself.

I admire the house and listen to him talk excitedly about everything he and Roman have done by hand, and while it is impressive, it's also depressing.

This is a house my daughter will spend time in, which means it's likely a house I'll never return to again. As much as I enjoy watching him show off his space, I also don't want to see it now that I'm here.

And to be honest, it kind of makes me sad to know that he won't be living across from Diem. I'm starting to really like him as a person, and knowing he's a constant in her life is comforting. But he won't be across the street from her when he moves out here, and it makes me wonder if that's going to make her sad.

The back door to the huge patio overlooking rolling hills opens up like an accordion. He pushes it to one side, and I walk out onto the back deck. The sun is about to set, and it's probably one of the best views of the sunset in this entire town. It lights up the tops of the trees below us and makes them look like they're on fire.

There isn't any patio furniture yet, so I sit down on the steps and Ledger takes a seat next to me. I haven't said much, but he doesn't need the compliments. He knows how beautiful this place is. I can't imagine what it's costing him to build.

"Are you rich?" It just comes out. I rub my face after I ask it and say, "Sorry. That was rude."

He laughs and rests his elbows on his knees. "It's okay. The house is cheaper than it looks. Roman and I have done most of the work by hand over the last couple of years, but I made good investments with the money I got from my football contract. It's mostly gone now, but I got a business out of it, and now a home. Can't complain."

I'm happy for him. At least life works out for some people.

We all have our failures, though, I suppose. I'm curious what Ledger's failures are. "Wait," I say, remembering at least one thing that didn't quite work out for him. "Weren't you supposed to get married this weekend?"

Ledger nods. "Two hours ago, actually."

"Are you sad about it?"

"Of course," he says. "I don't regret the decision, but I am sad it didn't work out. I love her."

He said *love*, as in present tense. I wait for him to correct himself, but he doesn't, and then I realize that wasn't a mistake. He loves her still. I guess realizing your life isn't compatible with someone else's doesn't erase the feelings that are there.

There's a tiny flame of jealousy suddenly flickering in my chest. "How did you propose to her?"

"Do we really have to talk about this?" He's laughing, like the subject is more awkward than sad.

"Yes. I'm nosy."

He exhales and then says, "I asked her dad for permission first. And then I bought her the ring she'd been not so subtle about wanting. I took her to dinner on our second anniversary and had this big proposal planned in the park down the street from the restaurant. Her friends and family were there waiting, and then I got down on one knee and proposed. It was your typical Instagram-worthy engagement."

"Did you cry?"

"No. I was too nervous."

"Did she?"

He cocks his head like he's trying to think back. "I don't think so. Maybe a tear or two? It was dark, which I didn't take into consideration, so the footage of the proposal came out kind of shitty. She complained about that the next day. That she wouldn't have good video and I should have proposed *before* the sun set."

"She sounds fun."

Ledger smiles. "Honestly, you'd probably like her. I keep saying things that make her sound bad, but we had a lot of fun together. When we were together, I didn't think about Scotty as much. Things felt light with her because of that."

I look away when he says that. "Do I only remind you of him?"

Ledger says nothing in response to my question. He doesn't want to hurt my feelings, so he just chooses not to answer, but his silence makes me feel like I want to flee. I start to stand up because I'm ready to leave, but as soon as I begin to stand, he grabs my wrist and gently pulls me back down.

"Sit. Let's stay until the sun sets."

I sit back down, and it takes about ten minutes for the sun to sink down into the trees. Neither of us talks. We just watch the rays disappear, and the tips of the trees return to their natural, fireless colors. It's dusk now, and without electricity, the house behind us is quickly growing dark.

Ledger has a contemplative look about him when he says, "I feel guilty."

Welcome to my constant state. "Why?"

"For building this house. I feel like Scotty would be disappointed in me. Diem gets so sad every time we bring up the fact that I'm putting my other house up for sale."

"Why did you build this house, then?"

"It's been my dream for a long time now. I bought the land and started drafting the design back when Diem was just a baby. Before I knew how much I would love her." He cuts his eyes to mine. "Don't get me wrong, I loved her then, but it was different. She started to walk and talk, and develop her unique personality, and we became inseparable. And over time, this place started to feel less like my future home and more like . . ." He tries to come up with the word, but he can't.

"A prison?"

Ledger looks at me like I'm the first person to understand him. "Yes. Exactly. I feel like I'm locked into it now, but the idea of not seeing Diem every day is really starting to weigh on me. It'll change our relationship. With my schedule, I'll probably see her once a week if I'm lucky. I think that's why I've been taking my time building it. I don't know that I'm really looking forward to moving out here."

"Then sell it."

He laughs, like that's an absurd idea.

"I'm serious. I'd much rather you live across the street from my daughter than clear across town. I know I can't be in her life like I wish I could, but there's some comfort in knowing you are."

Ledger stares at me for a long beat after I say that. Then he stands up and reaches out for my hand. "We should get to work."

"Yeah. Don't want to piss off the boss." I grab his hand and stand up, and when I do, I'm suddenly way too close to him. He doesn't back away or let go of my hand, and now he's looking at me from just a few inches away with an intensity I feel slide down my spine.

Ledger threads his fingers through mine, and when our palms touch, the feeling that surges through me makes me wince. Ledger feels it, too; I can see it in the way his eyes fill with torment.

Funny how something that should feel so good can feel so painful when the circumstances aren't right. And our circumstances are definitely not right. But I squeeze his hand anyway, letting him know I'm feeling exactly what he's feeling, and I'm just as torn as he is.

Ledger drops his forehead to mine, and we both close our eyes and just silently breathe through whatever this moment is. I can feel everything he's not saying. I can even somehow feel the kiss he's not even giving me. But if we slip back into the moment we shared last night, it would rip that wound open even wider, until that's all I am.

He knows just as much as I do that this isn't a good idea.

"What are you gonna do, Ledger? Hide me in your closet until she's eighteen?"

He looks down at our hands still linked together and shrugs. "It's a huge closet."

There's only a beat of silence before it's sliced in two by my laughter.

He grins and then leads the way through his dark house and back to his truck.

CHAPTER THIRTY

LEDGER

I'm in my office processing payroll, processing my thoughts, processing all the mistakes I've made in the last few weeks.

Roman was right when he said I could have paid her off if I really wanted her to leave. Maybe I should have, because the more I'm around her, the more false hope I'm giving her.

The Landrys won't come around to the idea of accepting her any-time soon. And if she stays here and continues to work, it's putting us both at risk of getting caught.

I don't know what I was thinking hiring her in the first place. I thought she could hide out in the back, but Kenna isn't the kind of girl you can hide. She stands out. Someone will notice her. Someone will recognize her.

And then we'll both feel the consequences of this lie.

I take out my phone and text Kenna. Come to my office when you have a second.

I stand up and pace for the entire thirty seconds it takes her to make her way back to my office. I close the door behind her and then walk over to my desk and sit on the edge of it.

She stands near the door, and her arms are folded. She looks nervous. I don't mean to make her nervous. I point to the chair in front of me, and she walks hesitantly toward it and then sits.

"I feel like I'm in trouble," she says.

"You aren't in trouble. I just . . . I've been thinking. About what you overheard Roman say. And I feel like I should let you know that you don't have to come to work anymore."

She looks surprised. "Am I being fired?"

"No. Of course not." I inhale a breath in preparation for the honesty I'm about to spill. "We both know I hired you for selfish reasons, Kenna. If you ever get to the point where you want to leave town and you need money, all you have to do is ask. You don't have to work for it."

She's looking at me like I've just punched her in the gut. She stands up and starts pacing while she processes this conversation. "Do you *want* me to leave town?"

Fuck. I brought her in here to try to make her life easier, but I'm saying everything wrong. I shake my head. "No." I reach out and encircle her wrist with my fingers to stop her from pacing.

"Then why are you telling me this?"

I could give her several reasons. *Because you need to know you have options. Because if you stay here, someone will eventually recognize you. Because if we keep working together, we'll shatter whatever is left of our flimsy boundary.*

I don't say any of those things, though. I just look at her pointedly while I run my thumb across her wrist. "You know why."

Her chest rises and falls with her sigh.

But then she jerks her hand from mine at the sudden knock on my office door. I immediately stand up straight, and Kenna folds her arms over her chest. Our reactions make us look really guilty right now.

Mary Anne is standing in the doorway looking back and forth between us. She grins and says, "What did I just interrupt? An employee evaluation?"

I walk around my desk and pretend to be occupied by my computer screen. "What do you need, Mary Anne?"

"Well. This suddenly feels like the wrong moment to mention this, but Leah's here. The woman you were supposed to marry today? She's out front asking for you."

It takes everything in me not to look at Kenna to see how she reacted to that. Somehow I manage to stay focused on Mary Anne. "Tell her I'll be right out."

Mary Anne backs away from the door, but she leaves it open. Kenna immediately follows her out without looking back at me.

I'm confused, because why would Leah be here? What could she possibly want? Is she having more of a reaction to what today was supposed to be than I am?

Because I've hardly thought about it. I think that proves it was the right decision. For me, at least.

I walk out of my office, but I have to pass by Kenna on my way to the front. We make two seconds of eye contact before she looks away.

I exit the kitchen and look around the room, but I don't immediately spot Leah. It's a lot more crowded now than when I went to my office to do payroll, so I glance around for a moment before making my way behind the bar. Mary Anne is at the other end of the room, so I can't ask her where Leah went.

Roman sees me and points at a group of guys. "I haven't taken their order yet."

"Where's Leah?"

Roman looks confused. "Leah? What?"

Mary Anne is walking toward me. She grins and leans over the bar when she reaches me. "Roman was getting swamped, so he asked me to grab you. I was kidding about Leah. I was just trying to build some angst for you because girls *love* angst. You're welcome." She picks up a tray full of drinks and glides over to a table to deliver them.

I shake my head in confusion. I'm irritated she lied, because now Kenna's mind is probably going in a thousand different directions. But I'm also relieved she lied. I didn't want to see Leah.

I stay and take a few orders and close out three tabs, but as soon as Roman is caught up, I head to the back. Kenna isn't in the kitchen. I look around for her, but Aaron motions toward the back door to let me know she's on break.

When I push open the door to the alley, I find Kenna leaning against the building with her arms folded over her chest. She looks up at me as soon as I walk outside, and I can see the immediate relief wash over her.

She was jealous. She tries to hide it by forcing a smile, but I saw the look on her face before she shoved it away.

I walk over to her and mimic her position against the wall. "Mary Anne was lying. Leah wasn't here; she made that up."

She narrows her eyes in confusion. "Why would she . . ." Kenna stops talking, and a small smile spreads across her lips. "Wow. Mary Anne is messy." She doesn't seem angry that Mary Anne lied. She appears impressed.

Her smile makes me smile, and then I say, "You were jealous."

Kenna rolls her eyes. "I was not."

"You were."

She pushes off the wall and heads for the stairs, but she pauses right in front of me. She faces me, and I can't tell what her expression means.

I don't know what she's about to do, but if she tried to kiss me, it would make my fucking night. I'm tired of the back-and-forth with her. I'm tired of hiding her. I'd give anything to be able to get to know her better without worrying about consequences, to be able to ask her questions that have nothing to do with Scotty or the Landrys. I want to openly kiss her, I want to take her home with me, I want to know what it's like to fall asleep next to her and wake up next to her.

I fucking like her, and the more I'm around her, the more I don't want to be apart from her.

"I'm putting in my two-week notice," she says.

Shit. I chew on my lip until I'm positive I won't drop to my knees and beg her to stay. "Why?"

She hesitates and then says, "You know why."

She disappears back inside the building, and I sit in my fucking feelings.

I stare at my truck with an intense urge to drive straight to Patrick and Grace's house and tell them all about Kenna. I want to tell them how selfless she is. I want to tell them what a hard worker she is. I want to tell them how forgiving she is, because every single one of us has been making her life a living hell, yet she somehow doesn't seem to resent us for it.

I want to tell Patrick and Grace every wonderful thing about Kenna, but even more than that, I want to tell Kenna how wrong I was when I told her Diem wouldn't benefit from having her in her life.

Who am I to say that to a mother about her own child?

Who the fuck am I to make that kind of judgment?

CHAPTER THIRTY-ONE

Kenna

It starts raining on our drive home. The rain hitting the windshield is the only sound right now, because neither of us is speaking. We haven't said a word to each other since we were in the alley earlier tonight.

I wonder if he's mad that I put in my notice. I don't know why he would be; he's the one who brought it up. But he's so quiet it's making things uncomfortable.

I can't continue to work for him, though. How do we plan for my potential departure when we're starting to crave each other's company? I thought this was messy before, but it's bound to get even messier if I let it continue.

There's an unresolved energy moving between us in the truck when he pulls into the parking lot. Sometimes when he drops me off, he doesn't even turn off the engine of his truck. But tonight he does, and he removes the keys, and his seat belt, and he grabs an umbrella and gets *out* of the truck.

It only takes him a few seconds to make it to the passenger side, but in that few seconds, I've decided I don't want him to walk me up. I can walk myself up. It's better that way. I don't trust myself with him.

He opens my door and I reach for the umbrella, but he pulls it back.

"What are you doing?" he asks.

"Give me the umbrella. I can walk myself up."

He takes a step back so I can get out of his truck. "No. I'm walking you up."

"I don't know if you should."

"I definitely shouldn't," he says. But he keeps walking. Keeps holding the umbrella over my head.

My breaths start to catch in my chest before we even reach the top of the stairs. I fish my keys out of my purse, unsure if he's expecting to come inside or if he just plans to tell me good night. Either choice makes me nervous. Either one is too much. Either one will do.

He closes the umbrella when we reach my door and waits for me to unlock it. Before I open it, I turn to face him as if he's going to let me say good night without inviting him inside.

He points at my door but says nothing.

I quietly inhale and then push open the door to my apartment. He follows me inside and closes the door behind him.

He's acting so assured right now. The complete opposite of what I'm feeling. I scoop Ivy up and take her to the bathroom so she can't get out in case Ledger opens the door to leave.

When I close the bathroom door and turn around, Ledger is standing at the counter, running a finger across the stack of letters I printed out.

I don't want him to read them, so I walk over and flip them over and shove them aside.

"Are those the letters?" he asks.

"Most of them. But I have digital copies too. I typed them all up a couple of months ago and put them into Google Drive. I was afraid to lose them."

"Will you read one of them to me?"

I shake my head. Those letters are personal to me. This is the second time he's asked if I'd read one, and the answer is still no. "You asking me to read you one of those letters would be like me asking you to play a tape of one of your therapy sessions."

"I don't go to therapy," Ledger says.

"Maybe you should."

He chews his lip with a contemplative nod. "Maybe I will."

I walk around him and open the refrigerator. I've slowly been stocking it, so I actually have more than Lunchables this time. "You want something to drink? I have water, tea, milk." I grab an almost-empty container of juice. "A swig of apple juice."

"I'm not thirsty."

I'm not, either, but I drink the rest of the apple juice straight from the container as a preventive measure, because I feel like I'm about to be parched with him standing in my apartment like this. Just his presence here is enough to make my throat run dry.

It's different when we're at work. There are other people around to keep my mind from moving in the direction it's moving right now.

But when it's just the two of us alone in my apartment, all I can think about is our proximity to one another and how many heartbeats will pass in the time it takes him to close the gap and kiss me.

I set the empty container of apple juice on the bar and wipe my mouth.

"Is that why you always taste like apples?"

I look right at him when he says that. It's an intimate thing to say. Admitting out loud that you know what someone else tastes like. I feel like a dazzled, inexperienced teenager under his gaze, so I look down at my feet because not looking at him is less draining.

"What do you want, Ledger?"

He calmly leans against the counter. We're just a couple of feet apart when he says, "I want to get to know you better."

I wasn't expecting him to say that, so of course I look over at him and then immediately regret it because he's standing so close to me. "What do you want to know?"

"More about you. Your likes, your dislikes, your goals. What do you want to do with your life?"

I can't help but laugh. I expected him to ask about Scotty, or something related to Diem, or my current situation. But he's just making casual conversation, and I have no idea what to do with it. "I've always wanted to be a locksmith."

That makes Ledger laugh. "A locksmith?"

I nod.

"Why a locksmith?"

"Because no one can be mad at a locksmith. They show up to help when people are in a crisis. I think it would be a rewarding job to make people's shitty days a little bit better."

Ledger nods appreciatively. "I can't say I've ever met anyone who wanted to be a locksmith."

"Well. Now you have. Next question."

"Why did you choose the name Diem?"

I turn his question around on him before answering it. "Why did the Landrys choose not to change the name I gave her?"

He works his jaw back and forth. "They were worried that maybe you and Scotty had discussed what to name her, and Diem was a name Scotty chose."

"Scotty never even knew I was pregnant."

"Did *you* know you were pregnant?" he asks. "Before Scotty died?"

I shake my head. My voice is a whisper when I say, "No. I never would have pleaded guilty if I knew I was pregnant with Diem."

He concentrates on that reply. "Why *did* you plead guilty?"

I hug myself. My eyes start to sting, so I take a moment to breathe through the memory before answering him. "I wasn't in a good head-space," I admit. I don't elaborate, though. I can't.

Ledger doesn't come back with another question right away. He lets silence fill the room, and then he empties it by saying, "Where would we be right now if I didn't know Scotty?"

"What do you mean?"

His eyes fall briefly to my mouth. It's a flicker of a gaze, but I see it. I feel it. "The night we met at the bar. You said you didn't know who I was. What if I was just some random guy who didn't know Diem or Scotty or you? What do you think would have happened between us that night?"

"A lot more than what did happen," I admit.

He rolls his throat as if he swallowed that answer. He stares at me and I stare back, waiting anxiously for his next question or thought or move.

"I sometimes wonder if we'd even be talking right now if I didn't know Diem."

"Why does it matter?" I ask.

"Because it would be the difference between you wanting to be with me for me, or wanting to be with me so you could use me for my connections."

My jaw tenses. I have to break our gaze and look at something besides him, because that comment makes me angry. "If I wanted to use you for your connections, I'd have fucked you by now." I push off the counter. "You should go." I start to walk toward the door, but Ledger grabs my wrist and pulls me back.

I spin around, but before I can yell at him, I see the look in his eye. It's apologetic. Sad. He pulls me to his chest and wraps his arms around me in a comforting embrace. I'm stiff against him, unsure of what to do with my lingering anger. He slides his hands to my arms and lifts them, wrapping them around his waist.

"I wasn't insulting you," he says, his breath grazing my cheek. "I was just working through some thoughts out loud." He presses the side of his head to mine, and I squeeze my eyes shut because he feels so good. I forgot what it felt like for someone else to need me. Want me. *Like* me.

Ledger keeps us wrapped tightly together when he says, "In a matter of a few weeks, I went from hating you to liking you to wanting the world for you, so forgive me if those feelings sometimes overlap."

I relate to that more than he knows. I sometimes want to scream at him for having been a wall between me and my daughter, but at the same time, I want to kiss him for loving her enough to *be* a wall of protection for her.

His finger meets my chin, and he tilts my focus up to his. "I wish I could take back what I said to you when I told you Diem wouldn't benefit from you being in her life." He slides his hands into my hair and looks at me with sincerity. "She would be lucky to have a woman like you in her life. You're selfless and you're kind and you're strong. You're everything I want Diem to be someday." He wipes away a tear that falls down my cheek. "And I don't know how I can change their minds, but I'm going to try. I want to fight for you because I know that's what Scotty would want me to do."

I have no idea what to do with all the feelings his words just brought out.

Ledger doesn't kiss me, but that's only because I kiss him first. I press my mouth to his because nothing I could say would convey how much I appreciate the validation he just gave to me. It's one thing for him to admit he wants me to meet her, but he took it a million steps further by saying he wants her to be like me.

It's the kindest thing anyone has ever said to me.

His tongue slides against mine, and the heat from his mouth seems to pulse into me. I pull him closer until our chests meet, but it's still not close enough. I had no idea that was the only thing holding me back from Ledger. I just needed to know he believed in me. Now that I know he does, I can't find a single part of me that doesn't want every part of him.

Ledger lifts me and walks me across the room to the couch without breaking our kiss.

The weight of his body feels so good pressed against mine. I start to pull off his shirt because I want to be against his skin, but he pushes my hand away. "Wait," he says, pulling back. "Wait, wait, wait."

I drop my head to the couch and groan. I can't take much more of this back-and-forth. I'm finally in a headspace to let him do whatever he wants to me, and now *he's* the one pulling away.

He kisses my chin. "I might be getting ahead of myself, but if we're about to have sex, I need to go down to my truck and grab a condom before you undress me. Unless you have a condom up here."

I'm so relieved that's why he stopped. I push him away. "Hurry. Go get one."

He's off the couch and out the door in seconds. I use the spare minute to check my reflection in the bathroom mirror. Ivy is asleep in her little bed that I've set next to the tub.

I take a small dab of toothpaste and brush it across my teeth and tongue.

I wish I could write a quick letter to Scotty. I feel like I need to warn him of what's about to happen, which is stupid because he's dead and it's been five years and I can have sex with whoever I want, but he was the last person I've ever had sex with, so this feels like a really big moment.

Not to mention, it's with his best friend.

"I am so sorry, Scotty," I whisper. "But not sorry enough to stop it."

I hear my front door open, so I leave the bathroom and find Ledger locking the door. When he turns to face me, I laugh because he's soaking wet from the rain. His hair is dripping water into his eyes, so he pushes it back. "I probably should have used the umbrella, but I didn't want to waste any time."

I walk over to him and help him out of his shirt. He returns the favor and helps me out of mine. I'm wearing my good bra. I wear it every time I work a shift at his bar because I've wanted to be prepared in case this happened.

I've been trying to convince myself it wouldn't, but deep down, I've been hoping it would.

Ledger leans forward and kisses me on the mouth with his rain-soaked lips. He's cold because he's wet, but his tongue is a scorching contrast to his frigid lips.

My stomach swirls with heat when he wraps his other hand in my hair and tilts my face back so he can kiss me even deeper. I lower my hands to his jeans and unbutton them, anxious to get him out of them. Determined to feel him against me. Fearful that I won't remember how to do this.

It's been so long since I've had sex I feel like I should warn him. He starts to walk me backward toward the inflatable mattress. He lowers me onto it and starts to remove the rest of my clothes. As he's working my jeans down my legs, I say, "I haven't been with anyone since Scotty."

His eyes meet mine after he pulls off my jeans, and there's a calming reassurance in his expression. He lowers himself on top of me and presses a soft kiss to my mouth. "It's okay to change your mind."

I shake my head. "I'm not. I just wanted you to know it's been a while. In case I'm not very . . ."

He cuts me off with another kiss; then he says, "You've already exceeded my expectations, Kenna." He moves his mouth to my neck, and I feel his tongue drag up my throat.

My eyes fall shut.

He removes my panties and my bra and his jeans while his tongue explores every inch of me between my neck and my stomach. When he crawls back up me to kiss me on the mouth, I feel him hard between my legs, and it fills me with anticipation. I give him a deep, long, meaningful kiss while he reaches between us and puts on the condom.

He positions himself against me, but he doesn't enter me. Instead, he slides his finger up the center of me, and it's so unexpected I arch my back and moan.

My moan is drowned out by the thunder outside. It's raining even harder now, but I like that the thunderstorm is our background noise. It somehow makes this even more sensual.

Ledger continues to work his finger over me, and then inside of me, and the sensation is so intense I can't even kiss him back. My lips are parted and I'm moaning in between gasps of air. Ledger keeps his lips rested against mine when he begins to push into me.

He isn't able to push into me with ease. It's a slow, almost painful experience. I move my mouth to his shoulder as he makes gentle progress.

When he's all the way inside me, I drop my head back to the pillow because the pain transforms into pleasure. He slowly pulls out and then pushes back into me with a little more force. He exhales sharply, and his breath falls over my shoulder, tickling my skin.

I lift my hips, opening myself up to him even more, and he shoves into me again.

"Kenna." I can barely open my eyes and look at him. His lips graze mine and he whispers, "This is too good. *Fuck.* Fuck, I have to stop." He pulls out of me, and when he does, I whimper. It's an immediate emptiness I wasn't prepared for. Ledger remains on top of me and slides two fingers inside of me, so I don't even have time to complain before I'm moaning again. He kisses the spot just below my ear. "I'm sorry, but I won't last long when I'm back inside you."

I don't even care. I just want him to keep doing what he's doing with his hand. I wrap my arm around his neck and pull him down. I want all his weight pressed against me.

He slides his thumb up the center of me, and it sends such an intense jolt through me, I end up biting his shoulder. He groans when my teeth clamp onto his skin, and his groan brings me right over the edge.

Our mouths meet in a frantic kiss, and he swallows my moans while he finishes me off. I'm still trembling beneath his touch when he thrusts into me again. The waves of my orgasm are still rolling through me when he lifts up onto his knees and grips my waist, pulling me to meet each thrust.

God, he's beautiful. The muscles in his arms flex with each roll of his hips. He pulls one of my legs up to his shoulder. We make eye contact for a few seconds, and then he turns his head and runs his tongue up my leg.

I wasn't expecting that. I want him to do it again, but he shoves my leg aside and lowers himself on top of me again.

We're at a different angle now, and he's somehow able to stab into me even deeper. It's only seconds before he starts to come. He tenses up and drops his weight on me. "Fuck." He groans and then says, "*Fuck*," a second time. Then he's kissing me. Intense kisses at first, but after he pulls out, the kisses grow sweeter. Softer. Slower.

I already want it to happen again, but I need to catch my breath first. Maybe rehydrate. We kiss for a couple of minutes, and it's so hard to stop because this is the first time we've been able to enjoy each other without things coming to an abrupt end.

It doesn't help that the rain against the windows is creating the perfect backdrop to this moment. I don't want it to end. I don't think Ledger does either, because every time I think he's finished kissing me, he comes back for more.

He does stop eventually, but only long enough to go to the bathroom and dispose of the condom. When he comes back to the bed, he adjusts himself until he's spooning me, and then he kisses my shoulder.

He threads his fingers through mine and tucks our hands against my stomach. "I wouldn't mind if we put that on the schedule again for tonight."

I laugh at the way he phrased that. I don't know why I find it funny. "Yes. Let's tell Siri to put it on the calendar for an hour from now," I tease.

"Hey, Siri!" he yells. Both of our phones go off at the same time. "Schedule sex with Kenna for one hour from now!" I laugh and elbow him, then roll onto my back. He lifts up and smiles down at me. "I'll last a lot longer the second time. I promise."

"I probably won't," I admit.

Ledger kisses me, and then he buries his head in my hair, tugging me closer to his side.

I stare up at the ceiling for a long time.

Maybe half an hour. Maybe even longer. Ledger's breathing has evened out, and I'm almost positive he's asleep.

The rain hasn't let up at all, but my mind is too active for it to make me sleepy. I hear Ivy meow from the bathroom, so I slip off the mattress and let her out.

She hops onto the couch and curls up into a ball.

I walk to the counter and slide my notebook in front of me. I grab a pen and begin writing a letter to Scotty. It doesn't take me long. It's a short letter, but when I finish and close the notebook, I catch Ledger staring at me. He's on his stomach with his chin resting on his arms.

"What did you write?" he asks.

This is the third time he's asked me to read him something. This is the first time I feel like conceding.

I open the notebook to the letter I just wrote. I run my finger over Scotty's name. "You might not like it."

"Is it the truth?"

I nod.

Ledger points to the empty spot next to him on the bed. "Then I want to hear it. Come here."

I raise an eyebrow in warning because not everyone can handle the truth as well as they think they can. But he remains steadfast, so I join him on the bed. He rolls onto his back, and I'm sitting cross-legged next to him when I begin to read.

> "Dear Scotty,
>
> I had sex with your best friend tonight. I'm not sure that's something you want to hear. Or maybe it is. I get the feeling if you can hear these letters from wherever you are, you would want me to be happy. And right now, Ledger is the one thing in my life that makes me happy. If it's any consolation, the sex with him was great, but no one can hold a candle to you.
>
> Love,
>
> Kenna."

I close the notebook and rest it on my lap. Ledger is quiet for a moment as he stares stoically at the ceiling. "You're just saying that so you don't hurt his feelings, right?"

I laugh. "Sure. If that's what you need to hear."

He grabs the notebook and tosses it aside; then he wraps an arm around me and pulls me on top of him. "It was good, though, right?"

I press a finger to his lips and drop my mouth to his ear. "The *best*," I whisper.

At the exact moment I say that, a loud clap of thunder rolls through the sky outside with perfect timing. It's so loud I can feel it in my stomach.

"Oh shit," Ledger says with a laugh. "Scotty didn't like that. You better take it back. Tell him I suck."

I immediately slide off Ledger and lie on my back. "I'm sorry, Scotty! You're better than Ledger, I promise!"

We laugh together, but then we both sigh and listen to the rain for a while. Ledger eventually puts a hand on my hip and rolls me toward him. He nips at my bottom lip before kissing my neck. "I feel like I need another opportunity to prove myself." His kisses move lower and lower until he takes one of my nipples into his mouth.

The second time is much longer, and somehow even better.

CHAPTER THIRTY-TWO

LEDGER

The kitten slept in Kenna's arms all night. Maybe it's weird, but I like watching her with Ivy. She's affectionate with her. She always makes sure Ivy doesn't have an opportunity to run outside when she isn't looking.

It makes me curious how she'll be with Diem. Because I'm confident I'll get to witness it someday. It might take us a while to get there, but I'll find a way. She deserves it and Diem deserves it, and I trust my gut feelings more than my doubts.

I move quietly as I reach for my phone to check the time. It's almost seven in the morning, and Diem will wake up soon. She'll notice my truck is gone. I should probably try to get home before they leave for Patrick's mother's house. I don't want to slip out while Kenna is asleep, though. I would feel like an asshole if she woke up alone after last night.

I press a gentle kiss to the corner of her mouth, and then I brush her hair out of her face. She begins to move, and moan, and I know she's just waking up, but her wake-up sounds are very similar to her sex sounds, and now I don't want to leave. Ever.

She finally gets her eyes open and looks up at me.

"I have to go," I say quietly. "Can I come back over later?"

She nods. "I'll be here. I'm off today." She gives me a closed-lips kiss. "I'll kiss you better later, but I want to brush my teeth first."

I laugh and then kiss her cheek. Before I get up, we have this brief moment of eye contact where it feels like she's thinking something she doesn't want to say out loud. I stare down at her for a minute, waiting for her to speak, but when she doesn't, I kiss her on the mouth one more time. "I'll be back this afternoon."

⸻

I waited too long. Diem and Grace are already awake and in their front yard when I pull onto our street. Diem sees me before Grace does, so she's already running across the street when I pull into my driveway and kill my truck.

I swing open the door and immediately scoop her up. I kiss the side of Diem's head right when she wraps herself around me and squeezes my neck. I swear to God, there is nothing even remotely close to a hug from this girl.

A hug from her mother does run a very close second, though.

Grace makes it to my yard a few seconds later. She shoots me a teasing look, as if she knows why I was out all night. She might think she knows, but she wouldn't be looking at me like this if she had any clue who I was with.

"You look like you didn't get much sleep," she says.

"I slept plenty. Get your head out of the gutter."

Grace laughs and tugs on Diem's ponytail. "Well, you have perfect timing. She was hoping to say goodbye before we left."

Diem hugs my neck again. "Don't forget about me," she says, loosening her grip so I can set her back down.

"You'll only be gone one night, D. How could I forget about you?"

Diem scratches her face and says, "You're old, and old people forget stuff."

"I am not old," I say. "Hold on before you go, Grace." I unlock my front door and head to my kitchen and grab the flowers I bought for her yesterday morning. I haven't let a Mother's Day or a Father's Day pass without getting something for her or Patrick.

She's been like a mother to me my whole life, so I'd honestly probably still buy her flowers even if Scotty were here.

"Happy Mother's Day." I hand them to her, and she acts surprised and delighted and gives me a hug, but I don't hear her thank-you through the loud regret piercing through me right now.

I forgot today was Mother's Day. I woke up next to Kenna this morning and said nothing to her about it. I feel like an asshole.

"I need to put these in water before I go," Grace says. "Want to buckle Diem into the car for me?"

I grab Diem's hand and walk them across the street. Patrick is already in the car waiting. Grace walks the flowers into the house, and I open the back door to buckle Diem into her car seat. "What's Mother's Day?" she asks me.

"It's a holiday." I keep my explanation brief, but Patrick and I trade glances.

"I know. But why are you and NoNo giving Nana flowers for Mother's Day? You said Robin is your mother."

"Robin *is* my mother," I say. "And your grandma Landry is NoNo's mother. That's why you're going to see her today. But on Mother's Day, if you know a mother that you love, you buy her flowers even if she isn't your mother."

Diem crinkles up her nose. "Am I supposed to give *my* mother flowers?" She's really been working through the whole family tree lately, and it's cute, but also concerning. She's eventually going to find out her family tree was once struck by lightning.

Patrick finally chimes in. "We gave your nana her flowers last night, remember?"

Diem shakes her head. "No. I'm talking about my mother that *isn't* here. The one with the tiny car. Are we supposed to give *her* flowers?"

Patrick and I trade another glance. I'm sure he's mistaking the pain on my face for discomfort at Diem's question. I kiss Diem on the forehead just as Grace returns to the car. "Your mother will get flowers," I say to Diem. "Love you. Tell your grandma Landry I said hello."

Diem smiles and pats my cheek with her tiny hand. "Happy Mother's Day, Ledger."

I back away from the car and tell them to have a safe trip. But as they're driving away, I feel my heart grow heavier as Diem's words sink in.

She's starting to wonder about her mother. She's starting to worry. And even though Patrick assumed I was just reassuring her by saying Diem's mother would get flowers, I was actually making her a promise. One I won't break.

The idea of Kenna going through the entire day today without her motherhood being acknowledged by anyone makes me angry at this whole situation.

I sometimes want to place that blame directly on Patrick and Grace, but that's not fair either. They're just doing what they need to do to survive.

It is what it is. A fucked-up situation, with no evil people to blame. We're all just a bunch of sad people doing what we have to do to make it until tomorrow. Some of us sadder than others. Some of us more willing to forgive than others.

Grudges are heavy, but for the people hurting the most, I suppose forgiveness is even heavier.

I pull up to Kenna's apartment a few hours later and am halfway to the stairs when I spot her out back. She's cleaning off the table I lent her when she notices me. Her eyes fall to the flowers in my hand, and she stiffens. I walk closer to her, but she's still staring at the flowers. I hand them to her. "Happy Mother's Day." I've already put the flowers in a vase because I wasn't sure if she even had one.

Based on the look on her face, I'm wondering if maybe I shouldn't have bought her flowers. Maybe celebrating Mother's Day before she's even met her child is uncomfortable. I don't know, but I feel like I should have put more thought into this moment.

She takes them from me with hesitation, like she's never been given a gift before. Then she looks at me, and very quietly, she says, "*Thank* you." She means it. The way her eyes tear up immediately convinces me bringing them was the right move.

"How was the lunch?"

She smiles. "It was fun. We had fun." She nudges her head up to her apartment. "You want to come up?"

I follow her upstairs, and once we're inside her apartment, she tops off the vase with a little more water and sets it on her counter. She's adjusting the flowers when she says, "What are you doing today?"

I want to say, "*Whatever you're doing*," but I don't know where her head is at after last night. Sometimes things seem good and perfect in the moment, but when you get hours of reflection afterward, the perfection can morph into something else. "I'm heading out to the new house to get some work done on the floors. Patrick and Grace took Diem to his mother's, so they'll be gone until tomorrow."

Kenna is wearing a pink button-up shirt that looks new, and it's topped over a long, white, flowy skirt. I've never seen her in anything other than a T-shirt and jeans, but this shirt reveals the tiniest hint of her cleavage. I'm trying so hard not to look, but holy fuck, it's a struggle. We both stand in silence for a beat. Then I say, "You want to come with me?"

She eyes me cautiously. "Do you want me to?"

I realize the hesitation pouring from her may not be because of her own feelings of regret, but rather her fears that *I* have regrets.

"Of course I do." The conviction in my response makes her smile, and her smile breaks down whatever was keeping us separated. I pull her to me and kiss her. She immediately seems at ease once my mouth is on hers.

I hate that I even made her doubt herself for one second. I should have kissed her as soon as I handed her the flowers downstairs.

"Can we get snow cones on the way there?" she asks.

I nod.

"Do you have your punch card?" she teases.

"I never leave the house without it."

She laughs and then grabs her purse and pets Ivy goodbye.

When we get downstairs, Kenna and I fold up the table and chairs and begin hauling them to my truck. It works out that I'm here today, because I've been meaning to move one of these tables to the new house.

I'm carrying the last armful of chairs to the truck when Lady Diana appears out of nowhere. She stands between me and Kenna and the truck. "Are you leaving with the jerk?" she asks Kenna.

"You can stop calling him a jerk now. His name is Ledger."

Lady Diana looks me up and down and then mutters, "Ledg*erk*."

Kenna ignores the insult and says, "I'll see you at work tomorrow."

I'm laughing when we get in the truck. "Ledg*erk*. That was actually really clever."

Kenna buckles her seat belt and says, "She's witty and vicious. It's a dangerous combination."

I put the truck in reverse, wondering if I should give her the other gift I have for her. Now that we're here in my truck together, it feels slightly more embarrassing than when I got the idea for it, and the fact that I spent so long on it this morning makes it that much more awkward, so we're at least a mile from her apartment before I finally work up the nerve to say, "I made you something."

I wait until we're at a stop sign, and then I text her the link. Her phone pings, so she opens the link and stares at her screen for a few seconds. "What is this? A playlist?"

"Yeah. I made it this morning. It's over twenty songs that have absolutely nothing to do with anything that could remind you of anything sad."

She stares at the screen on her phone as she scrolls through the songs. I'm waiting for some kind of reaction from her, but her face is blank. She looks out the window and covers her mouth like she's stifling a laugh. I keep stealing glances at her, but I eventually can't take it anymore. "Are you laughing? Was that stupid?"

When she turns to face me, she's smiling, and there might even be burgeoning tears in her eyes. "It's not stupid at all."

She reaches across the seat for my hand, and then she looks back out her window. For at least two miles, I'm fighting back a smile.

But then somewhere around the third mile, I'm fighting back a frown because something as simple as a playlist shouldn't make her want to cry.

Her loneliness is starting to hurt me. I want to see her happy. I want to be able to say all the right things when I tell Patrick and Grace why they should give her a chance, but the fact that I still don't truly know her history with Scotty is one of the many things I'm afraid might prevent the outcome we both want.

Every time I'm with her, the questions are always on the tip of my tongue. *"What happened? Why did you leave him?"* But it's either never the right moment, or the moment is right but the emotions are already too heavy. I wanted to ask her last night when I was asking her all the other questions, but I just couldn't get it out. Sometimes she looks too sad for me to expect her to talk about things that will make her even sadder.

I need to know, though. I feel like I can't fully defend her or blindly root for her to be in Diem's life until I know exactly what happened that night and *why*.

"Kenna?" We glance at each other at the same time. "I want to know what happened that night."

The air develops a weight to it, and it feels harder to breathe in.

I think I just made it harder for her to breathe too. She inhales a slow breath and releases my hand. She flexes her fingers and grips her thighs.

"You said you wrote about it. Will you read it to me?"

Her expression is filled with what looks like fear now, like she's too scared to go back to that night. Or too scared to take me there with her. I don't blame her, and I feel bad asking her to, but I want to know.

I need to know.

If I'm going to drop to my knees in front of Patrick and Grace when I beg them to give her a chance, I need to fully know the person I'm fighting for. Even though at this point she couldn't say anything that would change my mind about her. I know she's a good person. A good person who had one bad night. It happens to the best of us. The worst of us. *All* of us. Some of us are just luckier than others, and our bad moments have fewer casualties.

I adjust my grip on the steering wheel, and then I say, "Please. I need to know, Kenna."

Another quiet moment passes, but then she grabs her phone and unlocks the screen. She clears her throat. My window is cracked, so I roll it all the way up and make it quieter in the cab of the truck.

She looks so nervous. Before she begins to read, I reach over and tuck a loose strand of hair behind her ear as a show of solidarity . . . or something, I don't know. I just want to touch her and let her know I'm not judging her.

I just need to know what happened. That's all.

CHAPTER THIRTY-THREE

KENNA

Dear Scotty,
Your car was my favorite place to be. I don't know if I ever told you that.

It was the only place we could get true solitude. I used to look forward to the days our schedules would align, and you'd pick me up from work. I'd get in your car and it was like feeling all the same welcoming comforts of home. You always had a soda waiting for me, and on the days you knew I hadn't had dinner yet, you'd have a small order of fries from McDonald's sitting in the cup holder because you knew they were my favorite fries.

You were sweet. You always did sweet things for me. Tiny little gestures here and there that most people don't think of. You were more than I deserved, even though you'd argue with that.

I've gone over the day you died so many times, I once wrote every single second of that day down on paper. Most of it was an estimate, of course. I don't know if I *actually* spent a minute and a half brushing my teeth that morning. Or if the break I took at work really was fifteen minutes to the second. Or if we really spent fifty-seven minutes at the party we went to that night.

I'm sure I'm off in my calculations by a few minutes here or there, but for the most part, I can account for everything that happened that day. Even the things I wish I could forget.

A guy you went to college with was having a party and you had been his roommate your freshman year, so you said you owed it to him to make an appearance. I was sad to have to be at the party, but in hindsight, I'm glad you got to see most of your friends that night. I know it probably meant something to them after you died.

Even though you had made an appearance, it wasn't your scene anymore and I knew you didn't want to be there. You were past the parties and starting to focus on the more important pieces of life. You had just started graduate school, and you spent your spare time either studying or with me.

I knew we wouldn't be there long, so I found a chair in a corner of the living room and curled up into it while you made your rounds. I don't know if you knew this, but I watched you for the entire fifty-seven minutes we were there. You were so magnetic. People's eyes would light up when they would look at you. Crowds would gather around you, and when you'd spot someone you hadn't yet greeted, you'd have this huge reaction and make them feel like the most important person at that party.

I don't know if that's something you practiced, but I have a feeling you didn't even know you had that kind of power. The power to make people feel appreciated and important.

Around the fifty-sixth minute we were there, you spotted me sitting in the corner smiling at you. You walked over to me, ignoring everyone around you, and I suddenly found myself the focus of your sole attention.

You had me locked in your gaze, and I knew I was appreciated. I was important. You sat down next to me in the chair and you kissed my neck and whispered in my ear, "I'm sorry I left you alone."

You didn't leave me alone. I was with you the whole time.

"Do you want to leave now?" you asked.

"Not if you're having fun."

"Are *you* having fun?" you asked.

I shrugged. I could think of a lot more things that were more fun than that party. By the smile that spread across your face, I gathered you felt the same. "Want to go to the lake?"

I nodded because those were my three favorite things. That lake. Your car. *You.*

You stole a twelve pack of beers and we snuck out and you drove us to the lake.

We had a favorite spot where we'd go some nights. It was down a rural back road, and you said you knew of it because you used to go camping there with your friends. It wasn't far from where I lived with roommates, so sometimes you'd show up at my apartment in the middle of the night and we'd go there and have sex on the dock, or in the water, or in your car. Sometimes we'd stay and watch the sunrise.

That particular night, we had the beer you had taken from the party and some leftover edibles you had bought off a friend the week before. We had the music turned up and we were making out in the water. We didn't have sex that night. Sometimes we only made out, and I liked that about you so much, because one of the things I've always hated about relationships is how make-outs seem to stop when sex becomes a thing.

But with you, the make-outs were always just as special as the sex.

You kissed me in the water like it was the last time you would ever kiss me. I wonder if you had some sort of fear, or premonition, and that's why you kissed me the way you did. Or maybe I only remember it so well because it was our last kiss.

We got out of the water and we were lying naked on the dock under the moonlight, the world spinning above our heads.

"I want meatloaf," you said.

I laughed at you, because it was such a random thing to say. "Meatloaf?"

You grinned and said, "Yeah. Doesn't that sound good? Meatloaf and mashed potatoes." You sat up on the dock and handed me my dry shirt. "Let's go to the diner."

You'd had more to drink than me, so you asked me to drive. It wasn't like us to drink and drive, but

I think we felt invincible under that moonlight. We were young and in love, and *surely no one dies when they're at their happiest.*

We were also high, so our decisions were slightly more impaired that night, but whatever the reason, you asked me to drive. And for whatever reason, I didn't tell you I shouldn't.

I got in that car, knowing I had tripped on the gravel as I reached for the door. I still got behind the wheel, even though I had to blink really hard to make sure the car was in drive and not in reverse. And I still chose to drive us away from the lake, even though I was too drunk to remember how to turn down the volume. Coldplay was blasting so loud over the radio it was making my ears hurt.

We didn't even get very far before it happened. You knew the roads better than I did. They were gravel, and I was going too fast, and I didn't know the turn was so sharp.

You said, "Slow down," but you said it kind of loud, and it startled me, so I slammed on the brakes, but I know now that slamming on brakes on a gravel-top road can make you lose complete control of the car, especially when you're drunk. I was turning the wheel to the right, but the car kept going to the left, like it was slipping on ice.

A lot of people are lucky after a wreck because they don't remember the details. They have recollections of things that happened before the wreck, and after the wreck, but over time, every single second of that night has come back to me, whether I wanted it to or not.

The top was down on your convertible, and all I can remember when I felt the car hit the ditch and begin to tilt was that we needed to protect our faces, because I was worried the glass from the windshield might cut us.

That was my biggest fear in that moment. A little bit of glass. I didn't see my life flash before my eyes. I didn't even see your life flash before my eyes. All I worried about in that moment was what would happen to the windshield.

Because *surely no one dies when they're at their happiest.*

I felt my whole world tilt, and then I felt gravel against my cheek.

The radio was still blasting Coldplay.

The engine was still running.

My breath had caught in my throat and I couldn't even scream, but I didn't think I needed to. I just kept thinking about your car and how mad you probably were. I remember whispering, "I'm so sorry," like your biggest concern would be that we would have to call a tow truck.

Everything happened so fast, but I was calm in that moment. I thought you were, too. I was waiting for you to ask me if I was okay, but we were upside down in a convertible, and everything I'd had to drink that night was flipping over in my stomach, and I felt the weight of gravity like I had never felt it before. I thought I was going to puke and needed to right myself up, so I struggled to find my seat belt, and when I finally clicked it, I remember falling. It was only a couple of inches, but it was unexpected and I let out a yelp.

You still didn't ask me if I was okay.

It was dark, and I realized we might be trapped, so I reached over and touched your arm to follow you out. I knew you'd find a way out. I relied on you for everything, and your presence was the only reason I was still calm. I wasn't even worried about your car anymore because I knew you'd be more worried about me than your car.

And it's not like I was speeding too much, or driving too recklessly. I was only a little bit drunk and a little bit high, but so very stupid to believe even *a little bit* wasn't too much.

We only flipped over because we hit a deep ditch, and since the top wasn't even up, I thought surely it would be minimal damage. Maybe a week or two in the shop, and then the car I loved so much, the car that felt like home, would be fine. Like you. Like me.

"Scotty." I shook your arm when I said your name that time. I wanted you to know I was okay. I thought maybe you were in shock, and that's why you were so quiet.

When you didn't move, and I realized your arm was just dangling against the road that had somehow become our ceiling, my first thought was that you might have passed out. But when I pulled my hand back to figure out a way to right myself up, it was covered in blood.

Blood that was supposed to be running through your veins.

I couldn't grasp that. I couldn't fathom that a silly wreck on the side of a county road that landed us in a ditch could actually *hurt* us. But that was your blood.

I immediately scooted closer to you, and because you were upside down and still in your seat belt, I couldn't pull you to me. I tried, but you wouldn't budge. I turned your face to mine, but you looked like you were sleeping. Your lips were slightly parted and your eyes were closed, and you looked so much like you looked all the times I spent the night with you and woke up to find you asleep next to me.

I tried pulling you, but you still wouldn't budge because the car was on top of part of you. Your shoulder and your arm were trapped, and I couldn't pull you out or get to your seat belt and even though it was dark, I realized moonlight reflects off of blood the same way it reflects off the ocean.

Your blood was everywhere. The entire car being upside down made everything even more confusing. Where were your pockets? Where was your phone? I needed a phone, so I scrambled and felt around with my hands, looking for a phone for what felt like an eternity, but all I could find were rocks and glass.

The whole time, I was muttering your name through chattering teeth. "Scotty. Scotty, Scotty, Scotty." It was a prayer, but I didn't know how to pray. No one had ever taught me. I just remember the prayer you had given over family dinner at your parents' house, and the prayers I used to hear my foster mother, Mona, pray. But all I'd ever heard people do was bless food, and I just wanted you to wake up, so I said your name over and over and hoped God would hear me, even though I wasn't sure if I was getting his attention.

It certainly felt like no one was paying us attention that night.

What I experienced in those moments was indescribable. You think you know how you'll react in a terrifying situation, but that's the thing. You can't *think* in a terrifying situation. There's probably a reason for how disconnected we become to our own thoughts in moments of sheer horror. But that's exactly how I felt. Disconnected. Parts of me were moving without my brain even knowing what was happening. My hands were searching around for things I wasn't even sure I was looking for.

I was growing hysterical, because with each passing second, I became more aware of how different my life would be going forward. How that one second had altered whatever course we were on, and things would never be the same, and all the parts of me that had become disconnected in that wreck would never fully reconnect.

I crawled out of the car through the space between the ground and my door, and once I was outside and standing right-side-up, I puked.

The headlights were shining on a row of trees, but none of that light was helping us, and then I ran around to the passenger side of the car to free you, but I couldn't. There was your arm, sticking out from under the car. The moonlight glimmering in your blood. I grabbed your hand and squeezed it, but it was cold. I was still muttering your name. "Scotty, Scotty, Scotty, no, no, no." I went around to the windshield and tried kicking it to break it, but even though it was already cracked, I couldn't break it enough to fit through it, or pull you out.

I knelt down and pressed my face to the glass and I saw what I had done to you then. It was a stark realization that no matter how much you love someone, you can still do despicable things to them.

It was like a wave of the most intense pain you could ever imagine rolled right over me. My body rolled with it. It started at my head and I curled in on myself, all the way to my toes. I groaned, and I sobbed, and when I went back around the car to touch your hand again, there was nothing. No pulse in your wrist. No heartbeat in your palm. No warmth in your fingertips.

I screamed. I screamed so much, I stopped being able to make sounds.

And then I panicked. It's the only way to describe what happened to me.

I couldn't find either of our phones, so I started running toward the highway. The further I got, the more confused I grew. I couldn't imagine that what happened was real, or that what was *happening* was real. I was running down a highway with one shoe. I could see myself, like I was ahead of me, running *toward* me, like I was in a nightmare, not making any progress.

It wasn't the memories of the wreck that took time to come back to me. It was *that* moment. The part of the night that was drowned out by the adrenaline rush and hysteria that bowled through me. I started making noises I didn't know I could make.

I couldn't breathe because you were dead, and how was I supposed to breathe when you had no air? It was the worst realization I ever had, and I fell to my knees and screamed into the darkness.

I don't know how long I was on the side of the road. Cars were passing me, and I still had your blood on my hands, and I was scared and angry and couldn't stop seeing your mother's face. I had killed you and everyone was going to miss you, and you wouldn't be around to make anyone feel appreciated or important anymore, and it was my fault, and I just wanted to die.

I didn't care about anything else.

I just wanted to die.

I walked out into the street at what I'm guessing was around eleven at night, and a car had to swerve to miss me. I tried three times, with three different cars, but none of them hit me, and all of them were angry that I was in the road at dark. I got honked at and cussed at, but no one put me out of my misery, and no one helped me. I had already walked over a mile, and I didn't know how far away I was from my apartment, but I knew if I could just get there, I could step off my fourth-floor apartment balcony, because that was the only thing I could think to do in that moment. I wanted to be with you, but in my mind, you were no longer trapped under your car in that wreck. You were somewhere else, floating around in the dark, and I was determined to join you because what was the point? You were my whole point.

I began to shrink with every second that passed, until I felt invisible.

And that's the last thing I remember. There's a long stretch of *nothing* between me leaving you and me even realizing I left you.

Hours.

Your family was told I walked home and fell asleep, but that's not exactly what happened. I'm almost positive I fainted from shock, because when the cops beat on my bedroom door the next morning and I opened my eyes, I was on the floor. I noticed a small puddle of blood on the floor next to my head. I must have hit my head going down, but I didn't have time to inspect it because police were in my bedroom and one of them had his hand on my arm and he was lifting me to my feet.

That's the last time I ever saw my bedroom.

I remember my roommate Clarissa looked horrified. It wasn't because she was horrified for me. She was horrified for *herself*. It was as if she had been living with a murderer all this time and had no idea. Her boyfriend, *we could never remember his name*—Jason or Jackson or Justin—was comforting her like I had ruined her day.

I almost apologized to her, but I couldn't get my thoughts to connect with my voice. I had questions, I was confused, I was weak, I was hurting. But the most powerful of all the feelings flooding me in that moment was my loneliness.

Little did I know, that feeling would become perpetual. Permanent. I knew when they put me in the back seat of the police car that my life had reached its peak with you, and nothing that came after you would ever matter.

There was *before* you and there was *during* you. For some reason, I never thought there would be an *after* you.

But there was, and I was in it.

I'll be in it forever.

There's still more to read, but my throat is dry and my nerves are shot and I'm scared of what Ledger is thinking of me right now. He's gripping the steering wheel so hard his knuckles have turned white.

I reach for my bottle of water and take a long drink. Ledger directs his car all the way up his driveway, and when we reach his house, he puts his truck in park and leans his elbow against his door. He doesn't look at me. "Keep reading."

My hands are shaking now. I don't know if I can continue to read without crying, but I don't think he'd care even if I read through my tears. I take another drink and then start reading the next chapter.

Dear Scotty,

This is what it was like in the interrogation room.

Them: How much did you have to drink?

Me: Silence

Them: Who took you home after the wreck?

Me: Silence

Them: Are you on any other illegal substances?

Me: Silence

Them: Did you call for help?

Me: Silence

Them: Did you know he was still alive when you fled the scene?

Me: Silence

Them: Did you know he was still alive when we found him an hour and a half ago?

Me: Screams.

Lots of screams.

Screams until they put me back in a cell and said they'd come back for me when I calmed down.

When I calmed down.

I didn't calm down, Scotty.

I

think

I

lost

a

little

bit

of

my

mind

that

day.

They pulled me into the interrogation room two more times over the next twenty-four hours. I hadn't slept, I was heartbroken, I couldn't eat or drink anything.

I just. Wanted. To die.

And then, when they told me you would still be alive if I had just called for help, I *did* die. It was a Monday, I think. Two days after our wreck. I sometimes want to buy myself a headstone and have that date written on it, even though I'm still pretending not to be dead. My epitaph would read: *Kenna Nicole Rowan, died two days after the passing of her beloved Scotty.*

I never even attempted to call my mother through all of it. I was too depressed to call anyone at all. And how could I call my friends back home and tell them what I'd done?

I was ashamed and sad, and as a result of that, no one in my life before I met you knew what I had done. And since you were gone, and your entire family hated me, I had no visitors.

They appointed me a lawyer, but I had no one to post bail. I didn't even have anywhere to go if I *could* have posted bail. I found comfort being there in that jail cell, so I didn't mind it. If I couldn't be with you in your car, the only place I wanted to be was alone in that cell where I could refuse to eat the food they gave me and hopefully, eventually, my heart would stop beating like I thought yours had that night.

Turns out, your heart was still beating. It was just your arm that had died. I could go into more gruesome details about how it was so horribly crushed and mangled during the wreck that the blood flow was completely cut off and that's why I touched you and thought you were dead, and how, despite all that, you still somehow woke up and got out of the car and tried to get the help I never brought back to you.

I would have realized that if only I would have stayed with you longer, or tried harder. If I wouldn't have panicked and ran and allowed the adrenaline to pump through me to the point that I wasn't even functioning within the borders of reality.

If I could have been as calm as you always were, you'd still be alive. We'd probably be raising the daughter together that you never even knew we made. We'd probably have two kids by now, or even three, and I'd more than likely be a teacher, or a nurse, or a writer, or whatever you would have undoubtedly given me the strength to realize I could be.

My God, I miss you.

I miss you so much, even if it never showed in my eyes in a way anyone would have been satisfied with. I sometimes wonder if my mental state played a hand in my sentencing. I was empty inside, and I'm sure that emptiness showed in my eyes any time I had to face someone.

I didn't even care about the first court hearing two weeks after you died. The lawyer told me we would fight it—that all I had to do was plead not guilty and he would prove that I wasn't of sound mind that night and that my actions weren't intentional and that I was very, very, very, very, very, very remorseful.

But I didn't care what the lawyer suggested. I *wanted* to go to prison. I didn't want to go back out in the world where I would have to look at cars again, or gravel roads, or hear Coldplay on the radio, or think about all the things I'd have to do without you.

Looking back on it now, I realize I was in a deep and dangerous state of depression, but I don't think anyone noticed, or maybe there was just no one who cared. Everyone was #TeamScotty, like *we were never even on the same team*. Everyone wanted justice, and sadly, justice and empathy couldn't both fit inside that courtroom.

But what's funny is I was on *their* side. I wanted justice *for* them. I empathized with *them*. With your mother, with your father, with all the people in your life who were packed inside that courtroom.

I pleaded guilty, to my lawyer's dismay. I had to. When they started talking about what you went through after I ran away from you that night, I knew I would rather die than sit through a trial and listen to the details. It was all too gruesome, like I was living some horror story, and not my own life.

I'm sorry, Scotty.

I tuned it all out somehow by just repeating that phrase over and over in my head. *I'm sorry, Scotty. I'm sorry, Scotty. I'm sorry, Scotty.*

They scheduled another court date for sentencing, and it was sometime between those two court dates that I realized I hadn't had my period in a while. I thought my cycle was messed up, so I didn't mention it to anyone. Had I known I was growing a part of you inside me sooner, I'm positive I would have found the will to go to trial and fight for myself. Fight for our daughter.

When the sentencing date came, I tried not to listen as your mother read her victim impact statement, but every word she spoke is still engraved in my bones.

I kept thinking about what you told me as you were carrying me up the stairs on your back that night in her house—about how they wanted more kids, but you were their miracle baby.

That's all I could think of in that moment. I had killed their miracle baby, and now they had no one, and it was all my fault.

I had planned to give an allocution statement, but I was too weak and too broken, so when it came time for me to stand up and speak, I couldn't. Physically, emotionally, mentally. I was stuck in that chair, but I tried to stand. My lawyer grabbed my arm to make sure I didn't collapse, and then I think he might have read something out loud for me, I don't know. I'm still not clear on what happened in the courtroom that day, because that day was so much like that night. A nightmare that I was somehow watching play out from a distance.

I had tunnel vision. I knew there were people around me, and I knew the judge was speaking, but my brain was so exhausted, I couldn't process what anyone was saying. Even when the judge read my sentence, I had no reaction, because I couldn't absorb it. It wasn't until later, after I was given an IV for dehydration, that I found out I had been sentenced to seven years in prison, with the eligibility for parole even sooner than that.

"Seven years," I remember thinking. "That's bullshit. That isn't nearly long enough."

I try not to think about what it must have been like for you in that car after I left you there. What must you have thought of me? Did you think I had been thrown from the car? Were you looking for me? Or did you know I had left you there all alone?

It's the time you spent alone that night that I know haunts us all, because we'll never know what you went through. What you were thinking. Who you were calling out to. What your final minutes were like.

I can't imagine a more painful way for your mother and father to be forced to live out the rest of their lives.

Sometimes I wonder if that's why Diem is here. Maybe Diem was your way of making sure your parents would be okay.

But in that same vein, not having Diem in my life would mean it's your way of punishing me. It's okay. I deserve it.

I plan to fight it, but I know I deserve it.

Every morning, I wake up and I silently apologize. To you, to your parents, to Diem. Throughout the day, I silently thank your parents for raising our daughter since we can't. And every night, I apologize again before I fall asleep.

I'm sorry. Thank you. I'm sorry.

That's my day, every day, on repeat.

I'm sorry. Thank you. I'm sorry.

My sentence was not justice considering the way you died. Eternity wouldn't be justice. But I hope your family knows my actions that night didn't come from a place of selfishness. It was horror and shock and agony and confusion and terror that guided me away from you that night. It was never selfishness.

I am not a bad person, and I know you know that, wherever you are. And I know you forgive me. It's just who you are. I only hope one day our daughter will forgive me too. And your parents.

Then maybe, by some miracle, I can start to forgive myself.

Until then, I love you. I miss you.
I'm sorry.
Thank you.
I'm sorry.
Thank you.
I'm sorry.
Repeat.

CHAPTER THIRTY-FOUR

KENNA

I close out the document. I can't read anymore. My eyes have filled with tears. I'm surprised I made it as far as I did before crying, but I tried not to absorb the words as I was reading them aloud.

I set my phone aside and I wipe my eyes.

Ledger hasn't moved. He's in the same position, leaning against his driver's side door, staring straight ahead. My voice is no longer filling his truck. Now there's just a silence that's thick and uninviting, to the point that Ledger can't seem to take it anymore. He swings open his door and gets out of his truck. He walks to the back of it and begins unloading the table without so much as a word.

I watch him in the rearview mirror. Once the table is on the ground, he grabs one of the chairs. There's a pause before he chucks the chair onto the table. It lands with a loud clank that I feel in my chest.

Then Ledger grabs a second chair and angrily tosses it across the yard. He's so mad. I can't watch.

I lean forward and press my hands against my face, regretting ever reading a single word of that to him. I have no idea if he's mad at the situation, or me, or if he's just back there throwing chairs as a way to process five years' worth of emotions.

"Fuck!" he yells, right before I hear the crash of the final chair. His voice reverberates in the dense trees that surround his property.

The whole truck shakes with the slam of his tailgate.

Then there's just silence. Stillness.

The only thing I can hear is my shallow and rapid breathing. I'm scared to get out of the truck because I don't want to have to come face to face with him if any of that outburst was directed at me.

I wish I knew.

I swallow a lump that forms in my throat when I hear his footsteps crunching against the gravel. He stops at my door and he opens it. I'm still leaning forward with my face in my hands, but I eventually pull them away and hesitantly look up at him.

He's gripping the top of the truck, leaning in my doorway. His head is resting against the inside of his raised arm. His eyes are red, but his expression isn't filled with hatred. It isn't even filled with anger. If anything, he looks apologetic, as if he knows his outburst scared me and he feels bad.

"I'm not mad at you." He presses his lips together and looks down. He shakes his head gently. "It's just a lot to process."

I nod, but I can't speak because my heart is pounding and my throat feels swollen, and I'm still not sure what to say.

He's still looking down when he lets go of the roof of the truck. His eyes meet mine as he reaches into the truck and puts his right hand on my left thigh and his left hand under my right knee. He pulls me to the edge of the passenger seat so that I'm facing him.

Ledger then takes my face in his hands and tilts it so that I'm looking up at him. He blows out a slow breath, like what he's about to say is hard to get out. "I'm sorry you lost him."

I can't hold back the tears after that. It's the first time anyone has ever acknowledged that I lost Scotty that night too. Ledger's words mean more to me than I think he can comprehend.

Agony spreads across his face as he continues. "What if Scotty can see how we've been treating you?" A tear forms and spills down his cheek. Just one lonely tear, and it makes me so sad. "I'm part of everything that's been tearing you down all these years, and I'm sorry, Kenna. I'm so sorry."

I place my hand over his chest, right over his heart. "It's okay. What I wrote doesn't change anything. It was still my fault."

"It's not okay. None of this is okay." He's cradling me in his arms with his cheek pressed against the top of my head. He runs his right hand in soothing circles over my back.

He holds me like that for a long time. I don't want him to let go.

He's the first person I've been able to share the full details of that night with, and I wasn't sure if it would make things better or worse. But this feels better, so maybe that means something.

I feel like a weight has been lifted. It's not the weight of the anchor that keeps me tethered under the surface—that won't be lifted until I get to hold my daughter. But a small portion of my pain has attached to his sympathy, and it feels like he's physically lifting me up for air, allowing me a few minutes to breathe.

He eventually pulls back far enough to assess me. He must see something on my face that makes him want to comfort me because he presses a soft kiss to my forehead while brushing my hair back tenderly. He kisses the tip of my nose and then plants a soft peck on my lips.

I don't think he expected me to kiss him back, but I feel more for him in this moment than I ever have. I clutch his shirt in my fists and quietly beg his mouth for a much fuller kiss. He gives it to me.

His kisses feel like both forgiveness and promises. I imagine mine feel like apologies to him, because he keeps coming back for more every time we separate.

I end up on my back, and he's halfway into his truck, hovering over me, our mouths pressed together.

When we're in the thick of fogging up all the windows, he pulls away from my neck, and there's a split-second look he gives me. It's so quick; it's a flicker, a flash. But I can tell he wants more in that quick glance, and so do I, so I nod and he pulls away and opens his glove box. He grabs a condom and starts to open it with his teeth, bracing himself up with one arm. I take this opportunity to slide my panties off and bunch my long skirt up around my waist.

He gets the package open, but then he pauses.

The seconds begin to drag as he silently stares down at me with contemplation.

Then he tosses the condom aside and lowers himself on top of me again. He presses a soft kiss against my lips. His breath is hot against my cheek when he says, "You deserve a bed."

I drag a hand through his hair. "You don't have a bed here?"

He shakes his head. "Nope."

"Not even an inflatable mattress?"

"Our first two times were on an inflatable mattress. You deserve a real bed. And no, I don't have either one here."

"How about a hammock?"

He smiles at that, but still shakes his head.

"A yoga mat? I'm not picky."

He laughs and kisses my chin. "Stop it, or we'll end up fucking in this truck."

I wrap my legs around his waist. "And that's bad *how*?"

He groans into my neck, and then I lift my hips and he gives in.

He grabs the condom and finishes opening it. While he's doing that, I'm unzipping his jeans.

He slides on the condom and then pulls me to the edge of the seat. His truck is the perfect height for this. Neither of us even has to adjust ourselves or change positions. He just grips my hips and pushes into me, and even though it isn't a real bed, it's still just as good as it was last night.

CHAPTER THIRTY-FIVE

Ledger

I don't know how I found the strength to pull away from her long enough to go inside and get the floors started.

I figured she'd sit back and watch me, or write in her notebook, but as soon as I told her I needed to get some work finished, she asked how she could help.

It's been three hours. We've mostly worked, with the occasional short break to rehydrate and kiss some more, but we've finished most of what will be the living room floor.

We'd be done by now if she weren't wearing that shirt with that skirt. She's been crawling across the floor, helping me lock the flooring into place, and every time I look at her I can see straight down her shirt. I'm so distracted I'm surprised I haven't injured myself.

We haven't discussed a single thing of importance since we exited the truck. It's as if we left all the important stuff inside it and chose to carry nothing of weight with us into this house.

It's been such a heavy day already; I'm doing everything I can to keep things light. We both are. I haven't brought up the letter since we came inside. She hasn't mentioned the restraining order, I haven't mentioned Mother's Day under this roof, we haven't talked about what our new physical connection means or how we're possibly going to navigate it. I think we both know the conversations will come, but right now it feels like we're on the same page, and all we want out of today's page is to ride the high of each other.

I think Kenna and I needed today. Kenna especially needed today. She always looks like she's carrying the weight of the world on her shoulders, but today she looks like she's floating. She makes gravity seem powerless against her.

She's smiled and laughed more in the last few hours than she has since the day I met her. It makes me wonder if I've been a huge chunk of the weight she's been carrying.

Kenna locks the piece of wood in place on her end and then reaches for a bottle of water. She catches me staring at her chest, and she laughs. "You sure do have a hard time looking me in the eye now."

"I think I have an obsession with your shirt." She usually wears T-shirts, but this particular shirt is made out of a slinky material that dips down in the front, and now that she's been working for three hours, it's starting to stick to her in all the places where she's sweating. "That shirt is fucking lovely."

She laughs, and I want to kiss her again. I crawl over to her, and when I reach her, I press my mouth to hers so hard she falls backward against the floor. I kiss her through her laughter, until I'm on top of her.

I hate that I have no furniture. We just keep ending up on the hardwood floor we've been installing, and it's nice, but I'd give anything to kiss her on something more comfortable. Something as soft as her mouth.

"You'll never finish these floors," she whispers.

"*Fuck* the floors." We kiss for a few minutes, and we just keep getting better at it. There's a lot of pulling and tugging and tasting, and it gets a little chaotic, and her shirt that I love so fucking much ends up somewhere on the floor next to us.

I'm admiring her bra now, kissing her skin right above it, when she whispers, "I'm scared." Her hands are in my hair, and she keeps them there when I lift up just enough to look down at her. "What if they find out about us before you have a chance to tell them? We're being reckless."

I don't want her to think about this today because today is good, and they're out of town, so there's no point in dwelling on it until they return. I press a comforting kiss against her forehead. "Worrying won't make the situation any better," I say. "They're out of town. Whatever happens is going to happen whether we make out right now or not."

She smiles when I say that. "Good point." She wraps her hand around my neck and pulls me back to her mouth.

I lower myself on top of her, but then whisper, "What's the worst that could happen if I have to hide you forever? You've seen my closet, Kenna. It's huge. You'll love it in there."

She laughs against my mouth.

"I could install a minifridge and a television for you. When they come to visit, you can just go to your closet and pretend you're on vacation."

"You're terrible for joking about this," she says, but she's laughing. I kiss her until we aren't laughing anymore, and then I slide off her until I'm lying next to her, leaning over her.

It's the first time we've really looked at each other without feeling like we have to look away. She's so goddamn flawless.

I don't say that out loud, though, because I don't want to diminish any of the other wonderful things about her by giving her a superficial compliment about her face. It would take away from how smart I think she is, and how compassionate, resilient, and spirited she is.

I look away from her impeccable face and slowly trace the center of her cleavage until she has chills running across her skin. "I have to finish my floors." I slide my hand over to her breast and gently squeeze. "Stop distracting me with these things. Put your shirt back on."

She laughs at the same time someone clears their throat from across the room.

I quickly sit up, immediately scrambling to block the view of Kenna from whoever the fuck is in my house.

I look up to find my parents standing in the doorway, looking at the ceiling. Kenna immediately scrambles away from me and reaches for her shirt.

"Oh, my God," she whispers. "Who are they?"

"My parents," I mutter. I swear, embarrassing me is their favorite hobby. I raise my voice so they can hear me. "Nice of you to warn me you were showing up today!" I help Kenna to her feet, and my parents are still looking at everything but us as I help her back into her shirt.

My father says, "I cleared my throat when we walked in. How much warning do you need?"

I'm not as mortified as I probably should be right now. Maybe I'm growing immune to their shenanigans. But Kenna isn't immune.

Now that she's dressed and halfway standing behind me, my father motions at the work we've been doing. "Seems you've made a lot of progress . . . on the floors."

"In more ways than one," my mother says, amused. Kenna buries her face against my arm. "Who's your friend, Ledger?" My mother is smiling, but she has a lot of different smiles, and they don't always mean something sweet. This smile is her entertained smile. Her *this-is-so-much-fun* smile.

"This is . . . um . . ." I have no idea how to introduce Kenna to them. I don't even know what name to use. They'd definitely recognize her name if I said Kenna, but I'm not exactly sure they won't recognize her face, so lying to them would be pointless. "This is . . . my new employee." I need to ask Kenna how she wants me to confront this. I wrap my arm around her shoulder and lead her to the bedroom. "Excuse us while we go coordinate our lies," I say over my shoulder.

Kenna and I make it to the bedroom, out of their view, and she looks at me wide eyed. "You can't tell them who I am," she whispers.

"I can't lie to them. My mom will probably recognize you once she gets a better look at you. She was at your sentencing, and she never forgets a face. She also knows you're back in town."

Kenna looks like she's about to fold in on herself. She starts to pace, and I can see the weight of the world begin to return to her shoulders. She looks up at me with fear in her eyes. "Do they hate me?"

That question digs at my heart, mainly because she's starting to tear up. And it's only in this moment that I realize she assumes everyone who knew Scotty must hate her. "No. Of course they don't hate you."

I realize as I say those words that I don't necessarily know if they're true. My parents were heartbroken when Scotty died. He was as important to them as I am to Patrick and Grace. But I'm not sure that I've ever had a conversation with my parents specifically about their opinion of Kenna. It was over five years ago. I can't remember what conversations were had or what their thoughts were on everything that happened. And we barely discuss it anymore.

Kenna can see that I'm processing, and she grows a little panicked. "Can't you just take me home? I can sneak out the back and meet you at your truck."

Whether my parents realize who Kenna is or not, Kenna doesn't know what kind of people my parents are. She doesn't realize she has nothing to be concerned about.

I cup her face with my hands. "Kenna. They're my parents. If they recognize you, they'll have my back no matter what." Those words calm her a little bit. "I'll introduce you as Nicole for now, and then I'll take you home and deal with them and the truth later. Okay? They're good people. So are you."

She nods, so I give her a quick kiss and grab her hand and lead her out of the bedroom. They're in the kitchen now, inspecting all the things Roman and I have added since they were last out here. When they notice our return, they both casually lean against the counters, anticipating this introduction.

I wave a hand at Kenna. "This is Nicole." I wave a hand at my parents. "My mother, Robin. My father, Benji."

Kenna smiles and shakes their hands, but then she sidles back up to my side like she's scared to move too far away from me. I grab her hand that's at her side, and I move it behind her back and squeeze it to provide her with a little comfort.

"It's such a pleasant surprise that you aren't alone," my mother says. "We thought you'd be out here moping by yourself today."

I'm scared to ask. "Why would I be moping?"

My mother laughs and turns to my father. "You owe me ten bucks, Benji." She holds out her hand, and my father pulls out his wallet and slaps a ten-dollar bill in her palm. She shoves it in the pocket of her jeans. "We bet on whether you'd even remember you were supposed to be leaving for your honeymoon today."

Why am I not surprised? "Which one of you bet that I'd forget Mother's Day?"

My mother raises her hand.

"I didn't forget. Check your email. I sent a gift card because I had no idea where to send flowers to this week."

My mother takes the ten-dollar bill out of her pocket and hands it back to my father. She walks over to me and finally gives me a hug. "Thank you." She doesn't look at Kenna because her attention is stolen midhug by the patio door. "Oh, wow! It looks even better than I imagined!" She releases me and passes us to go play with the accordion-style door.

My father is still focused on me and Kenna. I can tell he's going to attempt to be polite and include her in conversation, but I know how much she wants to be ignored right now.

"Nicole has to get to work," I blurt out. "I need to give her a ride, and then I can meet you both at the house."

My mother makes a *hmph* sound behind me. "We just got here," she says. "I wanted a tour of everything you've done."

My father's attention is still on Kenna. "What do you do, Nicole? Besides . . ." He waves a hand toward me. "Besides Ledger."

Kenna gasps quietly and says, "Wow. Okay. Well, I don't . . . *do* . . . Ledger."

I squeeze her hand again, because that is *not* what my father meant. But if we're being technical . . . "I think he means what do you do other than . . . *work* . . . for me." She's looking at me blankly. "Because I said you're my employee earlier, but then I just lied and said you have to go to work, and they know my bar is closed on Sundays, so he assumes you have a different job besides the bar, and he said what do you do besides . . ." I'm rambling now, and it's just making the moment worse because my parents can hear this conversation, and I know they are enjoying the shit out of it.

My mother has returned to my father's side, and she's grinning with delight.

"Please take me home," Kenna pleads.

I nod. "Yeah. This is torture."

"It's such a treat for me, though," my mother says. "I think this might be my favorite Mother's Day yet."

"And here we were thinking he was going to be sad because he didn't get married," my father says. "What do you think he has in store for Father's Day?"

"I can only imagine," my mother says.

"You two are mortifying. I'm almost thirty. When will this stop?"

"You're twenty-eight," my mother says. "That's not almost thirty. Twenty-*nine* is almost thirty."

"Let's go," I say to Kenna.

"No, bring her to dinner," my mother begs.

"She's not hungry." I lead Kenna out the door. "I'll meet you both at the house!"

We're almost to my truck when I realize what leaving my parents alone means. I pause and say, "I'll be right back." I point to the truck so Kenna knows she can go ahead without me. I turn around and walk back to the house, and then I lean in at the doorway. "Do not have sex in my house."

"Oh, come on," my father says. "We would never."

"I'm serious. This is my new house, and I'll be damned if you two christen it."

"We won't," my mother says, shooing me away.

"We're getting too old for that anyway," my father says. "So old. Our son is almost *thirty*."

I step out of the doorway and motion for them to leave. "Get out. Go. I don't trust either of you." I wait for them to join me outside, and then I lock the front door. I point toward their car. "I'll meet you at the house."

I walk to my truck and ignore their chatter. I wait for my parents to back out, and then Kenna and I both sigh simultaneously. "They can be a lot sometimes," I admit.

"Wow. That was . . ."

"Typical of them." I glance over at her, and she's smiling.

"It was embarrassing, but I kind of liked them," she says. "But I'm still not having dinner with them."

I don't blame her. I put my truck in reverse and then point to the middle of the seat. Now that we've shattered whatever line we had drawn in the sand, I want her to be as close to me as she can get. She slides across the seat until she's right next to me, and I put my hand on her knee as I drive away from the house.

"You do that a lot," she says.

"I do what?"

"You point all the time. It's rude." She sounds amused rather than offended.

"I don't *point* all the time."

"You do too. I noticed it the first night I came into your bar. It's why I let you kiss me, because I thought it was hot. The way you kept pointing at things."

I grin. "You just said it was rude. You think rude is hot?"

"No. I think kindness is hot. Maybe *rude* was the wrong term." She leans her head against my shoulder. "I find your pointing *sexy*."

"Do you?" I let go of her knee and point at a mailbox. "See that mailbox?" Then I point at a tree. "Look at that tree." I tap on my brakes as we close in on a stop sign, and I point at the sign. "Look at that, Kenna. What's that? Is that a fucking pigeon?"

She tilts her head and looks at me curiously. When I come to a full stop at the sign, she says, "Scotty used to say that sometimes. What does it mean?"

I shake my head. "It was just something he used to say." Patrick is the only one who knows where that phrase originated, and even though there's no huge secret or story behind it, I still want to hold on to it. Kenna doesn't press me. She just lifts up and kisses me before I pull out onto the street. She's smiling, and it feels so good to see her smile like this. I look back at the road and put my hand on her knee again.

She rests her head against my shoulder, and after a quiet moment, she says, "I wish I could have seen you with Scotty. I bet you two were fun together."

I love that she admitted that out loud. It feels good to hear, because at some point, we're all going to have to move past the fact that Scotty died the way he did. I think I'm at a point where I want his memory to be accompanied by only good feelings. I want to be able to talk about him with people, especially with his father, but in a way that doesn't make Patrick cry.

We all knew Scotty, but we all knew him in different ways. We all carry different memories of him. I think it would be good for Patrick and Grace to get to hear the memories Kenna has of Scotty that none of the rest of us have.

"I wish I could have seen *you* with Scotty," I admit.

Kenna kisses my shoulder and then rests her head there again. It's quiet until I lift my hand and point at a guy on a bicycle. "Look at that bike." I point at an upcoming gas station. "Look at those gas pumps." I point at a cloud. "Look at that cloud."

Kenna releases laughter mixed with a groan. "*Stop.* You're ruining the sexiness of it."

I reluctantly dropped Kenna off at her apartment two hours ago. It might have taken fifteen minutes for me to stop kissing her long enough to walk back to my truck, but I didn't want to leave. I wanted to spend the rest of the evening, and possibly even the *night* with her, but my parents are assholes who don't believe in schedules, and they're always showing up at the worst times.

At least this time it was in the middle of the day. They once showed up at 3:00 a.m., and I woke up to my father blasting Nirvana in the backyard and cooking steaks on the grill.

My father made burgers tonight, and we just finished eating dinner about an hour ago. I waited throughout the whole dinner for them to ask me about Kenna. Or Nicole, rather. But neither of them brought it up. All we've talked about tonight has been their latest adventures on the road and my latest adventures with Diem.

They were disappointed to find out Diem and the Landrys are out of town. I suggested they call ahead the next time they feel like dropping in. It would make it easier on all of us.

My parents have always gotten along with Scotty's parents, but the Landrys had Scotty later in life, so they're a little older than my parents. I would say they're more mature than my parents, but *immature* isn't the right term to describe my parents. They're just a little more carefree and unstructured. But even though I wouldn't categorize the four of them as actively close, they share a bond because of Scotty and me.

And because Diem is like a daughter to me, she's been like a granddaughter to my parents. Which means Diem is important to them, and they want the best for her.

Which is probably why, as soon as my father goes to the backyard to clean up the grill, my mother slides onto the barstool and gives me one of her many smiles. This is her "*You have a secret, and you better spill it*" smile.

I ignore her smile, and her, and continue to wash the rest of the dishes. But my mother says, "Get over here and talk to me before your father comes back inside."

I dry my hands and sit across the bar from her. She's looking at me like she already knows my secrets. It doesn't surprise me. When I say my mother never forgets a face, I don't say that lightly. It's like a superpower.

"Do the Landrys know?" she asks.

I play dumb. "Know what?"

Her head lilts to the side. "I know who she is, Ledger. I recognized her the day she walked into your bar."

Wait. What? "The day you were drunk?"

She nods. Now that I think about it, I remember her staring at Kenna when she walked into my bar that day. Why would she not say anything to me about that? She didn't even bring it up when I spoke to her on the phone a few days later and told her Kenna was back in town.

"You told me she was leaving town last time we talked," she says.

"She is." I feel guilty when I say that because I'm hoping with everything in me that it isn't true. "Or she *was*. I don't know anymore."

"Do Patrick and Grace know the two of you are . . ."

"No."

My mother blows out a soft breath. "What are you doing?"

"I don't know," I say honestly.

"This isn't going to end well."

"I know."

"Do you love her?"

I blow out a heavy, slow rush of air. "I definitely don't hate her anymore."

She takes a sip of her wine and gives this conversation a moment to settle. "Well. I hope you do the right thing."

I lift an eyebrow. "What's the right thing?"

My mother shrugs. "I don't know. I just hope you do it."

I release a short laugh. "Thanks for the nonadvice."

"That's what I'm here for. To tiptoe around this thing they call parenting." She smiles and reaches across the bar to squeeze my hand. "I know you'd rather be with her right now. We don't mind if you abandon us tonight."

There's a moment of hesitation on my part, not because I don't want to go to Kenna's place, but because I'm surprised my mother knows who she is, yet she's still okay with it.

"Do you blame Kenna?" I ask her after a short pause.

My mother looks at me honestly. "Scotty wasn't my child, so I felt sorry for everyone involved. Even Kenna. But if what happened to Scotty had happened to you, I can't say that I would make a different choice than Patrick and Grace. I think there's room in a tragedy this size for everyone to be both right *and* wrong. However," she says, "I'm your mother. And if you see something special in her, then I know there must be something special in her."

I let her words ruminate, but then I grab my keys and my cell phone and I kiss her on the cheek. "Will you be here tomorrow?"

"Yeah, we're staying two or three days. I'll tell your dad you said good night."

CHAPTER THIRTY-SIX

KENNA

I'm in the shower when I hear a knock at my front door. It startles me because it's more like an incessant pounding. Lady Diana wouldn't knock like that, and she's the only person who has ever been here other than Ledger.

I've just rinsed the conditioner out of my hair, so I open the bathroom door and yell, "Hold on!" I frantically try to dry myself and my hair with a towel as much as I can so I don't drip water all the way to my front door.

I pull on a T-shirt and a pair of panties, and then grab my jeans and head to the door to check the peephole. When I see that it's Ledger, I unlock the door and then start pulling on the jeans as he makes his way inside.

He seems jarred that I'm not fully dressed. He just stands there and stares at me until I get my jeans buttoned. I smile. "You ditched your parents?"

He pulls me in for a kiss, but I'm caught off guard, because this kiss is more than just a kiss. There's so much behind the way his mouth presses against mine, it's like it's been weeks since he's seen me, but it's only been about three hours.

"You smell so good," he says, pressing his face into my wet hair. He slides his hands down my thighs and then lifts me, wrapping my legs around his waist. He walks us to the couch and lowers us onto it.

"This isn't a bed," I tease.

He nips at my bottom lip with his teeth. "It's okay, I'm not as thoughtful as I tried to be earlier today. I'd have sex with you just about anywhere right now."

"If this is happening, you might want to move me to that inflatable mattress, because this couch is questionable."

He doesn't miss a beat. He lifts me and drops me on the mattress, but as he's kissing my neck, Ivy begins to meow. She climbs up onto the mattress and starts licking Ledger's hand. He stops kissing me and looks at my kitten.

"This is awkward."

"I'll put her in the bathroom." I move the kitten to the bathroom and lock her in with her food and water. I lower myself on top of Ledger this time. I straddle him, sitting up, and he runs his hands up and down my thighs while his eyes scroll over me.

"Are you still feeling good about this?" he asks.

"About what? Us?"

He nods.

"I've *never* felt good about us. Us is a terrible idea."

He grabs the front of my shirt and pulls me down until our mouths are almost touching. He rolls his other hand over my ass. "I'm serious."

I smile, because he can't expect me to be serious while also pressing himself against me like this. "Are you trying to have a legitimate conversation while I'm on top of you?"

He flips us over so that he's hovering over me now. "I brought condoms. I want to take off your clothes. I want to have sex with you again, but I also feel like I should have a conversation with the Landrys before this goes any further."

"It's just sex."

He sighs and then says, "Kenna." He just says my name like he's lecturing me, but then he presses his mouth to mine, and it's sweet and soft and so very different from every kiss that has come before it.

I understand what he's saying, but I think I'm tired of circling around this discussion because I'd like to *not* think about it for a while. Every time I'm with him, my situation is all I think about. It's arduous, and to be honest, it's scary.

I lift a hand to his cheek and brush a piece of couch fuzz away. "You really want to know how I feel?"

"Yes. That's why I'm asking."

"We both keep going back and forth. You worry, and then I worry, and then you worry, but the worry won't solve this. I feel like this isn't going to end well. Or maybe it will. Either way, we like being with each other, so until it ends well or ends terribly, I don't really want to waste our time together going in circles about a future we can't predict. So just get me naked and make love to me."

Ledger shakes his head, but he's smiling. "It's like you read my mind."

Maybe, but everything I just said out loud isn't at all what I feel.

What I feel is terrified. I know in my heart that there's nothing he can say that will change the Landrys' minds about me. They aren't even wrong. The decision they're making for themselves is the right decision because it's the decision that will bring them the most peace.

I'm going to respect that decision.

After tonight.

But right now, I'm going to be selfish and focus on the one person in this world who sees me the way I wish everyone could see me. And if that means I have to lie to him and pretend this story can possibly have a happy ending, then that's what I'll do.

I pull off his shirt, and then my shirt is next, followed by our jeans, and within seconds, we're both naked and he's putting on a condom. I don't know why we're rushing, but we're doing everything with urgency. Kissing, touching, gasping as if we're running out of time.

He kisses his way down my body until his head is between my legs. He kisses both thighs before slowly separating me with his tongue. The sensation is so strong I dig my heels into the mattress and slide up it, so he has to grip my thighs and pull my body back to his mouth. I reach for something to grab on to, but there's not even a blanket, so I put my hands in his hair and keep them there, moving in rhythm with his head.

It doesn't take me long to finish, and as the sensations roll through me and my legs tense, Ledger intensifies the motion of his tongue. I tremble and moan until I can't take it anymore. I need him back inside me. I pull on his hair until he crawls up my body, and this time he pushes into me in one quick movement.

He thrusts so hard, over and over, until we somehow end up on the floor next to the inflatable mattress, covered in sweat and out of breath by the time it's over.

We wind up in the shower together, my back against his chest. The water is running over us as he holds me quietly.

The thought of saying goodbye to him at some point makes me want to curl up and cry, so I try to convince myself that I'm wrong about the Landrys. I try to lie to myself by saying things will work out between us. Maybe not tomorrow, maybe not this month, but hopefully Ledger is right. Maybe one of these days he can change their minds.

Maybe he'll say something to them that will plant a seed, and that seed will grow and grow until they start to feel empathy for me.

Whatever happens, I'll always be grateful to him for the forgiveness he gave me, whether I get it from anyone else or not.

I turn around and face him; then I lift my hand and touch his cheek. "I would have fallen for you even if you didn't love Diem."

His expression shifts, and then he kisses the inside of my palm. "I fell for you because of how much you do."

Dammit, Ledger.

I kiss him for that.

CHAPTER THIRTY-SEVEN

LEDGER

It's funny how life works out. I should be waking up in an oceanfront resort next to my brand-new wife, celebrating our honeymoon right now.

Instead, I'm waking up on an inflatable mattress in a barren apartment, next to a woman I've spent so many years angry at. If someone would have showed me this moment in a crystal ball last year, I would have wondered what could possibly have happened that would cause me to make a string of horrible decisions.

But now that I'm in this moment, I realize I'm here because I finally have clarity. I've never felt more certain about the choices I've made in my life than I do today.

I don't want Kenna to wake up yet. She looks peaceful, and I need a moment to formulate a plan for today. I want to confront this sooner rather than later.

I'm scared of what the outcome will be, so a huge part of me wants to wait a couple of weeks so Kenna and I can live in secret bliss, full of hope that things are going to go her way.

But the longer we wait, the sloppier we're going to get. The last thing I want is for Patrick and Grace to find out I've been lying to them before I can calmly confront them with my thoughts.

Kenna moves her arm to cover her eyes and then rolls onto her side. She tucks herself against me and moans. "It's so bright in here." Her voice is raspy and sexy.

I run my hand down her waist, over her hip, and then grip her thigh, pulling her leg over me. I kiss her cheek. "Sleep well?"

She laughs against my neck. "*Sleep* well? We had sex three times and then had to share a full-size inflatable mattress. I think I slept an hour, tops."

"It's after nine. You slept more than an hour."

Kenna sits up. "What? I thought the sun just came up." She tosses the covers aside. "I was supposed to be at work by nine."

"Oh, shit. I'll give you a ride." I search for my clothes. I find my shirt, but Kenna's kitten is curled up asleep inside of it. I lift her and set her on the couch and then start to pull on my jeans. Kenna is in the bathroom brushing her teeth. The door is open, and she's completely naked, so I freeze in the middle of getting dressed because she's got a perfect ass.

She sees me staring in the mirror and laughs, then kicks the bathroom door shut with her foot. "Get dressed!"

I finish getting dressed, but then I join her in the bathroom because I want some of her toothpaste. She scoots aside as she's rinsing, and I start to squeeze some toothpaste on my finger, but she opens a drawer and pulls out a package that has a toothbrush in it.

"I bought a double pack." She hands me the extra toothbrush and then leaves the bathroom.

We eventually meet at the front door. "What time do you get off work?" I pull her to me. She smells like fresh mint.

"Five." We kiss. "Unless I get fired." We kiss some more. "Ledger, I have to go," she mutters against my mouth. But we kiss again.

We make it to the grocery store by a quarter to ten. She's forty-five minutes late, but by the time we stop saying goodbye, she's fifty minutes late.

"I'll be here at five," I say as she goes to close her door.

She smiles. "Just because I put out now doesn't mean you have to be my chauffeur."

"I was your chauffeur *before* you put out."

She closes the door but then comes around to my side of the truck. I already have my window down, and she leans in and gives me one final kiss. When she pulls back, she pauses for a moment. It looks like she wants to say something, but she doesn't. She just stares silently for a few seconds, like something is on the tip of her tongue, but then she backs away and runs into the store.

I'm a mile from my house when I realize I've had a ridiculous smile on my face during the whole drive. I wipe it away, but it's the kind of smile that reappears with every thought I have about her. And all my thoughts this morning have been about her.

My parents' RV is occupying the entire driveway, so I park in front of the house.

Grace and Patrick are back already. He's out front watering his yard, and Diem is sitting in their driveway with a bucket of chalk.

I force the smile off my face. Not that a simple smile would give away everything that's happened in the last twenty-four hours, but Patrick knows me well enough that he might think my behavior is due to a girl. Then he'll ask questions. Then I'll have to lie to him even more than I have been.

Diem turns around when I close my truck door. "Ledger!" she looks both ways before meeting me in the middle of the street. I scoop her up and give her a big hug.

"Did you have fun at Grandma NoNo's house?"

"Yeah, we found a turtle, and NoNo let me keep it. It's in my room in a glass thing."

"I want to see." I put her back down, and she grabs my hand, but before we even reach the grass, Patrick and I make eye contact.

My heart immediately sinks.

His face is hard. There's no hello. It's the most resigned I've ever seen him.

His eyes fall to Diem, and he says, "You can show him your turtle in a minute. I need to talk to Ledger."

Diem can't feel the tension radiating from him, which is why she skips into the house while I'm frozen at the edge of the grass Patrick has been mindlessly watering. When the front door closes, he doesn't say anything. He just continues to water the grass, like he's waiting for me to admit my fuckup.

I'm worried for more reasons than one. His demeanor is making it obvious something is wrong, but if I say something first, I could be off the mark. Anything could be wrong. Maybe his mother is ill, or they received bad news he doesn't want Diem to hear.

The way he's acting could be completely unrelated to Kenna, so I wait for him to say whatever it is that seems so hard for him to say.

He releases the nozzle and drops the water hose. He walks closer to me, and each of his deliberate steps is aligned with the pounding of my heartbeat. He stops walking about three feet from me, but my heartbeats just keep pounding. I don't like how silent it is between us. I can tell he's about to confront me, and Patrick is not a confrontational person. The fact that he's not circling around what he wants to say with a *Welp* has me more than concerned.

Something is bothering him, and it's serious. I attempt to alleviate the tension by casually saying, "When did you guys get back?"

"This morning," he says. "Where were you?" He asks it like he's my father and he's pissed I snuck out in the middle of the night.

I don't even know what to say. I'm searching for whatever lie would fit this moment the best, but none of them seem to fit. I can't say I was parked in my garage, because my parents' RV is in the way. I can't say I was home, because obviously my truck hasn't been here.

Patrick shakes his head. His face is filled with galaxy-size disappointment.

"He was your *best friend*, Ledger."

I try to hide my inhale. I shove my hands in my pockets and look at my feet. Why is he saying this? I don't know what to say. I don't know what he knows. I don't know *how* he knows.

"We saw your truck at her apartment this morning." His voice is low, and he's not looking at me. It's like he can't stand the person standing across from him. "I was certain it was a coincidence. That someone who has a truck just like yours lived in the building, but when I pulled up next to it to get a better look, I saw Diem's car seat."

"Patrick—"

"Are you sleeping with her?" His voice is monotone and flat in an unnerving way.

I reach an arm over my chest and squeeze my shoulder. My chest is so tight it feels like my lungs are in a vise grip. "I think the three of us need to sit down and talk about this."

"Are you *sleeping* with her?" he repeats, much louder this time.

I run a hand down my face, frustrated that this is how it's coming to a head. I just needed a few hours and I was going to talk to them about it. It would have been so much better that way. "We've all been wrong about her." I say it unconvincingly, because I know nothing I could say right now is going to be absorbed by him. Not when he's this angry.

He releases a half-hearted laugh, but then his face just falls into the saddest frown, and his eyebrows draw apart. "Have we? We've been wrong?" He takes a step closer to me, finally looking me in the eyes. His expression is full of betrayal. "Did she not leave my son to die? Did your best friend not spend his last hours on this earth alone on a deserted road barely breathing because of her?" A tear escapes, and he angrily wipes it away. He's so angry he has to blow out a steady breath to keep from screaming at me.

"It was an accident, Patrick." My voice is almost a whisper. "She loved Scotty. She panicked and made the wrong choice, but she paid for that choice. At what point can we stop blaming her?"

He chooses to answer that question with his fist. He punches me hard in the mouth.

I do nothing, because I feel so guilty that they found out this way I'd let him punch me a million more times, and I still wouldn't defend myself.

"Hey!" My father is running out of my house, heading toward us. Patrick hits me again, right when Grace runs out her front door. My father pushes himself between us before Patrick can get in a third punch.

"What the hell, Pat?" my dad yells.

Patrick doesn't look at him. He's looking at me without even an ounce of regret. I take a step forward to plead with him because I don't want this conversation to end now that it's finally out there, but Diem runs outside. Patrick doesn't see her before he tries to lunge at me again.

"For Christ's sake!" my dad yells, pushing him back. "Stop it!"

Diem starts crying when she takes in the commotion. Grace reaches for her and starts to take Diem in the house, but Diem wants me. She's reaching for me, and I don't know what to do.

"I want to go with Ledger," Diem pleads.

Grace half turns and looks at me. I can tell by the look of betrayal on her face that she might even be hurting more than Patrick is right now.

"Grace, please. Just hear me out."

She turns her back to me and disappears with Diem inside her house. I can hear Diem cry, even after the door closes, and I feel like she just ripped open my chest.

"Don't you dare try to put your choices on us," Patrick says. "You can choose that woman, or you can choose Diem, but don't you *dare* try to make us feel guilty for a choice we came to peace with five years ago. You did this to *yourself*, Ledger." Patrick turns and walks back inside.

My father releases my arm. He moves so that he's in front of me, and I'm sure he's going to try to calm me down, but I don't give him the opportunity. I walk to my truck and I leave.

I go to the bar, but instead of going inside, I beat on the door to Roman's stairwell. I beat constantly until he opens it. He looks confused, but then he sees my busted lip, and he says, "Ah, hell." He steps aside and then follows me up the stairs to his apartment.

I go to the kitchen and wet some paper towels to wipe the blood from my mouth.

"What happened?"

"I spent the night with Kenna. The Landrys found out."

"*Patrick* did that?"

I nod.

Roman's eyes narrow. "You didn't hit him back, did you? He's like sixty years old."

"Of course not, but not because of his age. He's as strong as I am. I didn't hit him back because I deserved this." I pull the paper towel from my mouth, and the whole thing is covered with blood. I walk to the bathroom and inspect my face. My eye looks okay. It'll probably be a little bruised, but my lip is sliced up on the inside. I think he hit me so hard my tooth cut through my lip. "Fuck." Blood is pouring out of my mouth. "I think I need stitches."

Roman looks at my mouth and then winces. "Shit, man." He grabs a washcloth and wets it, then hands it to me and says, "Come on, I'll drive you to the ER."

CHAPTER THIRTY-EIGHT

KENNA

There's a little more bounce in my step as soon as I walk out of the store and spot Ledger's truck across the parking lot.

He sees me exit the store, so he drives across the lot to pick me up. I climb inside the truck and scoot across the seat to give him a kiss. He doesn't turn to face me, so my lips land on his cheek.

I would sit in the middle, but his console is down, and he's got a drink in the cup holder, so I sit in the passenger seat and pull on my seat belt.

He's wearing shades and hasn't looked at me since I got into the truck. I begin to grow concerned, but then he reaches across his console to hold my hand, and it puts me at ease. I was starting to worry that he spent the day regretting last night, but I can feel in the way he squeezes my hand that he's happy to see me. Paranoia is annoying. "Guess what?"

"What?"

"I got a promotion. Cashier. It pays two dollars more an hour."

"That's great, Kenna." He still doesn't look at me, though. He releases my hand and leans an elbow on his door, resting his head against his left hand while he drives with his right. I stare at him for a little bit, wondering why he seems different. Quieter.

My mouth is starting to run dry, so I say, "Can I have a sip of your drink?"

Ledger takes it out of the cup holder and hands it to me. "It's sweet tea. A couple of hours old."

I take a drink and stare at him the whole time. I put the cup back in the holder. "What's wrong?"

He shakes his head. "Nothing."

"Did you talk to them? Did something happen?"

"It's nothing," he says, his voice thick with the lie. I think he recognizes how unconvincing he sounds, because after a pause, he adds, "Let's just get to your place first."

I sink into my seat when he says that. Anxiety rolls through me like a wave.

I don't push him to tell me now because I'm scared to know what has him so stiff. I stare out my window the whole way to my apartment with a gut feeling that this will be the last time Ledger Ward gives me a ride home.

He pulls into the parking spot and kills his engine. I unbuckle and exit the truck, but after I close my door, I realize he's still sitting there. He taps his steering wheel with his thumb, looking lost in thought. After several seconds, he finally opens his door and gets out.

I walk around to meet him and get a better read on him, but I pause as soon as I'm face to face with him.

"Oh, my God." His lip is swollen. I rush up to him, just as he slides the sunglasses on top of his head. That's when I see the black eye. I'm scared to ask, so my voice is timid when I say, "What happened?"

He closes the gap between us and wraps an arm around my shoulders, pulling me against him so that his chin is resting on top of my head. He just tucks me to him for a beat and then gives me a chaste kiss on the side of my head. "Let's go inside." He slips his hand through mine and leads me up the stairs.

Once we're inside my apartment, I barely have the door shut before I ask him again. "What happened, Ledger?"

He leans against the counter and grabs my hand. He pulls me to him and smooths my hair back, looking down at me. "They saw my truck here this morning."

Any morsel of hope I left with this morning immediately dissipates. "He *hit* you?"

Ledger nods, and I have to back away and compose myself because I feel nauseous. I want to cry, because how mad would Patrick have to be to hit someone? The way Scotty and Ledger have talked about him, he doesn't seem like the type to lose his temper easily. Which means . . . they hate me. They hate me so much the thought of Ledger and me together made a generally kind, calm man lose his mind on him.

I was right. They're making him choose.

The panic begins spreading from my chest to all the other parts of my body. I take a sip of water, and then I pick up Ivy, who has been meowing at my feet. I pet her. I try to find comfort in her presence. She's my only constant now, because this story is ending exactly how I predicted it. No plot twists at all.

I came here with one goal, and that was to try to forge a relationship with the Landrys and with my daughter. But they've made it very clear that it's not something they want. Maybe it's just not something they can emotionally handle.

I put Ivy back on the floor and then fold my arms across my chest. I can't even look at Ledger when I ask him this question. "Did they ask you to stop seeing me?"

He exhales, and his sigh is everything I need to know. I try to hold it together, but I just want him to leave. Or maybe *I* need to leave.

This apartment, this town, this state. I want as far away from my daughter as I can get, because the closer I am to her without being able to see her, the more tempting it becomes to just go to their house and take her. I'm desperate enough that if I stay here too much longer, I might do something stupid.

"I need money."

Ledger looks at me like he didn't understand the question, or he can't process why I need money.

"I need to move, Ledger. I can pay you back, but I need to leave, and I don't have enough money to get a new place. I can't stay here."

"Wait," he says, stepping toward me. "You're leaving? You're giving up?"

His choice of words makes me angry. "I'd say I tried pretty damn hard. They have a restraining order against me—I wouldn't call that giving up."

"What about us? You're just going to walk away?"

"Don't be an asshole. This is harder for me than it is for you. At least you still get Diem in the end."

He grips my shoulders, but I look away from him, so he moves his hands to the sides of my head. He tilts my face and directs my focus back to his. "Kenna, don't. *Please.* Wait a few weeks. Let's just see what happens."

"We know what happens. We'll keep seeing each other in secret, and we'll fall in love, but they won't change their minds and I'll *still* have to leave, but it'll hurt a hell of a lot worse in a few weeks than if I were to just leave right now." I walk to the closet and grab my suitcase. I open it and toss it on the inflatable mattress and start throwing my shit in it. I can take a bus to the next town and then stay in a hotel until I figure out where to go. "I need money," I say again. "I'll pay you back every cent, Ledger. I promise."

Ledger stomps over to me and shuts my suitcase. "Stop it." He makes me turn and face him by pulling me in and wrapping me up in his arms. "Stop. *Please.*"

We're too late. It already hurts so bad.

I press my hands against his shirt and grip it in my fists. I start to cry. I can't bear the thought of not being around him, not seeing his smile, not feeling his support. I already miss him even though I'm still standing right here in his arms. But as much as the idea of leaving him hurts, I think my tears are for my daughter. They're always for her.

"Ledger." I say his name quietly, and then I lift my head from his chest and look up at him. "The only thing you can do at this point is go over there and apologize to them. Diem needs you. As much as it hurts, if they can't move past what I did to them, it isn't your job to repair or mend what's broken inside of them. It's your job to support them, and you can't do that with me in your life."

His jaw is clenched. It looks like he's trying not to cry. But it also looks like he knows I'm right. He takes a step away from me and then opens his wallet. "You want my credit card?" he asks, pulling it out. He removes several twenty-dollar bills too. He seems so upset and mad and defeated as he angrily yanks stuff out of his wallet. He tosses his credit card and the cash on the counter, and then he steps toward me, kisses me on the forehead, and leaves.

He slams the door as he goes.

I lean forward and press my elbows into the counter, and I hold my head in my hands and I cry even harder, because I'm angry I allowed myself to get my hopes up. It's been well over five years since it happened. If they were ever going to forgive me, they'd have done it by now. They're just not the forgiving type.

There are people who find peace in forgiveness, and then there are others who look at forgiveness as a betrayal. To them, forgiving me would feel like betraying their own son. I can only hope they change their minds someday, but until then, this is my life. This is where it's led me.

This is where I start over. *Again.* And I'm going to have to do it without Ledger or his encouragement or his belief in me. I'm sobbing now, but I'm still able to hear the front door when it swings back open.

I lift my head as he slams the door shut and strides across the room. He lifts me, setting me down on the counter so that we're eye to eye, and then he kisses me with a sad desperation, as if it's the last kiss he'll ever give me.

After breaking our kiss, he looks at me with determination when he says, "I am going to be the best person I can be for your daughter. I promise. I'm going to give her the best life, and when she asks about her mother, I'm going to tell her what a wonderful person you are. I'll make sure she grows up knowing how much you love her."

I'm a fucking mess now, because I'm going to miss him so, so much.

He presses his swollen mouth to mine, and I kiss him gently because I don't want to hurt him. Then our foreheads meet. It looks like he's struggling to keep his composure. "I'm sorry I couldn't do more for you." He starts to back away, pulling apart from me, and it hurts too much to watch him go, so I stare at the floor.

There's something beneath my feet. It looks like a business card, so I slide off the counter and pick it up. It's Ledger's snow cone punch card. It must have fallen out of his wallet when he took everything out of it.

"Ledger, wait." I meet him at the door and hand him his card. "You need this," I say, sniffling back tears. "You're so close to a free snow cone."

He laughs through his pain, taking the card from me. But then he winces and drops his forehead to mine. "I'm so angry at them, Kenna. This isn't fair."

It isn't. But it isn't up to us. I kiss him one last time, and then I squeeze his hand and look at him pleadingly. "Don't hate them. Okay? They're giving my little girl a good life. Please don't hate them."

He barely nods, but it's a nod. When he lets go of my hand, I don't want to watch him leave, so I go to my bathroom and close the door.

A few seconds later, I hear my apartment door shut.

I slide to the floor and fall apart.

CHAPTER THIRTY-NINE

LEDGER

I don't even go into my house when I get back home. I walk straight to Patrick and Grace's front door and I knock.

It was never a choice. Diem will always be the most important girl in my life, no matter what or who or when. But that doesn't mean I'm not torn the fuck up right now.

It's Patrick who opens the door, but Grace quickly joins him. I think she's afraid there might be another fight. They both look a little surprised to see the state of my injuries, but Patrick offers up no apologies. I don't expect him to.

I look them both in the eye. "Diem wanted to show me her turtle."

The sentence is so simple, but I'm saying so much. That sentence translates to, *"I chose Diem. Let's go back to how things were before."*

Patrick eyes me for a moment, but then Grace steps aside and says, "She's in her bedroom."

It's forgiveness and acceptance, but it's not the forgiveness I really want from them. But I take it.

Diem is on her floor when I get to her doorway. The turtle is a foot away from her, and she's trying to coax it toward her with a green LEGO.

"So, this is your turtle, huh?"

Diem sits up and beams a smile. "Yep." She picks him up, and we meet at her bed. I sit down and lean against the headboard. She crawls to the middle of the bed and hands me the turtle, then curls up at my side. I place him on my leg, and he starts to crawl toward my knee.

"Why did NoNo hit you?" She's looking at my lip when she asks this.

"Sometimes adults make bad decisions, D. I said something that hurt his feelings, and he got upset. It's not his fault. It was my fault."

"Are you mad at him?"

"No."

"Is NoNo still mad?"

More than likely. "No." I want to change the subject. "What's your turtle's name?"

Diem picks him up and lays him on her lap. "Ledger."

I laugh. "You're naming the turtle after me?"

"Yes. Because I love you." She says that in the sweetest voice, and it makes my heart clench. I wish Kenna could be the recipient of Diem's words right now.

I kiss her on top of the head. "I love you, too, D."

I put her turtle in its aquarium and then I crawl back onto her bed and stay with her until she nods off. And then I stay a little while longer just to be certain she's asleep.

I know Patrick and Grace love her, and I know they love me, so the last thing they would ever do is separate the two of us. They can be angry, but they also know how much Diem loves me, so even if the three of us can't work our shit out, I know I'll always be a huge part of

Diem's life. And as long as I'm a part of Diem's life, I'm going to fight for what's best for her.

I should have been doing it all along.

And what's best for Diem is having her mother in her life.

It's why I did what I did before I left Kenna's apartment.

As soon as Kenna closed her bathroom door, I closed her apartment door and pretended to leave. Instead, I grabbed her phone. The password was an easy guess—Diem's birthday. I opened her Google Docs and found the file with all the letters she's written to Scotty, and I forwarded the file to my email address before sneaking out.

I stay in Diem's bedroom and pull up Patrick and Grace's printer network on my phone. I open my email and find the letter Kenna read to me, and I skip over all the rest of the letters she's written Scotty. I've already violated her privacy enough by using her phone and forwarding these to myself. I don't plan to read any of the others unless she tells me I can someday.

Tonight, I just need one of the letters.

I hit print, and I close my eyes and listen for the sound of the printer to activate in Patrick's office across the hall.

I wait until it finishes printing, and then I sneak out of Diem's bed and wait a moment in her room to make sure I didn't wake her up. She's sound asleep, so I slip out of her room and into Patrick's office. I grab the letter off the printer and make sure all of it printed.

"Wish me luck, Scotty," I whisper.

When I emerge from the hallway, they're both in the kitchen. Grace is looking at her phone, and Patrick is emptying the dishwasher. They both look up at the same time.

"I have something I need to say, and I really don't want to yell, but I will if I have to, so I think we should go outside because I don't want to wake up Diem."

Patrick closes the dishwasher. "We don't really want to hear what you have to say, Ledger." He motions toward the door. "You should go."

I have a lot of empathy for them, but I'm afraid I've just met my limit. A wave of heat climbs up my neck, and I try to push down my anger, but it's so hard when I've given them so much. I recall the words Kenna said to me right before I left her. *Please don't hate them.*

"I've given my life to that little girl," I say. "You owe this to me. I'm not leaving your property until we talk about this." I walk out the front door and wait in their yard. A minute passes. Maybe two. I take a seat on their front patio. They're either going to call the police or they're going to come outside or they're going to go to bed and ignore me. I'll wait here until one of those three things happens.

It's several minutes before I hear the door open behind me. I stand up and spin around. Patrick walks out of the house just far enough to give Grace space in the doorway. Neither of them looks open to what I'm about to say, but I have to say it anyway. There will never be a good time for this conversation. There will never be a good time to take the side of the girl who ruined their lives.

I feel like the words I'm about to say are the most important words that will ever come from me. I wish I were more prepared. Kenna deserves better than to have me and my plea be the only hope left between her and Diem.

I blow out an unsteady breath. "Every decision I make is for Diem. I ended my engagement with a woman I loved because I wasn't sure she would be good enough for that little girl. That should tell you that I would never put my own happiness before Diem's. I know you both know that, and I also know you're just trying to protect yourselves from the pain Kenna's actions caused. But you're taking the worst moment of Kenna's life and you're making that moment who she is. That isn't fair. It isn't fair to Kenna. It isn't fair to Diem. I'm starting to wonder if it's even fair to Scotty."

I hold up the pages in my hand.

"She writes letters to him. To Scotty. She's been doing it for five years. This is the only one I've read, but it was enough to change my entire opinion of her." I pause, and then backtrack on my words. "Actually, that's not true. I forgave Kenna before I even knew the contents of the letter. But the second she read this out loud to me, I realized she's been hurting just as much as all of us have. And we're slowly killing her by continuing to drag out her pain." I squeeze my forehead and put even more emphasis on the words I'm about to speak. "We are keeping a *mother* from her *child*. That's not okay. Scotty would be so mad at us."

It grows quiet when I stop speaking. Too quiet. It's like they aren't even breathing. I hand Grace the letter. "It'll be hard to read. But I'm not asking you to read it because I'm in love with Kenna. I'm asking you to read it because your *son* was in love with her."

Grace starts to cry. Patrick still won't look me in the eye, but he reaches for his wife and pulls her to him.

"I've given the last five years of my life to you guys. All I'm asking for in return is twenty minutes. It probably won't even take you that long to read the letter. After you read it, and take time to process it, we'll talk. And I'll respect whatever decisions the two of you make. I swear I will. But please, *please* give me the next twenty minutes. You owe Diem the opportunity to have another person in her life who will love her as much as Scotty would have loved her."

I don't give them an opening to argue or hand the letter back to me. I immediately turn and walk to my house and disappear inside it. I don't even look out the window to see if they've gone inside, or if they're reading the letter.

I'm so nervous I'm shaking.

I look for my parents and find them in the backyard. My father has items from the RV spread out across the grass, and he's using the water hose to clean them. My mother is sitting in the patio love seat reading a book.

I take a seat next to her. She looks up from her book and smiles, but when she sees the look on my face, she closes the paperback.

I drop my head in my hands and I start to cry. I can't help it. I feel like the lives of everyone I love are hanging on this moment, and it's fucking overwhelming.

"Ledger," my mother says. "Oh, honey." She wraps her arm around me and hugs me.

CHAPTER FORTY

KENNA

I woke up with a migraine due to how much I cried last night.

I expected Ledger to text me or call me, but he never did. Not that I want him to. A clean break is better than a messy one.

I hate that my choices from that one night years ago have somehow created another casualty all these years later. How long will the after-shocks from that night continue? Will I feel the ramifications forever?

Sometimes I wonder if we're all born with equal amounts of good and evil. What if no one person is more or less malevolent than another, and that we all just release our bad at different times, in different ways?

Maybe some of us expel most of our bad behavior as toddlers, while some of us are absolute horrors during the teenage years. And then maybe there are those who expend very little malice until they're adults, and even then, it just seeps out slowly. A little bit every day until we die.

But then that would mean there are people like me. Those who release their bad all at once—in one horrific night.

When you get all your evil out at once, the impact is much bigger than when it seeps out slowly. The destruction you leave behind covers a much bigger circumference on the map and takes up a much larger space in people's memories.

I don't want to believe that there are good people and bad people, and no in-between people. I don't want to believe I'm worse than anyone else, as if there's a bucket full of evil somewhere within me that continues to refill every time it runs empty. I don't want to believe I'm capable of repeating behavior I've displayed in the past, but even after all these years, people are still suffering because of me.

Despite the devastation I've left in my wake, I am not a bad person. *I am not a bad person.*

It took five years of weekly therapy sessions to help me realize this. I only recently learned how to say it out loud. "I am not a bad person."

I've been listening to the playlist Ledger made me all morning. It really is just a bunch of songs that have nothing to do with anything sad. I don't know how he managed to find this many songs. It had to take him forever.

I slide Mary Anne's headphones over my ears, and I put the playlist on shuffle and start to clean my apartment. I want my security deposit back when I figure out where I'm moving to, so I don't need a reason for Ruth not to refund it to me. I'll leave the apartment ten times cleaner than I found it.

I clean for about ten minutes when I start to hear a beat in the song that doesn't belong. It takes me way too long to realize the beat is actually not in the song.

It's a knock.

I slip off my headphones and hear it even louder this time. Someone is definitely knocking at my front door. My heart rate speeds up because I don't want it to be Ledger, but I need it to be Ledger. One more kiss wouldn't break me. Maybe.

I tiptoe toward the door and look through the peephole.

It's Ledger.

I press my forehead to the door and try to make the right decision. He's having a weak moment, but I shouldn't do this. His weak moments will be my downfall if I cater to them. We'll just go back and forth until we're both completely broken.

I open my texts to him on my phone and type out, I'm not opening the door.

I watch him read it through the peephole, but his expression is unwavering. He looks right into the peephole and points down to the doorknob.

Fuck. *Why did he have to point?* I unlock the dead bolt and open the door just two inches. "Don't kiss me or touch me or say anything sweet."

Ledger smiles. "I'll do my best."

I open the door cautiously, but he doesn't even try to come inside once I have the door open. He stands up straight and says, "Do you have a minute?"

I nod. "Yeah. Come in."

He shakes his head. "Not for me." His attention moves away from me, and he points inside my apartment, but then he steps away from the door.

Grace walks into my line of sight.

I immediately slap my hand over my mouth, because I wasn't expecting her and I haven't been face to face with her since before Scotty died and I had no idea it would knock the breath out of me.

I don't know what it means. I refuse to let myself think this means anything at all, but there's too much hope inside me to keep buried in her presence.

I back into my apartment, but tears are spilling from my eyes. There's so much I want to say to her. So many apologies. So many promises.

Grace steps inside my apartment, and Ledger stays outside but closes the door to give us privacy. I grab a paper towel and wipe at my eyes. It's pointless. I don't think I've cried like this since I gave birth to Diem and watched them take her away from me.

"I'm not here to upset you," Grace says. Her voice is gentle. So is her expression.

I shake my head. "It's not . . . I'm sorry. I need a minute before I can . . . talk."

Grace motions toward the sofa. "Can we sit?"

I nod, and we both take a seat on the couch. Grace watches me for a moment, probably judging my tears, wondering if they're real or forced.

She reaches into her pocket and pulls something out. At first I think it's a handkerchief, but upon closer inspection, I realize it's a small black velvet bag. Grace hands me the bag, and I have no idea why.

I pull the strings to loosen the opening to the velvet bag, and then I dump the contents into my palm.

I gasp. "What? *How?*" I'm holding the ring I fell in love with all those years ago when Scotty took me to the antique store. The four-thousand-dollar gold ring with the pink stone that he couldn't afford. I've never told anyone that story, so I'm extremely confused as to how Grace is in possession of this ring. "How do you even have this?"

"Scotty called me the day you two saw the ring. He said he wasn't ready to propose to you, but that he already knew what ring he was going to propose with when the time came. He couldn't afford it, but he was afraid someone else was going to buy it before he got the chance. We let him borrow the money. He gave me the ring and made me promise to keep it in a safe place until he could pay us back."

My hands are shaking as I put the ring on my finger. *I can't believe Scotty did that.*

Grace releases a quick rush of air. "I'll be honest, Kenna. I didn't want that ring after he died. And I didn't want you to have it because I was so mad at you. But when we found out Diem was a girl, I decided to hold on to it. Just in case I wanted to pass it on to her someday. But after giving it some thought . . . that's really not my decision to make. I want you to have it. Scotty bought it for you."

There's too much coursing through me to process this, so it takes me a moment to recover. I shake my head. I'm too scared to believe her. I don't even allow the words to sink in. "Thank you."

Grace reaches over and squeezes my hand, prompting me to look at her. "I promised Ledger I wouldn't tell you this, but . . . he gave us one of the letters you wrote to Scotty."

I'm shaking my head even though she isn't finished talking. *How did Ledger get one of those letters? Which one did he give them?*

"He made me read it last night." Her expression falls. "After hearing your version of events, I was even more devastated and angry than I was before I read it. It was so hard . . . hearing all the details. I cried all night. But this morning when I woke up, it was as if an overwhelming sensation of peace had washed over me. Today was the first morning I didn't wake up angry at you." She wipes at the tears now sliding down her face. "All these years, I assumed your silence in the courtroom was indifference. I assumed you left him in that car because you only cared for yourself and didn't want to get in legal trouble. Maybe I assumed all those things because it was easier to have someone to blame for such a horrific and pointless loss. And I know your grief shouldn't bring me peace, Kenna. But it's so much easier to understand you now than when I assumed you never grieved at all." Grace reaches toward a strand of hair that's fallen loose from my ponytail, and she brushes it gently behind my ear. It's something a mother would do, and I don't understand it. I don't know how she can go from hating me to forgiving me in such a short amount of time, so I continue to be wary of this moment. But the tears in her eyes feel like the truth. "I am so sorry, Kenna." She says that with such sincerity. "I'm responsible for keeping you from your daughter for five years, and there's no excuse for that. The only thing I can do is make sure you don't go another day without knowing her."

My hand is trembling when I bring it to my chest. "I . . . I get to meet her?"

Grace nods, and then she hugs me when I fall apart. She runs a soothing hand over the back of my head and allows me several minutes to absorb everything that's happening.

This is everything I've ever wanted, and it's coming at me all at once. It's both physically and emotionally overwhelming. I've had dreams like this before. Dreams where Grace shows up to forgive me and lets me meet Diem, but then I wake up alone and realize it was a cruel nightmare. *Please let this be real.*

"Ledger is probably dying not knowing what's going on in here." She stands up and walks to the door to open it for him.

Ledger's eyes search frantically until they land on mine. When I smile at him, he immediately relaxes, as if my smile is the only thing that mattered in this moment.

He pulls Grace in for a hug first. I hear him whisper, "Thank you," against her ear.

She looks at me before she leaves my apartment. "I'm making lasagna tonight. I want you to come for dinner."

I agree with a nod. Grace leaves, and Ledger is wrapping me in his arms before she even closes the door.

"Thank you, thank you, thank you." I say it over and over, because I know this would never have happened if it weren't for him. "Thank you." I kiss him. "Thank you." When I finally stop thanking and kissing him long enough to pull back and look him in the eye, I see he's crying too. It fills me with a sense of gratitude like I've never known.

I am so grateful for him. *To* him.

This might be the exact moment I fall in love with Ledger Ward.

"I'm about to be sick."

"Want me to pull over?"

I shake my head. "No. Drive faster."

Ledger squeezes my knee reassuringly.

It was torture having to wait until this afternoon to make our way to Patrick and Grace's house. I wanted him to take me to Diem as soon as Grace left my apartment, but I want everything to be on their terms. I'll be as patient as I need to be.

I'm going to respect their rules. I'll respect their timeline, and their choices, and their wishes. I'm going to show them as much respect as I know they've shown my daughter.

I know they're good people. Scotty loved them. They're just also *hurt* people, so I respect the time they needed to come to this decision.

I'm nervous I'm going to do something wrong. Say something wrong. The only other time I've been inside their house was such a series of missteps, and I need this time to be different because there's so much at stake.

We pull into Ledger's driveway, but we don't immediately get out of the truck. He gives me a pep talk and kisses me about ten times, but then I become more nervous and excited than I've ever been, and the emotions all start to run together. If I don't get it over with, I might explode.

He holds my hand tightly in his as we cross the street, and walk across grass Diem has played on, and knock on the door to the house Diem lives in.

Don't cry. Don't cry. Don't cry.

I'm squeezing Ledger's hand like I'm in the middle of an intense contraction.

The door finally opens, and standing right in front of me is Patrick. He looks nervous, but he somehow smiles through it. He pulls me in for a hug, and it isn't just a forced hug because I'm standing in front of him, or because his wife encouraged him to hug me.

It's a hug full of so many things. Enough things that when Patrick pulls away, he has to wipe at his eyes. "Diem is out back with her turtle," he says, motioning down the hallway.

There are no harsh words from him, no negative energy. I don't know if now is the right time to apologize, but since Patrick is pointing us toward Diem's location, I feel like they want to save whatever sits between the three of us for later.

Ledger holds my hand as we walk into the house. I've been in the house before and I've been in the backyard before, so there's a sense of familiarity that's comforting. But everything else is frightening. *What if she doesn't like me? What if she's mad at me?*

Grace appears from the kitchen, and I pause before we head to the backyard. I look at Grace. "What have you told her? About my absence? I just want to make sure . . ."

Grace shakes her head. "We really haven't talked to her about you at all. She asked once why she didn't live with her mother, and I told her your car wasn't big enough."

I laugh nervously. "What?"

Grace shrugs. "I panicked. I didn't know what to say."

My car isn't big enough? I can work with that. In my mind, I had feared they had poisoned her against me. I should have known better.

"We thought we'd leave the rest up to you," Patrick says. "We weren't sure how much you wanted her to know."

I nod and smile and try not to cry. I look at Ledger, and he's like an anchor by my side, keeping me steady. "Will you come with me?"

We walk toward the back door. I can see her sitting in the grass. I watch her from the screen door for a couple of minutes, wanting to take in everything about her before whatever comes next. I'm scared of what comes next. Terrified, really. This is almost the exact same feeling as being in labor with her. I was terrified, in uncharted territory, but also full of more hope and excitement and love than I'd ever felt.

Ledger eventually gives me an encouraging nudge, so I open the door. Diem looks up and sees Ledger and me standing on the back porch. She gives me a quick glance, but when her eyes land on Ledger, she lights up. She runs to him, and he catches her in his arms.

I get a whiff of strawberry shampoo.

I have a daughter who smells like strawberries.

Ledger sits on the back porch swing with Diem and points to the empty seat next to him, so I take a seat with them. Diem is in his lap, looking at me as she curls up to Ledger.

"Diem, this is my friend Kenna."

Diem smiles at me, and it almost sends me to the floor. "Do you want to see my turtle?" she asks, perking up.

"I'd love to."

Her tiny little hand grips two of my fingers, and she slides off Ledger and pulls me. I glance at Ledger as I stand, and he gives me a reassuring nod. Diem takes me to the grass, and she plops down next to her turtle.

I lie down on the other side of her turtle so that I'm facing Diem. "What's his name?"

"Ledger." She giggles and holds up the turtle. "He looks just like him."

I laugh, and she's trying to get her turtle to come out of his shell, but I can't stop staring at her. Seeing her on video is one experience, but getting to be near her and feel her energy is like a rebirth.

"Want to see my jungle gym? I got it for my birthday—I turn five next week." Diem is running toward her jungle gym, so I follow her. I glance back at Ledger, and he's still sitting on the porch swing, watching us.

Diem pokes her head out of the jungle gym and says, "Ledger, can you put Ledger in his tank so he doesn't get lost?"

"Sure will," he says, standing.

Diem grabs my hand and pulls me inside the jungle gym, where she sits down in the center of it. I feel more comfortable here. No one can see us, and that puts me a little more at ease knowing people aren't judging how I interact with her in this moment.

"This used to be my daddy's," Diem says. "NoNo and Ledger put it back together for me."

"I knew your daddy."

"Were you his friend?"

I smile. "I was his girlfriend. I loved him very much."

Diem giggles. "I didn't know my daddy had a *girlfriend*."

I see so much of Scotty in her right now. In that laugh. I have to look away from her face because the tears start to fall.

Diem notices my tears, though. "Why are you sad? Do you miss him?"

I nod, wiping away my tears. "I do miss him, but that's not why I'm crying. I'm crying because I'm so happy I finally get to meet you."

Diem cocks her head and says, *"Why?"*

She's three whole feet away from me, and I just want to hold her and hug her. I pat the spot right in front of me. "Come closer. I want to tell you something."

Diem crawls toward me and sits with her legs crossed.

"I know we've never met before, but . . ." I don't even know how to say this, so I just say it in the simplest way. "I'm your mother."

Diem's eyes fill with something, but I don't know what her expressions mean yet. I don't know if that's surprise or curiosity. "Really?"

I smile at her. "I am. You grew inside my tummy. And then when you were born, Nana and NoNo took care of you for me because I couldn't."

"Did you get a bigger car?"

I release a laugh. I'm glad they gave me that tidbit of information, or I would have no idea what she's referring to. "I actually don't have a car anymore. But I will soon. I just couldn't wait to meet you, so Ledger gave me a ride. I've been wanting to meet you for so long."

Diem doesn't have much of a reaction. She just smiles. And then she crawls across the grass and starts flipping tic-tac-toe squares that make up a part of the wall of the jungle gym. "You should come to my T-ball game. It's my last one." She spins one of the letters on the wall.

"I would love to come watch you play T-ball."

"Someday I'm gonna do that thing with the swords, though," Diem says. "Hey, do you know how to play this game?"

I nod and move close to her so I can show her how to play tic-tac-toe.

I realize that this moment isn't nearly as monumental to Diem as it is to me. I've played out a million scenarios in my head of how this would go, and in every scenario, Diem was either sad or angry that it took me so long to be a part of her life.

But she truly didn't even know that I was missing.

I'm so grateful for that. All these years of worry and devastation have all been one sided, which means Diem has been whole and happy and fulfilled.

I couldn't have asked for a better outcome. It's like I just get to slip into her life without so much as a ripple.

Diem grabs my hand and says, "I don't want to play this, let's go to the swings." She abandons the game, and we crawl out of the center of the jungle gym. She climbs into a swing and says, "I forgot your name."

"It's Kenna." I say that with a smile because I know I'll never have to lie to anyone about my name again.

"Will you push me?"

I push her on the swing, and she starts telling me about a movie Ledger took her to see recently.

Ledger walks out onto the porch and sees us talking. He comes over to us and stands behind me, wrapping his arms around me. He kisses the side of my head, right when Diem turns and looks at us. "Gross!"

Ledger kisses the side of my head again and says, "Get used to it, D."

Ledger takes over pushing Diem's swing, and I sit down in the swing next to her and watch them. Diem tips her head back and looks at Ledger. "Are you gonna marry my mom?"

I should probably have a reaction to the marriage part of that question, but my brain only focuses on the fact that she just said *my mom.*

"I don't know. We still need to get to know each other better." Ledger looks at me and smiles. "Maybe one of these days I'll be worthy enough to marry her."

"What does *worthy* mean?" she asks.

"It means good enough."

"You're good enough," Diem says. "That's why I named my turtle Ledger." She tilts her head back again and looks at him. "I'm thirsty, will you bring me a juice?"

"Go get it yourself," he says.

I get out of the swing. "I'll get you a juice."

I hear Ledger mutter to her, "You're so rotten," as I walk away.

Diem laughs. "I am not!"

When I go inside, I watch them from the back door for a moment. They're adorable together. She's adorable. I'm scared I'm about to wake up and realize none of this actually happened, but I know it's happening. And I know I'll eventually embrace that I deserve this. Maybe after I finally have a real conversation with the Landrys.

I walk into the kitchen to find Grace cooking. "She wants some juice," I say as I enter.

Grace's hands are full of chopped tomatoes, and she drops them into a salad. "It's in the fridge."

I grab a juice and observe Grace as she prepares dinner. I want to be more helpful and interactive with her than I was the first time Scotty brought me to this house. "How can I help?"

Grace smiles at me. "You don't have to. Go spend time with your daughter."

I start to walk out of the kitchen, but my steps feel so heavy. I have so much I want to say to Grace that I didn't have the chance to say to her earlier today at my apartment. I turn around, and *I'm sorry* is on the tip of my tongue, but I feel like if I open my mouth, I'll cry.

My eyes meet Grace's, and she can see the agony in my expression.

"Grace . . ." My voice is a whisper.

She immediately walks over to me and pulls me in for a hug.

It's an amazing hug. A forgiving hug. "Hey," she says, soothingly. "Hey, listen to me." She pulls back, and we're about the same height, so we're eye to eye when she takes the juice from me and sets it aside. Then she squeezes both of my hands reassuringly. "We go forward," she says. "That's it. It's that simple. I forgive you and you forgive me, and we go forward together and give that little girl the best life we can give her. Okay?"

I nod, because I can do that. I forgive them. I've always forgiven them.

It's myself I've been hard on. But I think I've reached the point that forgiving myself finally feels okay.

So I do.

You're forgiven, Kenna.

CHAPTER FORTY-ONE

LEDGER

She fits. It's surreal and, to be honest, a little overwhelming. We just finished eating dinner, but we're all still sitting at the table. Diem is curled up in my lap, and I'm sitting next to Kenna.

She seemed nervous when we first sat down to dinner, but she's eased up a lot. Especially after Patrick started telling stories, giving Kenna a highlight reel of Diem's life. He's telling her the story of when Diem broke her arm six months ago.

"She spent the first two weeks thinking she had to wear the cast forever. None of us thought to tell her that breaks heal, and Diem assumed when a person broke a bone, it stayed broken for good."

"Oh, no," Kenna says, laughing. She looks down at Diem and runs a soothing hand over her head. "You poor thing."

Diem reaches a hand toward Kenna, and she accepts it. Diem effortlessly slips off my lap and onto Kenna's. It happens so fast and quietly. Diem tucks herself into Kenna, and Kenna wraps her arms around Diem like it's the most natural thing in the world.

We're all staring at them, but Kenna doesn't notice because her cheek is pressed against the top of Diem's head. I swear I'm about to lose it right here at the table. I clear my throat and push my chair back.

I don't even excuse myself because I feel like my voice will crack if I try to speak, so I silently leave the table and walk out back.

I want to give the four of them privacy. I've been somewhat of a buffer for all of them today, but I want them to interact without me there. I want Kenna to feel comfortable with them and not have to lean on me for that comfort, because it's important she have a relationship with them outside of me.

I could tell Patrick and Grace were pleasantly surprised at how different she is from what we all expected her to be.

It proves that time, distance, and devastation allow people enough opportunity to craft villains out of people they don't even know. But Kenna was never a villain. She was a victim. We all were.

The sun hasn't set yet, but it's getting close to eight, and that's Diem's bedtime. I'm sure Kenna is nowhere near ready to leave, but I'm looking forward to the aftermath of today. I want to get her alone and be near her while she processes what I'm sure has been the best day of her life.

The back door opens, and Patrick walks onto the porch. He doesn't sit down in a chair. He leans against one of the pillars and stares out over the backyard.

When I left him and Grace alone with the letter last night, I was expecting some sort of immediate reaction. I wasn't sure what it would be, but I thought I'd get something. A text, a phone call, a knock at my front door.

I got nothing.

Two hours after I left them, I finally worked up the courage to look out my window at their house, and all their lights were out.

I've never felt as hopeless as I felt in that moment. I thought my efforts had failed, but this morning, after an entire night of insomnia, I heard a knock at my door.

When I opened it, Grace was standing there without Diem or Patrick. Her eyes were puffy like she'd been crying. "I want to meet Kenna." That's all she said.

We got in my truck, and I took her to Kenna's apartment not knowing what to expect, or if she was going to accept Kenna or reject Kenna. When we arrived at Kenna's place, Grace turned to me before exiting my truck, and she said, "Are you in love with her?"

There was absolutely no hesitation when I nodded.

"Why?"

There was no hesitation after that question either. "You'll see. She makes it a hell of a lot easier to love her than hate her."

Grace sat in silence for a moment before finally getting out of my truck. She seemed almost as nervous as I was. We walked upstairs together, and she told me she wanted some time alone with Kenna. As hard as it was not knowing what was being said between them inside that apartment, it isn't nearly as hard as not knowing what Patrick thinks about all this.

We haven't had a chance to talk about it at all. I'm guessing that's why he's out here.

My hope is that he and Grace are on the same page, but they might not be. He might only be accepting Kenna because Grace needs him to.

"What are you thinking?" I ask him.

Patrick scratches his jaw, mulling over my question. He answers without looking directly at me. "If you would have asked me that question when you and Kenna arrived a few hours ago, I would have told you I'm still pissed at you. And that I'm not sorry for hitting you." He pauses and sits down on the top porch step. He clasps his hands together between his knees and looks over at me. "But that changed when I saw you with her. When I saw the way you looked at her. The way your eyes teared up when Diem crawled onto her lap at the dinner table." Patrick shakes his head. "I've known you since you were Diem's age, Ledger. Not one time in all the years I've known you have you ever given me a single reason to doubt you. If you're telling me Kenna is worthy of Diem, then I believe you. The *least* I can do is believe you."

Fuck.

I look away from him and wipe at my eyes. I still don't know what to do with all these fucking feelings. There have been so many since Kenna returned.

I lean back in my chair without a clue how to respond to him. Maybe I don't. Maybe his words are enough for this conversation.

We sit in silence for a minute or two. It feels different from the bouts of silence I've sat through with him before. This time, the quiet is comfortable and peaceful and not at all sad.

"Holy shit," Patrick says.

I look over at him, but his focus is on something in the backyard. I follow his line of sight until . . . *no. No way.*

"I'll be damned," I say quietly. "Is that . . . is that a fucking *pigeon*?"

It is. It's an actual pigeon. A real live white-and-gray pigeon just walking around in the backyard like this isn't the most miraculous timing a bird has ever had in the history of birds.

Patrick laughs. It's a laugh full of bewilderment.

He laughs so much it makes me laugh.

But he doesn't cry. It's the first time a reminder of Scotty doesn't make him cry, and I feel like this is huge. Not only because the chances of this random pigeon landing in this backyard at this very moment are probably one in a billion, but because Patrick and I have never had a serious conversation related to Scotty that didn't end in me sneaking away so he could cry alone.

But he laughs, and that's all he does, and for the first time since Scotty died I feel a sense of hope for him. For all of us.

The only other time Kenna has been inside my house was right after she showed up on this street unannounced. That wasn't a good experience for either of us, so when I open my front door and guide her inside, I want her to feel welcome.

I'm looking forward to getting Kenna all to myself tonight, in an actual bed. The few times we've been together have been damn near perfect, but I've always felt she deserved better than an inflatable mattress, or my truck, or a hardwood floor.

I want to show her around, but my need to kiss her is stronger. As soon as I close the front door, I pull her to me. I kiss her the way I've been wanting to kiss her all night. It's the first kiss without a little sadness or fear in it.

This is my favorite kiss so far. It goes on for so long I forget about showing her around the house, and I pick her up and take her straight to my bed. When I lower her to the mattress, she sprawls out and sighs.

"Oh, my *God*, Ledger. It's so soft."

I reach to the remote next to my bed and turn the massage mode on so the bed vibrates. It makes her groan, but when I try to lower myself on top of her, she kicks me to the side. "I need a minute to fully appreciate your bed," she says, closing her eyes.

I sidle up next to her and stare at the smile on her face. I lift a hand and gently outline her lips, barely touching them. Then I trace my fingertips across her jaw and down her neck.

"I want to tell you something," I say quietly.

She opens her eyes and smiles gently, waiting for me to speak.

I bring my hand back up to her face and touch her impeccable mouth again. "I've spent the last couple of years trying to be a good role model for Diem, so I've read a few books on feminism. I learned that putting too much focus on a girl's looks can be damaging, so instead of telling Diem how pretty I think she is, I put the focus on all the things that matter, like how smart she is and how strong she is. I've tried treating you the same way. It's why I've never complimented your looks before, or told you how fucking beautiful I think you are, but I'm glad I've never told you before this moment, because you've never been more beautiful than you are right now." I kiss the tip of her nose. "Happiness looks good on you, Kenna."

She touches my cheek and smiles up at me. "Thanks to you."

I shake my head. "I'm not responsible for tonight. I'm not the one who saved up every penny and moved to this town and walked to work every day to try and—"

"I love you, Ledger." She says it so effortlessly, like it's the easiest thing she's ever said. "You don't have to say it back. I just want you to know how much you—"

"I love you too."

She grins and then presses her lips firmly to mine. I try to kiss her back, but she's still smiling against my mouth. As much as I want to take off her clothes and whisper *I love you* repeatedly against her skin, I'd much rather just hold her for a while and give us both time to process everything that happened today.

So much happened today. And there's still so much left. "I'm not moving," I say.

"What do you mean?"

"I'm not selling this house. I'm going to sell the new one. I want to stay here."

"When did you decide that?"

"Just now. My people are here. This is my home."

Maybe I'm crazy, considering how many hours I've put into building that house, but Roman put those hours in too. Maybe I'll sell it to Roman for the cost of materials. It's the least I can do. After all, Roman might have been the catalyst for how today turned out. Had he not forced me to go back and check on Kenna that night, I'm not sure any of us could have gotten to this point.

Kenna is done talking, apparently. She kisses me, and she doesn't stop until an hour later when we're exhausted and sweaty and satiated and wrapped in each other's arms. I stare at her until she falls asleep, and then I stare up at the ceiling because I *can't* fall asleep.

I can't stop thinking about that fucking pigeon.

What are the chances Scotty had no connection to that? What are the chances he did?

It could have just been a coincidence, but it also could have been a sign. A message from wherever he is.

Maybe it doesn't matter whether something is a coincidence or a sign. Maybe the best way to cope with the loss of the people we love is to find them in as many places and things as we possibly can. And in the off chance that the people we lose are still somehow able to hear us, maybe we should never stop talking to them.

"I'm going to be so good to your girls, Scotty. I promise."

CHAPTER FORTY-TWO

KENNA

I unbuckle Diem from her booster seat and help her out of Ledger's truck. I already have the cross in my hand, so I grab the hammer from the floorboard.

"You sure you don't want me to help?" Ledger asks.

I smile at him reassuringly and shake my head. This is something I want to do with Diem.

I lead her to the edge of the road where I first found the cross, and I kick around in the grass and dirt with the toe of my sneaker until I find the hole the cross was in. I hand the cross to Diem. "See that hole?"

She leans forward to inspect the ground.

"Stick it right there."

Diem drives the cross into the hole. "Why are we putting this here?"

I push down on the cross, making sure it's stable. "Because it'll make your nana happy to know it's here, in case she ever drives by."

"Will it make my daddy happy?"

I kneel down next to Diem. I've missed so much of her life, which is why I want every minute we spend together to be authentic. I'm always as truthful as I can be with her.

"No. Probably not. Your daddy thought memorials were silly. But your nana doesn't, and sometimes we do things for people we love, even though we wouldn't choose to do those things for ourselves."

Diem reaches for the hammer. "Can I do it?"

I hand her the hammer, and she hits the cross a few times. It doesn't do much, so when she hands the hammer back to me, I hit it three times until it's secured into the ground.

I wrap my arms around Diem, and we stare at the cross. "Is there anything you want to say to your daddy?"

Diem thinks about it for a moment and then says, "What do I say? Do I make a wish?"

I laugh. "You can try, but he's not a genie, or Santa Claus."

"I wish for a baby sister or a baby brother."

Don't you dare grant her wish yet, Scotty. I've known Ledger for all of five months.

I pick up Diem and walk her back to the truck. "It takes more than a wish to make a sibling."

"I know. We have to buy an egg from Walmart. That's how babies grow."

I buckle her into the booster seat. "Not exactly. Babies grow in their mother's tummies. Remember how I told you that you grew in my tummy?"

"Oh, yeah. Then can you grow another baby?"

I stare at Diem, not sure how to answer that. "How about we just get another cat? Ivy needs a friend."

Diem throws her hands in the air, excited. "Yes! Another kitten!"

I kiss her on the head and shut her door.

Ledger is side-eyeing me when I open the passenger door. He points to the middle of the seat, so I scoot all the way over and buckle in. He grabs my hand and threads our fingers together. He's looking at me with a glimmer in his eye, as if the idea of giving Diem a sibling excites him.

Ledger kisses me, and then he starts to drive.

For the first time in a long, long time, I want to listen to the radio. I want to hear any song, even the sad ones. I lean forward and turn on the radio. It's the first time we've listened to anything in this truck other than the safe playlist Ledger made me.

He glances at me when he realizes what I've done. I just smile at him and lean against his shoulder.

Music still makes me think of Scotty, but thinking of Scotty no longer makes me sad. Now that I've forgiven myself, the reminders of him only make me smile.

The End

EPILOGUE

Dear Scotty,

I'm sorry I hardly write to you anymore. I used to write to you because I was lonely, so I guess it's a good thing the letters are few and far between now.

I still miss you. I'll always miss you. But I'm convinced that the holes you left behind are only holes felt by us. Wherever you are, you're complete. That's what matters.

Diem is growing so fast. She just turned seven. It's hard to wrap my mind around the idea that I wasn't here for the first five years of her life because it feels like I've always been here. I'm sure that has a lot to do with Ledger and your parents. They tell me stories about her growing up and show me videos, so it sometimes seems like I missed nothing at all.

I don't know that Diem even remembers a life without me in it. To her, I've always been here. I know that's because all the people who loved you gave her everything she needed when you and I couldn't be there.

She still lives with your parents, although I see her every day. She stays with Ledger and me at least two nights a week. She has her own bedroom at both houses. We eat dinner together every night.

I'd love for her to live with me full time, but I also know it's important she keep the routine she's had since birth. And Patrick and Grace deserve to be the major component in her life. I would never want to take that from them.

Since the day they accepted me into her life, I've never felt unwelcome. Not for one day or even one second. They didn't accept me with conditions. They just accepted me like I belong here with all the people who loved you.

You were surrounded by good people, Scotty. From your parents to your best friend to your best friend's parents, I have never met a family more loving.

The people that were in your life are now the people who are in my life, and I'll do everything I can to continue to show them as much love and respect as you gave them. I'll treat each of my relationships with the same level of significance and respect I give to the naming process.

You know how seriously I take naming things. I thought long and hard about what to name Diem when she was born, and I even took three days to name Ivy.

The last name I handed out two weeks ago was by far one of the more important ones, yet somehow the easiest name to come up with.

When they placed our newborn son on my chest, I looked down at him through teary eyes, and I said, "Hi, Scotty."

Love,

Kenna

KENNA ROWAN'S PLAYLIST

1) "Raise Your Glass"—P!nk
2) "Dynamite"—BTS
3) "Happy"—Pharrell Williams
4) "Particle Man"—They Might Be Giants
5) "I'm Good"—The Mowgli's
6) "Yellow Submarine"—The Beatles
7) "I'm Too Sexy"—Right Said Fred
8) "Can't Stop the Feeling!"—Justin Timberlake
9) "Thunder"—Imagine Dragons
10) "Run the World (Girls)"—Beyoncé
11) "U Can't Touch This"—MC Hammer
12) "Forgot About Dre"—Dr. Dre featuring Eminem
13) "Vacation"—Dirty Heads
14) "The Load Out"—Jackson Browne
15) "Stay"—Jackson Browne
16) "The King of Bedside Manor"—Barenaked Ladies
17) "Empire State of Mind"—JAY-Z
18) "Party in the U.S.A."—Miley Cyrus
19) "Fucking Best Song Everrr"—Wallpaper.
20) "Shake It Off"—Taylor Swift
21) "Bang!"—AJR

ACKNOWLEDGMENTS

You might have noticed there was never a location specified for where this story actually takes place. I've never had this issue in a book—solidifying a location for the characters. I just kept placing Kenna in different towns while writing her story, and none of them felt right because they *all* felt right.

There are people like Kenna everywhere, in every town. People who feel alone in the world, no matter where they're located. When I finished the book, I realized I still didn't pinpoint the exact setting, but the ambiguity of where Kenna's story unfolds somehow felt right. So this is your permission to imagine this story takes place wherever you are in the world. No matter how whole our neighbors appear on the outside, we have no idea how many broken pieces they're made up of on the inside.

Reading is a hobby, but for some of us, it's an escape from the difficulties we face. To all of you who escape into books, I want to thank you for escaping into this one. But I also want to apologize for never being able to write romantic comedies, no matter how much I try. I started this one thinking it was going to be a romantic comedy, but obviously the characters weren't in the mood for that. Maybe next time.

I also want to thank those who read this book early and gave me such helpful feedback: Pam, Laurie, Maria, Chelle, Brooke, Steph, Erica, Lindsey, Dana, Susan, Stephanie, Melinda, and I'm sure there are more who will read it and give me feedback after these acknowledgments are submitted, so this is also a thank-you to those who help me out last minute but don't get the public credit.

And a huge thank-you to two sisters, Kenna and Rowan. I saw your names in my reader group and stole them for this book because I thought they'd make a great character name, so I hope I did your names justice!

I want to thank my agent, Jane Dystel, and my foreign rights agent, Lauren Abramo. You ladies and your team of coworkers are so attentive and amazing and *patient.*

A huge thank-you to Montlake Publishing, Anh Schluep, Lindsey Faber, Cheryl Weisman, Kristin Dwyer, Ashley Vanicek, and everyone else who had a hand in the creation and distribution of this book. You guys have been a dream to work with, and I appreciate the entire Montlake team so much.

Thank you to my hype team, Stephanie and Erica.

Thank you, Lauren Levine, for believing in me. Always.

A huge thank-you to all the people who work so hard for the Bookworm Box and Book Bonanza. The charity wouldn't exist without any of you.

Thank you to my sisters, Lin Reynolds and Murphy Fennell. You're both my favorite sisters.

Thank you to Murphy Rae and Jeremy Meerkreebs for answering my early questions. Your advice resulted in the idea for this novel, so thank you both!

To Heath, Levi, Cale, and Beckham. Thank you for treating me like a queen. I've been gifted the best four men on the planet, world. Don't @ me.

To my mother. Thank you for being my first and most enthusiastic reader of every single book I write. Not sure most of them would get finished if it weren't for you.

Also, um, TikTok! What the heck? WHAT IN THE HECK? I don't even know what to say. Those of you on the BookTok side of that app have helped not only my books reach new readers, but the books of so many authors. Your love for reading has made new readers and has helped the entire publishing industry in huge ways. It's a beautiful thing to witness.

And lastly . . . thank you to the members of Colleen Hoover's CoHorts on Facebook. You guys brighten my day every day.

Thank you, world, and all who inhabit it!

ABOUT THE AUTHOR

Photo © Chad Griffith

Colleen Hoover is the #1 *New York Times* bestselling author of several novels, including the bestselling women's fiction novel *It Ends with Us* and the bestselling psychological thriller *Verity*. She won the Goodreads Choice Award for Best Romance three years in a row—for *Confess* (2015), *It Ends with Us* (2016), and *Without Merit* (2017). *Confess* was adapted into a seven-episode online series. In 2015, Hoover and her family founded the Bookworm Box, a bookstore and monthly subscription service offering signed novels donated by authors. All profits are given to various charities each month to help those in need. Hoover lives in Texas with her husband and their three boys. Visit www.ColleenHoover.com.